THE EXCALIBUR
CURSE

ALSO BY KIERSTEN WHITE

Paranormalcy

Supernaturally

Endlessly

Mind Games

Perfect Lies

The Chaos of Stars

Illusions of Fate

And I Darken

Now I Rise

Bright We Burn

The Dark Descent of Elizabeth Frankenstein

Slayer

Chosen

The Guinevere Deception

The Camelot Betrayal

THE EXCALIBUR
CURSE

KIERSTEN WHITE

DELACORTE PRESS

Text copyright © 2021 by Kiersten Brazier
Jacket art copyright © 2021 by Alex Dos Diaz

All rights reserved. Published in the United States by Delacorte Press,
an imprint of Random House Children's Books, a division of Penguin Random House LLC, New York.

Delacorte Press is a registered trademark and the colophon is a trademark
of Penguin Random House LLC.

Visit us on the Web! GetUnderlined.com

Educators and librarians, for a variety of teaching tools, visit us at RHTeachersLibrarians.com

Library of Congress Cataloging-in-Publication Data
Names: White, Kiersten, author.
Title: The Excalibur curse / Kiersten White.
Description: First edition. | New York: Delacorte Press, [2021] | Series: Camelot rising; 3 |
Audience: Ages 12 and up. | Summary: "The third and final book in the Camelot Rising trilogy
finds Guinevere facing off against those she loves most, but can she find the courage
to make the ultimate sacrifice?"—Provided by publisher.
Identifiers: LCCN 2020057286 (print) | LCCN 2020057287 (ebook) | ISBN 978-0-525-58175-8
(hardcover) | ISBN 978-0-525-58176-5 (library binding) | ISBN 978-0-525-58177-2 (ebook)
Subjects: LCSH: Guinevere, Queen (Legendary character)—Juvenile fiction. | CYAC: Guinevere,
Queen (Legendary character)—Fiction. | Magic—Fiction. | Arthur, King—Fiction. | Knights and
knighthood—Fiction. | Camelot (Legendary place)—Fiction. | Fantasy.
Classification: LCC PZ7.W583764 Exc 2021 (print) | LCC PZ7.W583764 (ebook) | DDC [Fic]—dc23

The text of this book is set in 11.5-point Fairfield LT.
Interior design by Ken Crossland

Printed in the United States of America
10 9 8 7 6 5 4 3 2 1
First Edition

To Kimberly

May you never come out of your shell

THE EXCALIBUR
CURSE

CHAPTER ONE

Once, not so long ago, Guinevere had ridden surrounded by armed soldiers and marveled at her power. Now she rode surrounded by armed soldiers and marveled at her smallness. She tried to hold on to both thoughts at once: her power *and* her smallness, each a comfort in its own way. She was only one girl, after all, in a world full of them.

Unfortunately, the armed soldiers around her at this precise moment were enemies of Arthur: Picts, led by their king, Nechtan; the sorceress Morgana, Arthur's half sister; and his nephew, Mordred the betrayer.

Guinevere had thought herself triumphant in sealing the city just before they arrived. But they had never been coming for the city. They had been coming for *her*. It was enough to drive her mad, but she was too tired for it. Guinevere half suspected the reason they had not dismounted and rested for the past twelve hours was to ensure that her nether regions were so painful that she would not try to escape. She had lost feeling in her toes, and her spine ached from sitting as straight as possible so as not to lean back against Mordred.

The least they could have done is give her a horse instead of forcing her to ride with him.

She had no idea how many leagues they had covered, but it was certainly more than she had ever traveled in a single stretch. Their pace was hurried without being frantic. The Picts were practiced soldiers. They were not going to risk their horses' health, but their horses had been trained to do exactly this.

Camelot falling farther and farther behind them as they rode into the night worried Guinevere less than the fact that they were galloping in the opposite direction of her goal. Merlin's cave would take her so much longer to reach now. She had planned on walking straight there, figuring out a way to free him from the Lady of the Lake's trap, and demanding answers about who she was. So she could finally know. If she could only know that, everything else would make sense. Would be easier. She was certain of it.

She focused on the cave, because that was less painful to think about than Camelot. About how she had left it. About who she had left.

The image of Lancelot on her knees behind the magical barrier they had created to keep armies out—but Lancelot in—lingered in Guinevere's mind like a wound. Guinevere knew what it meant to be denied crucial information. To be manipulated into a course of action without the freedom to decide. And she had done exactly that to Lancelot, not telling her brave knight until it was too late that Lancelot would be inside the city's shield, and Guinevere outside it.

It had been cruel, and unfair, and a betrayal of the trust Lancelot had always given her.

So she tried her best to not think about it. Fortunately, between the enemy soldiers and Mordred and this wretched, endless ride adding to the already long walk between her and Merlin's cave, she had an abundance of distractions.

At last, with dawn stretching pink and terrible across the sky, Mordred called out, "The horses need to rest."

It was the first time he had spoken the entire journey. The first time he had spoken since he had arrived at Camelot, begged her not to lose faith in him, and then announced he had successfully kidnapped the queen. Other than his chest at her back and his arms around her holding the reins, their only interaction was when he periodically passed her a canteen to drink from.

As soon as Mordred declared the horses needed to rest, word spread along the traveling party. Guinevere estimated there were two or three hundred soldiers. She slipped a hand into her pouch. All this long journey, she had tied knot after knot in her mind, from the most innocuous to the most vicious. It was time to choose.

A shudder rippled through her. She knew what she had to do. She would need her iron thread, and she would need blood, and it would be the worst knot she had ever tied. Worse than the protection she had placed in the river above Camelot that would kill anyone who ventured past it with intent to do her harm. Worse even than what she had done to Sir Bors, reaching into his mind and manipulating his memories. Perhaps not worse than what she had done to King Mark, destroying his mind but leaving his body, but certainly an evil enough magic that it would haunt her the rest of her days.

She was going to tie a death knot, loop it around herself so that any living creature that touched her would immediately die. And then she would walk out of the camp. It would not matter if they followed her all the way to Merlin's cave, because no one could touch her. The knot would mean she could not take a horse, but after twelve hours on one, that was almost a blessing.

She had to get away from Mordred first, though. Someone would touch her, doubtless, before they believed her threat. But it could not be Mordred. Not Mordred. It had to be someone whose name and face she did not know. A soldier sacrificed to a conflict Guinevere had not started.

A person, both small and infinite, ended because Guinevere valued herself more.

How did Arthur do this? How did he make these decisions? Her stomach churned, gnawing at its own emptiness. She squeezed her eyes closed. She could do this. She would do this.

Mordred's fingers circled her wrist, his grip gentle but insistent as he pulled her hand out of the pouch. He detached the pouch from her belt and tossed it to a tall, elegantly cloaked woman. His mother, Morgana. She caught it neatly and tucked it into her own bag.

Guinevere did not know whether she was about to cry out of frustration and disappointment or relief. Mordred had taken the choice from her. No one would die at her hand today. She would figure out another means of escape, hopefully one with a less desperate cost.

Feeling blurry with exhaustion, she watched as a camp appeared around them with practiced efficiency. Soldiers laughed and called to each other while they worked. Then everyone stilled as King Nechtan rode past them. He slowed, fixing eyes that had possibly once been wide and kind on Guinevere. Whatever they had been was hidden beneath bushy eyebrows and a permanent glower. He would have been intimidating even without the fur mantle he wore around his shoulders that quivered with black moths. Guinevere knew that each moth carried a bit of the Dark Queen inside it. A constant reminder of whom King Nechtan was working with, or for. It was hard to say which with the Dark Queen.

One moth rode on his earlobe like an ornament. Nechtan bent his head toward it, his gaze turning distant and unfocused, before snapping back to Guinevere with an almost physical force. She sighed with relief when he turned to Mordred. It was not only the presence of King Nechtan but also the knowledge that anything he did or said was not him alone. The Pict king and the Dark Queen were each a formidable enemy on their own, and now Guinevere had to contend with them both.

Nechtan said something in his language. Guinevere did not understand, but she did not need to. The way he spoke made it clear that Mordred was in trouble. If she were in higher spirits, she would tease him. As it was, she was grateful that King Nechtan continued riding past, his head bent once more toward the whispering wings of his passengers and the queen they were part of.

Mordred dismounted, then held up his hands to help Guinevere down. She deliberately threw her leg over the opposite side of the horse and slid off. But she had not accounted for how numb her legs would be after a ride that long. As soon as her feet hit the ground, her knees buckled and she fell gracelessly on her sore backside.

A woman laughed nearby. Guinevere looked up to see one of the Pictish soldiers—they were all dressed alike in leather and fur—hold out a hand. The woman who laughed was a *soldier.*

Guinevere took the offered hand and was pulled swiftly and unceremoniously to her feet.

"Your king should ride you more often." The woman winked. A bold blue cloth was wrapped around her head, and her face had freckles that put Guinevere's to shame. Her pale blue eyes were framed by nearly white eyelashes and eyebrows that were tinged with orange. She had two axes strapped to her back, and a belt full of knives.

"*Fina.* Enough." Another woman, taller than the first by a few inches with almost the same face and even more weapons, shoved Fina's shoulder. She looked down at Guinevere without curiosity, her expression cooler than even the icy blue of her eyes. "I am Nectudad. Most of the soldiers do not speak your language, so trying to speak to them will be a waste of energy."

"I learned your language to marry your husband." Fina grinned. She had a gap between her front teeth that made her smile seem even larger and happier. Guinevere did not know whether she was expected to apologize for marrying Arthur, but Fina's smile grew. "Lucky for him I did not. I do not think he would have survived me."

Guinevere's eyes narrowed. "Arthur is the strongest man I have ever known."

"I did not mean in combat. I meant in bed. Not if he prefers delicate morsels like you."

Mordred appeared next to Guinevere. "Oh, good, you have met the princesses." He bowed deeply. "They make princesses very differently in the north."

Even Nectudad smiled at that, a more reserved reaction than Fina's brash laugh, which was so loud the horse next to Guinevere startled, stamping its hooves. Mordred reached out a hand and put it on the horse's neck. The animal calmed immediately.

"My father wants to see you, fairyson," Nectudad said. "He has questions about how you came to join our party."

Morgana appeared again with a sweep of her black cloak. She looked none the worse for wear, even after such a grueling journey. Her hair, black with streaks of silver like metal woven through it, was perfectly plaited, and her eyes, a darker and older green than Mordred's, betrayed no weariness. "Of course. We have much to discuss with him."

Morgana held the two stones—the ones with which Guinevere had done blood magic, the ones that had failed to give her enough warning of Morgana's return to be of any use—in her hand. So she had found the stone hidden in Guinevere's pouch, and its mate.

How long ago had Morgana discovered the secret stone? Had she only realized what it was when she saw the same rock in Guinevere's bag, or had she kept it to warn Guinevere of the approaching army? Guinevere could ask, but how could she ever trust an answer from the woman who had disguised herself as Lily's maid, infiltrated Camelot, and tried to make Guinevere leave with her?

But then again, Morgana had had ample time to hurt Guinevere, or Lily, or even Arthur. None of them had suspected her. Even after Morgana had given Guinevere a potion to make her tell the truth, Guinevere had not feared her. She had felt compassion, sorrow for her losses, and confusion about what Morgana really wanted.

None of those feelings were likely to change soon. Particularly the confusion.

"Come, Mordred," Morgana said, her face inscrutable. "Fina, Nectudad, will you see our guest fed and settled? And watch her hands."

Fina raised a dubious eyebrow. "I should be afraid of this slip?"

"Make sure she does not sew or tie knots in anything. Bind her hands before she goes to sleep."

"Southerners," Fina muttered, shaking her head. "I do not understand you. Well, come along, Slip." She put her arm around Guinevere, forcefully guiding her. Guinevere looked over her shoulder. Mordred was watching, concern shaping his brows, but then he turned and followed his mother.

Mordred and Morgana were not her allies. She could not trust anything they did or said. But at least they were familiar. Nothing else here was. All around her, soldiers—men and women both—were bustling about. She could not understand anything they said. Even the scents of the meals being cooked over fires were unfamiliar.

Her despair must have shown on her face. Nectudad patted her shoulder roughly as they stopped outside a hide-covered tent in the center of camp. "We have no quarrel with you. Only with your king."

"And with our new queen," Fina grumbled.

Nectudad shot her a narrow-eyed warning, hissing softly.

Fina straightened, grinning once more. "And you have no need to worry about your virtue. Unless you want me to relieve you of some of it, in which case you can tell your king exactly what he missed. But you will never want to go back to him after tasting me, so be certain before you ask."

"Fina." Nectudad said the name like an exasperated sigh.

"What? She looks too tense. I am offering solutions, being a good caretaker."

"Go get food." Nectudad shoved Fina in the direction of the nearest campfire and then turned back to Guinevere. She lowered her voice so only Guinevere could hear. It was clear and calm as a lake on a windless afternoon. "I will protect you because I need you. But if you do anything that threatens my father or if you try to escape, I will break both your legs and all your fingers. Do you understand? Nod if you understand."

Guinevere nodded, her throat tight. She understood perfectly well. She had left Camelot to figure out who she was. She had left Arthur, Lancelot, Brangien and Dindrane and Lily, everyone who loved her. She had left behind the castle and the crown. Now she was surrounded by enemies. She had no allies, no one she could truly trust. Only herself. But that would have to be enough for now. With or without Merlin, she *would* discover her past.

Preferably with all her limbs intact.

CHAPTER TWO

Fina would not stop talking as she carefully bound Guinevere's hands together with strips of cloth. Her touch was as confident as everything else about her. In a lot of ways, she seemed like Arthur, but the sense Guinevere got of her was wilder, sharper, and . . . happier. If Fina were not currently binding Guinevere's hands to prevent her from tying any knots, and if Fina were not the daughter of the man who had stolen her to present her to the Dark Queen, and if Fina were not the sister of Nectudad, who had only an hour ago calmly threatened to break many of Guinevere's bones, Guinevere would like her quite a bit.

". . . unfair. They can just slide off a horse, untie their breeches, and piss away. We have to find somewhere to crouch. I complained to my father about it, but he told me even a king cannot change the way men and women pee. I thought we ought to make their breeches harder to untie to make it fairer. Nectudad banned me from the counsel for a week after that. Can you feel your fingers?"

Guinevere nodded.

Fina bound Guinevere's wrists together, tight enough that she could not free them, but not so tight that it would hurt. Then she pulled a leather pouch over Guinevere's hands and tugged it shut, tying it with such a complicated knot there was no way Guinevere could work it undone with her teeth before someone noticed. "What do they think you are going to do with your fingers that is so dangerous?"

"Shadow puppets," Guinevere said.

Fina frowned in confusion, then let out that horse-startling laugh. "I like you. I thought you would probably cry a lot. Or maybe faint. Actually, I placed a wager that you would faint. I am going to lose silver on you."

The tent flap opened, letting in a piercing shaft of light. Mordred ducked inside. "Hello, Fina."

"He did not kill you then." Fina sighed. "More coin lost. I need to stop gambling."

Mordred's eyes widened. "Was there a chance your father was going to kill me?"

Fina shrugged. "You were not supposed to be here. He did not like that you told him not to attack the city. And he does not know whether you support her." Fina waved vaguely. For a moment Guinevere thought Fina was talking about whether Mordred supported her, but then she realized Fina was mimicking a moth's flight. The Dark Queen.

Mordred scoffed. "She is my grandmother."

"That makes no difference. Nectudad killed our grandmother in combat."

"She *what*?" Guinevere could not help but be drawn into the conversation.

"Oh, yes. Our grandmother was supporting our uncle to supplant Father. She did not like that Father had no sons, only us. There was a war. We won. Barely."

Mordred apparently did not find this story remarkable. He moved away from the entrance, gesturing to it. "Speaking of Nectudad, she was looking for you. I can wait with Guinevere until my mother comes."

"Fina," Guinevere said. The other woman paused on the tent threshold. "If you tell me what your wagers are, I can help you win them."

Fina beamed. "Oh, you *are* dangerous, Slip. Fingers or not." She left, the flap falling back down and cocooning Guinevere and Mordred in the tent's dim interior.

They had been alone in a tent before.

Guinevere braced herself for whatever Mordred was going to try. He insisted he had come to Camelot to warn her, begged her to have faith in him, but how could she?

He had helped her once, in the forest after she was injured. He had proved he meant her no harm by crossing her magic line of defense. And he had gone out of his way to help Rhoslyn and her village escape the men who would have hurt them. But Guinevere's wrists still bore the scars of the trees he had tricked her into waking. And they were going to meet the Dark Queen, who Mordred had manipulated Guinevere into giving physical form once more.

He had held Guinevere between Excalibur and the Dark Queen, daring Arthur to end them or let them free. Arthur's fear—that she would be used against him, that he would be forced to choose between Camelot and Guinevere—had been realized by Mordred.

And now the Dark Queen was mounting some new threat, some new attack, and was it not Guinevere's fault, for being someone Arthur would choose to save instead of ending his most terrible foe? For being someone who *needed* to be saved?

It was her fault. But it was Mordred's fault more. She would not forget.

Mordred crouched, his ease gone. His posture was tense, his tone quiet but urgent. "Do not tell my mother anything. Do not tell anyone anything, but especially not her."

It was not what Guinevere had expected. She grasped for a response, but it was like walking down steps in the dark and missing the last one. Everything was a disorienting rush. If anything, she expected Mordred to be in league with his mother. To insist that Guinevere could trust only them.

"But—"

"Be patient. I beg you." There was a voice outside the tent. Mordred changed position, lying on his side, one leg bent, his head propped on his hand. "And do not go to sleep," he hissed before a playful mask descended over his face just as the flap opened and Morgana entered.

"Mordred," she said, sitting in a swirl of skirts. "That was close."

He waved one hand dismissively. "I do not understand why Nechtan was upset. I made it so much easier for everyone. No fight, no lives lost, the queen delivered."

"Mmm." Morgana adjusted her dress, sitting as straight as a woman carved from stone. "I think he hoped for an excuse to attack Camelot. He might be under the sway of your grandmother, but he is still a warrior king. Now." She pulled out Guinevere's pouch, dumping its contents onto the floor of the tent. Guinevere looked longingly at her iron thread, her dagger, all her supplies. Her handkerchief, embroidered with Arthur's sun, mocked her with its bright, hopeful colors.

Morgana swept her hand over Guinevere's belongings. "Where, exactly, were you off to? And tell me how Camelot was sealed. I am most curious." It was fascinating, how different Morgana was now that she was no longer pretending to be Anna, the lady's maid. Her identities were like distorted reflections of each other, Anna's practicality and warmth and Morgana's imperious forcefulness.

"Arthur did something with the sword." Guinevere could not let them know the truth: that if she crossed the magical shield she had placed over Camelot, it would break. All they had to do was take her home, and Camelot would fall.

Morgana sighed, slowly reaching into her own bag for something. "Liar. That accursed sword cannot create, only destroy. Who sealed the city?"

Guinevere's breath caught, waiting to see what Morgana would pull out of her bag. She had once given Guinevere a potion that made her tell the truth. If that happened again, they would know how to break the shield. How to get to Camelot before Arthur returned to protect it.

"Do not hurt me. It was Merlin," Guinevere blurted. If Morgana underestimated her and thought her incapable of such magic alone, she would play along.

"What?" Morgana's face paled. "I thought he was sealed away. She said he was sealed away."

"I thought so, too. That is where I was going. To find Merlin." The truth, or close to it. "I was the only person who could pass through the barrier. I assumed it meant he wanted me to leave."

"If Merlin is free, that means everything is at risk." Morgana stood, trembling with rage. "And it means I can still kill him. Come. Now. We have other purposes." She held out her hand. Guinevere nearly stood, too, until three dark shapes fluttered free from her back and went to Morgana's hand.

Moths. She had not even noticed them alight on her in the dimness of the tent, but she breathed easier as the weight of the Dark Queen left her.

Morgana stormed out, the air almost crackling in her wake. Guinevere could not forget that this was not Anna. This was Morgan le Fay, the sorceress. She had ripped power from the fairy world and imbued herself with it to fight Merlin. She was as single-minded as the wizard. Everything evil he did was to protect Arthur. And everything Morgana did was to fight Merlin.

Mordred sat up, rubbing his face. It was as though he rubbed away the easy mask he wore, replacing it with strain. "That was well played. I am surprised she assumed someone else made the shield. She should know better. What really happened? Where were you going?"

Guinevere gazed coolly at him. "I was recently advised to tell no one anything."

He let out a dry exhalation almost like a laugh. "You only listen when you want to. Do you know what I think?" He leaned back against one of the poles holding the tent up and considered her with tired, sad eyes. "I think you were running away. I think if I had gotten there before Nechtan, you would have let me join you."

"You are wrong."

"Am I? I saw the shield go up, Lancelot on one side, you on the other. If *I* were a very brave knight, I would have made certain my queen was on the inside and I was on the outside. Unless that queen planned it deliberately so no one could stop her from leaving."

Guinevere looked away. Mordred always saw too much.

"Guinevere, I—"

The tent flap opened again. "Your mother is scary," Fina said, ducking inside and flopping onto her back before kicking off her boots. "And you cannot be in here alone with Slip, because no one is allowed to touch her unless she wants them to, in which case she will undoubtedly choose me. I am a vigorously generous lover. Sleep time."

Guinevere remained sitting, her body and soul sore. Mordred did not move, either. The only things between them were their history of hurt and betrayal and the gentle snores of a Pictish princess.

§

Guinevere jerked her head up, forcing her eyes open. Thick clouds obscured the waning moon. The sounds of horses and soldiers were all around them, but she could not make out any details.

She had sat awake in the tent all day, hands bound, Fina sleeping sprawled out and Mordred sleeping—or pretending to sleep, she could not be sure—sitting with his back against the tent pole. Morgana had not returned. Nechtan had not appeared. No one else had disturbed them. The camp itself had been mostly quiet, everyone resting while they could. And then, in the late afternoon, the tents had come down as quickly as they went up, the horses were loaded with supplies and soldiers, and Guinevere was once again riding with Mordred. They had only unbound her hands for her to eat and relieve herself.

She wriggled her fingers as best she could, wishing she could pinch herself. Her spine ached where she kept it rigidly straight to avoid leaning back against Mordred's chest. She would touch him as little as possible. How long had it been since she had slept? She had stayed up to watch over the city when Arthur left to chase the letter that promised a son Guinevere was certain did not exist. Thoughts of Arthur made her heart ache far more fiercely than her spine. He was going to be devastated, and she would not be there to help him through it.

What was Arthur doing right now? Had the messengers found him in time to get him to turn back? Maybe he had already used Excalibur to undo Guinevere's magical shield around the city. Arthur and Lancelot—*oh, Lancelot,* Guinevere could not think of her knight without a stab of pain and regret—would be planning, ready to take action. And Brangien, Dindrane, Lily? What would they do? Lily would be so sad to hear her lady's maid "Anna" was responsible for all this. All those embroidered lilies left behind. Sashes. Belts. Pillows. Pillows.

Pillows.

Guinevere startled upright again. She was so tired she felt like she was losing her mind. No thread. No dagger. Morgana had taken all her things. And no one would let her use her hands. She could light her hands on fire. Burn away the bindings. Burn her way out.

Hild had died in a fire that was Guinevere's fault, for calling the dragon for help. And now the dragon was dead, too, and no one could come to her aid, and that was for the best. No fire. Not yet. Lull them into trusting her, thinking she was helpless, and then after she lulled them . . .

"Guinevere," Mordred said, his tone exasperated as she startled awake so hard he had to catch her from slipping off the horse. "Just go to sleep."

"Do not tell me what to do!" She tried to elbow him, but the knots at her wrists prevented her from doing more than nudging his torso. "You were the one who told me not to sleep!"

"All the Dark Queen's moths are chasing down your clever lie, so she cannot crawl inside your mind when your defenses are down. It is safe."

"*Nothing* here is safe."

Mordred sighed. "I know. But it is safe for you to sleep now. I will not let you fall."

She wanted to resist. To prove her point. But if she did not sleep soon, Morgana would not need a potion to addle Guinevere's brains; her brains would be perfectly addled and vulnerable on their own.

If she was going to find a way out, she needed to be ready. And that meant being rested.

"I am not sleeping because you told me to," she whispered, finally relaxing. Mordred's arms moved securely around her waist. She tipped her head back so it hit his shoulder, and before she could think of something mean to say to make certain he knew she hated this, she was asleep.

Or so she thought, until her eyes opened again.

"Guinevere!" Isolde shouted, running toward her and embracing her. "We thought you were dead!"

CHAPTER THREE

Guinevere was in a forest. Trunks rose around them like church pillars, leaves and branches forming delicate stained glass patterns against the sky. Insects droned in the warm air, everything smelling of life. Somewhere nearby was the gentle sound of water, which Guinevere had no desire to explore. And Isolde was here, too, hugging her.

"Where are we?" Guinevere asked, confused. It could not be a dream. She could feel Isolde's chest move with her breath, smell the rosewater scent of her hair. The only dreams she had ever had with this level of detail were not dreams at all, but memories belonging to the Lady of the Lake.

Isolde released her, beaming and wiping her eyes. She held out a portion of her hair. Black strands were knotted in with her auburn locks.

"Brangien." Guinevere's heart felt as warm as the day around them. Brangien had used Guinevere's dream magic to connect them.

"She wanted to come herself, but I could not get the knots right. I am sorry. I will practice."

Guinevere took Isolde's hands, squeezing them. "Do not apologize. I am so happy, so relieved to see you. Please tell me everything. How much time do we have?"

"Ever so much!" Isolde sat on a moss-covered log, and Guinevere did the same. "I have been sleeping almost constantly, but I could not find you. Brangien was worried that she had the knots wrong, and we were all worried that we could not find you because—well, here you are!"

"Not dead." Guinevere smiled gently.

"Where are you now?"

"Traveling north with King Nechtan's forces."

"Lancelot thought as much."

"Lancelot! How is she?" Guinevere leaned forward eagerly.

Isolde's face flushed. Her smile, normally blooming as easily as spring buds, faltered. "She is taking care of the city."

"How is she really?"

"She is devastated. And furious. Brangien suggested Lancelot be the one to try to speak to you here, but . . ."

"But she would not."

Isolde moved so they were side by side. She took Guinevere's hand and patted it. "Give her time. Deep love means everything is felt more fully."

"Including betrayal," Guinevere whispered. Because she could not deny it. She had betrayed Lancelot. Lancelot had made it clear that her first priority—her only priority—was Guinevere. And Guinevere had forced her to choose Camelot instead. It had been viciously selfish. At the time it felt necessary that Guinevere strike out alone. If she had known what was coming, though, would she still have done it?

Yes. She would not have left Lancelot alone to face King Nechtan's army. Lancelot was her protector, but Lancelot was also dearer to her than her own heart, and Guinevere did not regret keeping her safe.

Guinevere cleared her throat, trying to dislodge some of the pain there. "And the city, tell me how it is. The shield is holding?"

"Yes."

"And what do people think it is?"

"They are not certain. There are rumors it was the Dark Queen, other rumors that the Lady of the Lake has returned to protect them in Arthur's absence."

Guinevere had not thought of that one. It was a more positive spin. "Encourage that idea. Make up a story about the Lady doing something similar in the past and have it spread through the city. Has there been panic?"

"No, nothing disruptive. Lily, Brangien, and Dindrane have seen to that."

"How?"

"They declared everyone needed to spend as much time as possible in the church praying for the safety of the king and the return of the queen. And when they are not praying, they can attend free plays being performed in the theater, as well as training and entertainment bouts in the arena. And every citizen who helps with city sanitation or weapon preparation earns an invitation to a meal at the castle."

"All that in two days?" Guinevere was impressed, and mildly aghast. She would not have thought of any of it. She probably would have put soldiers in the streets to make certain there was no mischief. But keeping an entire city so busy that it could not fret was far smarter. Lily, Brangien, and Dindrane were so clever it made Guinevere want to cry. She was fortunate to have found women like them. And Camelot was even more fortunate, to benefit from their compassion and cleverness. "Any word of Arthur?"

Isolde shook her head. "Lancelot keeps a fire burning near the secret passage. The hope is that Arthur will see it and head directly there when he returns. That way, Lancelot can explain what happened. She is sleeping there, and has set a guard for all hours of the day."

"Good. That is good. Surely one of the messengers will have found him." Guinevere felt sick thinking about Arthur. Her most fervent hope was that the news would reach him before he arrived at his destination and discovered the cruel truth about his "son." The truth would not be easy to hear, but at least he would have less time to hope.

"Now," Isolde said, her expression serious, "I am supposed to ask for specific details about where they have taken you, how many people are with you, how fast they are traveling, and anything else that matters. Lancelot will be ready to come for you the moment Arthur returns."

Guinevere smiled, but she still felt like crying. Because despite what she had done to Lancelot, she knew it was true. Lancelot would be ready, always. "I hope it will not come to that. I will escape at the first opportunity and return south. Tell Lancelot that, if all else fails, I will meet her at the cave." Lancelot would know which one. It had been one of the first things they did together—Lancelot had saved her, then she had saved Lancelot, and then they had gone on a quest to find Merlin. It had resulted in him being sealed in a cave by the Lady of the Lake, but it had also sealed Lancelot and Guinevere to each other.

"All else will not fail." Isolde sounded determined. "And they will never forgive me if I come back without information. Tell me everything."

Guinevere detailed what she could about King Nechtan's forces, their numbers, their horses, their weaponry. "And Morgana is here, in league with the Dark Queen."

"And Mordred is still with you?"

Guinevere sighed. "Yes. But honestly, I do not know whose side he is on. I wonder if even he knows." Isolde would only know of Mordred through Brangien, who would never forgive his actions. Guinevere wished her own feelings were so straightforward, so she could declare him evil and resolve whatever hold he had on her. But she did not want to think about it or talk about it, and it was not information Lancelot needed. "Oh! Tell Lancelot many of their soldiers are women and Nechtan's daughters lead them."

"Is that important?" Isolde asked.

"I just thought she would like to know. If they were not my captors, I would be very impressed and want to know more about their society."

Isolde laughed, but then she grew somber. "And how are you being treated?"

"No one is harming me." Guinevere squeezed Isolde's hand, wanting to reassure her. "They are taking me to the Dark Queen in the north. I will not let it go far enough that I find out what she wants me for."

"Neither will we." After that, there were no more details to give regarding Guinevere's captors. Isolde tipped her head up, closing her eyes as sunlight dappled her features. "This is nice."

"Is it always like this? Is the forest part of the dream magic?" Guinevere had only connected her dreams to someone else once, with Merlin—and, as all things with the wizard, the normal rules did not apply.

"Oh, no. The dreamer sets the location. Brangien and I always met in front of the fireplace where we first kissed." Isolde sighed happily at the memory, then refocused. "I do not know how long we will have, but would you like to hear about how Dindrane had her sister-in-law put in a holding cell for breaking curfew?"

"Yes, please. I am so glad someone is living out their happiest dreams during this tumultuous time."

Isolde's laughter and stories filled the forest glen, and the dream sealed them in from all their troubles.

When Guinevere awoke, it was not on the back of a horse. She was lying in a tent diffused with light. It was at least late morning, if not early afternoon.

"Thank you!"

Guinevere sat upright, her head spinning. Fina was sitting across from her, sharpening a knife and beaming.

"You are . . . welcome?"

"You fainted!" Fina patted a pouch on her belt and was greeted with the clink of metal. "Or at least that is what I was able to argue. At any rate, you fell asleep and no one could wake you. It was good enough to win my wager. Mordred has been quite concerned, though I reassured him southern ladies are not meant for travel like this and we had probably just broken you, is all."

"Is that all?" Guinevere shook her head, reaching for a canteen next to her only to find her hands still bound. "Do you mind?" She lifted them.

Fina undid the various layers of wraps, and Guinevere stretched her aching fingers and wrists. "How long was I asleep?"

"We rode until midmorning and have been camped for several hours now. I only just woke up myself."

"Hmm." Guinevere tried her best to sound impassive. She had told Isolde she would try to sleep while riding at night. That felt the safest, and it meant Isolde would know when they could meet. Isolde promised to come back every night to get information. Guinevere did not care about giving information nearly so much as seeing her friend. Isolde was her connection to Brangien, Lily, Dindrane, and Camelot.

Lancelot.

Fina shrugged off her outer tunic, revealing arms covered in markings, as though an artist had lovingly used her skin as a canvas. The indigo paint was like threads of the night sky dancing over her freckled skin in bold patterns from her shoulders to her wrists. There were figures and animals, as well as lines and symbols that Guinevere did not know the meaning of. She leaned forward, intrigued. "What are those?"

Holding out her arms for Guinevere's inspection, Fina gestured. "These are for my family. These, my people. These show where I came from. See the lines of the rivers? My people sprang from that one. And these I just wanted so my arms were more covered than Nectudad's."

"They are *beautiful*." They reminded Guinevere of the carvings of Camelot, telling stories no one understood. But Fina knew her stories. Guinevere was struck with jealousy.

Mordred entered, relief washing over his face to see Guinevere awake. But then that honest flash of emotion was replaced with the expression he wore when slipping into his role as the eel. "When I told you it was safe to sleep, I did not expect you to take to it with quite that much enthusiasm."

"I prefer oblivion to your company. Fina, can we go eat? Or do I have to stay in the tent?"

Fina's eyes sparked with delight as she looked between the two of them. "You have kissed."

"What?" Guinevere sputtered, trying to look outraged instead of flustered.

Fina's eyes widened even farther, nearly invisible eyebrows rising halfway up her freckled forehead. "*More* than kissed?"

"*No!*"

Fina cackled in triumph. "So you have kissed. And you are married to his uncle. Maybe the south is more interesting than I thought. You have too many rules, so of course they are broken often."

"And you Picts have no rules?"

A flash of anger illuminated Fina's face. "We are not Picts. That is what the Romans called us, sneering at our art and our bodies. What you call the Picts are a vast people, free, bound only by tribes and family. The Romans could not defeat us, so they dismissed us. Your king will make the same mistake."

"I am sorry," Guinevere said, surprised to find she meant it. "I did not know. What is your tribe called?"

"You could not pronounce it, and it is not for you, anyway." Fina stood. "I will go get you food."

She left. Guinevere was still reeling at how quickly the conversation had turned.

"They are very proud people," Mordred said, sitting. "The Romans were brutally cruel, and they have not forgotten nor forgiven."

"But Arthur is not Roman."

"His father was. And he represents the same spirit of conquering that the Romans had."

"Arthur does not conquer people!"

Mordred lay back, putting one arm over his eyes to block out the light. "If you say so."

"I do say so!"

"The northern borders he has slowly but surely annexed will disagree."

Guinevere refused to be drawn into an argument about Arthur.

Not with Mordred. She sat, stewing and hungry, waiting for Fina to return. The tent dulled the noise of the camp but did not extinguish it. Guinevere startled as a couple of voices nearby launched into a heated argument. It sounded like Fina and a man.

"The soldiers want to take boats," Mordred murmured, translating. "They do not understand why we are going by horse. It is slower and more dangerous. We are not in Nechtan's lands anymore."

Guinevere put her hands over her stomach, suddenly less hungry and more ill. "Will we? Take boats?"

"No. My grandmother gave clear instructions to keep you away from water. Fina and Nectudad are presenting a united front with their father and shutting down all protest, but they do not trust my mother or grandmother, because the princesses are intelligent, unlike Nechtan."

"Do they trust you?"

Mordred sighed, not uncovering his face. But he sounded less playful and more . . . sad. "No one should." His breathing evened out as he drifted into sleep.

Guinevere wilted with relief, knowing that at least the Dark Queen's demands had saved her from a swift boat ride up the coast. But it left her puzzled. What did the Dark Queen have to fear from Guinevere and water? Was she afraid the Lady of the Lake would steal her prize?

And in that moment, Guinevere had a new plan. A terrible plan, one that filled her with dread but that just might save her from the foe she knew by delivering her to the one she did not. All she needed was a lake.

Fina reentered the tent, scowling as she shoved some dried meat and a hunk of coarse bread at Guinevere. A bird called from somewhere outside, and Guinevere longed to be out there with it.

"Can we—"

"Hsst," Fina hissed, holding up a hand. The bird called again. Fina threw herself out of the tent, shouting something in her language. Mordred sat up, hand bolting to his sword.

"What was she shouting?" Guinevere asked, at the same moment the first arrow sliced through the side of the tent and stuck in the ground at her feet.

CHAPTER FOUR

"Out!" Mordred shouted. He left the tent first, then gestured for Guinevere to follow.

The quiet order of the camp had been obliterated. Everything was motion, running, shouting, screaming. "Arthur!" Guinevere whispered to herself, her heart racing. How had he gotten to her so quickly? Perhaps he had never gone south. Or maybe one of the messengers had caught up to him and he came directly north instead of stopping at Camelot.

She took a step toward the cover of the trees, and that was when she realized Arthur could *not* have gotten here so quickly. These were not his men. In fact, it looked to Guinevere like Nechtan's own people were attacking. A man ran toward them from the trees, covered in fur, his face painted in streaks.

A knife appeared in his chest and he fell, face-first. "They are going for the horses!" Fina shouted, pulling out another knife, an ax in her other hand. She joined them, gesturing at Mordred. "If the horses panic, we will lose them! Get to them!"

"I am not leaving Guinevere." Mordred twirled his sword in a deadly arc as he looked around for threats.

"Without the horses, we are finished! I will keep her safe. Go, fairyson." Fina kicked him. Mordred growled in response.

He looked at Guinevere, torn, then jabbed his sword toward Fina. "If she gets hurt, I will hold you responsible." Then he ran.

"Who are they?" Guinevere asked. At least her hands were no longer bound. And this might prove an opportunity to escape. Chaos created openings. Arthur had taught her that when he explained the reason they had rooted the chaos of magic out of Camelot. Suddenly, Guinevere's nebulous, terrifying plan to walk into a lake as soon as they found one in hopes of summoning the Lady of the Lake was replaced with a much preferable plan, of slipping out on horseback. No water required.

"They are not friends." Fina threw another knife and it stuck deep into the thigh of a man sneaking up on one of her soldiers. He screamed and fell to the ground. The soldier turned and finished him off with an efficient strike to his throat.

Guinevere flinched from the life bleeding out into the dirt. She needed a horse. She could not escape fast enough on foot unless everyone in Nechtan's party was dead. Which might happen, for all she could tell. How did Arthur manage to fight his battles? There was so much noise and blood and violence. She felt frozen by the horror of it all.

Nectudad roared by, sweeping a path with the huge sword in her hands for the soldiers running in her wake toward the bulk of their attackers. Fina took a couple of instinctive steps toward them, distracted from the battle by her desire to join her sister. A man appeared from behind the tent, sword raised to strike her in the back.

"Fina!" Guinevere shouted. Fina turned just in time to block his strike with her ax. She danced around him, dodging his blows while trying to get close enough to deliver one of her own.

Guinevere ran for the horses, grateful there was a clear shot to them from her tent. One horse was already edging away from the others. Focused on her goal, Guinevere almost tripped over the body of one of Nechtan's soldiers. A bow was in the soldier's hand, arrows spilled on the ground.

Guinevere looked up again. Mordred was in the middle of the horses, hands out, eyes shut as he mouthed words she could not hear. The horses near him were not panicking, and calm seemed to radiate from them. The horse Guinevere had singled out was even closer to her, nearly within reach.

Two tents over, someone else was watching the horses with deadlier intent. There was a hiss as he drew an arrow, taking careful aim at Mordred.

The horse.

Escape.

Mordred.

Before she even realized what she was doing, Guinevere had the dead soldier's bow in her hands. She nocked an arrow and let it fly. It pierced the archer's neck. Gurgling, he put a hand over the wound.

Fina screamed in rage and Guinevere whipped in her direction, another arrow already nocked, then flying. It landed in the back of the man who had driven Fina to her knees, only the ax she held between them fending off his sword.

Guinevere reached for another arrow, and then another, and then another, picking off every attacker who approached the horses. She did not have time to think, to question. All she knew was that these men were going to kill Mordred, and she would not let that happen.

Her arms trembled as she turned, searching, ready, the last arrow nocked.

Fina, somehow beside her now, carefully took the hand that held the arrow taut and guided it so that the bowstring went slack. "The danger has passed, Slip."

The arrow fell, harmless, to the ground. It was over. Mordred was safe in the center of the horses, Fina was alive, and Guinevere had not escaped.

"Where did you learn to shoot?" Fina asked.

"I never did," Guinevere whispered. Her body had done it on its own. What had Lily said? *No one was better with a bow than my sister.* But Guinevere was not that sister.

She was not the real Guinevere. So how had her body known what to do? The action had been instinctive, muscle memory from countless hours of training. Guinevere dropped the bow as though it had bitten her.

"Guinevere." Mordred took her by her shoulders, searching her face. "Why did you do that? You should have hidden."

"She should have run," Fina said, patting Guinevere's back. "That was stupid. But thank you for saving my life. We will move as soon as the wounded are taken care of and the dead are honored. Now that we know we have enemies, we must change our course, which will add several days to the journey. That will be pleasant to command." She stomped away.

Guinevere tore her gaze from the bow and looked up, into Mordred's eyes. At the harvest festival, Morgana had told her that whatever she remembered, whatever she thought she knew, she *was* Guinevere. What made the sorceress believe that? What did she know, what could she see? "I need to speak to your mother."

Concern flashed across Mordred's face, then he smiled blankly. "Absolutely not." He pushed Guinevere toward the tents.

"No, I have questions, and I think—"

"You do not want any answers she can give you. Trust me."

"I will not!"

Mordred bowed as he held open the flap. "That is your right."

Nectudad had almost walked past them when she paused mid-stride and narrowed her eyes at Guinevere. "I saw you by the horses, trying to escape." She bent to pick up a large rock. Guinevere took a step backward, panic narrowing her vision until all she could see was the rock, all she could imagine was the damage it would do.

Fina popped her head out of the tent. "She saved me! And Mordred, unfortunately."

Nectudad nodded grimly, dropped the rock, and continued as though she had not been about to break both of Guinevere's legs.

"My grandmother just *had* to choose Picts," Mordred muttered.

Perhaps not going for the horse had been the best choice after all. And regardless of what Mordred said, Guinevere was going to speak with Morgana before she escaped. She had to. Morgana had promised to help her discover who she really was. If she could not get to the wizard, well, she had a sorceress. She *would* get answers, one way or another.

CHAPTER FIVE

Guinevere was sitting on the ground, the grass impossibly soft beneath her, Isolde's hands expertly twisting and braiding her hair, when something bit her arm. Guinevere yelped and looked down. But nothing was there.

"What is it?" Isolde asked.

"Something—ouch! Something is biting me!" Guinevere lifted her sleeves, but there was only her skin, smooth and unmarred by the scars the trees had left. The scar from where she had taken her own skin to heal Lancelot was still there, though.

"You should wake up," Isolde said.

"I do not know how!" Guinevere slapped at her arms, but the biting continued.

"Focus on the pain. Connect it to your body. Hurry. Something bad might be happening." Isolde wrung her hands.

Guinevere closed her eyes, focusing on the bites. And then the bites turned into sharp pinches, and the sun-soaked meadow around her turned into a chill dawn. No more soft grass, only the unforgiving horse and Mordred at her back.

"Guinevere," he hissed, pinching her arm.

"Stop it!" She shoved his hand away and sat up from where she had been curled against his chest. Her back went cold with the sudden rush of air. "What is wrong with you?"

"People are beginning to get suspicious when you do not wake up for the transfer to a tent. The soldiers think we are poisoning you, which is not doing my reputation any favors, but my mother and Nectudad know better. Nectudad has ridden by three times. If you are tying knots, they *will* find out."

"I am not." Guinevere lifted her bound hands as evidence. "I am just tired."

"Mmm." He did not sound convinced.

It had been two days since the attack. Guinevere endured the daylight hours in the tent, knowing that night would mean getting to spend time with Isolde. It also meant she had to rest against Mordred, but she tried not to worry what he might think about her willingness to sleep while he held her.

She knew the dreamspace was not helping her, but until she could talk to Morgana or enact her terrible plan, the escape was such a *relief.* And she was ravenous for news of Camelot, for the stories of how deftly her friends were managing the city, but always with the hope that one night she would see Isolde and find out Arthur had returned. It had to be soon. He had to be nearly back.

She imagined him riding toward Camelot, but her own landscape was far different. The terrain grew rougher with endless hills, gray rocks, weary green trees, and an utter absence of lakes. Traveling only at night slowed their progress, but Nechtan and his troops still preferred to camp during the day, when they had the greatest visibility to spy any approaching threats.

The visibility today was not in their favor, though. Thick, dark clouds rolled through the sky and a growing wind whipped

Guinevere's hair. With her hands always bound, she could not braid it, and it was impossibly tangled. She almost laughed, thinking of how livid Brangien would be. She would have to tell Isolde to mention the state of her hair, just to be certain that Brangien missed her.

Morgana rode past them. It was the first time in two days Guinevere had seen the sorceress, who always rode next to Nechtan. Mordred avoided Nechtan, perhaps because he did not wish to remind the king that he had considered killing Mordred. Or perhaps because he was trying to shield Guinevere from both Nechtan's and his mother's notice.

This was her chance. Before she could talk herself out of it, Guinevere called out. "Morgana!"

Mordred flinched, cursing under his breath.

His mother turned, raising an imperious eyebrow. "Yes?"

"I need to speak with you."

"My tent," Morgana said. There was a flash of triumph in her eyes that sounded an alarm in Guinevere's head, but what other option did she have? Morgana had told Guinevere she could give her information. Guinevere had no doubt there would be a cost; magic was transactional, and Morgana was a woman who would always extract what was owed to her.

They were camped atop a rocky hill. Men and women struggled to secure the tents as the wind picked up, bringing the first stinging drops of rain.

"Guinevere," Mordred said, tightening his arms around her waist. Before he could dismount or say anything else, Fina appeared and slapped Guinevere's leg.

"She lives!"

"Help me dismount?" Guinevere put her bound hands around Fina's neck and Fina helped her down. She had neatly avoided Mordred's attempt to have a conversation.

"Another wager lost," Fina grumbled. "I cannot figure you out."

"I am a mystery even unto myself." Guinevere tried to say it lightly, but it was the truth. It was the reason she had been outside of Camelot, outside of the shield. Perhaps if she had been able to accept her role, to be the queen Arthur saw her as—*wanted* her as— she would have figured out another way to protect the city. A way that kept her in the same castle as her dearest friends, a way that did not separate her from Lancelot. Then she would be awaiting Arthur's return, ready to comfort him, instead of pinning her hopes on either a sorceress or a wizard.

She took a deep breath. Answers. Morgana could give her answers, and hopefully those answers would give her courage. She was going to escape no matter what, but if she could do it armed with information, then she could make a better plan for what she did after escaping.

"Come on, Slip. This will be a bad storm." Fina started toward their tent, but Guinevere turned in the opposite direction.

"I am going to see Morgana."

"No," Mordred said. "Fina, take her to your tent."

"No." Guinevere glared at him. "I am going to see Morgana."

Fina frowned. "What for?"

"To braid her hair," Guinevere said. "I am very good at it. She is expecting me."

Fina looked from Guinevere to Mordred. Then she shrugged. "I will come. I want my hair braided, too."

Mordred followed as Fina led Guinevere through camp. "Change your mind," he said, his voice low and urgent.

"You are not invited," Guinevere snapped.

"And Fina is?"

Fina scoffed. "I can go anywhere I please. Morgana may think otherwise, but she is not in charge here. She is not one of us. If Slip is visiting the sorceress, so am I. No one will deny me entry, and if Morgana tries, there will be trouble. I deserve to know what she is doing."

Mordred let out a noncommittal noise. "It is my continual prayer that none of us get what we deserve in this life." But he did not try to stop Fina from ducking into Morgana's tent.

As soon as Fina was inside, he grabbed Guinevere's elbow. "*Please.* Whatever you think you want, it is not this."

"Never pretend you know what I want." Guinevere yanked her elbow free. If it were not for Mordred, she never would have picked up that bow. If she had not stopped to save him, she might have escaped. And she would not have the additional confusion of wondering how her body had known how to shoot when her mind did not.

Inside the tent, Morgana was sitting on a cushion, two cups set out in front of her. She smiled up at Guinevere. "Sit down. I am afraid I did not account for another visitor. Fina, you are welcome to leave. I am perfectly safe alone with the queen."

Fina shrugged, lowering herself to lounge on a cushion. "You have a nice tent." Mordred, too, ducked in. He said nothing, merely folded himself into sitting nearby.

Guinevere eyed the cups warily. "I am not thirsty."

Morgana laughed. "Oh, come now. I never try the same trick twice. Sit."

Guinevere did as instructed, tucking her legs beneath her. Her mouth was dry. She knew what she needed to ask, but she suddenly wished she had listened to Mordred. She stalled. "Do you have a spare dress? I would like to change." She had been forced to wash both herself and her clothing with a damp cloth. It was terrible. She missed her cleansing fire. As prickly and uncomfortable as the fire was, at least it was not a wretched piece of wet material.

"She will need a warmer cloak soon, too," Fina said.

"Mmm." Morgana took a cup and drank from it. Then she drank from the other one, too. "Is that why you came? To ask for a dress?"

Guinevere stared down at her bound hands. "I used a bow."

"I heard. Very heroic."

"I do not know how to use a bow. I have never held one before. But . . . I knew. My hands knew." She looked up into Morgana's impassive gaze. "You told me you could help me recover who I was. I want that." If Guinevere could get answers without going to Merlin, all the better. She would recover her past, and then she would escape. And then she would . . . what? Be satisfied with her life, and go back to Camelot to be queen? Did she want that?

A month ago she would have said yes. But she had been given a chance to claim, fully and completely, her identity as Queen Guinevere, and she had chosen to seal herself out. What did she really want?

Herself. She wanted herself. She would do what it took to find out who, exactly, she was.

Morgana smiled. On her stately face, the smile was disarmingly warm. Once more there was the Anna they had known in Camelot, the calm, experienced assurance. Against her better judgment, Guinevere let herself have a moment of hope and relief. This was the right choice.

"Unbind her hands," Morgana said.

Mordred leaned forward and did as instructed. Guinevere could feel his unease every time his skin brushed hers. Her relief evaporated. If Mordred was worried about what his own mother was doing, how much more worried should Guinevere be? Or did he simply not want her to get any answers?

"I told you a bit of what I could do. Do you remember?" Morgana's face was harsher than Mordred's, her features aggressive where his were elegant. She was still beautiful, but in a way that intimidated Guinevere, rather than—

Well, she did not want to feel one way or another about Mordred's looks.

"You are like Merlin. You can see through time."

"Not exactly." Morgana reached out and took Guinevere's hands in her own, looking down at them. Through their touch, Guinevere could feel Morgana's anger. It did not feel related to the moment. It was not a bright bonfire burst, but a smoldering heat, carefully banked, lovingly tended. This anger was as much a part of Morgana as her heart. "You lied to me. The cave is still sealed. Merlin did not create the shield around Camelot."

Guinevere swallowed. "Merlin is a wizard. Surely a little rock is nothing to him."

Morgana turned Guinevere's hands so the insides of her wrists were facing up, delicate tracings of veins peeking through the end of her sleeves. "Do not lie to me again. We are allies, you and I." Guinevere tensed, narrowing her eyes, and Morgana shook her head. "We *are* allies, whether or not you realize it. *Merlin* is our enemy. I will show you." She tapped one of Guinevere's wrists. "I am not like the wizard. I do not see through time. I see through people. I can see through those I am connected to." Her expression opened, eager and hungry. "And now I can also see through you, to those your heart is most bound up in."

Mordred rested one hand on his mother's arm. "Perhaps we should try something else."

"I want to unravel the young queen's past. And that is what she wants as well, is it not?" Morgana's gaze was piercing. Guinevere felt herself pinned in place, unable to look away. "I am going to pull you apart, connection by connection, until we find the source of it all.

Until we find the wizard. Until we solve the mystery of the *queen, not queen,* as my Dark Queen fondly calls you. You want that, too. To know who you really are."

Guinevere did. More than anything. If she was willing to go to Merlin, Merlin who had done unspeakable things time and again, how was it worse to go to Morgana? At least Morgana was human.

"Give me permission." Morgana's grip was as unyielding as stone. Guinevere wondered if she tried to pull away, would the sorceress let her?

"Do it," Guinevere whispered.

Morgana pressed a finger to a vein in Guinevere's wrist. "Passion," she whispered.

Guinevere screamed as something was torn from her and the world went white.

She was looking down at *herself.* Her head was tipped back, her mouth open in silent, frozen agony. She wanted to flee, wanted to return to her body, but her awareness made no difference. She could not do anything, only observe.

"Mother." Mordred's voice was sharp. "Not this." But it was not Mordred alone who spoke, because Guinevere was saying it along with him. As him. She was a passenger behind Mordred's eyes, a stowaway in his heart, thrown there by Morgana's magic.

Morgana's eyes were no longer green. They were the same color as Guinevere's. She was not trapped in another person like Guinevere was, but she was connected. She knew where Guinevere was, what she saw. "That was unexpected," Morgana said, flicking a pitying look at Guinevere's unmoving body.

Anger, far brighter than Morgana's, flared, and Guinevere's

hands—*no,* Mordred's hands, she had no control, she was nothing but a passenger—reached toward his mother. Roots snaked free of the earth, wrapping around his ankles and knees and tugging them down.

He ignored them, pulsing with rage. "You are not doing this for her."

"Be a good boy or I will not tell you where passion led her." Morgana frowned in concentration. Mordred watched, powerless. It was how he had always been, how he would always be. Guinevere felt it as he felt it, and wanted to cry for him.

He was powerless to reach her. Just as he had been powerless to reach Arthur. Powerless to save his father, to comfort his mother, to protect his grandmother. Powerless to feel loved by any of them. Desperation had driven him to that blood-soaked meadow on the night they resurrected the Dark Queen. Desperation to finally fix something, to finally help someone, to finally do something about all the pain that seemed to be the very core of himself.

And he had hurt her, had hurt Guinevere, and he could never fix it, and he did not deserve to ever fix it.

Despair overwhelmed him anew as he watched his mother tap another vein and say, "She is strong enough for more, I think."

"Mother. I am begging you." But he knew it would not matter. Nothing stood between Morgana and what she wanted, and what she wanted was never what her son wanted. He only wanted—

With a rush like that of blood returning to her fingers after she had tied them off in knots, Guinevere came back to herself. She gasped for air, blinking, disoriented, to find Mordred once again above her and herself lying on the tent floor. He was still bound by roots.

Morgana's gaze was flint, ready to spark a fire. "We will leave it up to Guinevere. Do you want to discover what connects you to Merlin? To see and feel as him? Or do you want to continue as a stranger to yourself?"

Guinevere licked her dry lips, trying to remember how to speak. Mordred had said his mother was not doing this for Guinevere. But if their goal—get to the wizard, figure out Guinevere's true identity—was the same, what did it matter if their reasons were different? "I want to unravel what he did to me."

"Good." Morgana squeezed Guinevere's wrist idly. "Hmm. I am thinking of what connection to tap into to try to find him."

"Did you really think it would be passion?" Guinevere asked, aghast.

Morgana laughed, a low, rich sound. "Well, no. I was just warming up. Passion lingers close to the surface, establishes an easy, intense bond between us. Would you like to talk about whom passion connected you to?"

Guinevere pushed her wrist into Morgana's hand, her head spinning and her cheeks burning with mortification. "Go on."

"You thought Merlin was your father, did you not?" Morgana took a deep breath and ran a finger along one of Guinevere's veins. The same itching rush as before, as though her vein were trying to lift from beneath her skin, made Guinevere certain she would go mad until Morgana tapped on it and said, "Family."

She was divided in three, her awareness like a river branching out.

CHAPTER SIX

On the first branch, Brangien.

"But which is it?" the kitchen maid Ailith, who had returned to Camelot instead of leaving with Rhoslyn's camp, asked, trembling, her hands stuck in dough but not kneading. "The Dark Queen trapping us, or the Lady of the Lake protecting us?"

It did not require any extra awareness to know that Guinevere was inhabiting Brangien. She could have laughed at the surge of intense annoyance Brangien felt.

"I was not aware you required that knowledge to finish baking bread for the day's meals. I will abandon all my many, many duties to rush down to the lake and get an answer for you, because that is my only priority for the day as I take care of an entire city."

Ailith's eyes widened. "Really?"

"No! And for your purposes, it could be the Lady of the Lake and the Dark Queen herself making passionate love to Merlin in the skies above Camelot, and it would not change the fact that the castle needs bread and you are the one responsible for making the bread. If you would like to give up that responsibility, I am certain there is someone in this city who would very much like your position and your bed in the castle and your coin. Someone who realizes that whatever is happening is a matter for kings and queens, and we need only busy ourselves with making sure this city runs in the meantime."

Ailith began kneading with terrified vigor. Brangien eyed the rest of the kitchen. It was exceptionally quiet, every person now intensely invested in doing their individual tasks.

"And seeing as how the sky has not fallen on our heads and none of us have been unceremoniously slaughtered, it should be quite obvious that the barrier around the city is a protection, not a threat. Regardless, it does not change our jobs and how we do them."

Brangien turned sharply on her heel and marched out of the kitchen. As soon as she was in the hallway, alone, she leaned against the wall, rubbed her face, and thought of her friends. Sir Tristan was in the south, fighting who knew what threats, and Guinevere was in the north, in the hands of Mordred and Morgana, and she herself was here, making kitchen maids cry. But someone had to keep this wretched city running while they waited for King Arthur to return and Guinevere to be rescued.

Brangien wished with a sudden, fierce longing that Isolde could do the knotting so she could speak with Guinevere, instead of having details relayed to her. Isolde was very good about describing Guinevere's mental and emotional states. But it was still unfair. Taking care of Guinevere was *her* job, not Isolde's.

Guinevere had given Brangien everything. A place in the castle, a friend, a safe space to be herself, and finally, most incredibly, Isolde. And Brangien had never let Guinevere know how much she cared about and valued her. Brangien hated that about herself, that she was good at snapping and criticizing, but kindness still felt like a muscle she had never used. She could manage kindness for Isolde, but that was easy because Isolde knew the ugliest things about her and still loved her.

When Guinevere came back, because she *would* come back, Brangien would work on being kind. Actually saying the nice things she thought. *After* she screamed at Guinevere and let her know how tremendously foolish her plan had been, and how livid Brangien was that she had not been consulted.

She straightened and marched up the stairs to Guinevere's room. In the meantime, Guinevere had left her in charge of the stupid city, and she would take care of it so well it would never recover. The king and queen would return to Camelot in the best shape it had ever been, every servant, every soldier, every single living creature doing exactly what they should because Brangien would destroy them otherwise. The Dark Queen had nothing on her determination and fury.

She tidied Guinevere's spotless room, then decided to do the same with King Arthur's. Brangien did not usually take care of his things, but she needed something, anything, to do until Isolde returned from her errands. She strode into the king's room and stopped cold.

The crown, in the center of the bed.

Guinevere's crown.

No, no no no. Guinevere, you fool. Cursing her best friend, Brangien grabbed the crown and took it back to Guinevere's room, setting it reverently on a table. She would protect her friend from herself. Whatever Guinevere's plan had been when she left the city, surely it was different now. And Brangien would make certain that when Guinevere returned, she did not return to questions and demands and heartbreak. She would be able to make a better decision then. One not driven by panic.

But.

What if . . . what if Guinevere meant to go with Mordred?

Brangien sat heavily on the end of Guinevere's bed. Had she been blind to what her friend needed? Guinevere had obviously wanted more with the king than the king was ready or able to give. Brangien had thought that, with time, they would figure it out. But she knew what it was to discover what you wanted, to damn every consequence, to abandon who you were and who you could have been in favor of what you could be with another.

And she was not a fool. She had seen the looks Mordred gave Guinevere, and the looks Guinevere had tried very hard not to give him.

Maybe if Brangien had been a better friend, she could have fixed this. Or, if she had been a better friend, she could have seen that it was not fixable, and helped Guinevere find her own way to happiness. But Camelot needed Guinevere. Arthur needed her. *Brangien* needed her.

There was a knock at the door. Brangien threw it open, scowling. "What?"

The page trembled, his voice squeaking. "There is a problem with the arena schedule, and I was told—we are supposed to—you are in charge?"

God help them all, she was. "Tell them I am on my way." She slammed the door in his face, then fastened her cloak. Her eyes lingered on the crown. This city was not going to break on her watch. When Arthur returned, Brangien would make certain the idiot king did not let Guinevere go without a fight.

Guinevere was slipping away. Something was cracking, something leaking between the fissures.

But before she could be properly afraid, she was swept along to the second branch and her feelings were swept into Lily.

Lily's cheeks hurt from smiling so much, but she kept her expression in place, waving at shopkeepers and cooing over babies and stopping to watch a ball game happening along one of the city's only level streets. The more Princess Lily was seen enjoying Camelot, buying fabric for new dresses, cheering on competitors in the arena, and laughing at the plays, the more the people would realize they had nothing to fear.

Guinevere had accused Lily of only associating with important figures, and that *had* been true while Lily was fighting for her place here. But now that the king and queen were gone, Lily had stepped into their place. They were a king and queen of the people, so she spent as much time among the common folk as she could.

If Guinevere could come to Camelot and become brave, Lily could come to Camelot and become whatever she needed to be to make a difference. Camelot was a place of opportunity. Of change. She would let it change her for the better, too.

"Do you miss Sir Gawain?" Isolde asked as she and Lily walked to a bakery. Isolde was also skilled at smiling, and her radiantly beautiful face was good for people to see.

"Oh! Yes? Yes." In truth, Lily had barely thought of him. It made her a little sad. She would love to be in love, to miss a brave knight and pray for his return, but . . . now that she did not have to marry to stay here, all the urgent affection she had built up for him had receded to passive fondness. It did not matter. Her father had been wrong. She was worth so much more as a person than becoming a wife and a mother.

At a bakery, she and Isolde bought every item, carrying the food out in baskets. "Good afternoon!" Lily called, handing out bread and honeyed buns to all they passed. The women clasped her hands, shining with gratitude, and she knew it was not for the bread. It was for the hope, the reassurance that Camelot was safe and everything would be all right.

It might not be. Lily was not a fool. She knew Guinevere had been taken by enemies, and that they had no idea when the king would return. Every morning when she awoke and remembered anew that her sister was gone yet again, she was equal parts devastated by fear and livid that she had been left behind.

But at the same time, she was confident. Proud. Guinevere had left her in charge. Guinevere trusted her. Believed in her. And Lily *liked* her work here. She loved spreading positive rumors, creating the lie that the Lady of the Lake was protecting them. She had no idea what the barrier was, but she could tell Brangien and Lancelot did.

Let them hold their secrets. It did not affect her job one way or another. Lily had a city to keep happy, and she was very, very good at it, and when Guinevere returned—because she had to return, Lily would not even think of the alternatives—her sister would be proud.

Guinevere wished she could let Lily know she already was proud, but then she was torn free, flung out, and she could feel pieces of herself falling away, dissolving into the darkness as she—

"Lady Dindrane!" Lionel, Sir Bors's youngest son from his first marriage, bowed to her. He was a tall sapling of a boy, just turned fifteen, with broad shoulders and long limbs. "Are you well?"

"Did you come from training?" Dindrane asked.

Guinevere was *not* Dindrane. She tried to peel herself away, to hold on to where she ended and Dindrane began, but it made her feel as though she were being carved open.

Dindrane considered her stepson. Lionel would become a knight soon, sponsored by his father. He was a handsome youth. His dark complexion favored his mother's, and he had a fine, straight nose and kind eyes. He had always been polite, he regularly attended church, and Dindrane had never heard him utter a sharp word to anyone.

And Sir Gawain was gone.

Surely Princess Lily was lonely. And how wonderful would it be to seal her bond with Guinevere by matching her stepson with Guinevere's sister? And what a triumph for Sir Bors for his son to marry so well.

There had been a time not long ago that Dindrane still lived in fear that Guinevere would one day realize she had been a fool to look at Dindrane and see anything worthwhile.

No one else ever had, after all. Dindrane was small and mean because the world around her was small and mean, and she became so used to striking back however she could that she had eventually started striking first, lashing out with her tongue before she could be hurt.

Yet Guinevere had laughed, and clasped her hands, and declared they would be friends.

Guinevere had meant it, too. In Guinevere's eyes, Dindrane was not small and mean, but clever and loyal. Being seen that way allowed her to see herself that way. She had grown. She was better because Guinevere loved her.

Guinevere would not stop loving Dindrane. But it never hurt to deepen alliances by gifting sweet Lily with an equally sweet boy.

"I have a task for you." Dindrane took Lionel's arm and turned him to walk with her. "Princess Lily is out in the city so much, without anyone to accompany or protect her. And since you are nearly a knight, it is only right that you should serve."

"Princess Lily?" Lionel's voice cracked ever so slightly, betraying a depth of excitement and emotion that did not surprise Dindrane but certainly encouraged her.

See how generous she could be?

❧

Morgana tore her hand away, scowling in annoyance. "I did not need to see that ridiculous woman."

At some point, Guinevere had fallen backward. Everything hurt, like her blood itself had been sunburned. She felt raw and exposed and scattered, trapped between dreaming and wakefulness, with a sudden fear that she would never wake all the way. That parts of her had been left behind in Brangien, Lily, Dindrane. Mordred.

"Are you dead?" Fina asked, concerned.

"No." Guinevere tried to move, but her body had not quite caught up. She blinked rapidly, trying to focus on the tent, on the feeling of being in her own mind again.

"Fina, get Guinevere something to drink," Morgana commanded.

Fina scowled down at Guinevere, worry creasing her brow. "I will, but not because you asked. Because she needs it." Fina left the tent.

"Dindrane never changes," Guinevere said with a rush of affection in spite of her disorientation. As awful as she felt now, she was glad for the few moments she had been able to spend with three women she loved. They were so strong, so smart. So complex and infinite and human.

"Release me, Mother." Mordred's voice was cold and sharp.

"Mmm." Morgana was holding her forehead, eyes squeezed shut. Guinevere bore the brunt of the magic, but it did not appear to be easy for Morgana, either. "She does change, though. They all do and have because of you. And none of it helps us because none of them are Merlin. Where are you connected to him?"

Guinevere wanted to sit up, but she did not think she could manage it. There was a feeling like a hive of bees in the back of her head, buzzing and droning, and she sensed a headache waiting to descend with as much torrential force as the storm outside. "If I knew how I was connected to Merlin, I would not need you." Guinevere's stomach clenched, and at last the feeling of being stuck in a dream was cut through with fear. If it had been that destructive to be in the heads of normal people, how would she feel in Merlin's?

Morgana sighed. "But you do need me, for more than this. I am not your enemy. We are allied against Merlin, whether you realize it or not."

"You want to give me to the Dark Queen so she can defeat Arthur."

"I want to find a new way of fighting Merlin. He used us all as unwilling tools in his quest to remake the world according to his desires. I—we—need to break the path he set us on."

Guinevere managed to sit up. The bees in her head were swarming, making room for the approaching pain. "I hold no love for Merlin or his methods." She thought of what had been done to Igraine, to Morgana, to herself. "But in fighting Merlin, you are also fighting Arthur, and I believe in Arthur. He has built something better in Camelot."

Mordred scoffed, his tone bitter, "Better for some. Not for all."

Guinevere could not deny that. Seeing Ailith in the kitchens with Brangien reminded her of it. But Rhoslyn and her camp had opted to reject Camelot, to cling to their traditions and their magic, and they had not been safe. Without Lancelot and Mordred, who knew what would have happened to them?

Arthur's way was not perfect, but the world was a vicious, dangerous place, and anything that countered that was better than nothing. It had to be.

"All he wants is Camelot."

Morgana lifted one eyebrow. "Really? How can you be sure? He wants what Merlin wants, and I promise you that monster is not satisfied with a single *perfect* city."

Guinevere tried to shake her head, but the movement made everything spin. Arthur was not Merlin, and he never would be.

"Here is her drink!" Fina said, her voice loud as she reentered the tent and passed a canteen to Guinevere. Guinevere swayed, nearly falling again. Her eyes weren't focusing.

Morgana pressed one hand against her own forehead. "Please be quiet, Fina."

"Oh, did the terrible magic you used Guinevere for wear you out?" Fina's voice grew even louder. "Does your head hurt? Does it hurt very much? How much would you say it hurts?"

"Hush, you wretched girl, or I will make all your hair fall out using my magic."

"Try it and I will make all your blood fall out. Using my ax."

"Enough." Mordred tore away the roots on his arms, pulled out a knife, and began cutting his knees and ankles free.

Morgana snatched Guinevere's wrist. Before anyone could stop her, she pushed on a vein and hissed, *"Duty."*

CHAPTER SEVEN

A booted foot kicked a body free from a sword. *The* sword. Excalibur. Guinevere had enough of herself remaining to marvel for a moment that she was near Excalibur without the sick dread that always left her shaking. But then her boundaries dissolved. She was bubbled breath released from lungs, floating to the surface to disappear, drowned in Arthur.

"Saxons," Sir Bors said, throwing a bloodied cloth onto the body. "And we found silver with Pictish scratchings on it." He held out a coin.

Arthur stared at the corpse. His knights had flown, almost by magic, their roads clear, their horses powerful, their brotherhood as strong as iron. They had crashed against the castle, the castle that held his past, his future, his son. A son and a wife, a family, all his own. He was going to have everything his heart had ever hoped for.

Instead they had found an ambush.

"Saxons." Arthur sounded hollow. "And Picts. Any sign of a child?"

Sir Bors shook his head, and though this knight was the least emotional of all of them, his mustache trembled as he answered, "No. None."

Arthur stared down at Excalibur. It was a lie. It was all a lie. The past four days of hope, of surety, of purpose. The burning joy of a quest, the quest that would atone for what he had done to Elaine, was never a quest at all.

He was a fool.

He stepped over the body and trudged through the castle hallways. The bloodied and ruined bodies of men registered as much as the moldy tapestries and the rush-strewn floors. Outside, he could breathe better. His knights gathered around him. Sir Percival had taken an arrow to the shoulder, Sir Gawain was limping, and Sir Bedivere was binding his torso where it bled freely. But their injuries were not the worst cost of his vain hope, his naive dream of the good he could force onto the world around him. The cost was Camelot. He had no doubt they would return to find Camelot under siege. Or, worse, captured.

He closed his eyes, tipping his face toward the sky. Returning as fast as he could would be the best protection for Guinevere. The city could hold against siege for a few days, at least. He could sneak back in through the secret passageway, in time to rescue his queen. Get her out if the attack was too far advanced to repel. She would not escape by herself, he knew. She would stand with the city to the end.

Guinevere. His Guinevere. Merlin's final gift to him. He stared down at the sword. It had been a gift, too. A gift and a curse. He was not yet free of the curse.

"We are close to King Mark's land, are we not?" Arthur asked, opening his eyes.

He could race back and save Guinevere, but that would not save Camelot. If he was going to defeat whatever they faced, he would need overwhelming force. Enough men that he could retake a stolen Camelot.

"Yes, my king," Sir Percival said.

What had Guinevere said when Arthur chastised her for destroying King Mark's mind and introducing chaos to his kingdom? *They do not have a King Arthur.*

Very well. He would give them an Arthur. He would give them *all* an Arthur. He would sweep through the south, and they would kneel because they must, but eventually they would be glad they had done so. They would see that his way was better as he rose like a flood through the land, washing away the Saxons, washing away the Picts, washing away all those who would sow chaos, who would destroy what he was working so hard to build. He would protect his borders by eliminating them. It was time to make this entire island Camelot.

He placed his sword before him and knelt, making an oath between himself and the future. He would do what needed to be done, and Guinevere would be safe because she had to be. Because he could not survive arriving at another castle and finding that piece of his heart gone, too. Merlin had promised him this was his duty. His right. And surely if he was fulfilling his destiny, what was right, fate would keep Guinevere safe until he returned.

It still took everything he had, every scrap of strength gathered over his lifetime, to stand and address his men instead of running for his horse and his queen.

"We are taking the south," he said, "and then the north. We are taking it all. For Camelot."

"For Camelot!" his men shouted as one, lifting their swords, and their confidence reassured Arthur that he was making the right choice.

There was no choice but him. Arthur was everything, and nothing else mattered. The last bubble of Guinevere, the last fragile piece of her, evaporated.

"She is not breathing!" she heard someone shout. Guinevere could not find herself, could not settle, did not want to. She wanted to be Arthur again, to feel so completely sure of who he was, of what he was supposed to do. Not this poor lost girl, lying on the floor of a tent. She was too tired to be that again. Why had she chosen this?

"No!" Mordred broke through the final root that bound him and threw himself over Guinevere. He pressed his lips to hers. She saw it without feeling, and in that moment she wanted to feel it—whatever else she would feel, she wanted to feel *that* again, one last time.

Guinevere took a breath.

CHAPTER EIGHT

Guinevere felt as though she had been picked apart at the seams and not quite sewn back together. Her mind kept leaping like a spooked horse, shuddering into motion and then jumping somewhere else entirely.

"We did not agree to this! The sorceress would have killed her!"

"Lower your voice, girl. I am worse for wear, too. But it was worth it."

A man was speaking, but she understood none of what he said. Why didn't her ears and her mind find their way back to each other? There was a whistling, a rattling. Something was trying to tear apart the tent, like her mind had been torn apart. She was being held, her cheek pressed against a chest with a heart beating terribly fast. So terribly fast. Why did hearts try to run themselves out of beats? They had so few.

"I do not want to go. Please. I want to stay," she whispered, pressing her face harder against the heart trying to find its way out of its cage to meet her.

"Shh," Mordred whispered, and she knew his voice, and she knew his soul, and when his hand pressed her cheek she could not feel which pain was hers and which was his, and she knew it did not matter to him, either. It was all the same pain.

The sorceress spoke. "Arthur is going to take the south. It will not be difficult. They are divided, small, most kings in name only. He thinks we are besieging Camelot, but when he finds it unharmed, he will sweep up the coast. He is coming for the north."

"And whose fault is that?"

"*Fina*," Nectudad chided. "Morgana, how do you know this?"

"I have seen it. Because I am a *sorceress*."

A trick. All a trick. Morgana had never been trying to help Guinevere. Perhaps she had never truly hoped to reach Merlin. She had used Guinevere to spy on Arthur. A new wave of pain crested, and this pain was entirely Guinevere's.

Fina spoke. "But surely when he finds Camelot unharmed, he will stop." Guinevere knew Fina's voice, and Nectudad's, and Morgana's. She understood them. Which meant the voice speaking words she could not translate was Nechtan's. The tent was very full. She wanted to be somewhere else, anywhere else, where she could peacefully sink into pain and despair.

"He will never stop," Morgana said. "He is as inevitable as the tide. We cannot stop him with men or armies. Only the Dark Queen can stand against him. Your father understands that. Translate."

"Translate it yourself, witch," Nectudad spat.

Wind whipped through the tent. Mordred shifted to shield Guinevere. She wanted to open her eyes, to wake up, to go to sleep, anything to stop feeling this way. To find herself fully or lose herself completely.

"Translate it, Nectudad," Morgana said, her voice as cold as the surrounding air and just as charged. "And my son will know if you translate it wrong."

The wind picked up again. The tent flap opened once more.

"Stay in or stay out, Fina," Morgana snapped.

Fina sounded angry. "Give her to me! Guinevere. Give her to me."

"No," Morgana said.

"Very well, continue talking our war strategy in front of the enemy queen! I will detail our numbers and the tribes we have alliances with, and you can tell her all about what your Dark Queen has in mind for her. This cannot possibly end badly."

Mordred moved to stand, still cradling Guinevere.

"You stay, Mordred," Morgana commanded. "I do not trust Nectudad to translate."

Nectudad's voice was low with disgust. "Only those without honor doubt the honor of everyone around them. If you do not trust me to translate, how can you trust me to lead my father's armies? We are all in this now. There is no hope without you. You have seen to that." Nectudad made a sound like spitting. "Fina, take Guinevere. Mordred, stay."

Mordred's arms tightened around her.

"I will be kind," Fina whispered, the sound of the storm against the tent keeping her words between the three of them. Guinevere was handed to Fina, and it was easier, being away from Mordred. Even the storm pelting them as Fina stumbled and struggled to get Guinevere to her tent felt like nothing compared to what she felt when she touched Mordred.

It was a relief to be numb once again.

Guinevere did not know how much time had passed. It could have been minutes, or hours, or days. Perhaps the storm would rage forever, and she would exist infinitely in this dark tent, unraveled in body and mind and spirit.

"I am going to brush your hair," Fina declared as she lit a lamp. She dragged Guinevere to sitting. "It is upsetting me." She worked out the tangles with the same brusque impatience Brangien would have. Guinevere cried, and as she cried, she felt herself restored. Bruised and battered, but still there.

Fina paused. "Sorry."

"No, please keep going." Guinevere wrapped her arms around her knees, hugging her legs and letting the tears trail down her face.

"So it did not work?" Fina whispered, barely audible over the storm pelting the tent's oiled cloth.

Guinevere had been Mordred, and then she had been her dearest friends, and then she had been Arthur, and then she had very nearly been nothing at all. "I am sure Morgana got what she needed. But I did not. Merlin—" Guinevere stopped, unsure how to continue. What to tell Fina, when so many secrets that were not hers to give had already been delivered to Arthur's enemies.

"I know who Merlin is. Long beard. Eyes like burning coals. Eats children."

"He does not— Well, maybe he does eat children. I do not know. I do not know anything. Merlin walks back and forth through time, seeing everything at once, and still he could not be bothered to give me anything true, anything real about myself. He pushed lies into my head and then sent me to Arthur."

"You saw him. Arthur. He really is building an army? Morgana is not lying?"

Guinevere should deny it, but maybe it was better they knew. They could not defeat him. She nodded. "He does not know what has happened in Camelot; he thinks he will have to fight to get it back."

"Maybe when he returns to Camelot and finds it unharmed, he

will stop." Fina suddenly sounded young, far younger than Guinevere had thought.

"He found an ambush instead of a promised son, and he will return home to a stolen wife. Do you think he will stop?" She had felt
his determination. Felt the confidence, the rightness of his choices,
settle onto his shoulders. She had lost herself in the sheer *power* of
his belief.

She believed in Arthur. She always had. But there was something terrifying about his certainty now. No one embarking on a war
should feel that certain of themselves. Arthur's world was good and
evil, right and wrong. And it was his to cut through, to judge good
and evil on the edge of Excalibur.

He had thought of Excalibur as both a gift and a curse. What did
that mean?

He had thought of her as a gift, too. But not that her life, her presence in his, was a gift. That she was a gift *from Merlin*. There was
a possessiveness to that belief that unsettled her. She had wanted
Arthur to be hers in every sense, but she had wanted that for both of
them, together. She no more wanted to belong to someone than she
wanted to possess someone.

How much of his anger had been at what he felt was taken from
him? At his desperation to have the family he had always wanted, but
could not give up Camelot for?

Fina let out an exhaled word that Guinevere did not understand
but felt instinctively was a profanity which she wanted to know.
"Nectudad is right. Morgana trapped us. And now Arthur will come
and take everything we are." Fina brushed Guinevere's hair slowly,
her pale eyebrows drawn in concern. "We are not perfect. There
is bloodshed and war between tribes. Not all are kind to the weak
among them. But we are *free*. We can leave a tribe if we do not love

it. Men and women can choose to fight if it is in their blood, or to stay home and care for their young. We can walk away from a partner if we do not love them. We do not need to be remade in Camelot's image."

Fina's people were violent. They had kidnapped Guinevere and cruelly tricked Arthur. But she had also experienced kindness from and friendship with Fina, seen women treated as equals. The idea of Fina being forced into a role that did not fit her, being restricted and diminished, filled Guinevere with tremendous sadness.

What if Lancelot had been born here? Would she have been happier? How many little Lancelots in the south would never be able to be true to themselves, would always have to become smaller to fit?

But how many people in the north suffered needlessly and died because of the lack of a core leadership, the absence of rules and justice, the constant warfare?

Fina wrapped Guinevere's hair in a long strip of blue cloth like her own. "This will keep your hair from tangling too badly when we ride."

"Thank you."

Fina hummed a low note in response. Then she slapped her thighs and stood, peeling off her outer tunic and exposing her arms. "I hate it when this gets wet. Easier to dry arms than leather. Do you want to get drunk?"

"*What?*"

"Did I say that wrong? Drunk. Drink too much wine. Make our brains slow and silly."

"No, you said it right."

"I want to get drunk. I think you should, too. You have earned it. I will be right back. I do not want to bind your hands right now." Fina crouched in front of Guinevere. "Please do not make me."

Guinevere did not have any reserves left. The idea of tying so much as a single knot of confusion made her want to cry again. "You have my word."

Fina nodded and disappeared through the flap, swallowed by the storm. Guinevere scooted to the center of the tent, trying to ignore the sound of rain pelting the flimsy shelter, desperate to get in. To get to her.

"I am not ready," she whispered to the water. She had hoped to leave behind her plan to find the Lady of the Lake, but it was all that was left to her now. Morgana had no desire to help her. She had taken Guinevere's desperation to know her own past and used it as a tool to get what the Dark Queen wanted: information on Arthur. Who knew what else she might try, might do?

Guinevere knew she should not be so hurt. She should have expected this from Morgana. A part of her had seen a woman—a mother—and expected help. But being a mother did not make someone nurturing. Morgana had her own plans and purposes, and she would do whatever she needed to in order to see them through to their bloody ends.

Guinevere could not give her any more tools. She would escape as soon as she had recovered enough to manage it.

After a few minutes, the tent flap blew in and delivered Fina in a burst of rain. Guinevere backed away from the water as Fina tied the flap shut again. She held up a stoppered clay jug, her expression triumphant.

"Your arms." Guinevere pointed to where water beaded on Fina's decorated arms. "How does the color stay? I thought it would wash away."

Fina laughed, lying down and propping herself on her elbows. "It does not wash away because it is not painted on my skin. It is under my skin."

"What?" Guinevere scooted closer, peering at it. "How?"

"Needles. They dip the needle in dye and then pierce the skin. The dye settles in."

"Forever?"

"The markings change as you age, but that is part of the beauty. Your history, told on your skin."

Guinevere reached out, then paused. "May I touch them?"

Fina held out her arm. Guinevere ran her finger over the designs. The skin was smooth, unscarred. "Beautiful," she said. She stared down at her own sleeves. "In Camelot, we do not even show our wrists."

"Why?" Fina unstoppered the jug and took a long drink.

"I honestly do not know." Guinevere accepted the jug and took a drink as well. The wine was spiced, unexpectedly familiar. She supposed wine was the same everywhere, which was comforting, in a way. "I wish I had my history written on my body. Though I suppose I have some of it." She rubbed at her wrists.

"What do you mean?"

Guinevere reached up and unlaced her sleeves, tugging them free from the bodice of her dress. She held out her arms, the delicate scars on them catching the lamplight. "The Dark Queen."

"And this one?" Fina pointed to the larger, flat scar.

"I took some of my own skin to save a stranger who had saved me." Guinevere smiled fondly. "She became dearer to me than my own flesh, so I have never minded that one." Guinevere sighed. "I did something terrible to her, and I think she will never forgive me, and I do not think she should."

"What did you do?"

"I deceived her. I deceive everyone, all the time, but not her. This time, though, I did. I thought I was protecting her." No one in Camelot knew the full truth of who Guinevere was, except for Lancelot and Arthur. And while she tried to be honest with Arthur, there was always pretense between them. She always tried to act how she thought she should to be the best person for him. To be the protector he needed, the queen he deserved, all while hoping to eventually be the wife he loved.

With Lancelot, she was allowed to simply . . . be. And she had ruined it.

Guinevere took another drink, then passed the jug back to Fina. The wine had been a good idea. She finally felt warm and safe.

"Sometimes we have to be false in order to be true." Fina lifted the jug in a salute.

"Yes! Exactly! Like when I went to Camelot and pretended to be the queen so that I could protect Arthur." Guinevere stared in horror at the jug. There was a reason the wine tasted familiar. She had had this exact brew before. "Oh, no. Oh, Fina, how could you?"

"How could I what?"

"You tricked me."

"I am confused."

"Morgana's wine."

"Yes! I stole it. The sorceress did not see that coming! I knew she would have something good hidden for herself."

Guinevere laughed, covering her mouth. "No! You did not know?"

"Know what?"

"It is a *potion*."

Fina's eyes went wide with fear. "What is going to happen to me? Am I going to turn into an animal? Or a man?"

"No. We are going to tell the truth."

Fina giggled. "So, definitely not a man. But now I am so curious, you simply must explain. How are you not the queen?"

"I am not a princess. And I am not Guinevere. I never was."

Fina's mouth made the same perfect circle her eyes were. "Does Arthur know?"

"Yes! He always knew."

"I was so wrong about things being dull in the south! Is he handsome?"

"Extremely." Guinevere frowned. "It is frustrating."

"But you do not need to be jealous of his looks! You are so beautiful. Tell me about Arthur, my almost husband." Fina flipped onto her stomach, perching her chin on her fists. "Is he a good lover?"

"I do not know!" Guinevere knew she should try to guard herself, but Fina was not a threat. And after so many months of pretending, it was more than just the potion that made her feel loose and happy. It was having an honest conversation.

"No! You have not—he has not—does he prefer men?"

Guinevere had never considered it. "No. I do not think so. I mean, he loves his knights. A lot. He loves them so much, and he spends all his time with them. But it is not romantic."

"Then why not?"

"He wanted to wait until I was ready."

"And you are not ready."

"No! I was ready! I was very ready. Especially after Mordred and I kissed."

Fina lifted a triumphant fist in the air. "I knew it! Tell me he is a good kisser."

"Yes, unfortunately." Guinevere felt a wave of sadness. He was. And as much as she had tried to break her heart away from him, feeling the pain that he felt, seeing herself in that same pain, made her feel closer to him than ever. He was a melody she felt in her soul.

Fina nodded smugly. "I should have put a wager on it. But wait, if you were ready, and Arthur wanted to wait until you were ready, then why are you still waiting? Is this the potion addling me, or is this confusing?"

"It *is* confusing! Everything in my whole life is confusing. But Arthur was being respectful."

"By not doing what you wanted."

"Yes."

"Does he control everything about your relationship?"

"No!" Guinevere frowned. "Well, sometimes when we are in my room, he tells people to enter or leave. Even though it is my room. That is because he is used to being king. But he leaves me in charge when he is gone." Guinevere was too chained to truth to deny how silly it sounded, that Arthur allowed her to rule when he was not there. Fina would not stand for it.

"I do not like that at all." Fina stuck out her tongue, confirming Guinevere's thought.

Guinevere wanted to push Fina, to make her see, but her hands would not obey. "Arthur *is* good, though."

Fina made a doubtful face. "He is good to you. He is not good to me. He is like the Romans, coming in and demanding the world remake itself in their image."

Guinevere frowned. That was not true. Was it? Arthur shaped Camelot, and determined how everyone there lived, but he did it for their own good. And now he was going to do the same to the entire south.

Was it good?

"I do not want to talk about Arthur anymore," Fina huffed.

"Are you angry that I married him? Did you want to?" Guinevere asked. Fina had said she was glad, but had she been telling the truth? Had Guinevere hurt her before they even met?

Fina shook her head energetically. "No. My father wanted me to, but the idea of becoming this"—she gestured at Guinevere—"made me want to throw myself off a mountain."

"It is not easy," Guinevere admitted. "There are so many rules."

"Like your sleeves!"

"Like my sleeves! I hate them! We should burn them!"

Fina eyed the lamp appraisingly, then shook her head. "You will get even colder. You should keep them."

Guinevere sighed, then scowled. "This is not fair. I told you I am not really a princess, and that Arthur and I have not—" She waved in the general direction of her lap. "Tell me something you should keep secret."

Fina put her hand over her mouth, but talked through her fingers, compelled to keep speaking as Guinevere was. "I do not want anything the Dark Queen wants. I cannot stand to even look at her. She is an abomination. And I hate that my father is under her sway. I love my father, but he does not believe in his people. He is afraid. And she found that fear and used it to wriggle her way inside him. Like a maggot."

"Like a thousand maggots," Guinevere suggested, remembering how the Dark Queen emerged from the ground in a swirl of insects.

Fina removed her hand from her mouth and shouted triumphantly, "Yes! And now Arthur is going to come with an army because she told us if we brought you to her, she would have a magic powerful enough to defeat him. But we would not need to defeat him if we had not taken you! It is like a snake devouring itself. The poison is the antidote. I do not want to take you to her. Especially not after what Morgana did today. She used you. It was terrible."

"You should not take me to the Dark Queen! It will be bad for all of us. I am going to try to get away. Oh, I did not want to tell you that!"

"How?"

"Right now my plan is to walk into the first lake I find."

"That is an awful plan. You have drunk too much."

"*You* have drunk too much!"

Fina giggled. "I have. But I am going to help you. I love my father and my sister and my people, and I will protect them however I can. I will be false in order to be true, just like you were with your friend."

"My Lancelot." Guinevere put one hand over her heart. "If she never forgives me, I—oh, Fina, I do not want to lose her. Sometimes I feel like she is the only true thing in my whole life. You would like her so much."

"Is she beautiful? I like beautiful women. And ugly men. Faces like rocks. Mmm."

"She is—" Guinevere grasped for the best way to describe Lancelot. "She is magnificent."

Fina nodded, lifting the jug to her lips.

"No! The potion, remember?" Guinevere giggled.

"Oh. I am so sad this is not really wine."

"You will still get a headache after."

Fina sighed. "Now I am even sadder. Why do we have to bind your hands?"

"I tie knots."

"That makes no sense."

"Magic knots." Guinevere wriggled her fingers. "I am a witch."

"That makes more sense. Maybe we can use that magic when we help you escape."

The tent flap opened. Guinevere could not quite manage to move or even be worried about who would appear.

"Who is going to escape?" Mordred said, shutting the flap behind him. His dark hair was drenched and curled around his shoulders, dripping water.

"At least when your hair is wet it is easier to resist running my fingers through it," Guinevere said, then slapped one hand over her mouth. Mordred's eyes widened in shock.

"Oh no!" Fina collapsed, laughing. Guinevere had not been so prone to laughter the last time she had taken this potion, but then again, Morgana had had a knife to her side. It was harder to feel threatened with delightful Fina. But Mordred! He could not be here, not now.

"Hit him!" Guinevere said. "On the head! So he cannot ask us anything!"

"I will." Fina did not move. "I am trying, really. I just cannot seem to care."

"Are you two drunk?" Mordred picked up the jug and sniffed it. "Oh *no*. Does she know?" He looked over his shoulder as though expecting his mother to appear.

"Fina stole it!" Guinevere pointed.

"Do you have any idea—"

"No!" Guinevere tried to lunge for him, but her limbs were not communicating with one another and she only managed to tip forward, narrowly catching herself from falling flat on her face. "You cannot ask us anything."

"Yes, because you are evil." Fina glared at Mordred.

Mordred reached down and gently helped Guinevere back to sitting. He stared at her bare arms, a spasm of pain twitching across his face. "Do you think I am evil?"

"I wish you were evil. It would make everything easier. I understand you, and it hurts so much." Guinevere stared into his horribly beloved moss-green eyes that caught the lamplight and looked like twin points of flame. "I wish I could trust a single thing about you. Even if it were trusting that you are evil. I could depend on that, at least."

Mordred sat on the floor. "Very well." He tipped the jug back and drained it. Guinevere watched, shocked.

Mordred, at last, could not lie.

CHAPTER NINE

"First," Mordred said, before Guinevere could formulate a question in her potion-addled brain, "I do not know what you remember from before in my mother's tent, but I promised you I would not kiss you again unless you asked. When I put my lips on yours, it was to force breath into your lungs, not to kiss you. I will not break that promise."

Fina giggled, pressing her face into a fur on the tent floor. "You two are so stupid. The whole south is so stupid. Inheritance should always go through the mother's lines so it does not matter who the father is, and that way everyone can worry less and just be with who they desire."

Mordred lifted an eyebrow. "I do not disagree." He looked back at Guinevere, his pupils dilated, the black eating away at the green. "Oh. This was a bad idea. I should not have done this. I am going to go." He stared at the tent's entrance, but did not move toward it.

"Were you really coming to Camelot to warn me?" Guinevere asked. "And not to take me for your mother and grandmother?"

Mordred sighed. "Yes, but it is still my fault. My mother was using me. She told me Nechtan's forces were coming for you because she knew I would try to get to you first. She was going to look through my eyes to find the secret passageway. I would have led them straight to you, regardless. I ruin everything I touch. Even when I am trying to be good. And I *am* trying, so hard."

"So that day with the wolves?"

"She killed my horse." Mordred's eyebrows drew together in pain. "My grandmother, in the meadow, the night we raised her. I felt it as my horse died. I was so frantic trying to make sure that you got out of there, and that Lancelot did not get killed, and then I was so angry with Arthur—so, so angry with him—that I could not even mourn it. But why did she kill my horse? There was no reason for it. And those wolves, too, their will stolen. The Dark Queen is—she is not what she was. She has been warped, twisted. She is on no one's side but her own. And still I love her, because she is part of me, and I do not want to see her destroyed. Which is why I am going to keep *you*"—he pointed at Guinevere—"far away from her. I am going to save you from Nechtan and my mother and my grandmother. And save *them* from Arthur by keeping you away. Let him chase us and leave them be. Save them all." He gestured vaguely. "A lot of saving. I can save people, you know. I can."

"I am going to get Guinevere out, too!" Fina flopped an arm out and tried to pat Mordred's knee, but she missed. "But I will do it before you do, and send her back to Arthur with an apology, to stop him from attacking my people."

"And I am going to get myself out and make my own decisions about where I go," Guinevere grumbled.

Fina blew air through her lips in a dismissive noise. "You cannot do it without me. And I am also going to get my father away from Mordred's mother and grandmother."

"You should," Mordred agreed. "My mother is consumed with thwarting Merlin's plans. The wizard took too much from her, and she is determined to take away the future he set in motion, however she can."

"You should fight her with me," Fina said.

Mordred shrugged. "Family is complicated."

"*You* are complicated!" Guinevere snapped.

Mordred nodded. "I wish I could be Arthur for you. I really do. Walk in the sunlight, cut through the world with a sword of justice and absolute surety. But I am the night. My eyes have always been open to the darkness, and there are so many shades once you get used to the dark. So many subtleties. I cannot unsee them, or unfeel them."

Fina raised her hand. "Why Guinevere, though? What does the Dark Queen want with her?"

"That, I do not know." Mordred shook his head. "Either my mother does not know, or she will not tell me. She keeps trying to make me leave. She knows I cannot be trusted."

"Because you love Guinevere?" Fina asked.

"Yes."

"No!" Guinevere groaned, closing her eyes. "This makes nothing easier! When I was Arthur, everything was simple. Right and wrong. Good and evil. Actions needed to be done because they were the right thing to do, and nothing else mattered. Mordred was only pain."

"When were you Mordred?" Fina asked, frowning in confusion. Guinevere slapped her hands over her own mouth once more, but it was too late.

Mordred's face shifted from despair to shock. "Passion," he whispered. "You saw me when she tapped passion! I dare to hope, now. I tried to want only your happiness, really, but I do not want you to be happy with Arthur. I want your happiness to be with *me*, and it makes it difficult to be good." Mordred reached out a hand toward Guinevere but then stopped, his hand inches away from her face.

His expression was painful to see, more open and hopeful than she had ever known him to look. "Were you leaving Camelot to find me, or were you leaving to leave Arthur?"

"Neither!" Guinevere blurted. "I was leaving because I tried to be a witch and people got hurt, and I tried to be a queen and people got hurt, and I have been in between for so long that I am *nothing*. I cannot keep flinging destruction around me because I do not know who or what I am. I have done such unforgiveable things. People have died because of me. Their minds have been destroyed. And not just bad people—I violated Sir Bors's mind, and he is a good man. I did it to protect my dragon, and then I got the dragon killed, too." Guinevere moved her hands from her mouth to wipe away the tears streaming from her eyes. Mordred slowly lowered his hand when it was clear she would not meet it with her own.

"Who taught you to alter minds?" Fina asked, frowning.

"Merlin. That is where I was going when I left Camelot: to his cave, to figure out how to drag him free and make him tell the truth about who I am. Who I was. Because when I try to remember, I—"

The worst truth, the truth she had not let herself see before, the truth only accessible to her now because of the potion, floated to the surface. She could not look away. She wanted to look away. That was the whole point of what had been done to her—to make her look away.

Guinevere shuddered, her whole body repulsed. "*He did it to me.* Merlin. He did the same thing I did to Sir Bors. When I remember being underwater, looking up—" Even referencing the memory made her want to fling her thoughts somewhere, anywhere else, but the potion demanded the truth. "The way I feel about water. He did not do it to protect me from the Lady of the Lake. He did it to hide my truth. He hid it from me, and he left absolute, devastating horror in its place so I could never get to it."

"We should kill him," Fina said, her voice sleepy.

"We are not strong enough to kill Merlin," Mordred answered. "Only the Dark Queen is."

"You have no idea how strong I am." Guinevere could feel the effects of the potion wearing off. Her body felt heavy, control of her limbs returning along with gravity's dreadful pull. Now she would have to feel everything. All the things Mordred had said, all the things she had said. All the truths that her mind had avoided for so long. Was it self-deception, or was it self-preservation?

Regardless, she no longer had the solace of simplicity. Not when it came to Arthur, not when it came to Mordred, not when it came to herself. Though that last one had never been simple.

"I know exactly how strong you are, and it terrifies me that your strength could be diminished at Arthur's side," Mordred said. "That he would subsume you. I hate that you could love him, and I also understand, because how could you not? I hate him and I love him and I wish I could walk away from all of this. I wish I were enough for you to choose to walk away, too."

"It is not about you. It has to be about me." Guinevere lay on her side, curling around herself. Fina snored softly. Guinevere closed her eyes for a moment, and then several moments more, and when she opened them, she was not sure whether she had slept. Mordred was still sitting nearby, watching her, his gaze inscrutable.

Guinevere looked up at him, wondering. "What would you have done that night, at the tournament, if I had not stopped us?"

"We would have run away to a cottage in the woods and it would not matter where I came from or who you were, because we would be together, and it would be enough for both of us."

Guinevere shook her head. "You are lying."

Mordred's smile was back, a secret he kept from the world. A secret she still wanted to know. "Yes. I am back to normal, it seems.

But I promise, I will get you out and take you far away from all this. We can find answers together. Just the two of us."

"And leave Arthur alone in Camelot?"

"God above, *yes*. Let Arthur be alone. Let him be alone forever." Mordred blew out the lantern, plunging them into silent darkness, the air heavy with the truths they had been unable to withhold.

When Guinevere finally fell asleep, she opened her eyes to the forest. "Isolde?" she called, desperate for the easy comfort of her friend.

"Guinevere!"

Instead of Isolde's warm embrace, Guinevere was nearly bowled over by Lancelot's crushing hug. Then Lancelot released her, pushing her to arm's length and gruffly examining her while avoiding eye contact. "Are you safe? Isolde said something happened last time, and she did not know what pulled you out of the dream."

"Lancelot. I—I am so sorry. Please let me explain." Guinevere tried to close the space between them, to embrace her knight, but Lancelot held her in place. Held the distance between them with all her firm strength.

"Tell me you are safe, and then tell me exactly where you are, how many men there are, how they travel, when they travel, and any landmarks you have seen."

Guinevere took a step back to allow Lancelot to determine how close they got. "Has Arthur returned?"

"No, but as soon as he does, I am coming for you."

Guinevere nodded, her throat painfully tight with how much she wanted to say. How it hurt that Lancelot would not let her. But if Guinevere demanded that her apology be listened to or accepted, she would be doing it for herself. Lancelot deserved to feel however she needed to, and Guinevere deserved Lancelot's anger.

"What are you wearing?" Lancelot asked, frowning and clearing her throat. "Is that part of the magic? Or did they take your dress?"

Guinevere looked down, surprised to find she was not in her usual clothing, her body covered from throat to toe. Her arms were bare in a sleeveless shift the same green as the forest that reached only as far as her knees. Her feet were bare, too, toes curling happily against the soft moss. "I suppose I am tired of my dress."

Lancelot was wearing her old patchwork knight leather armor, King Arthur's crest nowhere to be seen. She had a sword sheathed at her side. Had they both unconsciously chosen how they appeared?

Lancelot shook her head, refocusing. Perhaps reminding herself she was still angry. "Tell me about the organization of the camp and I will make my plan."

"I can help with that," Mordred said, stepping free of a gnarled tree.

"You!" Lancelot growled. Then she drew her sword and plunged it straight through his chest.

CHAPTER TEN

Guinevere stared, frozen, at the sword hilt protruding from Mordred's chest. Mordred, too, stared down at it. But less in horror and more in amusement.

"I missed you, too, Lancelot."

Lancelot drew her sword free. It came out of Mordred's chest gleaming silver. Mordred's tunic was still a resplendent green, no blood or gashes.

Mordred brushed his hands down the tunic fussily. "You do know we are in Guinevere's dream, right?"

Lancelot roared, swinging again. Mordred ducked, twisting and dancing and bending so that all Lancelot's attempts missed. Then a sword was in Mordred's hands, too, and he deflected a blow, the blades ringing off each other with a terrible noise.

"Do you want to know where Guinevere is?" Mordred leaned away from a strike intended to separate his head from his body.

"I want you to suffer!" Lancelot swung again.

Mordred blocked, but Lancelot had swung with so much force

he stumbled back a few steps. His smile grew. "Someone has been thinking about our fight."

Lancelot rushed him, and their blades clashed again.

"How are you here, Mordred?" Guinevere demanded.

"You talk in your sleep."

"How would you know?" Lancelot lunged as a distraction, then kicked Mordred, catching his stomach so that he backed away.

Mordred's face was infuriatingly innocent, which, for him, implied the opposite of innocence. "We are spending a lot of time together. Anyhow, I assumed Guinevere was meeting someone, based on her half of the conversations. I am the son of a sorceress and a fairy, so I invited myself in tonight, no knots necessary. I actually expected Brangien. Though I suppose she would have had a very similar reaction." Mordred attacked this time, and Lancelot was driven back.

Guinevere did not know what to say or do. It was stressful for the first few minutes, watching their battle, but eventually she sat, idly braiding her hair. "Will you be finished soon?" she called.

"No!" Lancelot shouted.

"Watch your feet. Faster." Mordred swept his blade toward her feet, and when Lancelot tripped to avoid the blow, he brought the hilt up and hit her in the forehead. "You are very strong, and very fast, but it is clear you never learned to dance."

"I hate dancing," Lancelot said through gritted teeth, launching herself at him once again.

"Nechtan has two hundred and thirty-seven soldiers." Mordred blocked a thrust, then kicked Lancelot's knee and skipped back, out of reach. "You do not use your legs enough. He had more, but there was an attack. It slowed us down. We are currently in the hilly lands one hundred leagues to the north."

"That is not Nechtan's territory!" Lancelot grabbed Mordred's wrist, yanked him downward, and kneed him hard in the torso.

He coughed, then twisted his wrist to break her grasp and pantomimed running his sword along her stomach to disembowel her. "You stopped moving. Never stop moving. We are not in Nechtan's territory. The Dark Queen hid herself as far north as she could. She wants to solidify power before going after Arthur. Though if Guinevere is her only prize, it would make more sense for a small group to get Guinevere there faster. The Dark Queen is insisting on all of Nechtan's forces. I do not know why."

"What do you mean *before* going after Arthur? She already has been. The trees, and the wolves."

Mordred jabbed toward Lancelot, and when she parried, he spun around her. "Feints," he said lightly. "To distract you." He slapped Lancelot's back with the flat of his blade.

"I am going to kill you," she said, and swung her sword to emphasize the point.

"Not with that form, you are not."

Lancelot rushed, throwing her shoulder low to tackle Mordred. He twisted, so she only grazed him, then shoved her so her own momentum carried her into a tree. She screamed, hacking at the tree with her sword, then turned to face him once more.

"Patience, Lancelot. Arthur is delayed. He is taking over the south, building an army. You will be waiting longer than you think."

"How do you know that?" Lancelot demanded.

"We travel with a sorceress, remember?"

"They have women soldiers," Guinevere blurted out, hating that Lancelot was interacting only with Mordred. She wanted to talk to Lancelot. To fix things between them. "There is no difference between men and women, at least among Nechtan's forces."

"What?" Lancelot stopped, staring at Guinevere.

"You would like Fina. She is Nechtan's second daughter. She fights with an ax and several long knives."

"I would not like her! She is my enemy. They are all my enemy."

Guinevere did not know how to explain that Lancelot was right but also wrong. "The Dark Queen is our enemy."

"*He* is our enemy!" Lancelot leveled her sword at Mordred's throat.

"You can move faster than they can," Mordred continued, ignoring Guinevere's interruption. "I recommend coming straight up the coast, then cutting inland. My grandmother will be in the oldest forest. Ask for directions to the Green Man's Chapel."

"Your father? But he is dead. Unless you abused Guinevere to revive him, too."

Mordred's face darkened, whether with anger or shame it was hard to tell. "The Green *Man,* not the Green Knight. An ancient earth god. There is more magic in the world than Camelot can manage to remember, but anyone in the north will know it. In the meantime, I am looking for an opportunity to—"

Lancelot swung, and Mordred only parried. "Very good!" he said. "I am looking for an opportunity to get Guinevere out. If we manage it, I will head to the eastern coast and travel down it. Ideally, we will meet somewhere in the middle."

"You are a liar."

"I am, yes. But we have the same goal: keeping Guinevere away from my grandmother. You can trust that I am highly motivated, as are you. Now, come at me again."

Baring her teeth, Lancelot did as instructed.

"How are you, Guinevere?" Guinevere muttered to herself. "You must be very lonely, very worried about your friends. Here is all the news." She stood and wandered into the trees. "I am sure you feel wretched about what you did, and I would love to let you explain it, since I am the only person who truly knows you. I will understand, eventually. When I am not too busy playing with swords. What do you think of our plan to go east and then south? What? It is the most obvious plan, and therefore bad? Well, what do you suggest then, Guinevere?" What *did* she suggest? Nechtan's forces would expect her to try to get back to Arthur along the quickest route possible. And if she had no way of letting her people know she was safe, it would make sense. But she had her own secret lines of communication.

When they were not too busy fighting Mordred in a dream, at least.

Regardless. She would free herself and head to the northwest. She would let Isolde or Lancelot know, to tell Arthur. And then she would gradually work her way back down the western coast and inland to Merlin's cave. It would take longer, but as long as Arthur knew he did not need to attack the north, she would have time. Time to figure out who she was. Time to sort through how she felt about Arthur, now that she had been inside his head and seen how he really felt about her.

The sounds of fighting followed her like birdsong, calling her back toward the meadow. She refused. If Lancelot wanted to use Mordred to ignore her, very well. She would make it easy for them. The forest was as pleasant as ever, if a bit false. No forest would have this soft blanket of moss on the ground for her feet, or trails that seemed to open up only when needed, dappled and inviting.

A cottage in the woods, Guinevere remembered, *and it would be enough for both of us.* Out of the corner of her eye, she saw one materialize. "No!" she exclaimed, turning sharply and walking in the other direction. She refused to look at the cottage, refused to acknowledge her brain putting it there.

Up ahead came a musical sound. It was not until she got close that she realized her mind had once again betrayed her. It was not music. It was a creek, babbling down into a still, silent pond. The pond was a perfect mirror, the trees and sky doubled.

"I am not afraid," she whispered, tiptoeing closer. "Merlin made me afraid, and I refuse to be."

She took another step and felt the same as when Excalibur was nearby. The cold, trembling terror of being unmade rippled through her. One more step and she would see her reflection. Clearer than she had ever seen it, on this crystal pond. She held out her hand and a pale, shaking hand mirrored her action. She took the last step.

There she was. Lying as still as death.

No. *Actually* dead. Because this was no reflection. Guinevere was standing, but the Guinevere in the pond was lying flat, eyes open but unseeing, lips the same blue as the sky. Guinevere could not breathe, could not look away.

Then the dead Guinevere twitched, fingers like claws, grasping upward.

Guinevere screamed and fell, scrambling away. Guided by the sounds of swords, Guinevere burst into the clearing. Mordred stopped immediately, lowering his sword in concern. "What happened?"

Lancelot stabbed him through the gut, shouting in triumph.

Mordred gave her a flat look. "You know that does not do anything, right?"

Lancelot took the hilt and drove the blade in even farther. "I know, but it still feels wonderful."

Mordred ignored her, turning back to Guinevere. "You should not wander."

Guinevere could not forget her face. Dead. Why would her mind show her that? "But this is my dreamspace."

"Exactly. I would not dare explore mine. I do find it curious, though, that you bring us to a forest instead of your beloved Camelot."

Lancelot twisted the sword.

"Honestly!" Mordred glared at Lancelot, then looked at Guinevere again. "I am only saying, you do not have a simple mind. There could be things lurking here you are not prepared to deal with. The knots of your dream magic do not contain or control this space. All they do is connect. Once you are in here, the landscape is as wild and dangerous as the dreamer."

"I am not dangerous, I am—" Guinevere looked over her shoulder, half expecting pursuit. The water, or whatever it held, rushing inexorably toward her to claim her. She suppressed a shudder.

"When *I* escape, Lancelot," she said, emphasizing the singular nature of her plan, "I will go northwest first. They will not expect that. Once I am certain I am not being pursued, then I will turn south along the western coast. I will let you know when I manage it."

Lancelot left her sword embedded in Mordred. She did not quite meet Guinevere's eyes. "I will be back tomorrow night."

"I am glad," Guinevere said, offering a sad smile.

Mordred gestured at the sword through his torso. "I am also looking forward to it. Work on your feet in the meantime."

"How do we wake up?" Guinevere asked. She wanted to be far away from the pond and what it held. Part of her wanted to ask Lancelot not to use the knot magic tomorrow night. She did not want to return here. Not now that she knew that abhorrent mirror was waiting for her.

The sun had disappeared behind a cloud, and the forest rippled with frost. Something cracked nearby. A twig snapping from the cold? Or something approaching?

"Let go of my hand," Mordred said.

Guinevere looked down. Her hand was empty. But . . . there was the sense of him, the spark she always felt at his touch. Her fingers twitched, and she felt his fingers between them, laced together. She straightened her fingers and pulled her hand away. Mordred disappeared, and she was alone again with Lancelot, who finally met her eyes for a single heartbeat. Guinevere woke up.

The pain in her knight's gaze would haunt her as much as the body beneath the water.

CHAPTER ELEVEN

The storm did not abate, turning to sleet in the coldest hours of the night. Which was precisely when Guinevere forced herself awake. Mordred was already sitting, still close. She could only make out the barest shape of him in the dark. Her hand was warm where he had been holding it. Everywhere else was bitterly cold.

"You are really going to keep barging in?" she snapped, shivering. Fina was nearby, in the same cramped position where she had fallen asleep.

"I told you, I am getting you away from all this. Lancelot will help."

"You do realize you are training her to be able to beat you."

"I am hoping by the time she finds us, she will realize she does not need to. Lancelot and I want the same thing."

"I sincerely doubt that. Unless you *also* want to see a sword through your chest."

Mordred held out a heavy fur. "We want your safety. Your happiness."

Guinevere snorted. "You have very poor ways of showing it."

Mordred lay down, tugging the fur over himself since she refused to take it. "It is hard to show something to someone who refuses to look. Lancelot understands that." He turned on his side, facing away from her.

"You are insufferable," Guinevere hissed. She grabbed the nearest furs, dragged them to Fina, and covered them both as she curled up alongside her.

Fina's warmth did not help Guinevere sleep. She was tormented with Mordred's familiar pain. The body in the water. Lancelot's anger and refusal to listen to her. And Arthur's troubling thoughts and actions. What was he doing now? What if something happened as he tried to take the south?

She had been in the south, and nothing there had made her think anyone leading was better than Arthur. Certainly the people would be safer and better cared for under his rule. But that did not necessarily make it *right* for him to take the south. Surely he could see that.

If he were not so angry over the idea of losing her in addition to the son who had never existed, would he have been inspired to go to war?

When dawn, waterlogged and frigid, finally sulked near, Mordred left without a word.

"Last night is our secret, right?" Fina asked as she bound Guinevere's hands.

"One of our many, many secrets."

Fina laughed. But then her brows descended, and she looked nervous rather than teasing. "Also, I do not remember going to sleep curled around you. Was there another part of the potion I am forgetting?"

Guinevere smiled gently and shook her head.

Fina sighed, her relief evident. "I hoped not. I am skilled at destroying friendships, and I need a friend far more than a lover. We are opposites in that way." She winked, then laughed again when Guinevere smacked her with her bound hands. "I am going to get food and discover our plans for the day."

Before Guinevere could miss her, or even finish stretching, Fina returned, pink-cheeked from the cold. "Would you like the good news or the bad?"

"I am not certain what would constitute good news at this point."

"That is fair! The good news is, we cannot continue until this storm lets up. It will slow our progress, but it will also slow Arthur's, so my father is not concerned. The bad news is, someone stole something from Morgana's tent."

"Did she discover the missing potion?"

Fina's face split into a smile. "No, someone stole this." She tossed Guinevere's pouch of supplies at Guinevere's knees. It radiated heat from the tracking stones. "And someone stole these, as well." She added a folded pile of clothes like her own.

"Fina," Guinevere gasped.

"They are having a council of war today. I will be there, along with Morgana and Mordred and Nectudad and my father. I anticipate it being contentious. I might encourage us to argue all day, which will be easy enough, since Morgana is still insisting we need to bring our entire force with us."

Mordred had mentioned the same thing. "That is suspicious. The Dark Queen should not need an army present if all she wants is me," Guinevere said.

"My feelings exactly. All an army does is draw attention and slow us down. I will try my best to convince my father. And, as I said, I will argue strenuously and at length. So, if I were to post my least favorite soldier as a guard, and something were to happen to him, I do not think anyone would check on you for several hours. And this storm is quite bad, so tracking you will be a challenge. But please tell me you have a better plan than walking into a lake."

Guinevere rubbed her face. "Ah, you remembered. I think it will summon the Lady of the Lake. I suspect she is my mother." Guinevere had dreamed memories of the Lady of the Lake, and seen first-hand how angry the Lady was with Merlin for taking something from her and giving it to Arthur. Guinevere seemed to be a possession to all of them. Her heart fell at that thought, but she did not have time to indulge her sadness. The Lady wanted her, and Merlin wanted to keep her away from the Lady, so to the Lady, Guinevere would go.

Fina poked Guinevere's shoulder. "You seem solid for someone who is half water."

Guinevere laughed. "I do not think it works that way. Look at Mordred. His father was the Green Knight."

"Ah, yes, the fairyson. He is not normal, though. He can talk to animals."

"What?"

Fina worked to unbind Guinevere's hands. "There is a reason I sent him to the horses during the attack. He does not talk out loud to them, at least I have never heard him do so, and I *have* tried to catch him so I could mock him. But he knows when they need rest, or how to push them just a little farther, or how to calm them. That is where he is right now, making sure the horses are not suffering in this weather."

"No wonder he kept it a secret. It would not have been accepted in Camelot." Guinevere was reminded of how tender Mordred was when they were around animals. And how heartbroken he had been last night talking about how the Dark Queen had killed his horse and taken away the wolves' ability to make their own choices.

Then another memory struck her. That night when he tricked her into raising the Dark Queen, when she pushed him from the horse and turned back to Arthur . . . he could have stopped her. He could have commanded the horse not to obey her.

He could have forced her to stay with him, and he let her go.

Guinevere stretched her freed fingers, wondering how this knowledge reshaped her relationship with Mordred. She felt a seismic shift quietly taking place but was uncertain where it would land her.

"It makes me sad that he would be rejected for that, when there are so many better reasons to reject him," Fina mused, helping Guinevere to undress. "Another fault of the south. We are wary of fairy folk, though apparently not as wary as we should be, but being fairy-touched is prized. I knew a woman whose mother was a fairy. The tattoos she created were magnificent. If you looked closely, the animals moved. What started as a fawn on a young woman became a doe as the woman aged. Flowers bloomed around loved ones' images, then wilted when that person was sick or dying. There was a man who had a serpent wrapped around his arm that bared its fangs in the presence of anyone who wished him harm. The woman died before I was old enough for my markings. I have always been sad about that. Do you have an ability like that?"

"My hands!" Guinevere held them up. "I can feel things."

"Yes, that is . . . what hands do. Are you still potion-drunk?"

Guinevere snorted. She would miss Fina. She had not expected to find a friend among her captors. "I can feel things about people, animals, sometimes even objects or places. An extra sense. It helps me understand people. Or not, in some cases." Guinevere glared at the space where Mordred's furs were stacked.

"Oh! I see. Maybe you are right! She could be your mother." Fina showed Guinevere how to lace the borrowed trousers around her waist so they would not fall.

"Exactly. And Merlin made me afraid of water and hid my memories, and the Dark Queen warned you against transporting me over water. I think the Lady of the Lake could find me if I was in water. And of course I will tell my friends in Camelot that I am free and Arthur does not need to come north."

Fina looked deeply dubious of Guinevere's plan. "Well, make sure it is a lake far from here. And please be careful. I will miss you. But always remember"—she leaned close, blue eyes plaintive—"that it was *me*, not Mordred, who got you out. I should have placed a wager on it."

Guinevere laughed. But then she hesitated. *Mordred.* She would be walking out on him, and it felt surprisingly cruel. She was forever turning her back on him, and he was forever returning to her. When would he finally give up on her?

The idea of never hearing that particular teasing note in his voice or seeing the shade of green of his eyes, never feeling that spark in his touch . . .

As though sensing her thoughts, Fina shook her head. "Life is short, death is swift, take what you want when you can. You did not take the fairyson, and you will regret it. Now you must focus on saving yourself and my people, Guinevere. Not on your loins."

"*Fina!*"

Fina shrugged. "All I am saying is I suspect he would be good in bed, and now you will never know. It would bother me, too. But you must go."

Guinevere hugged her friend tightly. "I promise I will never forget what you did for me. And I hope we meet again someday."

"Me too." Fina kissed her cheek, then ducked out of the tent and shouted something in an annoyed tone, delivering instructions in her own language. Guinevere put on the final layer of clothes. She had never worn trousers before, and it felt very strange to have her legs separated from each other by more than a thin layer. It did seem like it would make riding easier, though.

She would take a horse. Or at least she would make it look like she had. A plan came together as she finished wrangling herself into Fina's leathers and furs. Her hair was still tied in the blue cloth. It was raining and sleeting, which was less than ideal, but it created exactly the right opportunity.

Her pouch waited. Guinevere knew what she was going to do. It was a small wrong, when stacked against other potential wrongs. She still fought sick twists of guilt as she knotted the thread into the same loop she had once thrown around a bird to compel it to take her to Merlin. Any magic that stole the free will of another creature was one that sat heavily upon her. It was *violent* magic.

Steeling herself against her shame, she opened the tent flap and pulled the knot's wide loop over her guard's head before he had a chance to respond. His eyes, small and mean, went vague and his shoulders drooped.

"Go and steal a horse," Guinevere commanded. "Do not let anyone see you, but do not cover your trail. Ride southeast as fast as you can."

The guard nodded and walked stiffly away. He was quickly swallowed by the ferocity of the storm.

Guinevere stepped out of the tent. She threw on her cloak, then walked calmly in the opposite direction from the guard. She tugged out hairs as she went, her cold hands knotting them into confusion. Only a few, though, so she could keep her wits about her, but enough to make everyone overlook any trail she might leave.

She missed Fina already. She missed Mordred. She could not let that stop her. She owed it to herself, to Camelot, to accomplish what she had set out to do.

Now all she needed was a lake, and the courage to face it.

CHAPTER TWELVE

Guinevere supposed she would be just as miserable on a horse, but at least then she would have company. All she had now were her thoughts, which vacillated between misery over her current circumstances and vague terror over what her future circumstances might be.

The terrain was rough and unforgiving, even in the best weather. She slipped, and slid halfway down a muddy hill before catching herself. "Thank you, Fina," Guinevere said. The leather sleeves had protected her arms from being scraped. She was certainly bruised, though. And while the storm would make tracking her more difficult, she bore it no love. She was *wet*. All the water falling and puddling around her mocked her with what she had to look forward to.

Looking back at the mud, scarred where she had slid through it, Guinevere sighed and tied another confusion knot. Her head was fuzzy and pressure nagged behind her eyes, but she forced herself to focus as she dropped the knot. She shouldn't need to do any more. It had been at least eight hours since she left the camp. No one would have made it this far along her trail. Not with her magic obscuring it, and the soldier on horseback providing obvious tracks toward the southeast.

She put her hands over her pouch, the heat from the tracking stones radiating outward and keeping her fingers warm at least. Grateful as she was to Fina for the pouch and the clothes, Guinevere wished she had thought to steal some food. Her stomach complained with a low grumble.

The land around her was dotted with scrubby bushes, gray rocks, and hill after hill. She knew she was gradually making her way northwest, but without a destination in mind, all she could do was hope to wander across a lake. So far, though, there had been nothing but these wretched hills and bruising rocks. It was late afternoon and she had yet to see any sign of human habitation, which was why the crying baby startled her.

Her first impulse was to hurry away. But a baby meant people, and people meant food. She made her way carefully toward the sound. Sneaking behind a boulder, she peered around it. All thoughts of spying on a quaint village left her mind. This was not a village. It was not even a camp.

It was horror.

Guinevere moved free of her hiding spot and stepped haltingly forward. A woman sat hunched next to a bundle of wet wood, holding her arm where a wicked gash had torn straight through her beautiful tattoos. The stories of her life, disrupted and erased by violence. Next to her sat an old man. In his lap was a listless child bleeding freely from her head. There were forty, perhaps fifty people huddled on the ground and without shelter. Most were injured. A few lay prone, unmoving, and Guinevere was afraid they had already succumbed to their injuries.

Had she really thought she could prey on whoever was here? Steal from them? Ashamed, she knew these people had nothing to offer her, but they also presented no threat. She could offer them something, though. She crouched next to the woman and pulled the rocks out of her pouch. She pretended to strike the rocks together, then called fire to her fingers and sent it into the sodden wood. The wood sparked and smoked, but with her encouragement the fire caught.

The woman looked up, blinking in surprise. She said something in her language. Guinevere pointed to the woman's arm, then lifted her eyebrows questioningly. The woman sighed. "Saxon," she said. That word, Guinevere knew. These people were refugees in their own land, driven west by Saxons landing on the eastern shore.

Guinevere piled more wet wood onto the fire. The refugees who were able to wandered over. She used their distraction to light the other fires, spreading the warmth. Then she went back to the first group. They needed her cloak more than she did. She took it off and carefully tore it into strips. She bound the woman's arm first, then cleaned the little girl's head wound as best she could with her sodden cloak. But how could she stop there? She continued from group to group.

Another little girl sat in front of Guinevere, her father or grandfather propping her up. The man was knobby and thin, with a deeply lined face. The girl, whose flaxen hair was wet and plastered to her forehead, had an ugly wound in her leg from an arrow. Her eyes were glassy, her gaze dim and unfocused. How could this little girl have been seen as a threat to anyone or anything? Guinevere's fingers trembled from cold and rage as she carefully cleaned, then wrapped the wound. Heat radiated off the girl. After Sir Tristan had been bitten by one of the Dark Queen's wolves, a fever ate him up from the inside and he burned the same way.

Guinevere shook out her hands. She had not used her cleansing fire since she left Camelot, and she had not used it for this purpose since Sir Tristan. Arthur had warned her not to do it again.

But this was not Camelot. Fairy-touched abilities were valued here. People understood the difference between helping magic and harming magic.

Still, she needed permission. She called the sparks to her fingers and held her hand up so the man saw it. Then she pointed to the girl's leg.

The man frowned, puzzled, but nodded his head for her to proceed.

Guinevere closed her eyes, holding out her hand and calling more flame. It crackled to life, dry and hungry. Marshaling all her resolve, she put her hand on the girl's wound and commanded the flames to consume everything that was not the child. It took incredible concentration, never losing focus. If she did, the fire would rage and grow to devour the girl.

She would not let that happen.

When Guinevere sensed the girl's blood was cleansed, she pulled the fire back into her hand.

The little girl stretched as though waking up. The color in her cheeks returned to normal, and she put her arms around her caregiver's neck. Tears filled his eyes, and he whispered gratitude in a tone that Guinevere understood. Then he raised his voice and gestured.

Person after person lined up, some limping, some carried by others. Guinevere's heart sank. She had not planned on this. There were too many of them, too much need. But how could she say no?

She called back the flames and got to work. She could feel her palm blistering as she held fire for longer than she ever had before. But she forced it to obey, guided it precisely, ate away infection after infection to clean wounds and blood.

She had already walked so long and depleted her reserves with the confusion knots, and each effort drained her further. Finally, she was finished, at the end of her strength. Then three more people were added to the end of the line. Tears filled Guinevere's eyes. She could not do any more. She would have to tell them that. To turn them away.

Unbidden, Lancelot, Mordred, and Arthur all came to her mind. Lancelot would not give up fighting. Mordred would have enough burning anger at this injustice to sustain himself. And Arthur would never stop, not so long as he could help one more person.

Taking a deep breath, holding on to the three of them in her mind, Guinevere reached out once more. By the end, she sat on the ground and extinguished the flame with a small cry of pain. Her palm was raw and blistered, and she could not even summon the strength for tears, but she had done it.

The woman from the first fire limped over and sat gingerly next to Guinevere. She dropped several things into a bowl and then crushed them together with a rock to form a sticky paste. She carefully spread it over Guinevere's hand. The relief was almost instant.

Another woman passed her some dried meat. Another, a portion of bread. They sat in silence around the fire and ate. The first little girl Guinevere had healed laughed and splashed in a puddle, healthy enough to have a few moments of simply being a child.

Guinevere had an idea. She pointed to the puddle, then gestured to indicate something bigger. "I need a lake," she said, still gesturing. After several attempts at communicating the idea of a lake, the knobby old man nodded in understanding. He pantomimed walking, held up several fingers, and pointed directly east.

Now she had a direction to follow. Kindness could be just as powerful, just as useful as force.

CHAPTER THIRTEEN

Guinevere did not linger at the camp. She trudged up and down hills, hoping the old man had understood what she needed when he pointed her in this direction. The storm finally broke, the low rays of the sun piercing the clouds just as it set behind the nearest hill.

But not before the light revealed a hard gray lake.

Guinevere's feet stopped. She did not want to move forward. She did not have to do this. She could keep going, work her way south, get to the cave. If Merlin was evil, at least he was an evil she knew. And one that was not submerged in water.

But that was cowardly. She knew she was looking for any excuse to avoid the water. Merlin had erased so many parts of her, had deliberately planted this terror to keep her away from the Lady of the Lake. If that creature was her mother, she would have answers for Guinevere. And if Merlin wanted to keep them apart, that was a reason to seek her out. Guinevere no longer trusted that Merlin had anyone other than Arthur's best interests at heart.

She climbed down the rocky hill, going from scrubby tree to boulder to keep her descent slow and safe. The terrain was unfarmable, rugged, and unwelcoming. There was no habitation as far as she could see, and she had long ago left behind the refugees. It was just Guinevere and the lake.

She peeled off Fina's clothes, her hands shaking so hard she could barely manage, and set them atop a rock. She added her pouch and her boots to the pile. When she had stripped down to the thin shift she wore beneath everything, she stepped to the edge of the water.

The memory of the dream pool clawed at Guinevere, but the sun had set and the sky was cloudy. The lake held its secrets, offering only the dimmest of reflections. That, at least, was a relief. Guinevere did not want to see her soul-crushing fear reflected back at her, rippling in mockery.

Her toes curled around the sharp pebbles at the water's edge. The lake was in a basin of hills, pooling and gathering here for who knew how long. Waiting. Her lungs seized up, sealing themselves. Already she could not breathe, and she had not even touched the wretched water. No one would know if she ran from this. If she waited until morning.

But morning would not make this easier. Nothing would. She had to be strong enough now. She had walked away from Camelot, from being queen—from being with Arthur in every sense—because she could not be queen without knowing who she was. She had betrayed *Lancelot* for this. She owed it to Lancelot to see it through.

The first step was so cold, she gasped in shock. She did not know whether her violent shivers were from the temperature or from revulsion and fear. Her breath came out in a fog. Another step. Another. Another. The water was past her ankles now. Every step was an act of sheer will. Her hands curled into fists so tight they ached, and her burned palm pulsed with pain. She longed to have Arthur at her side to lend her his confidence. But if he were here, she would not be doing this.

Lancelot, then. Though Lancelot would probably drag her from the lake, insisting this was unnecessary.

Mordred. Guinevere wrapped her arms around herself and imagined his spark burning through her, giving her heat and arousing the hungriest, most desperate parts of herself.

Still, she was alone. There was no stirring of water, no glow, nothing to indicate the Lady was about to appear. "Where are you?" Guinevere shouted, her voice ringing off the surrounding hills. "I am right here!" Trying to feel angry instead of terrified, she took another step. Her foot came down on a sharp rock and she stumbled. Before she could right herself, her other foot slipped off a ledge and she went under.

The water was impenetrable, a blue so deep it was the icy sister of black. Guinevere reached for the surface, but her feet had nothing to push against. In her desperate flailing, she had lost all sense of direction. Bubbles trailed out of her mouth as she screamed, and she tried to follow them upward, but her frantic motions spun her uselessly. She was going to disappear, and no one she loved would ever know what had happened to her.

The water was everywhere, holding her in its cold embrace. But that was not right, either. The water was just water. There was nothing here to hold her, nothing here to drag her deeper. Nothing here to give her answers or care about her or help her.

She was alone.

She was a fool.

And, as her lungs burned and her vision dimmed, she knew with absolute certainty she had drowned before, and she was drowning again.

CHAPTER FOURTEEN

Guinevere did not know whether her eyes were open or closed. Everything was pressure and darkness.

Strong arms wrapped around her from behind. *The Lady!* her breath-starved mind thought. But these were not arms of water and magic. These were human arms, crushingly tight.

Legs behind hers kicked, and then her head broke the water. She coughed and gagged, hating the water, the feel of it still on her and in her. Worse was the knowledge—knowledge that she could not place or make sense of—*that this had not been the first time she had drowned.*

"Breathe!" Mordred commanded. Not the Lady. Of course it was Mordred. No one else appeared as relentlessly where he should not be to save her.

He dragged Guinevere to shore. She collapsed onto her hands and knees, trembling and coughing. She was cold, too cold, and she shook so hard she was unable to hold herself up.

Mordred picked her up and carried her. He paused to awkwardly grab her belongings, then made his way to where his horse stamped impatiently. "What do you see?" he asked, and Guinevere could not answer through her chattering teeth. But it did not matter. He was not talking to her. The horse whinnied and made its way halfway up the hill to a shallow cave. Mordred followed it. His horse stood at the entrance, blocking some of the bitter wind whistling through the valley. "Good girl," Mordred said.

He set Guinevere down and propped her against the far wall of the cave. It was so dark she could not see her hand in front of her face. Mordred grabbed his pack from his horse and laid out a bedroll, his silhouette black against the cave's entrance. Guinevere crawled onto the mat and curled into a ball. She could not speak. The shock of almost drowning combined with the frigid air was too much.

"We cannot start a fire," Mordred said, and she could hear the worry in his voice. "It would be a beacon to anyone searching. Take off your shift."

Guinevere squawked with as much indignation as she could manage, which was not much. She was cold to the very marrow of her bones. All she could think of was the unrelenting pressure of the water around her, the way it demanded entrance to her eyes, ears, nose, mouth. That she would still be there, would have been there forever, if not for Mordred.

The Lady had not come. Guinevere would have died, and no one would have known. Lancelot would have been left waiting, blaming herself. Brangien and Isolde and Lily and Dindrane would hope but eventually give up. Arthur would be alone, just as Mordred had wished.

But that was not true. Arthur would have his men—and his Camelot. He would remarry, and to someone better suited to his needs. Actually, after a couple of years for him to mourn and her to grow, Lily would be an ideal queen. Better than Guinevere, certainly.

The world would have continued on without her with little pause, her entire life a ripple on the surface of a forgotten lake.

"It is too dark for me to see anything," Mordred snapped, bringing her back to the present, precarious reality of living. "Not freezing to death is the priority right now."

Guinevere tugged off the clinging fabric. Mordred immediately draped a thick, scratchy blanket over her. It did nothing to warm her. "My pouch," she forced through her clenched teeth.

Mordred rummaged in the darkness before withdrawing the two stones, which radiated heat. He placed them next to her stomach and she curled around them. Then she heard more wet clothing drop onto the cave floor.

She gasped in shock as he lay next to her, pressing his cold body against hers. "What are you doing?"

"Trying to keep us both alive." His chest was against her back, his legs nestled against hers. But he kept his arms at his sides, not holding or touching her. His body was rigid, not just from the cold but also from barely contained rage. "What were you *thinking*? I told you I would get you out!"

"How did you find me?"

Mordred let out a harsh laugh. "You wanted me to."

"I did not!"

"You told Lancelot you would go northwest. I was right there! And you know I recognize your confusion trails. I have tracked you by them before."

Guinevere let the humiliation wash over her. It was true. She knew that Mordred was not only capable of but also experienced at finding her after she hid her trail using magic. Had she really forgotten, or had she secretly not wanted to lose him?

"And then there was the entire camp of refugees amazed at the tiny magical woman who stopped to heal them all."

"I had to!"

"You really did not. You chose to. Lucky for us both that I had a horse and caught up with you in time to hear you shouting nonsense before you fell in the lake. What were you hoping to accomplish? You hate water! You cannot even swim!"

Guinevere squeezed her eyes shut. Even her tears were cold. "I thought—" Her voice caught, trembling with her body. When she spoke again, it was in a whisper. "I thought the Lady of the Lake would appear. I thought she would give me answers."

"Why would she do that?" Mordred asked, aghast.

"Because I think she is my mother."

Mordred was silent for a few moments. When he spoke again, his voice was strained with the anger he was trying to hold back. "She does not simply *exist* everywhere all the time. Even mystical beings have a soul, a place where they are centered. The Lady has always dwelled around Camelot. Why would she be this far north? How would she even get to a lake unconnected to any rivers?"

Guinevere let out a small sob of humiliation and despair. Her grand plan, her brave sacrifice for answers, had been . . . foolish. She had thought herself so important that somehow an ancient being would know where she was and care.

When Mordred spoke again, the anger was gone. He sounded tired, and sad, and Guinevere felt both to her core. "You should have spoken to me about this. If anyone understands what it is to have a parent who is not human, it is me. And I am sorry you had to learn it this way, but . . . they do not care about us. They are incapable of it." He sighed, moving closer and brushing some of her wet hair away. She felt his breath on the back of her neck, a welcome warmth. "The story I told you of defeating the Green Knight? Finding him in the forest, the other knights trying to hack through him and failing until I brought a deer to devour him? That was true. And it is the happiest memory I have of him. For one brief, glorious moment, I had proof that I was clever enough to please my father. He was delighted with me. And then he was gone. Again. I never could hold his attention for more than a moment."

"I am sorry," Guinevere said through chattering teeth.

"We come to them with human hearts and emotions, and they break us, not because they are cruel but because they cannot meet us on that level. They do not exist there. Any parent soaked in the old world of magic is the same. My mother was poisoned by it, made new by what she took from it, both bigger and somehow smaller. It even poisoned Arthur the same way. They are all embroiled in things larger and deeper and older than themselves, and they cannot see anything small anymore. They *cannot* care about us. I spent so long thinking it was myself who was unlovable, who had not done enough yet to deserve their love. But it has nothing to do with me. . . ." His words were belied by the way his voice trailed off. Guinevere wondered whether Mordred really believed what he said or whether he only wanted to.

"Arthur cares," she said softly.

"He wants to. But he has devoted himself to Camelot, and anything less than that cannot ever take precedence. You know it is true."

Guinevere did. Arthur had told her as much once, that he would never put her before Camelot. And he had meant it. She did not hate him for it, or even think he was wrong, but that did not make it hurt any less that he had not come to rescue her from Maleagant, or that he stopped to take over the south and gather an army for the protection of Camelot rather than riding directly to save her.

If she had drowned tonight, the course of Arthur's life would not have been altered. She felt it like the release of a breath, like the ending of something that had only just begun.

She would never stop caring about Arthur. But she could not make caring about him her entire life. She deserved more.

Guinevere reached back and took Mordred's hand in hers, pulling his arm over her. He slipped his other arm beneath her, circling her waist. She wanted the spark of him, the heat of him, because she was so very cold and so very, very sad. Either she could not feel his emotions through her turmoil, or they were a perfect match to her own.

"Even if the Lady had come," Mordred said, "she could not have told you who you are. Neither can Merlin."

"But they know—"

"They are like my grandmother. Like my mother. When they look at us, they see plots and pawns and weapons. How could anyone who looks at you and sees only what you can do for them ever tell you who you are?"

"But if she is my mother . . ."

"If she is your mother, then I am glad she had a hand in creating you, and that brief gratitude is all we ever owe her. You do not owe her loyalty, just as you owe Merlin nothing, just as I owe my mother and my grandmother and the whole damned lot of them *nothing*." His voice became harsh. "We may have come from them, but we are not like them. You are not like them. That is why you are so unhappy, so lost. You are trying to be one of them, trying to offer your life on the altar of sacrifice to Merlin as Arthur has, trying to move through the world like an ancient power, unseeing and caring for nothing but your goals. You cannot help but care. You see people for what they are: tragic, wonderful, devastating individuals. Each with their own small worth and potential for good and evil."

"You do not give Arthur enough credit," Guinevere whispered. She had devoted so much of who she was to Arthur, and even now found herself rising to defend him. Worrying how it would hurt him to see her in this cave, in Mordred's arms.

"And you give him enough credit for both of us," Mordred snapped. "Go to sleep." He drew his arms away and turned his back on her.

They might be alone, but the specter of Arthur lingered, always between them.

CHAPTER FIFTEEN

"Lancelot," Guinevere said, relieved to see her knight in her dream-space, but still angry from her conversation with Mordred in the cave. Or angry about his anger.

"Are you safe?" Lancelot asked.

"That is open for debate," Mordred said. "You would probably not think she is."

She knew exactly what he meant—she was asleep in a cave, back-to-back with Mordred. But Lancelot did not and should not know that. "I got away," Guinevere blurted before Mordred could say anything else.

Lancelot's eyes widened with surprise and happiness. "You did?" Then they narrowed. "But he is still with you."

"Yes, well, he followed me."

"He *saved* you," Mordred trilled.

"Where are you now?" Lancelot asked.

"I went west, as I said I would. As soon as Arthur returns, make certain he knows I am free. No one holds me in the north."

Mordred raised an eyebrow as if he would disagree. Guinevere tightened her mouth into a line as sharp as a blade, daring him to.

"Right," Mordred said. "And I will keep her safe."

Lancelot's mouth twitched in an angry frown. "That is my job."

"And yet, I am at her side and you are safe in Camelot."

Lancelot unsheathed her sword and attacked without preamble. On the one hand, it was a relief that at least Mordred was not teasing and threatening to tell Lancelot the truth of their situation.

On the other hand, Guinevere was annoyed. This was supposed to be her time, but once again Lancelot had barely spoken to her, only confirming that Guinevere was safe before finding some flimsy excuse to spar with Mordred. Guinevere desperately wanted to speak with her friend, to tell her about the lake and what had happened, and what had not happened, and how confused and sad and lost she felt.

Mordred's words haunted her. If none of these powerful creatures actually cared about her as a person, the only answers she could look for were ones she could provide herself. Which meant she was back where she started.

A witch with false memories. A queen with no history. A girl with no past.

The formerly blue sky roiled with black clouds, and the birdsong had turned into the ominous snapping of twigs and rustling in the undergrowth. "Please do not make it rain on us," Mordred called. "I am quite happy being dry once more."

It was no use. The dreamspace made Guinevere nervous now. She could feel the pond, waiting somewhere. Maybe that had been the meaning of the body reaching up for her. A premonition of what awaited her in the water: an empty death.

Why, then, did she still desperately wish for someone to tell her who to be and how to be it?

"I need to go." Lancelot's voice was gruff. "I must be at my watch when the king returns so that he will know how to break the barrier."

"And so that he knows I am free," Guinevere insisted, not forgetting her debt to Fina.

Mordred sheathed his sword. "Yes, go and watch for the king and his army."

Lancelot had not stabbed him this time. Either she was softening or it had lost its novelty. "And why should he not have an army? His enemies will not leave him in peace."

Mordred raised his hands. "None of this was my idea."

"So you say. As soon as Arthur returns, I will meet you on the western coast. Guinevere is still not safe."

"So you say, Sir Lancelot." Mordred bowed with an exaggerated flourish.

Lancelot shoved her sword through his chest in response. Mordred smiled as she left it there and turned toward Guinevere, not quite meeting her eyes. "Would you like me to relay any messages?"

Guinevere was hit with a pang of longing to see her friends. She had seen through them, been a part of them, but it was not quite the same. What she would give to lay her problems at Brangien's feet and have Brangien dismiss them all with her brutal practicality! Or to spend the day just being a girl with Lily. Or even to listen to Dindrane's machinations and why, exactly, she had put her sister-in-law in a holding cell.

But thinking of them and what she had seen made her think of something she had *not* seen while looking through their eyes: chaos, disorganization, unrest. Guinevere, the queen, was not in Camelot. And Camelot was . . . fine. Better than fine. They had been more clever in running it than she would have been.

The storm's fury abated, turning into a sad smattering of drops.

What if the Lady *had* appeared? What answers could she give that would make Guinevere suddenly settled, ready to go back to the crown she had left behind, back to the role of queen . . . and capable of performing it?

There were bodies in Guinevere's wake. People and creatures killed because she wore a crown she did not deserve. She had chosen to walk away from Arthur and Camelot because she was not what they needed. But she also saw now that *they* were not what *she* needed. Knowing her past would not change that.

All was well in Camelot without her. Perhaps she needed to find a way to be whole without it. She forced a smile. "Only that Camelot is fortunate to have such champions and protectors. Oh! Tell Brangien to be a little gentler with the kitchen staff."

Lancelot frowned. "How do you know how she treats the kitchen staff?"

Guinevere flinched. She had not told Lancelot how Morgana had used her. "Morgana can see through others' eyes. She used my connections to people to see them. That is how we knew about Arthur's army."

Lancelot's eyes widened. "Who have you seen through?"

"Arthur, and Brangien, Lily, and Dindrane."

"And me," Mordred said, pulling Lancelot's sword free and tossing it to the ground. "Tell Lancelot the things that connected you to each of us." His smile was viciously flirtatious, a reminder of the old Mordred. Guinevere's face flushed as she remembered where their bodies were. He had not been coy or suggestive in the cave. Was this a performance for Lancelot? Or was he teasing Guinevere out of spite?

"Lancelot has to go," Guinevere growled.

With a flash of hurt illuminating her face brighter than any lightning, Lancelot disappeared.

But thinking about the connections did make Guinevere wonder:

Why, when Morgana had tapped into family, had Lancelot not appeared? Guinevere loved Brangien, Dindrane, and Lily. But her bond with Lancelot was deeper and stronger than any of those. If she had to pick the person who knew her best in all the world, she would name Lancelot without question.

Maybe Lancelot did not feel the same way about her. Maybe Guinevere's betrayal had forever broken their connection, and Morgana's magic knew that.

She did not question why passion had led her to Mordred. She understood it, even as she fought it. But the fact that it had been duty that led her to Arthur weighed heavily on her. She had wanted to be in love with him, wanted the validation of being loved by him. If he had loved her, desired her, would it have made her feel like she was enough?

Mordred sat on the forest floor and leaned back against the log that Guinevere was using as a seat. "Are you ready to wake up?"

"No," she said, resting her chin on her knees. "It is cold there."

Mordred gestured to the growing darkness around them. "It is not that warm here."

Guinevere closed her eyes, trying to focus. Trying to make it warm. "Can we just stay here? For a little while?" She did not want to be awake, to make a decision. To face the unknown future with no hope of knowing her past. She had no quest now. No direction. No purpose.

Mordred did not appear to be in a hurry to return to the cave, either. He began singing, almost as though he did not realize he was doing it. The tune was melodic and beautiful and deeply sad, in a language Guinevere did not understand.

"What does it mean?" she asked.

He stopped singing, and she realized the forest around them was warm once more. He turned his face toward hers. They were so close she could see the trees reflected in his eyes. "I do not know, but it makes me sad, and I love it. Some sorrows are sweet enough to be worth feeling."

"Mordred," Guinevere said, unable to look away from his eyes. Her forest had been designed to perfectly match the shade of them. He had followed her into the darkness, had saved her from drowning, had held her to keep the cold from claiming her.

Mordred had been told all his life who he was—the eel, Arthur's nephew, the fairyson, the Dark Queen's savior. And still he carved his own path, chose where to walk and followed no one. She had shied away from his pain because it was a mirror to her own. But he lived in it, did not run from it. He made mistakes and then kept going. And he always, *always* saw her.

"Mordred," Guinevere whispered with terror or something close to it dropping her stomach off the same drowning ledge, "I want to be kissed."

His eyes closed, and a spasm of pain altered his features. "You want to be kissed, but do you want me to be the one to kiss you? Here, in a dream, so you can wake and pretend it was not real?"

The heat of him against her here, in this forest, was real, and it was not. He was right. She was trying to steal a moment. Trying to avoid a choice.

Far away, she felt his hand release hers, felt the cold seep in. She was alone.

⚘

She awoke in the cave, to Mordred scooting away from her.

"No," she said, turning to face him.

Life is short. Death is swift. Some sorrows are sweet enough to be worth feeling.

She ran her fingers through his hair, put her hand on the back of his neck and drew his face to hers. It was not the same as the stolen kiss at Lancelot's tournament, all spark and exhilaration of the forbidden. It was not the same as being kissed by Arthur, with warmth and affection. It was a kiss of sadness, of fear, of pain, but also of desire. Mordred was neither here nor there, human nor fairy, good nor evil. He was a liar and a thief and a betrayer, and he was honest and fearless and loyal, and Guinevere saw all of him. Just as he had always seen her.

He pulled back. "Yes?" he whispered, and the hope in his voice broke her. She had no words to answer it, so she kissed him again. He crushed her to him, lips fierce and hungry as though he was afraid at any moment she would disappear.

She did not know what her future held or even what her past was, but here, in this moment, she knew what she wanted. And she took it.

CHAPTER SIXTEEN

Guinevere reached out a hand and trailed it along Mordred's jaw, then down his neck to his sharp, straight shoulders revealed in the daylight. That was the part hardest to believe, the part that filled her with the most giddy wonder. She could just . . . touch him.

And judging by his feelings, he was quite pleased with this development, as well.

Fina was right, after all. All this time spent wanting and denying, avoiding telling the truth, avoiding even *feeling* the truth, did not serve anyone.

Besides which, if she had known the sheer joy of touch that she had been missing out on, she would have made this decision a lot sooner. Mordred rested his face in the hollow between her neck and shoulder. It was warm now in the cave, with the sun streaming in and their body heat, but still they did not separate.

Guinevere almost wished they could stay in here forever. But of course that was neither practical nor possible. With a sigh, she extracted herself from Mordred's arms and went outside to take care of her bodily functions. Remembering Fina's ideas about how to make it difficult for male soldiers to pee outside made her giggle, and then she was laughing, head tipped back to the sun as she walked toward the cave, her soul dancing deliriously with joy.

"Did I miss something?" Mordred asked, stepping close to her. But then he hesitated, still unsure what the boundaries were.

Guinevere stepped toward him and fitted her back against his front, tucking her head beneath his. They looked out over the lake. His arms circled her waist, just as they had when he pulled her free. Saved her from drowning in pursuit of a past no one else cared about.

The lake was really more of a pond, water gathered in this depression between hills for who knew how many hundreds or thousands of years. Looking at it was like touching a bruise, and Guinevere looked away. She cast her eyes over the landscape instead, rugged and wild and empty.

"Should we move on?" she asked. "Is the rest of Nechtan's force coming here?"

"They are following the horse you industriously stole. Because of course it makes the most sense for you to go southeast toward Camelot."

"No one questioned why you went this way?"

"No one saw me. And I had a talk with the horses before I left. If any of Nechtan's people do decide to head in this direction, they will find their horses stubbornly opposed to the endeavor."

"How did you do that?" Guinevere asked, genuinely curious.

"I gave them all a very real fear that this direction was filled with snakes. Just endless snakes as far as the eye could see."

Guinevere laughed. "Poor horses."

"They will forget, eventually. Though, actually, they might forever hold an aversion to traveling west. For which I am sorry. But not too sorry." He tightened his arms around her, pressing his lips to the top of her head. "I cannot feel sorry for anything that brought me to this moment."

It was a sentiment Guinevere wished she could return, but she still carried a vast weight of regrets and guilt on her shoulders. Not about this, here, with Mordred. But about all the things she might have or could have or should have done. And the people she had left behind.

Had she left them behind, though? Would she never go back? In this empty, forsaken place, it was easy to imagine wandering forever. Camelot seemed impossibly far away.

As though sensing her tension, Mordred ran his hands down her arms, drawing her back to the present. "I have food."

"What about your mother?"

"I would assume she also has food."

Guinevere turned and scowled up at him. "You know what I mean. You left her."

Mordred's smile belied the pain she felt radiating from his touch. "It is nothing she would not have done to me in pursuit of her own goals. I learned from the best how to fixate on what I want and let everything else cease to matter."

"Mordred," Guinevere said, her voice softening. "I—"

"Breakfast!" Mordred walked to his horse. He provided the same rations they had eaten with Nechtan's people, and he and Guinevere sat, shoulder to shoulder in the sunlight.

"Stop," Mordred said, nudging her.

"Stop what?" Guinevere looked down at the remains of her food, confused. Had she done something wrong?

"Stop worrying about what comes next."

Guinevere tried to laugh. "Oh, now *you* can sense how I am feeling through touch? I thought that was my gift."

"I can sense how you are feeling by the incredible tension in the way you sit. Like you are about to run. Like you are bracing for a blow. We are safe."

Guinevere sighed. "But for how long? And for what purpose?"

Mordred raised one eyebrow, angling his body so they sat face to face. "Why does being safe have to serve any purpose other than . . . being safe?"

"Well, I just mean what are we going to do next? Do we continue north and west? Do we begin to work our way south again? Should I still try to speak with Merlin, or give that up entirely? What should I tell Lancelot the next time we speak? And then there is the issue of the Dark Queen. She might not have me anymore, but she is still plotting, and we do not know what her plans are or how—"

Mordred put a finger against her lips. "Why does it matter?"

"Because she is plotting against Arthur, and—"

"And Arthur is plotting against her, and my mother is plotting against Merlin, and doubtless Merlin saw all this and has his own plots that were put in motion seventy years ago and will somehow ruin whatever my mother is trying to do, while Arthur sweeps in with his damnable sword and cuts through the magic of my grandmother, who will retreat and plot anew, while Arthur goes and does Arthur things and my mother plots and Merlin interferes from afar. They are all a terrible river crashing down a hill. Nothing will stop them. Nothing will alter their course. If we remove ourselves from it, all we have done to affect the outcome is claim our own selves and our own happiness as more important than being drowned by their conflict."

Guinevere knew Mordred was right. That Arthur could and would fight these battles alone. That Merlin probably *had* seen all this, and that they could fight and worry and work in the background, and in the end the power of the Dark Queen, the wizard, and the sword would outlast them all. But . . .

"People will be hurt," she said. "And I don't mean people we care about, though they will be very hurt." Guinevere closed her eyes against the ache, thinking about how Lancelot would feel when she found out. For a reason she could not quite explain, being with Mordred this way felt like more of a betrayal of Lancelot than of Arthur.

She did not want to think about their feelings.

Guinevere swept her arm to encompass the land around them. "I mean the people who live here. The people of the south, and the north. The ones who are trying to go about living their lives, who do not deserve to be swept up in this violence and trouble."

"And why, my queen," Mordred said, brushing his lips along her knuckles and making her shiver with the depths of his feeling as he called her *his* queen, "do you deserve to be swept up in it?"

Guinevere opened her mouth to answer but found she had nothing to say. She had been sent to Camelot by Merlin with a false mantle on her shoulders. She had walked in thinking herself protector, to discover that she was the one to be protected. She had accepted her role as Arthur's wife and queen, even though neither had ever really been true. She loved Camelot, but she also felt trapped there. And she had seen firsthand that the city did not need her to thrive and be safe under the most trying of circumstances. Even the magical shield she had provided did not save the city, because she had been entirely wrong about what Arthur's enemies were planning.

She had thought she was waging war, when really she was just being moved around, a piece in a game controlled by more-powerful players.

Why *did* she deserve to be swept up in it? And what did she really think she could change?

"So what now, then?" she asked. Guinevere had left Camelot to find herself. Perhaps getting lost was the only way to do that.

Mordred's face brightened like dawn breaking after an infinite night. "Anything we want."

"And what if I do not know what that is?" She only knew she wanted to be with Mordred, to be touched and adored and to feel passion without fear or guilt. Maybe she would never recover the parts of herself that had been lost. She did not know if she could accept that. But she could at least try to be at peace with it, now that she had protected Camelot and helped avert war for Fina's people.

"Then we will figure it out, together. We could join Rhoslyn. She would take us in. Or we could stay in the north. I like it up here."

"And live in a cottage and be happy and content forever?" Guinevere teased.

Mordred laughed, but it was tinged with sadness. "You would not be happy or content with that. You care too much. But we can still do good together. Here, I can be a fairyson, and you can be . . . whatever you are. We can help people, like you did with the refugees."

"And like you did with Rhoslyn's camp."

"Exactly!" Mordred leaned forward, excited. "We did not ask to be who we are, but we can choose how we live. I thought I did not have choices before. I thought my life was a tragedy. But you are here, and I am . . ." He closed his eyes, an expression like pain on his face contradicting the exquisite happiness she felt in his touch. "I am made anew. Come. I want to take you somewhere and tell you the moment I fell in love with you."

CHAPTER SEVENTEEN

Guinevere rode with her arms around Mordred's waist, her head resting on his shoulder as she watched the landscape slowly change around them. They were moving from the rocky, relatively barren hills into land that increasingly sloped downward. She suspected it was sloping downward to the ocean, which she had no desire to visit or see again.

"Are you lost?" she asked. She realized she did not know whether Mordred had been to this region before. She doubted it. Which meant that he would not have a destination in mind, despite what he had said when they set out this morning.

Mordred squeezed her hands, and the brightness in his voice was impossible to conceal. "I am not lost. Wandering and lost are not the same thing."

She smiled against his shoulder. Wandering and lost were not the same thing. She would think of herself not as lost but as wandering. It certainly felt more romantic and less desperately lonely that way.

A happy sigh left her. She could not be sure how much of what she was feeling was her own happiness or Mordred's delirious joy, and she did not want to know. It was so nice to bask in a shared emotion with someone and not worry about where his feelings ended and hers began.

"There! We are almost there." Mordred's eagerness made Guinevere sit up. Maybe he really had known where they were going this whole time. But all she saw was a hardy, dull-green forest ahead of them. It was not the vibrant green of a summer forest, but the steady, tired green of trees that weather winter without losing their foliage. The trees were scraggly and spaced farther apart than those of forests in the south, the plants miserly and competing for water and sunlight. Their bark was dusty brown and gray. Still, the trees were beautiful in their determination, and Guinevere breathed deeply, inhaling the scent of bark and crushed needles as she and Mordred rode in.

"You knew this place?" she asked as they dismounted.

Mordred grabbed his pack, then patted the horse as it wandered off to forage for food. "I have never been in this region. I was looking for any forest at all."

"Because it provides better cover?"

"Because it will help me explain how I fell in love with you." Mordred tilted his head, eyes soft as he took her in. "That second day after we retrieved you from the convent. Among the trees."

Guinevere let out a shocked laugh. "You hated me!"

"I barely noticed you before then. You were yet another meaningless task. Stiff and veiled and boring." Mordred's smile got slyer and sharper. "And awkward. I felt sorry for you, actually. I assumed Camelot and the ladies there would eat you alive."

Guinevere hit his shoulder playfully, then nodded. "To be fair, they tried, but I had Brangien and Dindrane on my side." She had never been good at that part, the roles and the games women were expected to understand.

"Anyhow," Mordred said, as though eager to pull her out of reminiscing about her friends and place her back in his story, "there we were, under the trees. Everyone else was tense, watchful, desperate to get back to the cold stones and suffocating roofs of Camelot, safe from wonder and beauty and nature once more. But you tilted your head back. You relaxed and breathed deeply for the first time since we had retrieved you. I could see how it fed your soul, and in that moment I wanted—needed—to know you." He paused. "It did not hurt that you are very beautiful, I suppose."

Guinevere laughed. "Oh, well, I am glad it did not hurt." But she was also glad that her beauty was not the first thing he had liked about her. He had seen her and thought her beautiful, but he had not wanted to know her until he saw something familiar, something intriguing.

Mordred touched a strand of her hair that had escaped from Fina's blue wrap. "After that, I made any excuse I could to get close to you. Told myself I was spying on you to protect Arthur. Told myself I was spying on you for the Dark Queen. Told myself anything I could think of as a reason why I had to be near you, had to learn everything I could about you." He paused, lowering his hand and his eyes. "And eventually I let you get hurt, because in my head and my heart freeing the Dark Queen was the only way to separate you from Arthur. And I am sorry. I will always be sorry."

Guinevere put her hands on his cheeks and drew his face down. She kissed him, feeling his sorrow and guilt as dark undercurrents to the bright sparks of happiness and desire at her touch.

He pulled her close, holding her, their breath timed together.

For so long after he had hurt her, she thought her only options were to forgive him completely or hate him completely. But now she knew she could hold the wrongness of what he had done and at the same time forgive him, because people were so much more than the worst things they did. She had to believe that, otherwise how could she move through the world carrying the guilt of the harm she had done?

She understood Mordred's desperation to give his grandmother back her form, her being. She understood all their desperation, actually. Every one of their friends and foes alike. Morgana's actions were only bad because she was not working with Arthur, but against Merlin. And Merlin's own actions were far from good. He had hurt and killed and destroyed, all to create Arthur. So was he an evil being who did good things? Or a good being who did evil things?

Even the Saxons had to have their reasons for coming here, for invading. If Guinevere had been born a Saxon, how would she feel? Or if she had been born Fina's sister, or if she had been born . . . well, if she remembered anything about how and who she had been born, how would things be different?

Arthur had been born in violence, raised in it, instructed in it. And in spite of that, he tried to do what he thought was right. But who was there to tell him to think about other perspectives, other values? Who in his life told him to pause? Who in his life told him *no*? Certainly not his knights.

"What are you thinking about?" Mordred pulled back so he could search her face.

Guinevere could not admit she was thinking about Arthur. So she told part of the truth. "I am thinking about the nature of evil."

"You are such a romantic." Mordred sounded teasing, but she could feel the spike of dissatisfaction, of worry. She felt manipulative, knowing exactly how he was feeling and tailoring her responses to it.

He had just told her the story of how he fell in love with her. She should return the gift. But she did not have a story to tell him of the moment she fell in love with him, because she did not know if she *was* in love with him. She felt passion, yes. An attraction she had tried so long to deny. Understanding and connection. Maybe that was all love. But if she opened her mouth and said it, she worried she would always question whether or not it was true. Or whether she was simply mirroring back to him what he was giving her.

"The night of the play," she said, instead. "When you danced backward up the hill so you could keep talking to us without turning away. You teased about staying out after curfew and being locked up, and there was a moment where I very much wanted to know what we would—what we *could* do. I denied it then, and I continued denying it as best I could whenever we were together. You did not make it easy." Guinevere smiled up at him.

No trace of slyness or subtlety remained in Mordred's expression. He was a creature made entirely of open, heartbreakingly vulnerable happiness. It almost scared her to see him like this. Mordred had always survived, had kept safe the parts of himself that could destroy him. He was offering them all to her now.

"I am so glad you have stopped denying it." He kissed her as they lay gently down on the forest floor.

She was glad she had stopped denying it, too, because this—this desire, this passion—was part of her. No one had magically placed it in her mind, or taken it away from her. It was not someone else's memories or feelings. So much had been taken away or lost or hidden that she refused to ignore or deny any part of herself that she had left.

Time passed in a dreamy haze punctuated with sparks of laughter. Want turned to drowsy satisfaction. She watched as his features relaxed. She had never before seen him sleeping. He always fell asleep after her and woke up before she did. Careful and cautious.

His face while sleeping looked so much younger than when he was awake. Fragile even, though she knew he was one of the most dangerous men on the entire island.

She reached out to touch his cheek, wanting to reassure herself that it was real and he was real and they were real together, when his eyes opened. It took her a few moments to process what she was seeing.

Because they were not Mordred's eyes.

Guinevere had spent enough time looking at—and desperately avoiding gazing into—Mordred's eyes to know that these green eyes were not his. His were the green of the deepest forest, verdant and lush. These were the weary green of lichen clinging to ancient rocks, refusing to be washed away.

"Oh, my poor, foolish son," Mordred's voice said in a tone that matched the Morgana green. "You took him away from me."

"Yes, it must be devastating to have someone you love taken," Guinevere snapped. "But he walked away from you because you refuse to see beyond your own desperate quest for vengeance."

Morgana's glare was colder than the wind cutting through the valley. "*Everyone* I love has been taken from me by the monster who puppets your precious Arthur." Morgana had lost her father and mother to Merlin's plotting. She had lost her half brother Arthur to the same. Her lover, the Green Knight, had been killed by Arthur, and now Mordred had broken with her.

"What do you want with me?" Guinevere sat up and wrapped her arms around her knees. It made her skin crawl, looking at Mordred and seeing his mother. She stared at the trees instead.

"I must break the wizard's stranglehold on this island. And you, silly, selfish girl, are the only piece of his handiwork that I have access to. The Dark Queen will rip what she wants from you, regardless of the consequences. But if I can unravel you first, I can find a better way. An easier way. A way you are more likely to survive. Come back to me."

"I will not. And neither will your son. He deserves better."

"And I do not?" Mordred's hands shot out and grasped Guinevere's wrists. "I *will* discover Merlin through you. One more to try. *Love.*"

Guinevere had a single heartbeat of fear and hope to wonder whom love would connect her to—Mordred? Arthur? Her life before either?—and then she was flung out of herself and into—

CHAPTER EIGHTEEN

Lancelot. Guinevere was Lancelot.

Lancelot waited on the narrow strip of rock-strewn beach between the secret passage and the border of Guinevere's shield.

It was an almost physical pain, staring out through the blue shimmer. Guinevere felt it alongside Lancelot, truly understood what it meant to her knight to be trapped. Lancelot replayed over and over the moment when Guinevere stepped back, away from her. Left her behind. Tasked her with protecting a city that did not love or want her while the queen she would do anything for was taken.

Guinevere felt it, and she wanted to cry, to apologize, but she was not Guinevere right now. She was Lancelot, and Lancelot was quickly taking over her sense of self.

Lancelot prowled, taking three steps in either direction. She would as soon kill Mordred as take his side, but . . . she trusted him to keep Guinevere alive. He had proved that was a priority at least. And Guinevere with Mordred was safer than Guinevere with Morgana and Nechtan.

Safer, but still not safe.

Her mind ran through strikes and blocks and parries, her limbs twitching in half-hearted attempts to keep up with it. Tonight in Guinevere's dream she would fight Mordred again, and she would beat him, because she had to. She would defeat the whole world if she had to, over and over, as many foes as there were between herself and her queen.

She would see Guinevere again tonight, and it would hurt, but as long as it hurt it meant that Guinevere was still alive and unbroken, and as long as Guinevere was alive, Lancelot would get her back.

She *would*.

Guinevere wished Lancelot could feel her, too. Could feel her relief at knowing that Lancelot had not given up on her in spite of the pain she had caused. But she was merely a passenger.

Twisting to dodge an imaginary blow, Lancelot's eyes swept the horizon and she stopped. Horses. They approached Camelot's lake at a ferocious speed. Lancelot threw more branches on the fire, stoking it so high that it hurt to be so close to it. "Come on, come on," she whispered, her eyes watering from the smoke but still fixed on the horses.

They changed course, heading straight for her.

The king, and Excalibur, and the end of her interminable watch. Lancelot grabbed her bag and slung it over her shoulder. She would alternate between her horse and a spare one, push them as fast as she safely could. Alone, she could cover the same amount of ground that Nechtan's forces had in a couple of days, cutting west to find Mordred and Guinevere.

Guinevere, I am coming.

One horse pulled away from the rest. Lancelot recognized King Arthur's silhouette in the twilight as his knights hung back. He dismounted and approached the barrier, staring up at it.

Guinevere's thoughts—muted and confused, but not overwhelmed as they had been with Arthur—juddered. Arthur through Lancelot's eyes looked so different. Stronger. Harder. There was no affection in Lancelot's gaze, only impatience and a surprising burst of anger toward the king who had ridden away from Guinevere so easily.

"My king!" Lancelot bowed quickly, a hand to her heart. "There is much to say and little time. Guinevere has been taken, but she escaped. I know where she is and I have a plan."

"What is this?" King Arthur gestured at the shield. "Is the city overthrown? Is the Dark Queen here?"

Lancelot felt another flare of anger that the king asked first about the city, not about who had taken Guinevere or where she was. "It is Guinevere's magic. As long as she was on that side and I on this, the city could not be reached."

"Why was *Guinevere* outside the shield? Why not you?"

Lancelot wanted to slump, to give her shame physical expression, but she forced herself to stand tall. "She did not tell me that was how it would work." *She tricked me. She protected me and I will never forgive her for not allowing me to protect her,* Lancelot thought. *No one has ever tried to protect me before. Not since the Lady.* No one else had ever looked at Lancelot and found someone worth protecting.

Lancelot forced the thoughts away. "Morgan le Fay and the Dark Queen are in league with Nechtan. They are heading north to a forest known as the Green Man's Chapel where the Dark Queen is hidden. But Guinevere escaped with—" Lancelot stumbled over the name. She did not want to say it, and she did not want King Arthur to know. But she was a knight, and she told the truth. "Guinevere escaped with Mordred. Fina, one of Nechtan's daughters, helped her so that you would not attack her people."

The king's eyes flashed with an emotion Lancelot did not understand. She had expected anger, and there was anger but something else as well. Sadness? Regret? Jealousy? It seemed both softer and more complicated than rage.

"How do you know this?" King Arthur asked.

"Guinevere has been talking to us. Through dreams."

The king frowned. "Who knows about this?"

"Only myself, Isolde, and Brangien."

"And what does the city think of the barrier?" King Arthur gestured at it. "Do they know Guinevere did it?"

"No. We started rumors that it was the Lady of the Lake, protecting Camelot in your absence. All you have to do is break the spell with Excalibur and then I will go to the queen. I will bring her home." As night fell, the barrier had a subtle glow to it. Their safety robbed them of the stars in the black night sky, and Lancelot missed them fiercely. Soon she would be out. Free to save her Guinevere.

The king rubbed the back of his neck, staring up at the dome over all of Camelot. "It stands, as long as you stay on that side?"

"Yes, but Guinevere was certain Excalibur would break through. She wanted you to do it on the lakeside, where everyone could see, but there is no time to lose. Mordred is not on Nechtan's side, but I do not trust him, not for a moment, and—"

"I did not expect Camelot to be safe. I thought I would have to besiege my own city. This changes things." King Arthur did not unsheathe Excalibur.

Lancelot was explaining things wrong. Or the king was in too much shock to understand. "We kept it safe for you, yes. And I swear, I will not return without the queen."

King Arthur took a step back. His voice softened with wonder. "What a gift Guinevere has given me. The city has everything it needs for the winter. All my people are protected, so I can do what needs to be done without fear. Merlin must have known when he sent her. He prepared the way for me." He fixed his eyes on Lancelot. "I have an army. This attack against the very heart of Camelot, *my* heart, will not stand. Nechtan and the Dark Queen must fall."

"But they do not have Guinevere anymore." Lancelot understood his anger, but there were more important things. Getting Guinevere to safety was the priority. "She and Mordred went west, and—"

"Mordred will never go against his mother and the Dark Queen. He is manipulating Guinevere. The only way to save her is by destroying the enemies that would use her against me."

If the king insisted on traveling with an army, it would slow him down. And if he went after Nechtan and the Dark Queen, he would miss Guinevere entirely. Which meant more time with Guinevere and Mordred on their own, and Lancelot could not stand for that.

She trusted Guinevere. But she did not trust Mordred to let Guinevere make her own decisions. He would manipulate her, however he could. King Arthur was right about that.

"Very well," Lancelot said. She could not tell the king what to do with his army, even if she thought he was wrong. "I will find the queen while you lead your men against Nechtan. I swear she will be protected."

"No. Camelot is safe, and you will see that it remains that way by keeping the barrier in place."

"But—"

The king's eyes turned as hard and cold as iron. "You are a knight of Camelot, and I command you to keep my city safe until I return. Go and fetch the captain of the guard. I need to give him instructions before I leave."

Lancelot did not understand what had just happened. She had a plan. *She* had the connection to Guinevere, the way to see where she was, to speak with her. King Arthur had—

He had an army. He was riding to war, and Lancelot could do nothing to help Guinevere or help the king . . . or stop him. This time Lancelot did not fall to her knees in despair. She was numb beyond feeling as she turned and obeyed the orders of Arthur Pendragon.

CHAPTER NINETEEN

When Guinevere finally clawed her way back to her wits, it was night. Mordred was sleeping, and, as far as she could tell, he was once again entirely himself.

He had warned her that she would be vulnerable to the Dark Queen when she was sleeping. Perhaps it was the same with Morgana. Guinevere nearly woke him, but realized the conversation they needed to have—now that Morgana knew about Lancelot, knew Arthur was coming with his army, knew everything they did—was one that had to include Lancelot. Weary and troubled by what Lancelot had seen, Guinevere cut a lock of her own hair and knotted it into Mordred's to make certain his dreams were hers as well.

Guinevere's forest was no longer green. It was winter and summer and spring and autumn. Trees flamed with orange and red leaves that were entwined with spring buds and shadowed by winter-bare skeletons piercing the sky.

Mordred and Lancelot were there, and the wind whipped them with punishing lashes as Guinevere explained to Mordred what had happened. Which meant explaining to Lancelot that Morgana had used Mordred to fling Guinevere into her.

"I am sorry," Guinevere whispered, fully aware that she possessed insight into and knowledge about Lancelot that had not been willingly given. It was unfair at best, a violation at worst. She felt it more keenly than she had with the others. Perhaps because Lancelot was deeply private, or because Guinevere knew that Lancelot forgave her even though she was unwilling to talk about it yet. "It was not my decision. I would have stopped her if I could have."

"A warning that you could be possessed by your mother might have been nice," Lancelot snarled, turning her rage on Mordred instead.

"Had I known, I certainly would have warned Guinevere! It was not a pleasant surprise for me, either."

"Please," Guinevere said. "We need to figure out what to do about Arthur. Morgana knows he is coming. Besides, I made a promise to Fina." Guinevere had left Arthur a perfectly protected Camelot, sent word that she was safe, yet he was still coming.

With an entire army.

Guinevere shivered, remembering how Arthur, her Arthur, had looked so different through other eyes.

And *why* had love taken her to Lancelot? She stole a glance at her knight. When Fina had asked if Lancelot was beautiful, Guinevere had described her as magnificent. And it was true. She admired Lancelot, was continually impressed by her, depended on her. Were it not for Lancelot, she really might be able to disappear into the wilderness with Mordred and leave Camelot behind.

But she had not been able to tell Mordred she loved him. And she had not been able to imagine a future with him, because it meant a future without Lancelot. It broke her heart that Lancelot thought no one had ever valued her enough to try to protect her other than the accursed, faithless Lady of the Lake. Guinevere would not, could not leave her behind.

In many ways, she had been fixated on Lancelot since the first time she saw her fight. Even then, she had known Lancelot was something exceptional. And they had been fighting for each other since that day in the forest with the Dark Queen's boar and spider. Protecting and saving and supporting in equal measure. It was more than friendship, more than passion, more than duty.

Lancelot's hand in hers had always felt *right*.

"The king should be warned they know he is coming," Lancelot said.

"It will not deter him. Arthur is a fool." Mordred shook his head.

Arthur was not a fool. He had been set on this path by a wizard who saw all of time at once. Was it any wonder that Arthur viewed his every decision as necessary and right? Because surely if he were choosing wrong, Merlin would have seen it. Prevented it.

But Arthur *was* choosing wrong. This was not about Camelot. Camelot was safe, safer than ever now, with all of the south united under Arthur. The Dark Queen was not formidable enough to face Arthur on her own. And Lancelot had delivered the message that Guinevere was free, thanks to Fina. The only purpose coming north served was revenge. That was not the Arthur she had known, or at least the one she hoped for when she looked at him.

"What if I go back to him?" Guinevere asked, her voice soft. "We could intercept him. Turn him around."

"Oh, yes, he is likely to listen to me," Mordred snapped.

"I would not feel safer with you in the middle of an army. I should—" Lancelot ran her hands through her curls, growling in frustration. "I should be with you. I should be riding to you right now."

"Then why are you still in Camelot?" Mordred leaned against a skeletal tree, arms folded.

"You would like that! For me to break the barrier and leave Camelot without sword *or* shield!"

"I could not care less about Camelot."

"So you say. But you encourage me to leave it and break the barrier."

"Actually, I do not want you to join us, Lancelot. Believe me, I prefer you and Arthur far away. But an army is sweeping northward. My mother can still reach us. Our enemies grow every day. If it were just Nechtan, or just my mother, or even just my wretched grand-mother, I might have a chance. But I cannot protect Guinevere alone from so many threats. I need your help."

"I do not need protection," Guinevere said. So many people were going to get hurt, and though she was not the cause, she could not help feeling responsible.

Lancelot ignored her. "I cannot leave the city."

Mordred closed the distance between him and Lancelot and jabbed her shoulder with a finger. "You swore to protect her!"

Lancelot punched Mordred so hard he fell. "Do you think I do not know that? I would give anything to be riding for her. But if I leave, I will have betrayed the king."

Mordred laughed bitterly. "It gets easier with practice, I promise."

Lancelot moved to kick Mordred, then stopped. She turned to Guinevere, her face tortured. She crossed the meadow and knelt in front of Guinevere. "Please. Command me. Tell me what you would have me do."

"Do not—do not kneel. Please. Not for me." Guinevere dropped to her knees and took Lancelot's hands in her own. "I already made a decision for you, and I know how it hurt you, and it will haunt me until the end of my days. If you leave, you turn your back on knight-hood, and no one has ever been more deserving of that title than you. It would break my heart to see you lose it. You are the best of all of them."

"But if I do not leave, I break my vows to you. And those vows are more sacred to me than any I have made to the king." Lancelot's dark eyes were flooded with emotion as she searched Guinevere's face. Usually the height difference separated them; they had never been this close face to face. Guinevere was filled with the sudden impulse to kiss Lancelot.

Confused and jumbled by panic, desperation, fear, and hope, Guinevere wrapped her arms around Lancelot's neck instead, pulling her close. She closed her eyes against the intensity of her feelings, against the relief of being forgiven. She had not lost Lancelot. Lancelot's curls tickled Guinevere's face as she pressed her lips near her knight's ear. "I know you would fight the whole world for me. And I would for you as well, which is why I cannot tell you what to do. I will be safe, one way or another. And we will be together again." Guinevere whispered it like a promise, like a prayer.

"We will go to the western coast," Mordred said. "Hide. No one will find us."

Guinevere released Lancelot, flushing with embarrassment even though no one knew how close she had come to kissing Lancelot. Indulging her impulses with Mordred was one thing. She would have to get better control of herself.

Guinevere stood. "And leave Fina's people to be overthrown by a vengeful king?"

Mordred shrugged, but his expression conveyed regret. "They are the ones who stole you in the first place."

"Do you really think that when Arthur defeats them all—because it is a when, not an if—he will leave you be? That he will give up on finding Guinevere?" Lancelot turned to Guinevere. "Do you *want* him to find you? What was your original plan?" Lancelot's eyebrows shifted as she considered for the first time that Guinevere might not want to return to Camelot. Guinevere braced herself to be berated, or told what to do.

Instead, without judgment or expectation, Lancelot simply asked, "What do you need?"

"I—" Guinevere said. "I need . . ." She did not know what she needed. She *wanted* to know who she was. She *wanted* to pretend it was only herself and Mordred in the whole world, to get lost in the dreamy heat. She *wanted* to be reunited with Lancelot. She *wanted* to be with her friends, both those in Camelot and in the north. She *wanted* to be at Arthur's side, helping him, guiding him away from becoming his father's son.

But those wants could not all exist together.

"I need to take a walk," Guinevere said, unable to breathe, unable to look either Mordred or Lancelot in the eyes and face their questions.

Guinevere hurried away.

She had claimed a delirious present with Mordred, but when she tried to see a future, it was as riddled with emptiness and questions as her own past.

She loved so much of Camelot and the people there. It was not perfect, and neither was Arthur, but she still loved them. She did not want to be separated from them forever.

And any future that did not include Lancelot was not a future she wanted.

But the future was coming for them all with violent speed. Images of her friends hurt, dying, ran through her mind in an inescapable loop. Arthur, pulled underground by the devouring roots of the Dark Queen like Maleagant's men had been. Fina, gored by one of

Arthur's soldiers, her bright light gone forever. Lancelot, breaking her vows, hunted down by the other knights in the name of honor. Mordred, killed by Arthur, killed by his mother, killed by Nectudad. So many possibilities, all of them ending with the people she held dearest dying because she could not save them.

Because she did not know what she wanted. Because she was still lost. Wandering was a luxury she did not have. She did not have years or even months to discover herself. She needed answers. Some way she could make sense of herself and her place in the midst of all this conflict so that she could do her part to fix it.

Guinevere stopped. Her feet had carried her to the pond. As still and calm as a breath held in terror, it reflected the dark sky above, a pool of perfect, ominous storm.

Merlin had placed the certainty that water would unmake her so deep within her soul that she could not push past it, could not find whatever lay beneath the surface. And everyone and everything she cared about was now at risk. Mordred was right. She would not find the answers from Merlin, or Morgana, or the Lady of the Lake.

Only she had them.

Guinevere walked to the edge of the pond. Her reflection screamed toward her as she tipped straight into the water. When she hit the surface, it did not ripple. It shattered.

And so did Guinevere.

THE LADY/THE GIRL

She touches everything, flowing over and through and around. She is in the clouds, the rocks, the dirt, the trees. She is deep and still and powerful and rushing, a drop and an ocean.

And a lake.

She likes being a lake best of all.

There is no such thing as time, but there are *moments,* and the moments shape her. The first time a human kneels on her banks and drinks from her. The first time a human breathes their last in her depths, taking her into their lungs before ceasing to exist. She is part of their life, part of their death, part of them, but she cannot feel it.

She wants to feel it.

She gathers these moments, treasuring them, stealing them away on droplets of sweat from lovers' skin, tears from women pushing new life from their bellies, even the blood that dyes her puddles violent red.

They are, all of them, *life.* And she feeds it and nourishes it and treasures it.

And envies it.

Without her, none of it would be possible, and yet she cannot be any of it. No matter what forms she takes, how far she flings herself, what she touches and helps, she always, always comes back to herself.

She makes family, of a sort. She tells herself they are family, because she wants more. Always more. She names herself, and she names Nynaeve, the part of her that she split off in the deepest of winter with a resounding crack, moving through the ice.

Sister, she calls, and Nynaeve answers.

In the forest, the deepest, wildest parts, she finds a riot of chaos and life shaping itself into something real, and recognizes herself there, too. The darkness has no name, and she wants to name it, but the darkness just laughs.

I am life and I am death and I am everything in between, it says. *How can I be named? If you are a lady, I am a queen. The dark queen, the true queen, the only queen of this land.*

A lady. Yes. That is what she wants to be. So the Lady claims the queen as sister, friend, washing over her and greedily carrying away all the bits of life she can. She is ravenous, desperate, and the desire for more does not end. She builds humans a city, a perfect city so they will always reflect on her, so that she can grasp at those reflections and walk among them, pretend to be one of them.

It is not enough.

Nynaeve does not understand. Nynaeve took all their calm, unknowable depths. She is content to exist, to observe, to flow in endless cycles. Water always finds a way back to itself, and Nynaeve assumes that eventually they will become one once more.

But the Lady does not want that. Anything but that. She fixates on humans. In them, she sees her hunger, her desire. They are endlessly striving, endlessly trying. Swarming over the land and through the water, consuming and creating and dying in almost the same breath. Such fragile, glorious creatures. She is holding several of them in her depths, waiting for that ecstatic moment when life becomes nothing, when she is completely part of them for that infinite, infinitesimal moment between *something* and *nothing,* when the wizard appears on her shores.

She abandons her pursuits and rises to meet him. Because he is something new. And, for the first time in her existence, she has reason to hope for something she never thought was possible:

Change.

🦢

Another baby is born three years after the baby who was meticulously planned, violently created, and immediately stolen by the wizard.

No one has plans yet for this baby, because she is a girl, and her father already has sons.

She is small and quiet, with large brown eyes that take in the world. And what she sees breaks her tender heart as soon as she can understand. A castle takes care of her, but no one cares *for* her. A thousand observed or experienced acts of carelessness, cruelty, or indifference cut her. She is only one very small person. One very small person whom no one listens to.

She has a sister, and she finds what joy she can in the golden determination of her tiny companion, but even that fills her with fear. Because they will be separated. Because her sister's spark will be smothered by a father who deems girls best seen and not heard and, best of all, sold to the highest bidder. Because she knows she cannot protect her sister or herself.

She learns to shoot, each arrow that finds its target soothing her. She does it for hours, whenever she can get away from lessons or obligations. Nock, pull, release. Nock, pull, release. She pretends herself the arrow, flying far from here, finding safety buried in a target.

Sometimes it is all too much and she retreats deep inside herself, so far inside that she almost cannot feel it when her father strikes her sister, almost cannot feel it when every person in the castle looks the other way, almost cannot feel it when he praises her for her behavior when she knows she is a coward and part of the problem. Almost cannot feel it when her *sister* comforts *her*.

But she still feels terror when her father turns on her, and her sister gets between them. Guilt when her younger sister has to take care of her. Maybe the problem is not her father or her sister. Maybe it is her. Without her, what would they fight over?

She is the one hurting everyone. Her weakness, her sadness, her constant fear.

The convent is her idea. She presents it meekly to her father, how much more desirable it will make her as a bride. He agrees. Her sister is devastated, bereft, and though she promises she will return for her, she knows it is a lie. A lie she is telling both of them. Because she will never be able to help anyone, and that is the truth of her world. One girl alone is nothing.

The convent is easier. All she has to do there is exist. They like her silent and pliant, mistake her wide-eyed gaze for attentiveness instead of absence. The nights are long, though. She cannot sleep, feeling her sister's absence like a wound that has festered, fearing everything that is happening to her sister while she is here, safe. Dreading the unknown void of the future waiting to swallow her whole when she is given to another castle, another man.

She retrieves her bow and arrows from where she hid them in the false bottom of her trunk, and sneaks out. In the dark, the forest is her friend. She can breathe here, can simply exist like a creature of the wild. Every night she escapes herself. Every day she sleepwalks through her tiny, selfish life.

Then one night an arrow goes wide. She cannot afford to lose it; she has so few. She follows its path, her way lit by the full moon, and finds herself on the bank of a lake as brilliant and glowing as the moon itself.

It is so unexpectedly beautiful that it pierces her numb haze. She sits and weeps, her tears trailing down her face and falling to the ground. A wave laps up from the still lake, carrying her arrow on it. When she touches the water, it is as warm and comforting as a bath.

The next night, her path to the lake is lit by winking lights. She does not question the magic, only follows it, feeling at last like an arrow flying toward an unknown target. She is not surprised to find a boat on the shore. It pulls her to the center of the lake. Leaning over, she sees herself, perfectly reflected. But not herself, not exactly. Because this girl's eyes are the color of the lake. This girl is strong. Determined. Happy. This is a girl who can help others.

This is who she wants to be, who she knows she can never be.

And then, behind her, another reflection appears. A young man, handsome and kind and so real as he smiles and puts his hand on her reflection's shoulder that she looks behind herself, certain he is in the boat with her.

The two of them, together. When she looks at them, she knows: they could change the world. And she wants that. She wants them, wants to be that girl, that version of herself, more than she has ever wanted anything. The water ripples under her outstretched hand

and the reflections disappear, leaving only her own horrible, weak face, her brown eyes always afraid.

The boat takes her weeping back to shore. She grips the sides of the craft, unwilling to step out, unwilling to leave what she has seen. A woman waits for her. She has long silver hair, hands gnarled like an old oak tree, but eyes that are terrifyingly, vitally alive.

"His name is Arthur," the old woman says. She sounds as tired as the girl's soul feels, but her eyes pin the girl in place. "He is the greatest king this island has ever or will ever know. He will change everything. And he needs a queen. Are you willing to become that woman?"

She wants the man in the reflection, but more than that, she wants the *Guinevere* she saw there, the one who was not afraid, the one who was powerful, the one who could be deserving of a man such as Arthur. There are no words to express how this feels, that she finally has a purpose, that she can become someone other than herself. She nods silently.

The old woman sighs, and for a moment her eyes fill with tears. Then she blinks and the tears are gone. She steps into the boat. For a moment, the girl could swear the old woman's reflection does not have long silver hair, but a long silver beard. She does not have time to think on it, though, because the boat carries them swiftly across the lake. Then the lake turns into a river, sweeping them along a forest path before abruptly stopping in front of a cave.

"Seven days," the old woman says, stepping nimbly out of the boat. "Much to prepare in seven days." She points to a tiny cottage. For a moment, in the silver of the river, it looks like an abandoned shack, rotting and wretched. But the river recedes and it is a cottage once more.

The girl pushes aside fear, pushes aside doubt, imagines herself an arrow. At last she has a target to bury herself in. She will not miss.

And so she spends seven days sweeping and sleeping and walking the woods.

Haunted by and hungry for the Guinevere she had seen, the Guinevere she could be, she agrees to do terrible things. She sits perfectly still in a meadow until a young deer trusts her enough to walk close. And then she plunges a knife into its neck, letting the blood of a stolen life pulse over her, dyeing her skin scarlet. The old woman takes a needle and traces the knots and patterns across her bloodied skin while Guinevere closes her eyes against the iron scent of guilt.

She has to become the Guinevere from the lake. She *has* to.

Finally, the seven days are over. The old woman takes her hand and leads her into the cave. Guinevere weeps with gratitude that at last she can become someone new. Someone who will not hurt. Someone who can help others, be more than just a girl.

The cave is the blackest space she has ever been. The lack of light is so complete she almost cannot breathe. But the old woman's hand guides her to take off her clothes and lie down. She does, closing her eyes against the darkness.

Water comes rushing around her, warm and comforting. The salt of her grateful tears mixes with it. "Thank you," she whispers. Her tears will wash away who she was, and she will emerge strong and good and right.

"Are you certain?" the old woman asks. "There will be no return. It is the beginning of everything that we *are* becoming everything that *never was* and *never again will be*. It is the beginning of being unmade, never to return to yourself. It is life, true and real, and therefore it is also inevitable death."

"That is what I want," she says, and the water echoes her, saying the same thing.

"Very well. I am sorry," a man says.

She opens her eyes. The cave is luminescent with glowing water. An old man with a long silver beard watches her. She tries to scramble away, to cover herself, but the water is all around her and she cannot move. What was like being held in an embrace has become like being crushed in a vise.

She tries to scream and the water rushes in, filling her mouth, her throat, her lungs, her ears, her eyes, pushing against all the magic that had been written on her body to contain it. For a brief moment she sees another woman's face above hers, as glowing and clear as the water. The woman smiles with love and affection, and then presses herself against and into and through and there is no air

and there is no light

and there is no *her* anymore.

The thing that is neither sits on the floor of the cave, shivering, her black hair knotted and curled around her. The wizard searches her face. "You are not there, are you?" He frowns, puzzled. "It was not supposed to work like that. You should still be Nimue. How could I not have seen this?" He scratches at his beard, tugs on the long silver strands. "I should not have trusted your magic with mine. Perhaps you knew this would happen." He sounds deeply troubled, tilting her chin this way and that, trying to find something that is no longer there.

Finally, he sighs. "Still, he needs his queen and I made you a promise." He puts his fingers to the new thing's forehead. "This should be enough," he whispers. "Do not look for more."

He pushes and she opens her eyes, no longer brown but reflective like a lake. Black as the cave around them, waiting to be green as a forest, blue as a sky, gray as the stones of Camelot.

"Oh, Nimue," Merlin says, sitting next to her. "What have we done?"

CHAPTER TWENTY

The scent of blood clung to her sinuses. She was sticky with it, covered in it, drenched in it.

It was the smell that brought her to her senses. The smell of life. Of violence. Of death.

Of theft.

"Guinevere!" Someone was shaking her.

She was not Guinevere. She was not Nimue.

She was *not*.

She opened her eyes. The pond and the forest were gone. There was only blackness and herself in the center of it, floating, hair drifting around her on a lazy, invisible current. No clothing covered her knotted and scarred and haunted body, but it did not matter, because this was not her body.

This was not her body.

"No, no, no, no," she moaned, tearing at her hair, staring down at herself in horror.

"Guinevere." Lancelot's tone was sharp, her fear contained and channeled into action. She grabbed Guinevere's hands and held them, forcing Guinevere to look into her eyes. "What happened?"

"I am not Guinevere."

"Yes, I know." Lancelot's tone was careful.

"No, you do not! I *was* Guinevere. And I was the Lady of the—" Guinevere gagged, her throat seizing up, the memory of warm water rushing in and drowning her so vivid she could taste it. Water poured from her throat, spilling down her body, an unending stream of it.

Lancelot cried out in dismay. "What is wrong? How can we help?"

Mordred grabbed Guinevere's face and turned it so she was looking at him. "Focus! You have to focus! Tell us what happened."

"I have to take it off." Guinevere pulled her hands free of Lancelot's and raked them down her arms, clawing at the skin. "I have to get out of her."

"Get out of who? What do you mean?"

"This is not me! This is not my body! They tricked her. They used her. And they stole her. I am not Guinevere, but this body—this body is. I am nothing. I am an *infection*." Like the Dark Queen's poison raging through Sir Tristan's body, eating him from the inside. That was what she was. That was all she was. Something foreign, destroying and taking over.

The water had stopped coming out of her mouth, but it poured from her eyes, it would never stop, it could never stop.

"Who are *they*?" Lancelot demanded.

"Merlin and Nimue. The Lady of the Lake. Your Lady of the Lake, Arthur's Lady of the Lake, she made herself into this, into me, so that she could have him, and I—I cannot—I cannot be this, I cannot. Guinevere was *real*. This was Guinevere." She tore at her face, the face she had smiled and spoken and kissed with, the face she had worn like a mask to walk through a world that had never been hers, would never be hers, should never be hers. "I can burn myself out. Rid her of the infection of me. I will do it now, and then—"

Mordred cast a desperate look at Lancelot. Lancelot once again took Guinevere's wrists, holding them fast in her hands. "Did *you* do this to her?" she asked Guinevere.

"I *am* this."

"But did you do it? Did you lure Guinevere? Did you cast the magic and steal Guinevere's life to create yourself?"

"I did not exist until that cave. It was Merlin, and the Lady, and—"

"So it was not *you.*"

"It was not me because I am not real! I am the greedy dream of the Lady who had everything and wanted more, the experiment of a wizard who reshaped reality to his own liking. And I was not even supposed to be this! Something went wrong and Nimue was lost, too. I am neither Guinevere nor Nimue. I am nothing."

"But you are—" Lancelot shook her head, frowning. "You are you. I know you. I have known you since the first moment we met."

Guinevere felt as though she had been struck. Lancelot. Their connection. Their bond. Their love. It was not theirs at all. "Because you recognized Nimue. Because she set you up, groomed you, raised you to be who you are, and then made certain you would continue to be hers!"

"No. You are taking the choice from me again. The Lady—" Lancelot's voice broke, then grew strong again. "It is not the same. I do not feel the same for her that I do for you. I never loved her."

"You do not love *me,*" Guinevere said, and her heart could not break because it was not her heart, but still, it hurt so much. "There is nothing to love. You were tricked, just like Guinevere was tricked, just like Igraine was tricked, just like Arthur was tricked."

"And me?" Mordred's voice was terribly soft. "Why should I have loved you? How was I tricked?"

"I should not be here, that is how! I did not ask to exist."

Mordred laughed, the sound landing dully in the black void with no echo to carry it back to them. "None of us did. Do you think I would have chosen to be born to a capricious fairy, or a mother obsessed with vengeance? That Lancelot would have chosen a life of unending battle to be seen as who she is?"

"It is not the same! I am an abomination. My very existence is a violation of Guinevere, of who should be here, of what she should be." Guinevere—how could she still think of herself with that name? but what else did she have?—searched herself for the real girl, that broken, desperate creature. She even searched for Nimue, that greedy, desperate creature. But it was only herself, only whatever she was, whatever false soul had rushed in to fill the emptiness that flooded between Guinevere and Nimue.

And yet could she not see some of them in herself? They were knotted into her soul. Guinevere's tender heart, seeing pain and wishing desperately to be able to fix it. Nimue's hunger and desire for more: more experiences, more life, more love. She had none of their memories, but she had been carved into this body by both of them. Guinevere's humanity, Nimue's magic.

"She had brown eyes," Guinevere whispered, and then Mordred caught her as she collapsed, sobbing.

"We need you, Lancelot," Mordred said. "She needs you."

"I will leave as soon as I wake," Lancelot answered.

"No." Guinevere looked up, shaking her head. "Please. Camelot should not suffer because of me."

Lancelot burned with anger. "How would that be because of you? Arthur is the one who left to go north. My vow is to you. Not to him, not to Camelot."

"Your vow was to the queen. And we both know I am not the queen. I am nothing."

Lancelot's voice was twisted and raw with anger. "You are not nothing."

"I forbid you to leave Camelot." She would not let Lancelot risk herself, not for her. If the only thing she could do was keep Lancelot and Camelot safe, it would not be enough to atone for what she was, but at least it would save some of what she loved. Some of what she had no right to love.

"If you are not the queen, you cannot command me in anything. I will do what I wish." Lancelot turned to Mordred. "Get to the coast. I am coming to meet you."

Mordred nodded, and Lancelot disappeared. With a sigh, Mordred stroked Guinevere's hair. "Be patient. Be gentle with yourself. We will figure this out together."

Guinevere did not answer. As soon as she awoke, she would burn herself out of this body, restore it to the real Guinevere.

As though reading her thoughts, Mordred continued. "If you do something rash, you risk destroying everything. Yourself, and whatever might be left of her." He did not say Guinevere's name, and she knew he was avoiding calling the other person, the real person, Guinevere. "It took two of them—Nimue and Merlin—to do this. Their magic is more powerful and complex than anything you know. If you feel responsible for what happened to that girl, do not make it worse by destroying even more. I swear we will figure this out."

"How to free her?"

Mordred pressed a kiss to her forehead.

It was not lost on Guinevere as she opened her eyes to the enormity of daylight that Mordred had not promised to help free the girl whose life she had stolen. She knew his voice when he was lying, and he had lied when he said they would figure this out. He had no intention of helping her. He had already made up his mind that she would never free the real Guinevere.

Mordred stirred beside her. She tore hairs from her head, knotted them for sleep, and threw them on his chest.

She did not need Mordred, or Lancelot. She needed Morgana, Morgan le Fay, the sorceress, the most powerful woman who had ever bridged the divide between human and fairy.

At last Guinevere knew who she was. And she would do anything to fix it.

CHAPTER TWENTY-ONE

Standing on the outskirts of a camp, the men there not yet alerted to her presence, Guinevere was hyperaware of the body she wore. She could not let it get hurt again. She had done so much to it, so much with it.

She would not think about it.

The journey to Morgana would have been easier if Mordred's horse had let her take it, but the mare had refused to leave without him. Four hours of walking back toward Nechtan's camp and she had at last stumbled on a group of men. They had three horses. They also had an excessive amount of weapons.

The language they spoke was the same Hild and her brother had. Saxons. Perhaps they were the group that had attacked the refugees she had found. Or perhaps they were simply looking for a place to set up home. Regardless, she needed a horse.

The men looked up, surprised, as she stepped free of the trees. Then the surprise mutated into something darker, something hungrier. It was a comfort to see exactly what their intentions were. She felt no guilt when she lit her hands on fire and watched them scramble away, terrified.

She chose the healthiest-looking mare, though she wished she could take them all. They did not look well cared for. If Mordred were with her, he could persuade all the horses to follow him. But if Mordred were with her, he would stop her.

She could not think about Mordred right now. About leaving him behind. About the brief, bright, delusional dream of a life together that she had allowed herself to indulge in.

She rode as fast as she could without injuring the horse. She knew she was traveling in the general direction of Nechtan's forces, but they had probably moved since her escape. She did not know how long it would take to find them. It felt urgent, desperately so, to find Morgana. Morgana's entire goal in life was to unravel Merlin's magic. Surely she would leap at the chance to undo whatever bound Nimue to this poor girl's body. Immediately. There had already been so much time lost, so much stolen from the girl who had been Guinevere. Every breath through her lips, every beat of this counterfeit heart, every stolen thought and hope felt like a violent act.

Who was she to judge the Saxons, after all? Or even Arthur? Her very existence was an act of conquest.

Up ahead she saw the smoke of many campfires. "Please," she whispered, urging the horse faster. It was nearing nightfall. She had not paused to rest or eat. The thought of putting food into this body made her ill. But if she did not take care of it, she was harming the real Guinevere even more.

"Stop!" a voice called from behind her. She knew the voice; she knew his kiss and his touch. Her horse obeyed just as someone else shouted from the direction of the campfires.

"God above, Guinevere," Mordred said, his voice twisted with anguish and frustration. He rode next to her, grasped her horse's reins, and, to her surprise, urged both horses forward. "Do not contradict me, I beg you." He straightened in his saddle, his posture easy and arrogant. "Hello!" he called out. "I bring a gift!"

Nectudad herself appeared, eyes blazing. "You left," she said, pointing a knife at Mordred.

"Because I had the best chance of finding her. And find her I did. Here we are." Mordred yawned and stretched one arm high over his head. Nectudad's expression indicated that she did not believe for one moment that Mordred had left to bring back Guinevere. But they were both here, and she could find no reason to argue with him or deny the proof of his words.

She grunted and gestured for them to follow. Guinevere dismounted and continued on foot. Fina stood by the nearest campfire. When she saw Guinevere, her eyebrows rose in shock and dismay. "You are back," she said.

Guinevere shook her head slightly. She did not know how to tell Fina how badly she had failed. Arthur was still coming. Nothing she had done had protected anybody. But she would fix the one thing she still could.

Mordred leaned close to Nectudad, speaking in a low voice. "There was a camp of refugees from the eastern coast. Men, women, children. Old and young. All injured and driven out of their homes by Saxons."

Nectudad's steps slowed. "When?"

"They told me it happened three days ago. At least two hundred Saxons, by their estimate. No women or children on the boats. It was not a group of settlers. It was a war party."

Nectudad gestured sharply to Fina. Before Fina could follow her sister, Guinevere grasped her arm and whispered, "It did not work. Arthur is coming. You should all run."

Fina gasped as though struck. "When?"

"He left Camelot last night. Did Morgana not tell you?"

"No. Nectudad! We must prepare!" Fina said. Guinevere did not know why Morgana would keep that information to herself. Had she been wrong to reveal it? But she wanted Fina to be safe.

"I know," Nectudad said. "War with the Saxons."

"With Arthur! He is coming for us with an army."

Nectudad frowned. "How do you know?"

"I told her." Guinevere met Nectudad's fierce gaze. "I do not want you to die."

Nectudad's face opened in surprise, but then hardened again. "It does not change what we do next. We must speak with Father." Ahead of them, a tall, regal figure in a dark cloak was talking to the fur-shrouded bulk of Nechtan.

"Morgana!" Guinevere called.

The sorceress turned, a single imperious eyebrow lifting the only hint of her surprise at seeing them here.

"Hello, Mother." Mordred waved cheerily. "Our plan worked. Here she is again, safe and sound."

Morgana's lips twitched in a wry smile, but she did not betray her son. "Yes. Well done."

"I need your help," Guinevere said. "Can we speak privately?"

Nectudad grasped Guinevere firmly by the elbow. "No. You are under my watch now, until we get to the Dark Queen. Father, we have dire news."

"Do you really think I am going to let her out of my sight?" Morgana waved dismissively. "This is my plan, Nectudad. Not yours."

"I am aware of that," Nectudad said through gritted teeth. She spoke to Nechtan in a hurried, urgent cadence. Moths fluttered around his ears, and even now he seemed only half present, tilting his head toward the moths instead of his daughter.

Nectudad finished. Nechtan grunted, muttering a reply.

Morgana folded her arms, cross. "Well?" she demanded.

Mordred translated. "There is a war party of Saxons on the eastern coast. Nectudad wants to fight them. They made an alliance with the Saxons to trick Arthur, and this breaks that alliance. And if they change course, Arthur will not find them. Nechtan said that these are different Saxons, and that it does not matter anyway, because they did not attack Nechtan's lands or people. Nectudad argues that outsiders attacking anywhere in the north is an attack on all of them, and that an army of Saxons is a threat to everyone."

Nechtan spoke again, his voice a low rumble, but an oddly dreamy-sounding one.

Mordred's jaw twitched. "The king declares that it does not matter, because the Dark Queen will save us all."

Nectudad threw her hands in the air, her voice finally rising. She pointed to Fina, then gestured behind herself. Nechtan waved again and ambled away. He had lost the intensity from when Guinevere had first met him, as though the moths of the Dark Queen were keeping him in a disconnected, half-awake state.

Nectudad let out a low string of curses. "He will do nothing, not fight back against the Saxons, not lay a trap for Arthur. It is on us now. I will take the majority of our forces to the coast to fight the Saxons and draw Arthur off your trail. If we are lucky, we can make them fight each other instead."

"No!" Guinevere said. That was not what she meant to have happen.

Nectudad ignored her. "Fina, you stay with Father and see that the sorceress and the fairy queen do not betray him."

Fina whirled, turning to Nectudad. "I will come with you!"

"It is the best way. The only way."

"The Dark Queen has requested all your father's soldiers," Morgana said. "She is expecting them."

"That is what I am afraid of." Nectudad was as tall as Morgana. Unbending and unafraid, she stepped up to the older woman and they stood face to face. "You have poisoned my father. You will not destroy my people or my land. My father said he did not care what I do, so I am taking my soldiers to the coast. And you can thank me for throwing Arthur off your trail as you take the little queen to your fairy queen and do whatever it is that you have promised will *save* us." Nectudad spit on the ground.

Fina shook her head, her voice high with emotion. "I am going with you to the coast to fight."

"Father needs someone to protect him from the Dark Queen and the sorceress," Nectudad said. "And from himself."

Fina folded her arms. "I will not take Guinevere to that abomination."

Nectudad stepped forward, so close to Fina that her sister was forced to take a step back. Fina lowered her head, cowed, as Nectudad spoke. "You will do what is best for our people. Enemies are pouring forth from the sea, and Arthur is rising from the south. If there is *any* chance the Dark Queen can help us, we must take it. And if they betray us, you will see that they pay for it."

Fina pointed to Guinevere. "She will help us. She is Camelot's queen!"

Guinevere lowered her head. Fina's faith in her was misplaced.

Nectudad had no such false faith. "An alliance with a southern queen is a house built of sand, washed away with a single wave of the king's sword."

It stung Guinevere almost as much as her burned palm had. "I tried to stop him," she said. "Maybe I still can." Maybe the real

Guinevere could, once she was returned to her body. She could go meet Arthur, and he would see how fragile she was, how desperate to help. It might be enough for him to turn around.

"I will not risk my people on that hope. Fairyson," Nectudad said, turning to Mordred, "you are coming with me."

"What?" Mordred smiled to cover his panic. "No, thank you. I am not fond of the coast."

"It is not a discussion. If the sorceress is staying with my father and sister, you are staying with me to ensure she does not betray us."

"This is absurd," Morgana said. "I came to *you* with the offer to help. I am not your enemy. Besides, you do not command us."

Nectudad whistled sharply. Soldiers swarmed. Before Guinevere could react, three had Mordred on his knees with a knife against his neck.

CHAPTER TWENTY-TWO

Mordred's life pulsed beneath the blade at his neck, one jab away from bleeding out. Guinevere's heart squeezed in panic. She had left him. She had chosen to walk away from him and the life he wanted with her, because he would not have let her do any of this. But she did not want him dead.

"I do not need you or your son," Nectudad calmly informed Morgana. "Fina and my father can take Guinevere to the Dark Queen without help."

Mordred cleared his throat. "I have changed my mind. I would very much like to accompany them to the coast. Suddenly I am eager to see the ocean."

Morgana flicked her eyes upward in annoyance, then nodded at Nectudad. "Just keep Arthur busy for as long as you can and be certain to return to the Green Man's Chapel. I do not know why the Dark Queen wants your father's army, but if she wants it, she will have it."

Nectudad gestured and the soldiers released Mordred. "We leave within the hour."

Mordred stood and held out his hand to Guinevere. "Come, I will get you settled."

"No," Nectudad said. "I will speak with her alone."

She led Guinevere to a tent and pushed her inside. "I know you care about my sister," Nectudad said, packing her things efficiently. "Do not put her in danger or ask her to betray her family and her people again."

So Nectudad knew, or at least had guessed, that Fina was the reason Guinevere had escaped. Guinevere knelt, exhausted, on the floor of the tent. If Nectudad tried to hurt her body, she would do what she had to in order to protect it. "Or you will break my bones?"

"Or *you* will break Fina's spirit. If Fina goes against our father, she will be banished. They will burn away her tattoos, leaving her without claim to any family or people. I think you know what it is to have no place where you truly belong. Do not do that to my sister."

Guinevere had never wanted to hurt Fina. And she did know what it was not to belong, more than Nectudad could ever understand. "Forgive her. She only wants to help. To protect you all from war."

Nectudad hefted her bundle of belongings over her shoulder. "War is here. It is always here. If I could save you from the Dark Queen, I would, but not at the cost of my people or my sister. Do you understand?"

"I do."

Arthur had talked with Guinevere about this. The cost of leadership. The price that a ruler had to pay, again and again, sacrificing some for the good of many. Killing so that the most vulnerable would remain safe. But Guinevere could not be the sacrifice that saved Fina and her people. She had to be the sacrifice that restored the true Guinevere to her body.

As soon as Nectudad left the tent, Mordred rushed inside. His face was contorted with anger. "Guinevere, why?" he demanded, dropping to his knees and grabbing her arms. "Why did you do this?"

"I have to save her," she whispered.

"No! You do not!" Mordred put his forehead against hers and closed his eyes. "We could have been free. Of all of it."

"It is not mine to be free of. *Nothing* is mine."

"I was," he said, his voice breaking. "I am. You think you are responsible because of what the wizard did? He has done violence to this entire damnable island. I will not lose you because of it."

Guinevere shook her head, pulling back from Mordred's touch. She did not need to feel his desperate anguish. She had enough of her own.

"You were always going to lose me," she whispered. "At least this way, a wrong will be righted."

Mordred's voice grew harsh. "And what of Arthur?"

"He will still have a queen. A better queen. A real one."

"And Lancelot?"

Guinevere turned her head away. "I cannot put anyone above the life of this girl."

"What did my mother use to connect you to Lancelot? Tell me."

Guinevere finally met his gaze. "It does not matter. Nothing that connects me to anyone is mine to keep."

Mordred's jaw twitched, but he forced out the words. "I know what it is to look on you and want nothing more than to have you look back. Lancelot watches you the same way. If you love me at all, if you love her as she loves you, do nothing. Wait for us. I will escape from Nectudad. Lancelot is already on her way. Imagine what we will feel if we are too late to save you."

Guinevere closed her eyes against the pain. Mistaking that for a lack of resolve, Mordred wrapped his arms around her once more, his voice soft and urgent. "Run away with me. Right now. Between the two of us, we can escape again. Please, Guinevere, please."

She did not move, did not lean against him or return his embrace. The passion that had connected her to Mordred was gone, killed by the realization that this had never been her body to experience. They had talked about protecting the innocent, daydreamed a simple life where that was their only purpose, their only goal. She was still going to do that. But there was only one innocent that she could help now.

"I will save you in spite of yourself," he whispered into her ear. "I will save you even if I am saving you for someone else."

Nectudad shouted his name from outside and he growled in frustration. "I wanted more. We should have had more."

"More is the only thing I ever knew I wanted," Guinevere whispered. It was the thing she could no longer hope for. She pressed a kiss to Mordred's cheek. He might have viewed it as a promise, but she felt it as a farewell.

As soon as Mordred was gone, Guinevere found Morgana's tent and stepped inside.

Morgana looked up from her sewing. "I am very curious to hear why you returned, because I know my son did not bring you back."

Guinevere sat and told her everything, her voice as hollow as her heart.

By the end, Morgana was pacing back and forth in a tight line. "And you are certain about the details of Merlin and the Lady's magic?" A frown pulled all the elegant lines of her face into a severe mask.

"Yes." Guinevere stared at her hands. Her stolen hands. She had held lovers with these hands, had destroyed minds, had ended lives.

She had scarred this body that was not hers. She would return it damaged, changed. Would the real Guinevere remember any of it, or would this time simply be gone?

"And you are certain you want it undone?"

"How could I not?" Guinevere looked up, despair pooling in her eyes. "They lied to her. They *tricked* her. You of all people understand this violence. Whatever I am, I am because Nimue wanted a body and Merlin wanted a queen for his chosen king. I know the Lady of the Lake is still in here somewhere; I have power and magic I should not, dreams of her memories. I think she is what is blocking the real Guinevere. We need to take Nimue out, restore this body to what and who she was."

Morgana's frown did not relax as she sat. "The Dark Queen must have tasted this magic. I thought she wanted you just to lure Arthur out of Camelot. But no, it is because you are entirely new."

"I am entirely stolen."

Morgana took Guinevere's arm and peered at it, then sighed in frustration. "I wish I could see the knots. He must have used his magic, Nimue's magic, and human magic, as well."

"But you are human and use fairy magic. You can undo it."

"It is beyond me."

"So it cannot be fixed?" Guinevere could not quite draw a full breath. She kept remembering the real Guinevere's face, her shattering terror as the water invaded her lungs.

"I did not say it could not be fixed. I said it was beyond me." Morgana rubbed her face. "The Dark Queen is the only one who can rival Merlin for power, now that—"

"Now that Nimue has bound herself into a stolen body," Guinevere finished. "Merlin did not realize she would be erased, too. I think he thought she would wear the real Guinevere like a dress to walk around in and playact as a human." Guinevere shuddered, the feeling of water invading her mouth impossible to forget. Then another idea occurred to her. "What about Nynaeve? The other Lady? She was split off from Nimue, so they must be the same. Maybe she could undo it! She wants her sister back."

"Nynaeve has never meddled in the affairs of humans. Whatever it was that drove Nimue to obsess over them, the part of her that became Nynaeve had none of it. Maybe that is what split them to begin with. No, I believe the Dark Queen is your only hope. We must be clear, though. I will not pretend I am doing it for you or to help whoever held that body before you. I will do it because if Merlin made you this, unmaking it will hurt him. Merlin created you for a reason and at last I have a chance at undoing his work." Morgana's eyes burned, not with the coal of Merlin's gaze, but with a feverish need.

Guinevere did not care what Morgana's motivation was, so long as it ended with the real Guinevere restored. "Promise once Merlin's magic has been broken that you will return me—" Guinevere caught herself. "*Her* to Arthur. I do not want her hurt. And once he has a queen again, hopefully that will settle things with the north."

"I will keep the girl safe." Morgana's voice was as gentle as Guinevere had ever heard it. "She deserved none of this."

At last someone understood. "Oh, I should warn you. Mordred will try to rescue me."

Morgana clucked her tongue. "My poor son. You make him wish to be a hero, and I am so afraid it will be the end of him."

Guinevere stood and helped Morgana roll up her sleeping furs. "Soon I will not be here to make anyone wish to be anything, and then things can be as they should have been."

Without her.

CHAPTER TWENTY-THREE

Fina gave Guinevere worried looks all the long ride toward the Green Man's Chapel. During a stop to rest the horses, she took Guinevere's arm and marched them into the cover of the few hardy trees that survived in this area. "Even queens need to piss!" she declared loudly enough for everyone to hear. "What happened?" she whispered. "What did Mordred do to you?"

"What do you mean?" Guinevere asked, avoiding her friend's gaze.

"When you returned, it looked as though someone had murdered you, and your body had not realized yet that it was walking about without its soul."

Guinevere laughed dryly at how close to the mark Fina was. Her soul really did have no place in this body. If she had a soul at all, that is, and was not just a twisted knot of destruction with a human face.

"Listen, we can still escape. I know this land, and—"

"No." Guinevere finally looked up into Fina's clear blue eyes. Blue eyes that were her own, that had always been blue, that should be blue. "You should never have risked helping me to begin with. You know who you are, Fina. You love who you are, and you love your people. Nothing, and no one—especially not me—is worth betraying that."

"But Arthur, and the war—"

"I sent word that I was safe. He is still coming. I cannot fix that now, but maybe things will change after the Dark Queen helps me."

Fina's brows lowered in suspicion. "Helps you *what?*"

"It does not matter. When we get there, you should leave as fast as you can. Do whatever you have to do to make your father join you. And then get Nectudad and your people out of Arthur's way and hide. If there is no army to meet him, there cannot be a war. This is not your fight. It never should have been. Just take me to the Dark Queen and then get out and never think of any of us again."

Fina looked stung by her words. "But you are my friend."

"I am not real. Do not give up who you are for someone who is nothing." Guinevere turned and went back to her horse.

She did not sleep that night. She could not find the strength to face Mordred or, worse, Lancelot. She had left Lancelot behind once, and now she was doing it again. It was selfish of her not to say goodbye, but she needed all her strength for the sacrifice ahead. Seeing Lancelot would break her.

The next morning dawned clear and cold and terrible. Autumn's grasp came earlier at this elevation. The trees were brown, the hills endless and empty. After a few hours' ride, though, they drew to a surprised stop.

Ahead of them, summer was in full, riotous bloom. A forest had settled into a canyon between two hills, as though dropped there from another land. Guinevere had wondered how they would know the Green Man's Chapel when they saw it, but it was obvious why the Dark Queen had fled to this place of ancient power. This was no natural forest. This was *magic*. Guinevere slipped off her horse and walked toward the trees, then paused at an unexpected sensation.

The forest was breathing.

Guinevere could feel the warm, humid life of it, exhaling and inhaling. Somewhere inside it, a heart was beating. Waiting for her.

She put a hand out and touched one of the smooth trunks that formed an archway, the branches overhead braided as delicately as if Brangien had done it herself. Inside, the air was green. There was no other way to describe it. Guinevere understood now why Fina had said it was a sacred place, why it was called a chapel. She had been in Camelot's chapel, but that was a worship space for men. This was a worship space for nature, and as such was more beautiful and more dangerous.

Nechtan, Fina, and their ten remaining soldiers had dismounted. They all stared, wide-eyed, no one moving. Their awe was both overwhelming and a warning: this was not a place made for humans, and humans who did not tread lightly might not walk back out.

Nechtan took a step toward the Green Man's Chapel. Fina put an arm out to block him. Her fists were clenched as she considered the trees and what threats might be found inside the chapel.

Morgana cut her eyes toward Fina. "Tell your father the Dark Queen will come out to him. He cannot enter this space."

"Very well," Fina said. "But Guinevere stays out here with us, too."

Guinevere tried to sound reassuring. "I am not afraid." That was a lie. She was terrified. Devastated. But also determined. And glad that Fina at least would not see whatever happened in there. Fina would be safe.

Guinevere needed Morgana and the Dark Queen in order to undo Merlin's abominable magic, but she did not need them to succeed elsewhere. She wanted them to fail in their quest to overthrow Arthur. That meant Fina getting Nechtan out of their clutches and away from whatever the Dark Queen had planned for him.

Guinevere walked to her friend, going up on her tiptoes to press a kiss to Fina's cheek. "Get your father out of here, however you must," she whispered, remembering Mordred's poor slaughtered horse, and how careful Mordred had been to remove Lancelot from the meadow before the Dark Queen was raised. There was no telling what she would do from malice or even indifference. "I have loved knowing you. Take good care of your people."

Ignoring Fina's protests, Guinevere walked into the trees. Outside, the day had been chilly. In the warm, living air, she barely needed a cloak. Something about the heavy green ceiling and elegantly twisted trunks made her want to shed her clothes, shed her skin. To lie on the ground and stare up, content to simply breathe, to simply be.

The real Guinevere had felt safe in the forest, too, but predators had found her.

Morgana walked with confidence through the trees, which leaned to create a wider path, ushering the two women to their goal. The trilling songs of birds and rustling sounds of small burrowing things were undisturbed by their passing. These creatures had never been given a reason to fear humans.

Moths fluttered free from trees, dancing through the air ahead of them, guiding them. It was like following drifting ash toward a raging fire. One landed on Guinevere's shoulder, and she did not brush it off. It quivered and twitched, whether with excitement or because its tiny, fragile body could not contain the portion of the Dark Queen it held, Guinevere could not say. Feather-soft antennae caressed her cheek and she shuddered.

Up ahead, an ancient tree had been split in two, scorched tendrils marking the path of lightning that ended its life. Sitting in the center of this throne was a writhing mass in the shape of a woman.

And though the Dark Queen was as terrible as the last time Guinevere had seen her, formed from the forest floor by a swarm of beetles and a tangle of roots, she was also magnificent. Here, on her throne, where she belonged, Guinevere could see the core of magnificence, of what the Dark Queen had been and should be.

She understood Mordred at last. Because the Dark Queen was extraordinary, and she did not want the jeweled black beetle mass of her to disappear.

When Guinevere lowered her eyes to the forest floor, though, she saw the rot that was the result of the Dark Queen's form. Tuberous growths, corrupted with black mold, twitching and writhing, surrounded where she was connected to the ground. And spreading out from her throne were tendrils of the same foul growth. But *growth* was not the right word. Growing implied health, life. This was not life. This was infection. The Dark Queen was leeching power from the forest but giving nothing back.

At last. The words vibrated and clicked through Guinevere, formed with bodies never meant to speak. She looked up, to the Dark Queen's head. Two moths, their wings patterned like eyes, fluttered gently in the center. Black beetles scuttled and stirred, holding the form of a human but leaving Guinevere dizzy with their constant motion.

"I need your help," Guinevere said.

The Dark Queen hummed with the buzz of insect wings.

"Merlin made me. He used this girl"—Guinevere gestured to her body—"and bound Nimue into her. I need you to undo it, to take out Nimue and restore the girl."

A hand of scurrying insects and tendrils of root reached out, taking Guinevere's chin and tipping her face up toward the light. The Dark Queen was ferociously alive, a part of everything around her. No wonder the Lady of the Lake had loved her. It was hard to breathe, connected to that much magic and wonder and terror.

Show me. Show me what he did.

Guinevere could feel the power of that need pulsing out of the Dark Queen. But there was something else, something she was not saying. The sense of a swarm of ants, flooding out from their queen, covering—

The Dark Queen's grip tightened, holding Guinevere in place. *Make her show me.*

Morgana grasped Guinevere's wrist. In Guinevere's single-minded appeal to the Dark Queen, she had forgotten about Mordred's mother.

"Promise me first. Promise me you will free her. The Guinevere that was, before Nimue—" Guinevere choked on her name, fighting back the warm taste of water spilling down her throat. "Before *I* became."

The Dark Queen's moths fluttered from her face to Guinevere's, leaving the queen without eyes but not without sight. She laughed, a sound like a thousand birds taking wing. *I will free everything. Now show me.*

"Think about what you saw," Morgana said to Guinevere. "What they did to her."

Guinevere trembled with revulsion as the Dark Queen's moth eyes fluttered over her own, covering everything in soft black. Morgana's grip tightened and then all three of them were in the cave. This time, though, Guinevere observed from above. It did not make the scene any less horrifying. The girl looked so fragile, laid out in the lightless cave. Naked and shivering and hopeful. It was the raw hope that hurt the most to see. Guinevere knew how this story ended, and she did not want to watch it again. She wanted all of this to be over.

But before the story could flow on to its devastating conclusion, everything froze. Her wrist hurt as she was tugged lower, closer to the real Guinevere. Closer. She saw the patterns drawn and knotted onto her skin, so faint they were nearly invisible.

Merlin leaned in, and a low hiss slithered around the cave. But it did not come from the memory. It came from the Dark Queen peering through Guinevere. She wanted to cry out in agony, to beg Morgana to make it stop. Staring at the young princess, still hopeful, was somehow worse than watching her be overrun with water.

Finally, an eternity later, time began moving again. The noise of the Dark Queen vibrated through the cave like laughter as they watched Nimue bathe the girl and then pour herself inside her. As the real Guinevere's eyes went wide, and then dead, and then—

And then a part Guinevere had not seen, because she had not yet existed. Merlin sighed and looked up toward the ceiling of the cave. Right at them.

His voice rumbled like the passage of time. "I am not gone. Nor am I powerless. *Fear me*," he commanded, his eyes burning red and gold.

The new Guinevere opened her eyes, and they were no longer brown. They were the black of the cave. Clear. Ready.

"No," she said.

Merlin frowned in confusion and looked back down at her.

The image swirled and swarmed away. Guinevere came back to herself gasping, on her knees, the warmth and life of the Green Man's Chapel around her a stark contrast to the bleak emptiness of that horrible cave.

The Dark Queen was shaking. She shivered and trembled, coming apart and re-forming. Guinevere thought she was upset or scared, until she realized the Dark Queen was laughing.

Nimue, the fool, she buzzed. *She gave everything. She held nothing back. She could have infected, and instead she became.*

Morgana's voice thrummed with urgency. "Did you see everything you needed to?"

Yes.

"So undo it," Guinevere said, shivering and wrapping her arms around herself, haunted by the way she had sounded when she opened her eyes and refused to be afraid of Merlin. She had lost that. The bravery. The assurance. The power. She had lost every piece of the stolen life she had built. And now she would be gone entirely.

The black mold of the Dark Queen had crept onto the knees of Guinevere's leather leggings. A single spider, elegant and sinister, each leg like a needle, descended from the Dark Queen and followed the rot's path toward Guinevere.

I wonder if Nimue meant for you to happen. If she meant to undo herself, to become something new. The Dark Queen leaned closer, the moths fluttering back to her face so she stared, wide-eyed and unblinking. *Or if you were a mistake. It was not like her to make mistakes. Until she betrayed me and sided with the wizard and his puppet king.*

The spider crawled onto Guinevere's leg and moved up her with luxuriously slow intent. It took everything in her not to scream, not to fling it away. The spider spun the knot of a web, intricate and delicate, as it laid the shimmering threads on Guinevere's hand.

I will unmake you, the Dark Queen said with a skittering lilt.

Guinevere tried to feel relief. Gratitude. Happiness that she had gotten right at least this one thing, this most important thing. But she was so afraid. She was not about to die. She was going to simply cease to exist. She wished she had slept last night, had stolen a few last moments with Mordred, with Lancelot. With herself.

I will unmake you and take this body you sealed yourself into, Nimue.

Horror seized her. "No. No, you promised. You promised to free the real Guinevere!"

I promised I would free everything. And I will keep my word. I will liberate your entire race, dear child. Free them from themselves, forever.

What had she done? What had she given to this creature, this corruption? Guinevere twitched, lighting her hands on fire and incinerating the spider that was about to pierce her skin in the center of the knot it had made. But there were more spiders—dozens, hundreds—dropping free of the Dark Queen and swarming toward Guinevere.

"Do you hear that?" Morgana asked. She stood on the edge of the clearing, staring into the trees.

All the spiders stopped as one. The droning hum of the Dark Queen's mass went silent.

Morgana's face was bloodless when she turned back toward them. "There is . . . nothing out there."

There was no longer birdsong. No soft, sibilant breeze. The temperature, too, was dropping, as though someone had opened a door into autumn.

Excalibur, the Dark Queen moaned in a voice like a small body decaying slowly into the forest floor. She fell into a thousand insects, roots writhing back into the ground, moths fluttering upward in frantic circles. She was disappearing. Running.

Guinevere felt her say one last thing in a lingering moth's brush against her ear.

I will be everywhere.

"No!" Morgana shouted. "Do not leave me!" But the Dark Queen was already nearly gone, the only trace of her the blackened ground that surrounded the ruined tree. Morgana looked at Guinevere, her face lined with so much sorrow that she seemed older than when they had entered. "Please," she said, "tell Mordred that I—"

The tip of a sword appeared through her chest.

CHAPTER TWENTY-FOUR

Morgana, the sorceress, lover of the Green Knight, mother of Mordred, champion of the fairies, and determined foe of Merlin, capable of seeing through other people and commanding more magic than any other mortal woman, died in a single breath.

Guinevere could not even scream. The swirling dread of being unmade, the inescapable sickness of Excalibur, seized her, and she fell, back into the cave, back underwater, the end of herself.

She was scooped up by arms she knew, arms she had been destined for, created for.

"I have you," Arthur said, his voice a confident rumble, his heart steady and sure, his hands covered in Morgana's blood.

He carried her swiftly through the trees. The trees that had been verdant and ageless minutes ago were now dropping their leaves in the full, sudden grasp of autumn. They had been something sacred, something special. But Excalibur had walked their paths and devoured it all. Now, they were just trees.

And because of Excalibur, Guinevere did not have the strength to get down, to shout at Arthur, to process what had just happened. "Why?" she whispered. "Why did you kill Morgana?"

"Because I had to." There was no satisfaction in his voice. He sounded sad. "Merlin told me that I must never let her speak to me, and he has never led me to harm."

Guinevere closed her eyes against the nausea that the memory of Merlin's face triggered. She could only see him standing next to the real Guinevere, watching. He had harmed Arthur in countless ways, and brutally harmed too many women in Arthur's life. She could not have this argument with Arthur now, though. She did not have the strength for it. After what Morgana had done to her and now, close to Excalibur, it was all she could do to stay conscious. Part of her despaired and longed for oblivion.

Morgana was dead. The Dark Queen was gone. And Guinevere was still herself—this terrible possession.

"Where is Mordred?" Arthur asked.

"I do not know." At least Excalibur had only claimed Morgana, and not her son, too.

Guinevere was still trying to claw her way back from the cold void where Excalibur wanted her to be when they broke free of the trees. Men were everywhere. An incomprehensible number of men and horses and swords and shields, all in Arthur's colors, a field of yellow and blue against the dusty green and gray of the land.

Nechtan, the king who had sold himself to the Dark Queen to avoid serving another king, lay on the ground, his throat slashed, his heavy fur mantle sodden and blackening with blood.

"Fina!" Guinevere cried. She shoved Arthur so hard that he dropped her. She stumbled when she landed, but kept going. She found Fina kneeling at the end of a line of corpses, her face bloodied, shoulders sloped with defeat, eyes down so she would not have to look on the body of her father. A soldier was lowering a knife to her neck.

"No," Guinevere commanded, at last finding the tone she had used when she refused to fear Merlin. The soldier stopped.

"Fina is mine." Guinevere grabbed the other woman's arm and helped her stand, though she was so unsteady it might well have been Fina who was helping her. "No one harms her."

Arthur frowned. "Who is she?"

"Nechtan's daughter. She helped me escape."

Fina did not look at Arthur, her expression as hollow as if her throat, too, had been slit.

"Where are the rest of your men?" Arthur asked. "Reports said between two and three hundred."

"My soldiers," Fina said, finally lifting her chin. "They are not all men. And they are gone. They followed my sister, not my father, and are of no concern to you."

Guinevere swayed on her feet. Her adrenaline was spent, and so was she.

A familiar face that Guinevere could not quite place appeared in front of her. It had round, ruddy cheeks. Gawain. Sir Gawain, solemn and concerned. "My queen. What are you wearing?"

Guinevere laughed and laughed, because Morgana was dead and Nechtan was dead and the Dark Queen had fled and Guinevere could not free the girl who had been tortured to bring her existence about, and this boy's worry was that she wore *trousers*.

Arthur pressed her to his chest and she was no longer laughing, she was sobbing, and he was so real and exactly as she remembered him, but nothing else was the same and it never could be again.

CHAPTER TWENTY-FIVE

Guinevere did not remember falling asleep. All she knew was that one moment she was curled around herself in abject misery, and the next, Brangien was yelling at her.

"You leave me for a few days and the entire world falls apart!" Brangien stormed around the black depths of the cave, glaring at the darkness. "This place is absurd. You can do better than this. At least give us a fire, or something nice to eat."

"Brangien?" Guinevere could not understand what her friend was doing here. "Where is Lancelot?"

"Lancelot is in chains. Give me a chair."

Guinevere was too stunned to protest. Two chairs and a table appeared. Apparently Brangien could enforce her will even on someone else's dreamspace. She sat with a scowl, gesturing to the other chair. Guinevere took it, and only then did Brangien explain.

"After the king spoke with Lancelot, he left commands with the captain of the guard. Commands that should Lancelot try to leave the city, she was to be locked in a cell until Arthur's return. At least she had the sense to cut the knots from her hair, lest the charge of witchcraft was added to that of treason, or whatever it is they will charge her with after catching her in the secret tunnel. It took a dozen men to bring her in."

Guinevere shook her head, stunned. "But I told her to stay."

"Yes, well, according to her you have lost your mind and are in immediate danger."

"What else did she tell you?" Guinevere was unable to look Brangien in the eye.

"Something about Merlin and the Lady of the Lake and magic making you decide you have no right to exist."

Guinevere stared at the cave floor. "This is Guinevere's body. She was real. They bound Nimue into it and I am the result, an infection, a plague, and—"

Brangien huffed and folded her arms crossly. "And you are just as innocent as that other girl, because you did not choose to have this done to you. It was forced on you as well."

"But part of me is the Lady of the Lake! And I benefited from what she did!"

"Oh, yes, your life is wonderful! What a dream, to be married to a bullheaded, intractable king, to have to run a city, to be constantly threatened and manipulated and outright abducted as a pawn in stupid men's wars. You have certainly benefited."

Guinevere finally looked up. Brangien was furiously embroidering a piece of cloth. She did not understand. Guinevere had to make her understand. "Brangien, I am an abomination."

"You are a *girl*. Just because violence shaped you does not make your very existence an act of violence."

"But—"

Brangien stabbed her needle into the cloth with more force than was necessary, but her tone was gentle. "I am sorry for the other Guinevere. I am. It breaks my heart. But it does not make you less real, less deserving of life."

"It does, though. I should never have been here."

"And the world would have been poorer for your absence! That other Guinevere never would have married Arthur. Merlin would not have chosen her. Arthur would have had some other queen, someone who was raised to be queen, someone cold and delicate, insulated from life and pain and suffering. Someone who would never look twice at a lady's maid, much less protect her and care about her and rescue her dearest love. Someone who would have let Sir Tristan die because she would never have been able to heal his fever. Someone who would have never fought for Lancelot to take her rightful place as a knight. Someone who would have never known or cared about Lily, dooming that poor girl to Cameliard and to her father. Someone who would have looked on Dindrane with disdain instead of compassion, leaving her to a life of misery at the hands of Blanchefleur and Percival. Someone who would be unable to guide and direct our king toward compassion and unable to help him see the nuance and complexity of life because she herself had been raised to be blind to it all. And someone who would doubtless require a *lot* more of me, forcing me to poison her and be executed for murder."

Guinevere did not know how to respond.

Brangien reached across the table and took Guinevere's hands in hers. "I do not care how you got here. That was not your doing. But I can tell you what you have done, and what you do, and who you are. You look at people, and you see what they can become. You reflect the best versions of themselves, and, in doing so, you allow them to grow into what they could have been but never would have without you. You are not an abomination. You are a miracle, in my life and in the lives of everyone who has been fortunate enough to know you."

"Not everyone," Guinevere whispered, remembering the dragon, Hild, Hild's brother, King Mark, the innocents and the guilty who had suffered and died because they crossed paths with her.

"Such is the cost of living. Such is the cost of moving through the world and rejecting apathy. Such is the cost of being human, which you are. You are the most human person I have ever known, and I will not hear you say otherwise." Brangien sniffled, wiping roughly under her eyes with her embroidery, which dissolved as soon as she no longer needed it. "And I will nag and harass you until you agree with me, because I am always right and you should know that by now."

The table between them disappeared, and Guinevere knelt at Brangien's feet, resting her head on her friend's lap. Brangien stroked her hair, far more gently than she had ever combed it in real life.

"I have to try," Guinevere whispered. "I have to try to make it right."

"I know you do, because you are an idiot, and I hate you for it. But please do not forget that if every life has value, yours does, too. I cannot tell you what to do, but please, please take care of my best friend."

Guinevere nodded, closing her eyes. "I have missed you terribly."

"Of course you have. I am wonderful company."

Guinevere allowed herself to exist in silence with her dear Brangien for a while. She dreaded the thought that Mordred might appear and she would have to tell him the unspeakable truth. That he was, once again, alone. As long as she could avoid talking to him, he would go on believing he still had a mother. However complicated his and Morgana's relationship had been, Guinevere was certain Morgana had loved him.

She wished Morgana had been able to finish her request. What was Guinevere to tell Mordred? That his mother wanted vengeance?

Demand that he take up her mantle in the fight against Merlin? Or was she simply leaving this world with love for her son?

Guinevere would lie. She would tell Mordred that Morgana had died saying she loved him. It was the only kindness she could offer.

"Are you safe at least?" Brangien asked.

"I am with Arthur. But I will try to get away and to the cave. Only Merlin can undo this now."

Brangien's fingers tightened in Guinevere's hair, tugging it, before she let go. "Merlin has never helped anyone but himself."

Guinevere knew that was true. She had tried to seek help from the Dark Queen, had trusted that the fairy would do something because it was the right thing. Instead, Guinevere had shown her how to do the same harm that had been done to the real Guinevere. "If I do not come back, or if I come back as someone else, help Lancelot. Tell Arthur I bewitched her, or Morgana did, or whatever you have to. She must be free. I need to know she will be free."

"If I have to help her fight her way out with nothing but my needle and thread, I swear, Lancelot will be free. But I will not have to do that, because I refuse to believe you will not come back and do it yourself."

"Will you braid my hair?" Guinevere asked, because she could not answer or make promises. For once, Brangien, showing a grace Guinevere had not known she possessed, did not argue.

CHAPTER TWENTY-SIX

"Where is Arthur?" Guinevere demanded, peering out of her tent to find Sir Tristan standing guard. She paused, smiling through her heartbreak, and said, "I am glad you are safe."

Sir Tristan answered her smile with one of his own. "I am glad *you* are safe. The king is trying to catch the Dark Queen before he loses the trail."

Guinevere hoped Arthur did catch her. The knots to do Merlin's magic—the knots she had inadvertently handed over to the Dark Queen—nagged at her. Would the fairy find some other vulnerable girl since Guinevere was no longer in her reach? Take over a human body, as Nimue had done? The Dark Queen seemed to think she could do so without losing herself in the process. Would she be stronger as a human? Why would she even want to become human? She was not like Nimue, watching and wanting for all those aching ages. The Dark Queen had no love for humans at all.

Guinevere could not hold back a shudder, remembering how the Dark Queen had promised to be everywhere. Maybe she would try for Guinevere's body again. Had she not only *not* saved the real Guinevere but also doomed her to more invasion?

Guinevere reached up to nervously adjust her braid before realizing that Brangien had only fixed her hair in the dream. She undid the mess under her blue fabric wrap and ran her fingers through it. "How did you get here so quickly?" she asked Sir Tristan. It should have taken days for Arthur's forces to catch up to them, and she could not understand why they were here instead of following the obvious trail of Nectudad's forces.

"We sailed up the coast and cut inland from there," Sir Tristan answered.

That explained how they had missed Nectudad. "But where did you get the ships?" Guinevere still felt shaky and off balance from both Morgana's magic and her proximity to Excalibur. She needed to gather her strength, to prepare for her journey to Merlin.

Sir Tristan's expression was inscrutable. "Saxons."

"Arthur is working with Saxons now?" Guinevere was aghast. Aside from the fact that Saxons had conspired with King Nechtan to ambush Arthur, they had also tried to kidnap and ransom Guinevere. And she had seen firsthand what Saxon raiders did to people whose land they wanted.

"No. We raided several village settlements and took their ships."

"Oh." Guinevere understood Sir Tristan's reluctant tone. It was not like Arthur to attack first.

Guinevere stood, trying to feel the warmth of the sun, but it did not seem to want to settle on her. She wrapped her arms around herself. She needed Arthur to return so they could speak. So she could explain why she had to leave for Merlin. A phantom spider twitched on her arm, and she kept looking down to make sure there was nothing crawling on her. She had to restore the real Guinevere before the Dark Queen found her again.

But first, she had to make certain her friend was safe. "Where is Fina?"

"Who?"

"Nechtan's daughter." Guinevere walked out into the camp, Sir Tristan at her side. There were so many men and horses. But she knew from what Lancelot had seen that Arthur had even more soldiers. He must have left them behind to guard Camelot. Guinevere scanned for Fina. Her eyes snagged on a tree at the center of camp.

Guinevere rushed over to where Fina sat chained to the tree, her hands and feet bound with rope. A soldier with a blunt face and a sharp sword stood guard.

"Release her," Guinevere said.

The soldier frowned. "But—"

"You heard your queen," Sir Tristan said, his normally soft voice brooking no dissent.

"Of course." The soldier bowed, fumbling for a key to the chains. He undid them, then grabbed Fina's arm to haul her roughly up.

"Do not touch her," Guinevere commanded, and this time the soldier listened to her. Sir Tristan bent down and reached for the rope binding Fina's wrists. She flinched.

Guinevere crouched next to her. "He is my friend," she said, and put a hand on Fina's shoulder as Sir Tristan cut her hands and feet free. Guinevere helped Fina stand, then walked her back to her tent. Sir Percival stood nearby, leaning on a spear. There was something heavy and threatening in the way he licked his lips while watching Fina that turned Guinevere's stomach.

"Bring me clean water and some cloth," she snapped at him.

Sir Percival's face folded into a frown. Before he could say no or inform her that knights did not do such tasks, Guinevere guided Fina into her tent and let the flap drop behind them. "I am sorry. I am so, so sorry," she said.

When Fina spoke, she sounded empty, all her brash fire turned to ashes. "I know my father started this fight. But he is—he was—"

"I will mourn him with you." Guinevere helped Fina sit. She would mourn Morgana, too. A person did not have to be *good* for there to be loss when they left this world ahead of their time.

Sir Tristan, not Sir Percival, brought the supplies. He handed them to Guinevere, and then bowed respectfully to Fina. Fina let out a strangled half laugh of surprise at the gesture. Sir Tristan smiled and then left. Guinevere cleaned Fina's bloody face and did her best to soothe any visible wounds. It was the ones she could not see that would be the hardest to heal.

"What happened in the trees?" Fina asked, staring at the floor of the tent as Guinevere cleaned her ragged and swollen knuckles.

Remembering what had taken place triggered dread and fear and also shame. Shame that she had thought the Dark Queen would help her. Shame that she had not been able to do what she swore to and restore the real Guinevere. Shame that she had watched another woman die and been unable to stop it.

Guinevere gave the simplest account she could. "Morgana is dead. The Dark Queen escaped. Arthur is pursuing her."

"It was always going to end this way."

Guinevere could not comfort Fina over the death of her father, but she could at least send her back to her sister. "We will reunite you with Nectudad and make peace. Arthur's conflict was with your father, not with you."

Fina made a hopeless noise in the back of her throat. She was rubbing her tattoos without thought, tracing the intricate triangle that Guinevere knew represented her family. One point of that triangle was gone now. "Do not make promises you cannot keep."

"I will make sure you are safe. I *will*."

Fina finally met her eyes. "Guinevere, I watched you trust Mor-

gana. I watched you walk into the trees with her. You let her manipulate you, just like my father did. He also promised me we would
be safe. That our people would be safe. And now he is dead and
Nectudad is fighting without me by her side and you are back with
your king, who came for us even though you said he would not. We
cannot stay friends if you lie to me. If you lie to yourself."

"You are right," Guinevere whispered. She could make no promises to Fina, because she was not staying. Not here in this camp, or
even in this body. "Come, we will get you a horse and—"

The tent flap opened once more and Arthur stepped in, taking in
the scene with no small amount of confusion. "I thought you were
resting?"

"Can we get a horse for Fina?" Guinevere asked, not pausing in
her careful tying of the cloth wrap around Fina's hair. Her stomach
clenched with dread about what Arthur might say. "She wishes to
rejoin her sister."

Arthur frowned. Before he could speak, Fina got on one knee and
bowed her head.

"No," she said. "I wish to pledge my fealty as a knight."

CHAPTER TWENTY-SEVEN

"What?" Guinevere and Arthur asked at the same time.

Fina's head remained bowed, but her voice was strong and clear. "As evidence that my people wish you no harm, and as atonement for my father's actions in league with the Dark Queen, I will serve you as a knight."

Arthur scratched the back of his neck, his eyes searching the tent as if it might hold answers. "You cannot—you see, first of all—well, there are rules for becoming a knight."

"Yes, you have to win the right in combat. I understand. I am ready." Fina looked up, her eyes blazing. "I will win that right, and then I will serve you and Camelot and the queen. I understand she already has a lady knight. I will join Sir Lancelot as the queen's guard."

Guinevere's heart raced. It was a brilliant gambit. Fina would sacrifice her place among her people to protect them. To atone for what her family had done and to keep Arthur away from Nectudad. Guinevere knew Fina, knew how she valued honor. If Fina did this, she would do it with absolute commitment.

"I will consider it." Arthur's voice was cautious, but Guinevere could tell from his expression that he was turning the proposition over in his mind. He really was considering it.

Arthur did not sit. He seemed to be waiting for something else to happen. After a few seconds, he held out his hand to Guinevere. "Walk with me?"

Guinevere turned to Fina. "You can stay in here until your tent is ready." She wanted to say more, but this was not the time. She took Arthur's hand and walked out of the camp with him. Several soldiers hovered on the periphery, guarding the king and queen while allowing them privacy.

"I could not find the Dark Queen," Arthur said, frustration radiating from his touch.

Guinevere rubbed her forehead with her free hand, but the phantom touch of moth wings lingered. She shuddered. "She is terrified of Excalibur." Maybe that was why the Dark Queen wanted Guinevere's body. If she was shielded by flesh and blood, Excalibur could not easily unmake her. But it could still kill her the way any sword could kill.

Guinevere sat on a lichen-splotched boulder. The memory of the warmth that had existed in the Green Man's Chapel made the day feel even colder. And now her mind was back in that horrible cave as she prepared to tell Arthur everything. She wished he were Lancelot, or Mordred. That she did not have to explain this *again*.

Arthur surprised her by putting his hand on the back of her neck and pressing her close in an embrace. "I was so afraid. Knowing they had you, it was—it has been—"

She had been viewing him as a warrior, but this was a reminder that he was barely a man. Still so young. And he had already lost so much. As much pain as she was in, Arthur had been through a lot, too. "My heart broke for you. I really wanted you to have your son," she said.

He nodded, his cheek against the top of her head. "I wanted that, too. And I nearly lost you because of it. I am sorry. I should have waited, should have sent someone else."

"You did the best you could with the information we had."

"You figured it out, though." He sighed and sat next to her. "At least one of us is clever. But why did you seal yourself outside the city?"

It was tempting to go back to the way things had been. To look at him through a confident haze of belief and admiration. She wanted to return to that moment at the table in the castle, sitting next to Arthur, certain in the decision she was about to make. Certain that they were about to become king and queen, husband and wife in reality and not just name.

But she could never go back. She knew now she was not that person, had never been that person, could never be that person. And she could not ignore the realizations she had had about Arthur and Camelot, either. Neither the man nor his kingdom were perfect, and idealizing him did no one any good.

"I sealed myself outside because I was going to free Merlin. I wanted answers about who I am. Who I was."

Arthur put an arm around her. "We were both chasing ghosts. We should make a pact to only look forward, together. For the sake of Camelot, and for our own safety."

Guinevere opened her mouth to tell him the truth. To tell him that she had found the answers. She *was* the ghost, and she could not move forward. But before she could speak, he continued. "Do you know where the rest of Nechtan's people are?"

Guinevere nodded, then paused, remembering Nechtan lying dead on the ground. She had not been there. She had not seen what had happened. Whether Nechtan had been executed as summarily as Morgana, or whether he had fought and forced Arthur's hand.

Fina did not think Guinevere could protect anyone, but Guinevere had to at least try. One last gift before she gave up being Guinevere forever. "If I tell you, will you kill them?"

Arthur leaned away from her, confusion reshaping his strong features into something more boyish. "Guinevere, they abducted you. They delivered you to our greatest enemy. They told me my son was alive and then ambushed me. They engineered both our deaths, and it is only through our strength that we survived. They do not deserve your protection or your compassion."

"*Nechtan* did all that, yes. Under the direction of the Dark Queen, direction his daughters did not approve of or support. You know perfectly well how a corrupt king can drive an entire people in a violent direction. They did not choose this, and the man who did is dead. Fina is a genuinely good person. She and her sister were never unkind to me." Guinevere paused. "Well, Nectudad did threaten to break many of my bones. But she did it to protect her family and her people."

"Nectudad? Nechtan's oldest daughter? I have never met her."

"She is a good leader. I think you would respect her. She did what she could to correct her father's course and protect her people. She even broke away from her father to defend other tribes from a Saxon invasion."

"So she is on the coast."

Guinevere flinched, scowling in frustration. She had not meant to give Arthur any details about Nectudad's location. It felt like betrayal.

He did not fail to notice her expression. He took her hand, covering it with his. "I love your compassion and that you can find good in anyone."

"Take Fina up on her offer, then. Nectudad loves her fiercely, and if Fina is part of Camelot, we will have an alliance."

"Mmm." Arthur frowned, thoughtful. "But I cannot leave an army at my back."

"Nectudad has fewer than two hundred soldiers. And the people of the north are not a united kingdom. For the most part they want only to be left alone."

"But they provoked this fight. I will never leave Camelot vulnerable again."

"Even if it means locking Lancelot up?" Guinevere asked, remembering the plight of her friend with a spike of pain and resentment. In her worry about Fina, Lancelot had slipped to the background, and Guinevere felt herself heating with anger.

Arthur's face fell. "She tried to leave, then. That is disappointing."

"And you had her arrested!"

He looked genuinely baffled by her reaction. "You are the one who laid the shield so that it only worked if she remained in the city."

Guinevere stood, pacing. She did not want to feel Arthur right now. Perhaps that had been part of her inability to truly see him. She understood him so well because she constantly felt how he felt about things. She needed to focus on how *she* felt now. "She wanted to save me."

"And I told her she did not need to. Knights serve the crown. If she cannot follow direct orders from both her king and her queen, then she is a danger to everyone."

Guinevere's hands fluttered uselessly. Everything was broken. "She is a danger to no one."

Arthur stood, again pulling her close. "I can see you are upset. You have been through so much. I will fix everything, I promise."

Guinevere breathed him in, breathed in how much she cared about him, how deeply she believed in him, how much she loved him. And it hurt. She could see all his flaws now, all the flaws of Camelot and justice and Excalibur. How much of what she felt for him was real, and how much was that horrible destroyer Nimue, who loved him so much she gave him a city and a sword and created a new self just so she could be with him?

And then an even worse thought seized Guinevere. Did Arthur know? Had he always known?

She grabbed his hands. He looked down at her, his affection turning to alarm at her expression. "What is it?" he asked.

"Who am I?"

"You are . . . Guinevere?" His confused frown matched the feelings pulsing from him. He had never been capable of deception, never gifted in telling or showing people what they wanted to hear or see.

"And who was I before I was Guinevere?"

His confusion became tender amusement. "You were a forest witch, and I do not care. I would not trade you for all the real princesses in the world."

There was no lie in him, no deceit. He genuinely believed what Merlin had told him about Guinevere. He had no idea what had been done to create her. He had lost his son once again, and now she would take away his wife.

"No," Guinevere said. "I was never *anything* before I was Guinevere. *This* was the real Guinevere." She gestured limply at her body. "She was real, and this is her body. Merlin and the Lady of the Lake lured her away from the convent. They promised her a life of strength and love and purpose, and then they destroyed her."

"I do not understand. You are the real Guinevere? But . . . you are also not?"

"They destroyed her to create me. There is a reason I do not know who I was before, because I was no one. I am—I am Guinevere and I am Nimue. The Lady of the Lake. She wanted to be real, to be yours, to be your queen. Merlin and Nimue bound her into Guinevere's body, but it went wrong and the Lady and the girl were both erased. I am the result. Arthur, I am not real. I am a stolen body with a false soul. And I have to fix it. I have to get to Merlin and figure out how to give the real Guinevere her body back."

She expected shock. Demands for more explanation. Even horror at what his wife truly was. Nothing could have prepared her, then, for Arthur's reaction.

"Absolutely not," he said, his voice trembling with barely contained fury.

CHAPTER TWENTY-EIGHT

Arthur marched back toward the camp.

Guinevere grabbed his arm. "We need to talk. You are angry, but—"

"I am *hurt,* and I do not have time for it. We have been away too long. We need to get back to Camelot." He kept walking.

"Stop!" she demanded.

"We are going home." Anger radiated off him in such intense waves that Guinevere wondered if everyone else felt it. He might be hurt, but somewhere in his life—perhaps under the cruel tutelage of Sir Ector and Sir Kay, or at another point along his journey as an orphaned young man—he had learned to turn hurt into anger. She had felt him do just that when he discovered he did not have a son. Instead of pausing to mourn, he had decided the solution was to take over the entire south.

How might things be different if he had been raised by a caring family? Been taught that pain and anguish and hurt were things he was allowed to feel, that sadness was not something to be fought but something to move purposefully through?

If the real Guinevere had been taught that, too, maybe she never would have made that devastating agreement on the lake.

Guinevere followed Arthur into the camp's center. He gestured to the tent where she had left Fina. Sir Tristan opened the flap and Fina emerged.

"Get the others," Arthur said to Sir Tristan, and then he addressed Fina. "Write a letter to your sister. Tell Nectudad that you are coming to Camelot, and she can send an emissary to discuss our terms. And tell her that if either of you betray me as your father did, if she sends more than one solitary emissary to Camelot, I will not hesitate to bring the full might of the south against every tribe in the north."

Fina's mouth was a hard line, but she nodded and was led away to write her letter.

"That is hardly fair," Guinevere said. "Nectudad does not rule the north. No one does."

"Maybe that is the problem." Arthur's voice was curt. "It certainly was in the south."

"My king," Sir Bors said, standing at attention along with Arthur's other knights. "Is it wise to leave the Picts at our back?"

"I spoke with a scout from the coast just now," Sir Gawain said, his round cheeks flushed with pleasure at being the one with news. "The Picts and a settlement of Saxons are engaged in a skirmish near an inlet. The Picts are pinned against rocky terrain and outnumbered."

"We have ships nearby," Sir Percival said. "Let the Saxons kill them all and then clean up whoever is left."

"No!" Guinevere said. All the men turned toward her, frowning. "This is an opportunity. Nectudad, Nechtan's daughter, is a good leader. Make a deal with her. You cannot hold the entire eastern shore against the Saxons, and many of the tribes here are skilled sailors who already have ships."

Sir Caradoc waved dismissively. "If these Picts die, there are always more."

"But Nectudad is the type of leader who could unite tribes."

"Why would we want that?" Sir Percival said, aghast at both the suggestion and the fact that Guinevere was talking.

"They could be united in purpose *with* you. To hold the coast against Saxon invaders."

"It would be easier to just kill them," Sir Caradoc said, yawning. Guinevere was glad Fina had gone to write her letter and did not hear how casually and cruelly the extinction of her people was being discussed.

Sir Bors surprised her, though, when he spoke, his tone thoughtful. "We will already be stretched thin, consolidating your rule in the south and transitioning all the cities and lands there to our laws. Anything that makes a northern campaign easier is worth exploring."

Arthur nodded but did not appear swayed. "I am sending word that Nectudad can deliver an emissary, and we will discuss terms then."

"But they could die. We should go help now," Guinevere said. "I can speak with Nectudad once we reach her."

Sir Caradoc laughed. The sound boomed from his chest. "All this work to save you, and we throw you into battle against a Pictish warrior princess?"

Arthur's voice was as firm as the foundation of Camelot. "I will not spill my men's blood to protect Nechtan's people. We are going home."

Arthur continued talking with his knights, and it was clear Guinevere's suggestion had been dismissed. She was hurt and angry that the knights had not listened to her. But why should they? When had she ever led in Camelot? The most she had done there—at least that *they* knew of—was plan a harvest festival. She had worked so hard to keep her powers and abilities secret that they truly saw her as nothing but Arthur's wife.

Was it this way for all women? The rules and laws in Camelot were made and administered by men, always. The ways that women had power were subtle and quiet, overlooked. Or, in the case of using magic, outright banned.

"It will not be a treaty," Fina said, no emotion in her voice, when she joined Guinevere. They both stared at where a scout was riding away to deliver the letter to Nectudad. Fina scuffed one heel through the dirt in a circle. "It will be terms of surrender. We will survive, but we will not be our people anymore. We will be *his* people, and everything will change. It is another kind of death."

Guinevere took her hand and Fina did not rebuff her. But the sense of Fina was so much lessened, so dampened compared to the wild and confident Fina that Guinevere had met. Was life nothing but a series of dying and being remade? Being lessened each time? No. She could not think that, because it let her think that perhaps what had been done to the real Guinevere had not been a violation.

Guinevere longed to have her funny, lively Fina back. "That was clever, the offer to be a knight."

Fina's grin was not quite at full force, but it was lopsided and proud. "I needed to take control before he decided to kill me. Or, worse, marry me to one of his knights."

"Guinevere!" Arthur called.

Guinevere squeezed Fina's hand and returned to Arthur. "We need to talk," she said. "I need to explain."

"You need rest."

"Do not tell me what I need!" Guinevere hissed.

But Arthur was already speaking to Sir Tristan. "I will leave you here with a significant force. Meet up with the soldiers from our ships, and hold the borders to the south until I decide what to do."

Sir Tristan bowed his head. He had once told Guinevere all he wanted was to go on adventures and fight at King Arthur's side. But now he was being left behind to patrol a land that was not theirs. How did he feel about it?

"Come, my queen, we will get you changed for our journey back." Arthur led her to her tent before she could speak to Sir Tristan.

"You cannot leave him here!" Guinevere said as soon as they were inside. She knew she was speaking loudly enough to be overheard, but she did not care.

Arthur threw his hands in the air. "What would you have me do? What is a better solution than this? There is no perfect path. We can only do the best with what we have, and this is the best I can do for the most people. The Picts are being killed. Saxons will not stop coming, and the way the Picts are now, scattered and isolated, they will not survive. I am not being cruel. I am being practical. Did you notice the bands of people on the outskirts of our camp?"

Guinevere frowned. "No." She had been too focused on protecting Fina and trying to speak to Arthur.

"We have at least a hundred refugees who begged for permission to accompany us south. The north is not *free,* it is lawless and dangerous even for those who love it. I will not let the instability bleed down and threaten Camelot."

"But the people here are not united. They cannot mount a large enough attack to threaten you."

"If Nectudad is as you describe her, perhaps she could unite them. I am less worried about that, though, than I am about more Saxons. Sir Tristan will stay here to protect against a Saxon invasion as much as Pict attacks."

"They do not like being called Picts," Guinevere said, because it was the only argument she had left.

Arthur's eyebrows lifted in surprise. "I was not aware."

"Well, now you are," she snapped. At least Arthur was not attacking Nectudad. And she had seen the destruction inflicted by malicious Saxons. If anyone was going to oversee the men left in the north, it should be someone kind and true like Sir Tristan. But it broke her heart, thinking of leaving him here. He was her friend, and more than that, he was Brangien and Isolde's friend. She could not imagine Camelot without him.

Her heart seized. She should not be imagining Camelot at all. She was letting herself be drawn into decisions that were not hers to make, battles that were not hers to wage. She could not go back to Camelot. Not ever. She had to do right by the real Guinevere.

Brangien and Isolde would have to mourn Sir Tristan's absence along with Guinevere's. She was certain they would be kind to the real Guinevere, but it would not be the same for them. And who would look after Fina? She would need a friend and ally in Camelot. Guinevere would make sure Lily, Brangien, and Dindrane stepped up to the task. Though she could not imagine Dindrane and Fina getting along.

She wished she could watch them try, though. Doubtless it would be hilarious. And she wished she could watch Fina's trials, see her knighted alongside Lancelot. She wished so many things. Knowing what she knew now, she almost regretted her decision to seal the city and then walk away from it. If she had known those would be her last moments there, she would have done things differently. Said better goodbyes.

Arthur scooted closer and brushed away a tear. "Why are you crying?"

"Because I cannot stay, and I want to."

"You are not going anywhere."

"But the real Guinevere—"

"Is not here and I have never known her. I do know the Lady of the Lake, and—"

"And you do not want to lose her? Is that it? The Lady of the Lake crashed over that scared girl like a wave, erasing everything they both were. And I felt the real Guinevere's fear, her horror, her pain. I *drowned* with her. Your beloved Lady drowned her, and still you do not want to give her up?"

"I did not love her that way. I knew nothing of this plan. If Merlin had asked, I would have told him not to do it."

"Then why are you angry at me for wanting to undo it?"

Arthur rubbed his forehead as though he could push into his mind and find the right words. "I am *angry* because I am here due to Merlin's magic, too. I have worked my whole life to make certain my place on this earth is worth what it cost. Meanwhile, you want to tear yourself out of existence for a princess none of us know. You, who became a queen because you were needed, who figured out how to protect all of Camelot in my absence." Arthur pressed her hands to his heart. "I need you. And I am sorry for the way you were created, but I am not sorry you are here. You deserve to be here."

"It is not about what I deserve." Guinevere blinked back tears. "The real Guinevere was innocent. You protect the innocent. If I can save her, should I not try?"

"Would you go back and save Igraine, if it meant I was never born?"

"No!" Guinevere lowered her head. "It is different. This is different. You were a baby, and Igraine died. The princess Guinevere did not. She is here, somewhere, in this body." Guinevere hoped it was true. Her body at least remembered being someone else; her skill with the bow proved it. The girl could not be totally gone. After all,

Nimue lingered in Guinevere's magic and dreams. "I know you think I am real, but before we met, I was nothing. I still am."

Arthur let out a dismissive huff. "You only think it is different because this time you are the one who has to shoulder the guilt of your existence. *Everyone* who lives does so at the cost of others, in one way or another. For some of us, the cost is higher. You excuse it in me because you love me, so allow me to love you and keep you here."

Guinevere looked him in the eyes. His warm brown eyes, that should have been a match to the real Guinevere's. "I understand. And I am sorry. But you cannot forbid me from trying to find a way to save her."

His face fell, and the pain there was not sharp but soul-crushingly weary. "I absolutely can and do forbid it."

Guinevere flared with anger. "I am not your subject to command. Nor am I your wife. I am not anything, and therefore can do as I think best."

"Very well. If you think it is easy to make decisions about who deserves to live and who does not, I will give you what my mother and the princess never had: a choice. If you promise to never pursue this course, I will pardon Lancelot and let her remain a knight. And if you do not, she will be tried as a traitor."

"That is not fair! You cannot threaten someone I care about!"

"Says the woman informing me she will be removing herself from existence!" He took a deep breath, calming himself, once again becoming Arthur the king. "And I am not threatening Lancelot. There are consequences for treason. I am offering to show her mercy because she matters to you, just as I hope you will show yourself mercy because you matter to me."

"How can I live with this, though?" Guinevere whispered.

Arthur wrapped his strong arms around her. "We will figure it out together."

She wanted to laugh at how similar Arthur and Mordred were. They made promises, but really they were both asking her to wait until the guilt faded and the pain lessened and she could live with what she was. She knew that was exactly what would happen, and it terrified her.

CHAPTER TWENTY-NINE

Arthur rode beside Guinevere, but they were surrounded by knights and could not speak. He let her stew in silence over the choice he had given her. She was afraid they would go to the coast and sail home, but at least he pitied her enough to avoid a boat.

They made camp when it got dark, and Guinevere sat in the tent, watching Arthur write letters.

"Do you want to know what the Dark Queen wanted with me?" Guinevere asked.

Arthur looked up in surprise. It was clear it had not occurred to him to ask. "What?"

"To find out how I was made. Does that worry you?"

Arthur paused, a thoughtful frown pulling his lips down. Mordred smiled when he was caught off guard. Arthur frowned. "Does she want to become human, too?"

"I do not know. Maybe."

"It would limit her. And she would be much easier to kill than when she—" He wiggled his fingers and moved his hands like they were insects scurrying away. "I cannot imagine that was her goal.

She wanted to hurt me, to distract me, and knew she could do it by taking you from me."

Guinevere did not agree. She could understand why Arthur assumed everything was about him, but the Dark Queen had been so specific in what she wanted to see, so gleeful with the knowledge. There must be an advantage to becoming human that she and Arthur were not seeing, not understanding.

He returned to his letters. He was sending them out as quickly as he wrote them, communicating with the men he had left all over the south. Occupying the south.

Arthur Pendragon, Lancelot had thought when looking at him. The name of his conqueror father.

Guinevere could see perfectly well the bad in Camelot, the ways it destroyed. But she could also see the good, the ways it built and would build. Arthur was the bridge between the old and the new. But what would happen if he continued to give in to anger when he felt pain? If he grew more like the father he never knew? Would that bridge collapse and bring down Camelot with it?

"Who are you writing?" she asked.

"I left Sir Kay in charge in Cameliard."

"You *what?*"

Arthur sighed. "Believe me, he was not my first choice."

"What happened to King Leodegrance, Lily's father?" Guinevere realized with a sickening lurch that Leodegrance was her father, too. Or at least the father of the body she wore.

"He is dead," Arthur said. "He did not accept our unification of the south."

Guinevere did not know how to feel. Lily bore the man no love, and Guinevere had seen firsthand what a cruel, destructive father he had been. Arthur was a better person, a better king. But did that justify Leodegrance's death?

"And his sons?" she asked, remembering that Lily and the real Guinevere had brothers.

"They accepted. I knighted them both and gave them command of several ships to patrol and guard the coast. I thought it best not to keep them in Cameliard."

"Oh, certainly Sir *Kay* is better." Guinevere had been around Sir Ector and Sir Kay only once, and that had been more than enough. They were crude, opportunistic mercenaries: if not actively malicious, then certainly passively harmful.

"He is a temporary measure while I decide what the permanent solution is."

"Lily." Guinevere said the name before she had thought it through, but as soon as it came out of her mouth, she knew she was right. "If anyone should rule Cameliard, it is her."

"But she is so young."

"And you are so old?"

Arthur gave a grudging shrug. "Still. She will need to be married."

"No. Absolutely not. She is too—" Guinevere bit her lip before she could say Lily was too young, given that she had just declared her old enough to rule an entire city.

Arthur visibly held back a smile, and when he spoke his voice was gentle. "They will not accept an unmarried maiden as ruler. Besides which, her lack of a husband would make her a target for predatory men seeking power." He paused, then scratched out whatever he had been writing. "But married to one of my knights, she is the visible link to their past and he is the connection to Camelot's rule. You are brilliant. Of course it should be Lily. And she can marry—"

"Lionel!" Guinevere hurried, before Arthur could say a name. If he said someone old and terrible like Sir Caradoc, she would never forgive him. "Sir Bors's son. He can be knighted alongside Fina. And you should send Sir Bors and Dindrane with Lily to help her rule Cameliard. No one is more loyal than Sir Bors, and Dindrane is wickedly intelligent. She will make certain Lily and Lionel are taken care of."

"Are you sure? You will miss Lily and Dindrane." Arthur kept his voice even, but she could still hear the note of happiness in it. Because if she missed them, it meant she was still in Camelot. It meant she was still in this body.

"I am sure," Guinevere snapped. If Arthur was going to rule the island through his knights, there should also be smart, compassionate women present to lead, guide, and direct them.

"We are settled, then. That was a good idea. Thank you. We have a long ride tomorrow. You should try to sleep," Arthur said, his voice warm and affectionate.

Would he feel warmth and affection if he knew there was a chance she would close her eyes and open them to Mordred? Would he feel that way if he knew she had held Mordred in her arms, had been closer to him than she had ever been to Arthur? If she told him, would he let her run to Merlin? Or would his pain crystallize into an anger so complete that there would be no turning him away from his Pendragon destiny?

Guinevere did not want to sleep. She did not want to face Mordred, or even Brangien, and she certainly did not want to open her eyes in that accursed cave once more.

"I am going to check on Fina." She hurried from the tent before Arthur could ask why. Fina's tent was next to theirs, and Guinevere ducked inside.

Fina had been given material to sew skirts and sleeves, but she sat, staring blankly, with the supplies untouched. Guinevere sat next to her and was surprised when Fina rested her head on Guinevere's shoulder.

"I have never been without my family," Fina said. "Not one night in my whole life. You will help me, right? You will be my friend and help me. I am—I am scared."

Guinevere could hear how much the admission cost her warrior friend. "I will," she promised, then her throat caught. She was making more promises, tying herself in knots of loyalty and obligation to people in Camelot. Tying herself tighter and tighter to this body and this life that were not hers to claim. Lancelot's freedom. Fina's success in Camelot.

Fina needed her, though. And Fina had risked her life to help Guinevere.

"One of the knights seems particularly interested in me," Fina said, her tone deliberately light. "He kept making excuses to ride next to me and helping me with things I did not need help with. He even set up my tent."

"Oh no, Sir Percival?" Guinevere's stomach dropped in dread.

"A young one. Round face. Red cheeks. He is not very ugly," Fina said with a disappointed sigh.

Guinevere let out a relieved laugh. "That is Sir Gawain." Apparently he, too, had gotten over Lily in their time apart.

"If I do not pass the trial to become a knight, I am afraid my only other option is to marry. Perhaps Arthur would marry me, too, and we could be wives to each other?" Fina lifted an eyebrow. Her efforts at teasing made Guinevere want to both laugh and cry, knowing how hard it must be for her friend right now.

"I am afraid they do not do that in the south."

Fina let out a dramatic sigh. "It is going to be very boring."

"Probably." Guinevere picked up the material left for Fina. She needed a new dress of her own and had a few ideas for adjustments.

Fina nodded, steeling herself. "Our father wrote our death

sentences. I was ready to die. I am glad I did not have to. I will find a way through this, too. Alongside my friend." She took Guinevere's hand and Guinevere felt all the knots tightening so that she could barely breathe. How was she ever going to do what needed to be done with so many people holding her here?

CHAPTER THIRTY

The shimmering magic barrier looked like waves of heat, though the day was barely warm. Through the haze, Guinevere could see the distant shore of Camelot teeming with people waving flags of blue and yellow. Camelot was safe and their king was returning, a triumphant conqueror.

She had always viewed Arthur as a protector, not a conqueror. She did not particularly like the idea of him being both.

Fina and Guinevere wore blue and yellow. Guinevere had done her best to sew them dresses using Arthur's flags, the only material a traveling army had. And she sewed a secret into both the dresses.

Fina looked over at her and smiled. She bent her elbows and the sleeves, slit from just above the wrist to the shoulder, opened. "Our wrists *are* still covered," she said.

"Indeed. Who better to create new fashion standards than the queen?" Guinevere wrinkled her nose in a smile, moving so that her own sleeves opened as well. But her smile was false. Fina's beautiful arms revealed her history, written onto her skin. Guinevere could not look at her own skin without knowing she wore another girl's life like an obscene costume.

And what could she do about it? She had no one to talk to. Arthur would not hear any more discussion on the topic, and she had had no more dreams on their journey, either because no one had been trying to reach her or because she slept so near to Excalibur that she could feel the nagging pain of its magic-devouring presence even when it was sheathed.

Where Mordred was, what he was doing, Guinevere had no idea. She suspected he knew what had happened to his mother. Perhaps he was grieving, or perhaps he was rightfully livid that Arthur had killed his mother and Guinevere was back at his side.

Maybe it was for the best. She did not regret her time with Mordred, but the relationship felt broken in her heart. A fault line had appeared, separating her from whom she had believed she was. There was no room in her life now for desire like that, for throwing all caution aside in favor of passion.

"I never thought I would go inside Camelot," Fina said, drawing Guinevere's attention back as she gestured toward the other side of the lake. Guinevere remembered her first sight of Camelot. The twin waterfalls protecting the steep gray city where the Lady of the Lake had carved it from the mountain.

Fina waved her hand at the shore ahead and frowned. "Why does it look so strange? Like a bubble?"

"That is a shield of magic," Guinevere said.

"I thought magic was against the rules in Camelot?" Fina darted a worried glance at Guinevere. Guinevere trusted that Fina would never use her knowledge of Guinevere's truths against her. It touched her that, even now, Fina was on her side.

"It is." Arthur joined them in staring at the city. Guinevere expected him to look excited or happy. He just looked tired. His voice did not match the exhaustion on his face, though. It projected warm confidence to everyone gathered around them, pitched loudly enough for them to overhear. "This was left by the Lady of the Lake to protect the city in our absence. Her final gift to help us unite the south and rescue our queen."

Guinevere braced herself for Arthur to ride forward and draw Excalibur. She was certain the sword would make her very sick and leave her in incredible pain. Not only because it always had that effect on her but because this time it would be undoing magic that she had set with her own blood.

A thought struck her. If Excalibur devoured magic . . . could it devour the magic that bound Nimue to this body and had erased the real Guinevere?

She had no time to consider it further. She hurried to dismount, sliding down so quickly she practically fell. Fina copied her. "If I faint," Guinevere whispered to Fina, "catch me."

Fina looked even more confused. But Arthur did not ride forward as expected. He, too, dismounted, then held his hand out and took Guinevere's.

"I cannot be next to you when you use the sword," she whispered, smiling to keep nerves from showing. But maybe she should encourage it. What if being so close to Excalibur when it was used snapped all the knots of Merlin and Nimue's magic? What if it could release the real Guinevere? Her heart raced with both hope and fear.

"We are not using the sword. They will see the magic make way not for Excalibur but for their king and queen," Arthur said.

He had listened when Guinevere said the barrier would only work if she was on this side and Lancelot on the other. And rather than taking the moment to showcase his power as king, he was taking it to show unity with his queen. That they returned in peace and happiness, not on the edge of a sword. That he really could be both conqueror and protector.

It was just as well. She would set a date with Excalibur privately. After Lancelot was free, and everyone was settled. It was cowardly and a betrayal of Arthur's trust, but it gave her time for goodbyes.

Nodding, she squeezed his hand and they strode forward. Passing through the barrier felt like releasing a breath held too long. Cold rushed through her veins, and, just like that, the air was clear and the shield was gone. They were home.

CHAPTER THIRTY-ONE

Guinevere heard the roar from Camelot as its newly freed people cheered in unison. Arthur held up his and Guinevere's hands, still clasped. He did not release her as his men split. Some would camp here while they waited to be sent to different parts of the island. Others would take care of the horses. Arthur directed them all while staying with Guinevere as they waited for the ferry.

Guinevere finally understood why the lake was a cold, dead space, devoid of any magic. It had all been ripped away to wash through and overwhelm the real Guinevere as the Lady of the Lake took possession of her body.

Perhaps crossing the lake would feel different, now that she knew who she was. Maybe she would even feel some sense of the water beneath her. But as soon as she stepped onto the ferry, fear once again overwhelmed her. She had meant to stay beside Fina and show Camelot that Fina was her guest. All of that fled her mind, replaced with terror. It was worse than ever, now that she had actual memories of drowning.

Arthur embraced her and she pressed her face into his shoulder. The fear of water had never been put into her by Merlin after all. It was an echo of the real Guinevere, screaming through her forever. *She* was the dark cave in which the real Guinevere had been imprisoned. She was the water that had drowned another life.

"Almost home," Arthur murmured, stroking her back in reassurance.

The ferry rocked and he held her tighter. Then the ferry did not rock so much as shudder, a tremendous blow coming from beneath.

"What did we hit?" someone shouted.

The shout was followed by more as the ferry flew a couple of feet into the air before smashing back down into the water. Guinevere fell to her knees, and someone landed roughly on top of her. The person was tossed aside by Arthur. "Guinevere! We—"

The ferry splintered into pieces, knights and wood and water flying through the air as Guinevere and Arthur plunged straight down.

Guinevere tried to scream, but water filled her mouth. She clung to Arthur. He pushed her, trying to pry her fingers off him. Panicking, she clung even tighter. He shoved her away and she watched as he sank, frantically trying to undo his chain mail.

Guinevere hung, suspended. Mordred was not here to drag her to safety. How many times could one body drown before it never took another breath?

There was movement around her, bodies flailing, knights peeling off swords and armor so they would not sink, but she remained still. There was nothing she could do. This was always going to be her end. Now both she and the real Guinevere would be gone forever.

Something else was moving in the water, though. Bubbles and ripples coalesced into a humanlike form, and a face horrible in its lack of features appeared in front of her. A single watery hand reached toward her face. *Nimue,* a voice pulsed in her ears. Guinevere had seen this being once before, when Nynaeve, the other Lady of the Lake, the sister broken apart and left behind, had sealed Merlin into the cave.

Arms grasped around her waist and Guinevere was dragged upward. Nynaeve bubbled in fury.

Beneath them a terrible void opened. Not water, not earth, not *anything,* swirling upward to swallow them. Nynaeve broke apart, a whirlpool tearing through the water so fast it spun Guinevere in its wake.

But the arms did not let her go. They held her and their ascent continued. Guinevere's head broke the surface of the lake and she gulped air greedily, desperately.

"I thought *you* were going to protect *me* in Camelot," Fina said, huffing. "Stop struggling! You will drown us both. Just lie flat on your back. Like that. I have you. I have you. Good. Just like that." She paused. "I was not under long enough to begin seeing things, but that was definitely a face in the water. Right?"

"Yes," Guinevere gasped, keeping her face turned up toward the sun, trying to ignore the water slapping at her ears and washing over her body as it tried to find its way back into her throat, her lungs, her entire self. There were shouts around her, but she could not understand them.

"Here!" It was Arthur's voice. Guinevere wanted to cry with relief that he had surfaced, too. Suddenly the void beneath her made sense. He had unsheathed Excalibur to banish Nynaeve. Nynaeve had fled, and Guinevere was still here.

A long, jagged piece of the ferry was shoved toward them. Fina helped Guinevere throw her arms and shoulders over so she could cling to it.

Arthur hung opposite her. Water streamed down his face, and his thin tunic clung to his body. His armor was gone, but he still held Excalibur, thankfully sheathed once more. "Are you all right?"

Guinevere shook her head, eyes wide. She was still in the lake. She could breathe, but her lungs struggled to remember how to do it correctly.

"I am sorry I had to push you away. My armor would have dragged us both down. And then I looked up and saw—"

Guinevere nodded.

Fina was still next to Guinevere, keeping herself afloat while barely moving her arms and legs. "Maybe Guinevere's escape plan of walking into a lake was not as silly as I told her it was, if that creature was what awaited her. Who was it?"

"The other Lady of the Lake." Guinevere shuddered violently.

"How many are there?" Fina eyed the water around them as though expecting an army of ladies to come bubbling up. Guinevere could not tell her there was only one other, bound inside her body.

Arthur, too, looked at the water, frowning as though it held answers if only he could see them. "I do not think anyone else saw her. Why come now, though?"

"She wants her sister back. I used my blood for the shield, so it went into the water. I wonder if that drew her." Guinevere suspected Nynaeve had been here, waiting, the whole time. If Mordred had not followed her, Guinevere really would have died alone in a pond in the north, because she was a fool.

Arthur nodded thoughtfully. "And when the shield went down, she knew exactly where you were. It is a problem. But a problem for another day. We will keep this between us. Thank you, Fina." Arthur changed the subject by clasping Fina's hand. "Guinevere was right to call you friend. Stay with her."

Arthur left to help others and make sure everyone had something to hold on to while the next ferry was frantically steered toward them. They had capsized not far from shore, and many of the knights had opted to swim to solid ground once divesting themselves of their chain mail.

The blacksmiths would be working overtime to replace all the lost armor. Guinevere tried to imagine the heat of the furnaces, the ringing of metal, the smoke billowing upward. She tried to imagine anything other than what was lurking beneath her as she clung helplessly to a mere matchstick.

Sir Gawain splashed toward them. "Are you unharmed?"

Guinevere thought he was asking her, but his eyes, large and worried, were on Fina.

"I can swim." Fina gestured toward Guinevere, making the plank bob and Guinevere squeal with fear. "I was helping our queen, who does not seem to be fond of water."

"That was noble of you." Sir Gawain's face lit up in wonder and a touch of pride. "Such selflessness. I will go see if anyone else needs help!" He swam away.

"He is a fool and a child," Fina muttered. "But I suppose he is at least uglier than King Arthur."

Guinevere opened her mouth to answer and lake water splashed in it. She gagged, coughing and clutching the piece of wood while Fina patted her back in a decidedly unhelpful manner. At last the other ferry arrived. Arthur lifted her aboard, placing her squarely in the middle of the deck. When they finally bumped into the docks, he helped her off. The crowd was silent, no doubt wondering how to interpret the bizarre destruction of the original ferry.

Arthur put his arm around Guinevere and laughed loudly. "What a kindness that you were all spared the scent of unwashed knights after such a long ride!"

The crowd erupted into raucous laughter and cheers. Guinevere forced a smile onto her face, her cheeks trembling from the effort. Brangien broke free from the mass of people and rushed to her, taking off Guinevere's sodden cloak and putting her own dry cloak around Guinevere's shoulders. She paused for a moment, searching Guinevere's face with genuine fear in her expression. Then she sighed in relief. "It is you," she whispered.

Guinevere realized Brangien's fear was not that Guinevere might have been injured but rather that Guinevere might have been successful in restoring the real princess. Brangien was checking to make certain she knew the woman standing before her. It was both touching and devastating.

Brangien pulled Guinevere close, hugging her fiercely, then released her. "Your hair is an embarrassment. I cannot bear for you to be seen in this state and for people to think it had something to do with me." Brangien tugged Guinevere's hood over her head, shielding her face so she could be freer with her expressions.

"How is Lancelot?" Guinevere whispered.

"I told her the magic was down before I rushed to the dock. She knows you are back and safe."

Guinevere could not ask more at the moment. A blur of pink rushed toward her and then she was in Lily's embrace. "I prayed every day for your return. I am so happy, oh, I am so happy." Lily pulled back, tears spilling from her eyes as she beamed.

Guinevere wanted to cry, too, both because she was genuinely happy to see Lily and because she now knew the truth of what had taken the innocent girl's sister from her. How would Lily feel about her if she knew that Guinevere was merely a *thing* wearing the body of her beloved sister?

Misinterpreting Guinevere's tortured expression, Lily took her hands and squeezed them. "You will be all right," she whispered.

"I will take care of you, just like I took care of Camelot. We kept it safe."

It was difficult to speak around the pain lodged in her throat, but Guinevere forced herself to. "I never feared for the city, knowing you would be here to see that everyone was cared for. I am so proud of you."

Lily's smile was as bright as the sun above them. "Did everyone make it back safely?" She looked surreptitiously around, her gaze settling on Sir Gawain. Sir Gawain, who stood next to Fina, gallantly putting a cloak around her shoulders as she gave him a witheringly dismissive look.

Lily's eyes twitched narrowly, but then it was as though her face shrugged. Just like that, she let him go. Guinevere remembered Lily's feelings about him—how she did not have many, after all—and was relieved that at least there would be no suffering on her part. Lily glanced back at the waiting crowd. Dindrane was wrapped around Sir Bors, kissing him in spite of his sodden state and the very public location. Next to them stood a tall youth whom Guinevere recognized from her time spent in Dindrane's head. He was handsome, still growing into his frame, with Sir Bors's strong jaw but his mother's larger, prettier eyes and brown skin that complemented his black hair.

"Much has happened in your absence," Lily said, a bit breathless, her cheeks blooming pink as she tore her eyes away from Lionel.

At least Lily seemed flexible when it came to giving her heart away. Guinevere felt a burst of gratitude toward Morgana for the gift of insight into her loved ones' lives, but it was quickly punctured by sadness as she remembered Morgana's end. She did not have time to dwell on it, though. Dindrane disentangled herself from Sir Bors and rushed to embrace Guinevere.

"We must speak," Dindrane whispered in her ear. "I have meddled, and—"

"And I am glad. I unquestioningly trust your meddling. We will have a tournament immediately so we can get Lionel knighted, if he passes the trials."

Dindrane pulled back, shocked, then smiled slyly. "Tell Brangien that bit about trusting my meddling. She is still reluctant."

"Brangien is right here," Brangien snapped.

Dindrane continued as though Brangien had not spoken. "But of course Lionel will win his tournament. He is Sir Bors's son. Anyway, I am so glad you are safe and you are home." Dindrane's eyes shone with sincerity as she hugged Guinevere once more and then returned to her husband.

Arthur reappeared at Guinevere's side, taking her arm in his and leading her up the hill toward the castle through a veritable tunnel of cheering citizens. He bent his head so only she could hear him.

"Are we releasing Lancelot?"

She knew what he was asking. Would she agree to stay in her stolen place as Guinevere, agree not to pursue a way to restore the real Guinevere, undoing Nimue and herself at the same time? Would she live with this guilt and pain, live with the atrocity of what had been done to that poor girl, so that she could protect the people she loved? Arthur was leaving the decision to her. She knew if she said no, she could go. She could release Merlin, try everything to make this right. Arthur was letting her decide, but not letting her forget the consequences of giving herself up.

In the water this time, the fear that seized her had not been the real Guinevere's. It had been entirely her own. She did not want to be unmade. She wanted to live.

She was a wretched, selfish creature, and Arthur was trying to make it easier for her by allowing her to think she was saving others by letting the real Guinevere be lost. But he did not know what she did: Excalibur was still here. She did not have to leave to figure out a way to undo this magic. It was right there.

"I will stay," she whispered.

CHAPTER THIRTY-TWO

It felt like grinding her teeth, being back in an unchanged Camelot when, for Guinevere, everything had changed.

Crossing the threshold of the castle for the first time actually knowing who she was, where she had come from, was like all of her knots unraveling at once. She wanted to scream and cry and sleep. But first, she wanted to retrieve Lancelot. She was only holding herself together for that, and because with Arthur, Fina, Brangien, Lily, and Dindrane all accompanying her, she could not very well lose her composure.

"Brangien, will you take the queen to her rooms and help her into dry clothes?" Arthur said. "I have to see to a knight." Arthur squeezed Guinevere's hand and then strode away. Before Guinevere could hurry after him, Fina took her arm and leaned close.

"Where am I supposed to go?" she whispered.

"Right. Yes. Come with us." As they walked upstairs behind Brangien and Lily, Guinevere imparted crucial details to Fina in a hushed voice: who already knew which truths, and who must not know anything about their time away and what Guinevere had done and whom she had done it with.

Mordred.

Fina's smile was grim. "I will feign ignorance. I suspect everyone will expect ignorance from me anyway, so it will not be hard."

Guinevere felt yet another pang of sorrow for her friend, now living among enemies who held everything from mild prejudice to utter hatred of the northern people. "I do not have space in my rooms for you, but Lily does." Lily's maid Anna, Morgana in disguise, was gone forever. Guinevere shuddered, trying to move her mind away from the memory of the sword. The blood. The light going out of Morgana's eyes.

Hearing her name, Lily turned around. "What was that?"

"Fina is my dear friend. Can you take her to your rooms? She is a princess, too. You have a lot in common."

"What is your preferred weapon?" Fina asked, eyeing Lily.

Lily laughed. "Embroidery."

"You can teach me," Fina said. "And I will teach you axes and knives."

Lily's eyebrows lifted, but she nodded. "That sounds fair."

To Guinevere's surprise, not a single one of her retinue left her at the threshold of her bedroom. They all came in, joining Isolde, who had prepared the room. Guinevere had missed Brangien and Isolde and Dindrane and Lily, but with Guinevere and Fina as well, there were far too many *and*s for one room.

Guinevere walked toward her bed, exhausted, then stopped short. The crown was on her table, where Brangien had put it. It sat like a burning brand, filling her vision no matter where she looked. She was back where she had started. She had all her answers, yet nothing had changed.

No. That was not true. Everything had changed. She had made

the right choice to come back; it did not mean she was giving up. She would *never* give up on the real Guinevere. But while she was here, she would use this time as best she could. To take care of her friends. To prepare them and the city for whatever might come if Guinevere succeeded in cutting away Nimue and Merlin's magic with Excalibur.

Waiting was not the same thing as idleness. She took a deep breath. *Use this time.* The thought assuaged her guilt a little, and she vowed to think of it as a gift of grace from the real Guinevere instead of further theft of the princess's life.

"I do not need help," Brangien said, waving away Dindrane's efforts to pull out new clothes for Guinevere. "Really, I am certain the queen wants to rest. I can manage alone."

Brangien clearly wanted to speak with Guinevere privately, darting glances heavy with intent at her, but none of their companions listened as Brangien repeated comments about how they were not required. Isolde industriously peeled Guinevere's wet clothes off and wrapped her in a robe. Dindrane examined Fina, who had her face pressed against the window, staring down at the city. Lily chattered, filling Guinevere in on how the city had been in her absence.

At first, Guinevere was annoyed that Lily would not stop talking, but then she realized it was for her own benefit. Lily was watching her carefully, and every time it seemed as though Brangien or Dindrane were going to ask Guinevere about her time away, Lily would burst out with another anecdote of organizing actors to travel through the streets performing a play after curfew that everyone watched from their windows, or which young men were preparing for the next tournament, or how the watchman rotations had been improved. Inane, unimportant things, all of which Lily wove into a blanket to wrap Guinevere in until she was ready to talk.

As Fina and Brangien argued over Fina's hair wrap and whether aggressive brushing was needed, Guinevere sat next to Lily and rested her head on the other girl's shoulder. She did not deserve Lily. Tears burned as she imagined telling her the truth.

"Would you like us to stay and take an evening meal with you?" Dindrane asked, looking up from her examination of Guinevere's new sleeves with a critical but curious eye. "I will need to send word to Blanchefleur not to wait for me."

Guinevere remembered that Isolde had said Blanchefleur was locked up. "You eat with Blanchefleur now?"

Dindrane set down Guinevere's dress. "She is living with me."

"What? But you hate her! She was awful to you!"

Dindrane smiled, toying with a lock of her shiny chestnut hair. "Well, I did give her the worst room in the whole house. It looks out on the privy." Then she sighed. "You have been a bad influence on me. I took her in after we had a heart-to-heart about my brother's many mistresses whom she was breaking curfew to check on."

"How is that Guinevere's influence?" Fina asked, leaning forward curiously and then yelping as Isolde's brush caught on a particularly stubborn tangle.

"Because a year ago I would have been giddy over Blanchefleur's miseries. But Guinevere has taught me compassion. It is just as well. Since I am family, my wretched brother cannot claim Blanchefleur has abandoned him or force her to return to him without causing gossip. If I have to be generous to her, at least I will be a thorn in Percival's side."

"She cannot simply leave him?" Fina asked, yanking the brush away from Isolde.

"She is his wife," Dindrane said, as though that explained every-thing.

"Sir Percival is the knight with the eyes like hands, right?" Fina turned to Guinevere.

"Eyes like hands?" Isolde asked.

"You can feel them pawing you even when he is far away." Fina made her hands into claws and aggressively grabbed at the air.

"That would be him," Brangien said, her tone dark. Had she had problems with Sir Percival? Or with any of the men in Camelot? Why did Guinevere not know about this?

"Where is Sir Tristan?" Brangien asked, deftly changing the subject, though it lingered in Guinevere's mind. "He was not on the barge. Is he overseeing the soldiers' camp?"

Guinevere's heart sank. Of course they would not have heard yet. "He stayed in the north. I do not know how long he will be there."

Isolde's face fell. Brangien squeezed her hand. "He will be fine," she said.

Isolde nodded bravely. "I know. But I was so longing for us to all be together again."

There was a knock on the door, and Guinevere sprang to open it, her heart racing as she readied her apology to Lancelot. But she stopped in surprise when she saw it was not her knight behind the door, but her king.

Arthur smiled at the full-to-bursting room. "May I borrow Guinevere?"

"Make it quick, she needs to rest," Brangien snapped, then her eyes went wide as she realized whom she was commanding. "My king," she added hastily.

"Of course." Arthur's smile did not budge. And, Guinevere thought, the look he shared with Brangien was oddly familiar. Conspiratorial, even. They had never spoken much. Had they talked to each other on the docks, when Guinevere was distracted?

Arthur offered his elbow and she took it, but he only escorted her to the next room. She had expected him to take her to Lancelot. As soon as his bedroom door was closed, she turned. "Well?"

"Well?" Arthur echoed questioningly.

"Where is Lancelot?"

"Ah." Arthur sat. But it was not his posture that made her insides tighten in fear and dread. It was the look of determined anticipation on his face. She had seen that look only a few times before—when he was midfight, bracing for a blow.

Guinevere clutched her stomach. "What did you do?"

Arthur held up his hands at the accusation in her voice. "I freed her, as promised."

She more collapsed than sat in the chair opposite him. "Then why do you look like I am about to attack you?"

"Please understand. I knighted Lancelot. She represents the kingdom and the crown. We are only as good as the worst of us, only as strong as the weakest of us."

"Lancelot is neither of those things! She is the best of them!"

"But she lost sight of Camelot, of knighthood. And I understand, I do."

Guinevere knew for a fact he did *not* understand. She had been inside his mind, had felt what he felt. He never lost sight of Camelot, of the kinghood. He had lost a promised son and faced the fear of losing Guinevere, then decided to take over the south to make Camelot stronger.

Arthur moved through the world like his sword, every judgment cutting through nuance and complexity, turning the world into right and wrong, good and evil, living and dead. And he was sincere in his belief that his choices were what kept Camelot going. Sincere, and probably accurate. Guinevere knew Camelot existed because of his determination.

And she knew the costs. So did Arthur. But it was possible to know a cost and still not *understand* it.

"What did you do?" Guinevere asked.

"I sent her north, to aid Sir Tristan."

"What? You cannot do that! She is my knight!"

"She is a knight of Camelot," Arthur said, his voice firm. "That is what you demanded, and what she wanted. I see now I did her no favors by allowing her to be separate from the rest of the knights. It created division, made everything harder for her. I know you think I do not care about Lancelot, but I do. I admire her tremendously, and want what she wants: for her to be the greatest knight and defender of Camelot that she has the potential to be. This is how we do that for her."

Guinevere trembled with rage. Arthur had made this decision without her. He had sent Lancelot away before Guinevere could see her, could discover whether she was forgiven. Could throw herself into Lancelot's embrace, hear her reluctant laughter, see her curls or the dimple in her chin or her determined intensity again.

Guinevere missed Lancelot. All of her, in a way that struck Guinevere with its intensity and specificity.

"Lancelot can never be like the other knights because she is *not* like them. She is my knight, and this is a punishment. I wonder which of us you were intending to punish, though. This was the wrong decision, and you made it alone," Guinevere snapped. She stood. Nectudad saying she knew exactly how much power queens had in the south tugged on her mind, haunting her. "It was the wrong decision *because* you made it alone."

CHAPTER THIRTY-THREE

Guinevere considered her work. Brangien let out a dubious noise. Dindrane, however, seemed pleased. She bent her arms, watching as the split sleeves opened. "And you will all be wearing them, too?"

"Yes. I had hoped to make a bigger impact with them when we arrived at the city," Guinevere said, "but it was overshadowed by the ferry mishap."

"You did make a splash, just not the type you were hoping for." Dindrane laughed. "Well, I like it. It is very coy, covering the wrist but baring the arm."

"Wait until you see my plans for the summer."

Dindrane covered her mouth in mock outrage, then smiled. "I cannot wait."

"Next summer will be wonderful," Brangien said, with slightly more force than was necessary. Guinevere tilted her head and sighed at the unsubtle subtext that she would be here for it. She had been back in Camelot for less than a day, and Brangien had taken every possible opportunity to emphasize how much they all needed her here.

Isolde had taken Fina into the city to explore. She was due to meet Sir Gawain at the arena that afternoon and begin training. Arthur was as good as his word. She would be given a fair chance in the trials. Or an ostensibly fair chance. Guinevere did not doubt that the knights would be much harder on Fina than they would on Lionel, the son of one of their own. But she suspected Fina would not want it any other way. Lancelot certainly would not have.

Lily opened the door. "Oh, hello!" she said. Her cheeks were flushed prettily. Brangien had already altered the pink dress Lily wore so that it had the sleeves Guinevere was determined to make fashionable and acceptable.

"I thought you were with Lionel?" Dindrane said, a note of worry in her voice.

"I was! But he and Sir Bors had a meeting with Arthur, so they escorted me home."

"When?" Guinevere said, suddenly alert.

"They are meeting him now."

Not without Guinevere, they were not. She knew exactly what the meeting was about, and she would be damned if she let it take place without the women it would affect the most. "Dindrane, Lily, with me." Guinevere grabbed the crown, mashed it on her head, and swept down to the throne room.

She threw open the door just as Arthur, Sir Bors, and Lionel sat. They all stood, puzzled.

"My queen?" Arthur asked, taking in her expression with mild alarm. "What is wrong?"

"I was worried we would be late for the meeting," Guinevere said, striding into the room and sitting in the chair next to Arthur's without preamble. "We are discussing the plans for Cameliard, are we not?"

"Uh, yes." Arthur sat. He leaned close to Guinevere while Sir

Bors and Lionel held out chairs for Dindrane and Lily. "You do not need to be here for this."

"If I do not get to make unilateral decisions about my own fate, you do not get to make unilateral decisions about the fates of others. This is not an assignment, this is a *discussion,* and everyone will have a say in their own lives. Especially Lily." Guinevere lifted her chin, not looking at Arthur to gauge his reaction. She would not be guided by his feelings anymore.

Guinevere smiled at the table. "Sir Bors, you are one of the king's most valued and trusted knights. You have proved your valor both on and off the field. Dindrane, you are one of my closest friends and allies, and a powerful force in this city. Lionel, I do not know you, but I hear of your kindness and bravery and very much look forward to watching you complete the trial for knighthood." The young man— only a year younger than Guinevere, but without her burdens— flushed and ducked his head modestly. Guinevere liked him already. But clearly not as much as Lily did. The princess beamed at him with unabashed pride and affection.

"And, Lily," Guinevere said, her own affection warring with deep shame and sadness at the information about herself she was keeping from Lily, "you are my beloved sister. Intelligent, compassionate, and infinitely capable. As you all know, King Arthur decided to extend the borders of Camelot, which means Cameliard is also included."

Lily frowned. "Our father would never accept that."

"He did not," Arthur said, his voice soft. "He was killed in combat."

Lily took several seconds before she spoke again. "And our brothers?"

"They agreed to my terms and joined the ranks of my knights. They are overseeing our ships along the northeastern coast to protect against Saxon invasion."

Lily nodded. "I see."

Guinevere wanted to ask her how she felt. Guinevere herself had no love for the man who had been Lily's father. The memories she had of him—the memories belonging to the real Guinevere—had been bleak at best, violently cruel at worst. Lily had essentially fled Cameliard. But he had still been her father, and now he was dead.

Everyone was watching Lily in gentle anticipation, waiting for her to cry, or rage, or demand more explanation.

"My brothers should not have Cameliard," Lily said.

Arthur leaned back in surprise. "I agree."

"What are your plans for it, then? The people are good, but they have lived a long time under a tyrant, and that poison seeps downward. They need firm guidance as they transition to the rule and order of Camelot."

Arthur glanced at Guinevere. He was asking permission. Both relieved and gratified, she gave him a slight nod. He turned back to Lily. "We would like the four of you to provide it. Sir Bors and Dindrane will go to bring experience, and, Lily, by stepping into the role your father left, you will provide reassurance to your people that they are respected, joining us as part of the kingdom, not as a conquered people."

To Guinevere's surprise, Lily laughed brightly. After how hard the princess had worked to escape Cameliard, Guinevere had expected her to fight returning there, or at least express consternation. Instead, she clapped her hands in delight.

"Oh, he would die all over again if he could hear this. His worthless daughter, in charge of shepherding Cameliard into a new era of peace." Lily's smile was incandescent, but her expression quickly turned determined, accompanied by a tilt of her chin. "I can do this, King Arthur. I promise."

"We know you can." He beamed at her.

"What is Lionel's role?" Dindrane asked, her voice as carefully uncurious as Guinevere had ever heard it. But she could see the hopeful anticipation in her friend's eyes.

Guinevere spoke first. "That is up to Lily. The people are less likely to accept the leadership of an unmarried girl. If it is acceptable to everyone, we will bind the love and alliance between our two families through marriage. But if anyone objects, for any reason, we can find an alternative."

Lionel was sitting as straight as a sword, absolutely rigid, whether with hope or terror, it was impossible to tell. His face was nearly purple. Guinevere suspected he had not drawn a breath since Dindrane asked her question. Dindrane coughed and elbowed Lionel in the side.

"Yes," he gasped. "Yes, I am—I would—that is acceptable. Very acceptable. The most acceptable. I have never heard a more acceptable plan."

Dindrane elbowed him in the side again and he stopped babbling.

Sir Bors was fighting a smile underneath his mustache. He nodded solemnly. "It would be the greatest honor I could ask for."

Guinevere looked at Lily. "It is your decision. I promised you as much, and I will never break that promise."

Lily's strong expression faltered, her lips quivering. "We will be separated."

Guinevere nodded. That was going to happen regardless. Lily was not hers to claim, not forever. But when the real Guinevere was restored, they would be reunited. She was *jealous* of that, jealous she would not get to have Lily's love and fierce protection forever. "We will, for a time."

"But you do not need me." There were tears in Lily's eyes, but a smile in her voice. "Not like you used to. And now Cameliard does."

"It does."

Lily nodded, lifting her chin once more. "As long as Guinevere and

I get to visit each other often, I am both honored and delighted"—she shot a glance under her lashes at Lionel, who looked liable to boil over with happiness—"to serve my king and Camelot in this way."

"Good." Arthur hit the table with an open palm. "That is settled then, and—"

"Lily and Dindrane will be included in all ruling decisions," Guinevere interrupted. "When situations arise and there is not time to wait for letters to and from us, we trust you to represent Camelot with compassion and judgment. We trust the four of you, *together*. Lily and Dindrane are not decorations, they are there to lead alongside you."

Lionel's head bobbed with eager nods. Guinevere looked at Sir Bors. He was older, and the most experienced at the table. She expected him to be flustered, or to disagree. She was surprised when he bowed his head and put his good hand on his heart. Guinevere realized Dindrane was holding his withered hand beneath the table.

"As my queen wishes, and as Cameliard deserves, we will work together."

"Excellent." Guinevere stood. "I will leave the four of you to work out the logistics of the wedding and travel while I take a walk with my sister." Guinevere held out her hand to Lily.

She glanced at Arthur over her shoulder as they left. He was watching her, eyebrows raised, a conversation waiting. She let the door close between them. He could keep waiting.

As soon as they were outside and on the stairs, where they would not be overheard, Guinevere turned to face Lily, taking both her hands in her own so she would be able to feel if Lily was scared or worried or lying.

"I am so sorry. I meant to tell you before. I did not realize he would act so quickly. And now we are alone and there is no pressure. Do you—"

Lily was laughing. She pulled Guinevere in for a hug. Guinevere felt her tension melt away. Lily was happy. Genuinely happy. "I always knew I would marry strategically. Marrying someone I actually like feels like a miracle. And he is not old! And he is so kind. He writes me poetry, Guinevere."

"Is it good poetry?"

Lily laughed, snorting against Guinevere's shoulder. "No, and that makes me like him all the more. And Cameliard! I will get Cameliard." She pulled back to search Guinevere's face. "I am sorry. I feel awful for being so excited, when it means we will be separated."

"Do not feel any guilt at all." Guinevere tucked a strand of Lily's beautiful golden hair behind her ear. "You were born to lead. My only regret is that you should be queen outright, not a representative of Arthur's."

"I disagree. I would much rather rule Cameliard as part of Camelot than try to manage it on my own. What we have here is worth protecting, and I get to bring it to our people. To our home. I get to give them the same haven I found."

"But never forget, it is not a haven for everyone. It can be better. It *should* be better." All this time, Guinevere had tried to be here for Arthur, when really, she should have been here for Camelot.

Lily nodded. "And I will make you visit me, and plot to have you come right before the rainy season, so it is too dangerous to travel for months and months. And I will not feel sorry in the least for stealing you away from your husband." She pressed a kiss to Guinevere's cheek. "Of course you will have to bring Brangien and Isolde. And also Fina. She is very wicked. I like her ever so much. Come, we should plan my wedding dress! I am assuming we will be wed as soon as Lionel is knighted. The tournament is in two weeks. That is not much time!"

Guinevere had not known when she would tell Lily the truth, but hearing Lily make these plans with her *sister* was too much betrayal for Guinevere to manage. If anyone deserved a say, deserved to know what had happened to the real Guinevere, it was the girl who had always fought to protect her. "I need to tell you something. We should go to your rooms."

Lily's expression grew troubled, but she followed Guinevere to her rooms. Guinevere made her sit down. And then Guinevere carefully explained what she had seen. What she had felt. And what had been done to Lily's real sister. It felt like cutting herself open.

No. Worse than that. It felt like cutting *Lily* open. Because not only had the real Guinevere been hurt but now Lily was being hurt, too. Being forced to know what had been done. Maybe it had been a kindness for her not to know, but it was too late.

"Oh," Lily said, when Guinevere was finished. She stared at the floor. For once, her open face was unreadable. "I thought I had gone mad. Your eyes really were brown, as I remembered."

Guinevere nodded, tears filling her eyes as though they could wash away the evidence of the violence that had been done. The evidence of herself, infecting this body. "I am going to fix it, if I can. I will undo this magic and restore your sister."

Lily shook her head. "I think you are wrong. About not being my sister."

Guinevere's heart hurt. Of course Lily would try to find a way to make Guinevere feel better about this. She was still trying to protect her, however she could. But Guinevere could not accept it. "I told you what I saw. What happened to her. I am not that same girl."

"So you changed. We all change. Sometimes those changes are forced on us by the choices of others." Lily held a hand to cut Guinevere off before she could interrupt. "Yes, you are not the same, but you are not so different. You *feel* like my sister."

A soft sigh escaped Guinevere's lips. She loved Lily far more fiercely than their brief acquaintance should account for. But that did not make it right for her to claim the place of the real Guinevere. "But what if I can bring your real sister back?"

"My real sister was taken from me years ago. And even if that wizard and watery witch had not done this, I would not have gotten her back. She would never have married Arthur. Our father would still be alive in Cameliard, and my future would be a bleak nightmare."

"But—"

Lily held up a hand again. She would make an excellent ruler if the way she controlled this conversation was any indication. "Whether you can undo this magic or not, I—I am not certain I care. I appreciate that you want to protect who she was, too. She is worth protecting. But whatever happens, please make sure I have a sister when it is over. And do not forget that *you* are my sister, one way or another."

Guinevere nodded, her chest tight. No one else had listened to her need to restore the real Guinevere. Lily alone understood what—who—had been lost, so Guinevere did not know how to handle having her permission to bring back the real Guinevere . . . or stay.

"I have only ever wanted you to be happy." Lily squeezed Guinevere's arm. "Now, I am going to go see Brangien about my dress. My sister will be by my side when I wed. Right?"

"I promise." Guinevere cleared her throat. She had more to accomplish before she could keep her date with Excalibur. "Brangien will complain about the extra work, but do not listen. She likes making perfect dresses."

"Things do not have to be perfect to be *good*," Lily said, and Guinevere knew she was talking about far more than dresses.

CHAPTER THIRTY-FOUR

Night had long ago fallen. Guinevere and Arthur sat on his bedroom floor to be nearer to the fireplace and its heat. Their voices were rough from speaking for hours, debating Guinevere's ideas for Camelot.

"We do not need that." Arthur rubbed his hands over his face. His slumped, his normally perfect posture gone, and there were shadows under his eyes.

"We *do* need that."

"But the laws are the same for everyone!"

"Tell me, then. What would you do if a woman came to you and told you her husband was beating her?"

"I would bring the man in as well and question him. If it was true, then I would punish him."

"And do you not think that punishing him would make him angrier, and that he would increase his cruelty tenfold?"

Arthur frowned, considering it. "Perhaps."

"And what if the man denied it, and said that his wife was practicing magic?"

"Is she?"

"Does it matter?"

"Well, magic is not allowed."

"Neither is beating your wife, I would hope. What if a man came to you and said his wife had abandoned him, denying him the opportunity for heirs?"

Arthur threw his hands in the air. "I do not know. Why did she leave him?"

"What if a woman came to you and confided that her husband not only beats her but also keeps several mistresses around Camelot? He is unfaithful in both heart and body, and she has no recourse, because she cannot leave him, she cannot marry another, she cannot protect herself?"

"I would protect her. We would take her into the castle."

"And what if the man denied the allegations? What if he was a man you trusted with your very life? A man you had fought side by side with, a man who had vowed to protect you and uphold your laws? Who would you believe?"

Arthur's gaze sharpened. "This is a real example."

Guinevere nodded. "Sir Percival."

Arthur's expression wavered between disgust and disbelief. "He is a good knight."

"That does not make him a good man."

"Where did you get this information?"

"From someone who has no reason to exaggerate on Blanchefleur's behalf. If Blanchefleur were to come forward with these complaints, are there laws that will support her?"

Arthur opened his mouth, then paused before speaking. "Women are protected by their husbands. I never thought to protect them *from* their husbands." He pulled his knees up and wrapped his arms around them. "And the men who would judge her case are men who have fought side by side with Sir Percival, many of whom owe him their lives."

"So now do you see why we also need a council of women? Not to merely advise, but with actual power to make or change judgments? You took away magic, which I understand." Guinevere did understand. Better than anyone, she understood the violence that magic made possible. "But it left many women without tools to protect themselves, and you replaced those tools with the rule of men."

When Arthur looked up, his expression was one of genuine anguish. "Why can people not be good?"

"Because they are complicated. Flawed, and messy, and disastrous, and wondrous." Guinevere smiled sadly. She had once thought Arthur wholly good. Her love for him, her support, her admiration, had been simple. But now she knew him—and herself—better. And it was dangerous to think of anyone as entirely good. Or entirely evil. She suppressed a shudder thinking of Morgana's fate. Thinking of what might have been Mordred's fate, had he not been taken away by Nectudad.

Arthur stretched his long legs out. "It all used to be easier. I had a goal: to overthrow my father and create Camelot. And I did it. But the work has not ended. It has only gotten harder, and more confusing."

Guinevere nudged his leg with her knee. "And you keep making more work for yourself, too." She softened her next statement with a teasing note. "You could have left the south to its own devices."

"Should I have?" His question was so earnest it knocked the wind out of her. He leaned toward her, searching her face. "Did I make the wrong choice?"

Guinevere had no answer for him. She had no doubt that some of the kingdoms—Cameliard, for one, as well as King Mark's, which her own actions had left in turmoil and chaos—were better off. But surely some had been fine before and would now experience devastating growing pains during the transition.

Guinevere placed a hand on Arthur's cheek. "Only time will tell, so we must use that time as best we can to make life on this island better for everyone."

Arthur closed his eyes and sighed. She wished yet again that she could make others feel her the way she felt them. But did she really want Arthur to know how she was feeling? How torn she was, staring into the face she had loved, had wanted to love, and feeling tenderness but no desire? Affection warring with sadness? He would feel her sadness and her regret, and he would know the truth: she was not planning on staying long enough to find out whether he had made the right choice.

Her eyes drifted to Excalibur where it rested against the wall next to the door.

Soon.

Her heart beat faster and harder, racing with fear at the mere thought. But she had made a promise. Things would be settled here soon, as good as she could leave them. She wanted to wait for Lancelot to return, to say goodbye to her knight, but that felt like cheating. Because who was to say that when Lancelot returned, Guinevere would not set another goal, another timeline, pushing the real Guinevere further and further away until she could accept living this stolen life forever?

"When I chose to stay in the south instead of racing back for Camelot," Arthur said, his voice soft, "I knew the risk was losing you. And I did lose you, in a way. Things have changed between us." He put one hand over hers, then smiled sadly. "Whenever I used to look at you, you were waiting. You are not waiting anymore. I am sorry I missed my opportunity."

He did not need magic to understand her after all. Guinevere withdrew her hand, unable to hold both her own feelings and Arthur's. "I wish—" What did she wish? That she had not discovered who she really was? That she and Arthur had come together as husband and wife before she was taken? That she had kept running with Mordred, leaving everything behind?

No. She wished she had known how limited her time was. That she had used all of it better. Loved more fiercely, without fear. Claimed power as queen instead of trying to work always in the shadows. She had squandered so much.

It was not her fault. But that did not make it sting any less.

"I used to wish," she said, finally, "that you were just a boy and I was just a girl and we could meet and fall in love and have a simple life. But then you would not be *you,* and I could not bring myself to wish that."

Arthur's heavy gaze drifted to Excalibur. "That fate was never ours to choose."

Guinevere stood and walked to the sword. She brushed her fingers along the hilt, a cold spike in her head at the touch. "Why can you have magic when no one else can?" she asked, wrapping her hand around the hilt and gritting her teeth against the pain.

"The sword is not magic." Arthur moved to her side and gently pried her fingers from the hilt. "We should sleep. We have a lot of work to do in the morning."

"How is it not magic?"

Arthur sighed and sat on the end of his bed. "It is the opposite of magic. It was made only to end magic, not to create or control or do anything else. It is night swallowing day. Winter ending growth. The silence at the end of a song."

"Who made it?" Guinevere did not take her eyes off the sword. She had to know, had to understand more about it. "I know the Lady left it here, but who crafted it?"

"She did," Arthur snapped, his voice so angry that Guinevere looked at him in surprise. "Is that what you want to hear? It was made by her. Even Merlin did not know how. He tried to replicate it and could not. She made it for me. She gave it to me. If you want to know why, well, we cannot ask her." He lay on his bed, turning so he was not facing her.

The conversation was over.

CHAPTER THIRTY-FIVE

"But is Fina our prisoner?" Lily asked, leaning close to Guinevere. They were walking along Market Street toward the arena. Fina strode confidently ahead of them, and Sir Gawain was struggling to keep pace with her. "No one knows whether they should invite her to dine with them or shun her, or something in between."

Guinevere shook her head. "Arthur brought her here as leverage against her sister, Nectudad. So in a sense, she is a prisoner. But she pledged loyalty and vowed to become a knight. Our goal is to support that, and encourage everyone else to support it, as well. I am treating it as an alliance in the hopes that someday it can turn into that. Regardless, I love her very much and want her to be happy here, if she can be."

"You certainly do like to collect the odd ones," Lily said, wrinkling her nose with a laugh. "No one can figure you out."

Guinevere's smile was tight and false. "There is very little to figure out." There was so little to her, after all. How many months had she existed? Each of them taken from someone else. "Thank you for your suggestions for the women's council, by the way. You have such good judgment."

Lily beamed and drew Guinevere closer so that they walked arm in arm. "Really, all we need is Brangien. She has been training her entire life to judge everyone who crosses her path."

Guinevere laughed. "Her skills are unparalleled."

"Will you tell me?" Lily asked, her voice suddenly soft. "Before you try. So I know. Every time I see you, I am afraid that you will be different."

"I will try soon," Guinevere said. "I am sorry I cannot be more specific than that. I have to be careful, because Arthur and Brangien would try to stop me."

Lily nodded. "I understand."

Brangien was waiting for them up ahead, cutting off their conversation. She and Arthur had teamed up to make sure Guinevere was never alone. But there was no chance of being alone at the arena.

Fina practically skipped inside. Sir Gawain was going to show her how the combat was structured. Though she had been in many battles already in her young life, this type of fighting was different. Guinevere did not want to leave Fina's success to chance. Fortunately, neither did Sir Gawain.

Brangien and Lily began discussing wedding plans as they settled into the booth overlooking the arena floor but soon left to buy fabric, with several reassurances from Guinevere that she would not leave the arena alone.

Guinevere watched Fina training. Axes could be used, but knives could not, so Gawain was helping her with swordplay. Fina was a quick study and always managed to look like she was having fun down in the dirt flinging weapons around. Her turn was up quickly, though. The arena floor was on a carefully scheduled rotation. During Camelot's brief time sealed away from the world, young men had needed something to do, and the next tournament would be filled with a record number of aspirants.

Fina loped up to the box to join Guinevere. She snorted with laughter as she watched the new group. "Nectudad would whip them silly, posturing like that instead of focusing on the actual attack."

"How are you doing?"

Fina shrugged, rolling out her shoulders and neck. "It is a different style than I am used to, but I like learning it. And I am confident I can beat at least three knights. Especially if Gawain is one of them. He is quite in love with me."

"Who can blame him?"

Fina smiled slyly. "Certainly not me. I am very desirable."

"But how are you *really* doing? With everything?" Guinevere turned so they were facing each other, not the arena floor.

"It is . . . a lot." Fina's smile dropped away, her gaze turning inward. "When it is too much, I imagine I am where I want to be and who I want to be with. It gives me strength. Here, try it with me." She reached out and took Guinevere's hands, then closed her eyes.

Guinevere did the same.

"You can be anywhere you want," Fina said, her voice soft and dreamy. "Look around. Where are you? Who are you with?"

The where was nebulous. Guinevere could not settle on a place. Camelot, a forest, a golden field, all blurred together. But when she turned, the person her mind gave her was both a shock and no surprise at all.

"Is it Arthur or Mordred?" Fina whispered mischievously.

Guinevere opened her eyes and lost the image of Lancelot standing in front of her. She was the person whom Guinevere longed to be with, the one she did not want to leave behind. She had been able to walk away from both Arthur and Mordred, but giving up herself without one last moment with Lancelot? Guinevere could barely breathe, thinking about it.

"Neither," she said with a sad smile.

"Really." Fina leaned back, a puzzled look on her face. "Was it me? Because I do not like you that way, but I understand my allure."

Guinevere laughed. "It was not you."

Fina nodded. "Well, I am sorry for both Arthur and Mordred. But there are all different types of love. Some burn so hot and bright they devour themselves. Some flare and then settle into friendship. Some build for years, becoming the foundation of a life. My parents had that. I think that is what broke my father, losing my mother. It turned him hard and brittle, and the Dark Queen seeped into the cracks."

Guinevere nodded. What she had had with Mordred was real and wonderful, but even then she had known she could not build a life around being with him. He had known it, too, she suspected. And while she still loved Arthur and cared about him, she realized now that she had been trying to form an identity based on her belief in him. It was wrong, and it hurt them both.

When she had been in the north, Lancelot was the one person she could not bear to be apart from forever. Maybe because Lancelot had always seen her and accepted her. There had been no expectations of what Guinevere would be to her, no demands other than that Guinevere be the best version of herself. The one most deserving of a knight like hers.

Mordred had not held her here. Arthur would not, either. But the more Guinevere thought about leaving Lancelot, the more she wanted to stay. To keep this body and life forever.

"Are you crying?" Fina asked, worried.

Guinevere wiped beneath her eyes. If it were possible to expel the Lady of the Lake by crying her out, surely that would have happened by now.

Guinevere had to try Excalibur tonight, or she never would.

❧

One last time she slipped through the secret passage between her room and Arthur's. She ran her fingers along the stone, thinking of the Lady who carved it all. Thinking of the girl who stood in this same passage on her first night in Camelot, so certain of herself and her purpose. The girl who gave her name to the candle's flame and blew it out.

It did not matter what that name had been. It had never been hers.

She hated the Lady and she pitied that nameless girl, and tonight she would end both of them.

Arthur's room was dim, the fire burned down to flickering embers. Guinevere could see his dark shape in the bed, the broad span of his shoulders, the trim waist. She knew how it would feel to curl up next to him, to revel in closeness, to hope for more. She really would miss him. But she had done everything she could for now. She dared not risk more delay.

I am sorry, Lancelot, she thought.

Excalibur was propped against the wall, where it would be easy for Arthur to spring up and grab it. He never hung it, never displayed it. It was odd, now that she thought of it, how little he showcased his wondrous sword.

Taking a deep breath, Guinevere sat on the cold floor and set the sheathed sword on her lap. If she fell when the magic was undone, this way it would not injure the real Guinevere's body. Guinevere had not been the most careful steward, and she regretted that. But oh, she had loved life. She gathered her memories close to her heart, trying to live one last moment in them.

The first time she saw Arthur.

The look on Mordred's face as he danced backward up the hill, teasing her.

The sense of rightness that had flooded her when she took Lancelot's hand.

Laughing with Brangien. Watching Isolde and Brangien in quiet moments. Making Lily smile. Dindrane's joy during her wedding. Fina's horse-startling laugh.

Kisses both stolen and freely given.

She wished she had been able to get word to Lily that tonight was the night. She selfishly wished Lily were here with her now, so she did not have to do this alone. But she was not alone, not with all her memories held so tightly.

She filled her heart with Camelot and who she had been here, and drew the sword.

Nausea overwhelmed her instantly and she fell backward, clutching the sword, trying not to vomit and wake Arthur. She held on to consciousness, fighting against the swirling dread and numbness that radiated from the blade. But she was still herself. There was no sense of loosening, of being pushed out by the real Guinevere, of plunging toward nothingness.

The hateful sword was not doing its job.

Guinevere gritted her teeth. The Lady had made this wretched thing, and Guinevere *would* use it to rid this body of the Lady and her magic.

She slid her hand along the blade, letting it bite into her skin. A terrible cold flooded her. It was not the same as the Lady flooding into the real Guinevere, washing her away and replacing her with something else. Or even the poison of the Dark Queen, or the possession of Morgana. It was the cold of a void, the finality of death.

Guinevere had made a mistake.

She fell into darkness.

CHAPTER THIRTY-SIX

A hushed argument pulsed through Guinevere's pounding head, each wave of sound creating a wave of pain. It took her several bleary seconds to remember. The sword. Her determined attempt to restore the real Guinevere. Determined, but failed. She was still here. At least she was not dead. She twitched with horror at the idea that she might have killed this body that was not hers, and the movement sent a rush of nausea through her system.

"Guinevere?" Brangien snapped.

Guinevere peeled her eyelids open. It was still night. Brangien was hovering over her, her candlelit face a mask of cold rage.

"Come get me if her bandage needs to be replaced," Brangien said over her shoulder. "And *you* have lost the right to sleep alone," she added, delivering a sharp pinch to Guinevere's arm. The fear Brangien felt was delivered in far sharper form in that brief touch than in her words.

"I am sorry," Guinevere whispered. And she was. Both for the pain she had caused her friend and for her failure to release the real Guinevere.

Brangien left, and the bed shifted as Arthur sat on the edge of it, his back to her.

"What were you thinking?" he said, exhausted.

"I thought—" Guinevere swallowed hard as her head swam. She lowered her voice to a whisper again. "I thought if the Lady did this magic to bind herself in this body, the magic of the sword could undo it."

"You are human, Guinevere. The only way Excalibur will unmake you is if it stabs you. Is that what you want? To bleed to death? To take yourself away because you cannot live with the guilt of what happened to bring you here?"

"No. No." Guinevere curled around herself, drawing her knees up and cradling her bandaged hand. It throbbed with her heartbeat. "But Excalibur always makes me sick. And in the meadow, when I woke the Dark Queen, it was going to end me, I could feel it." Mordred had used it against Arthur, putting Guinevere between Excalibur and the Dark Queen as a shield.

"That entire meadow was filled with magic," Arthur said. "It was pouring off you and the Dark Queen, because she was using you. So yes, it was enough that the sword might have ripped the rest of the magic out of you and killed you. It devours unbound magic, wild magic. It makes you feel sick because you have magic all around you. But it does not *end* you, because most of the time the magic is contained in your body. Your very human, very fragile body."

Guinevere closed her eyes. This had been her last hope. Short of freeing Merlin from his cave and somehow forcing his hand, she had no other recourse. No way to save the innocent girl whose body she inhabited. "I cannot save her."

"Did you really think a sword could save anyone? Swords do not save. They kill, Guinevere."

She reached out and placed a hand on Arthur's back. He did not move. "Why do you think of the sword as a curse?" she asked.

"What?" At last he turned. It was too dark to see his face, only his shape.

"Morgana sent me into your head when I was with her. And you thought of Excalibur as a gift but also a curse. What is the curse? Is it that it ends magic?" Maybe if she understood more about the sword, they could figure something out together. If Arthur would help her, if he could understand why she needed to do this . . .

"The curse is that because I was given Excalibur, I *have* to wield it. I cannot turn my back on the sword or what it represents. I carry the weight of Camelot, the weight of this entire island, every moment of every day. The curse is not that it ends magic. It is that it ends *lives*. But only the lives I choose. I have to make that choice again, and again, and again. And it gets easier. That is the worst part of all."

Guinevere felt understanding settle on her, so heavy she could barely breathe. The sword was only a tool. It was useless without someone to wield it. And that burden had fallen on Arthur alone.

No, not fallen. Falling was passive. This burden had been carefully, deliberately put on Arthur's shoulders by Merlin and Nimue.

Tonight, she had tried to leave Arthur even more alone than he already was. Sorrow and guilt flooded her. They tasted like the warm water of the Lady, washing away a fragile, scared girl. Guinevere knew, without question, that the real princess, the one she had replaced, would not have been able to help Arthur bear this weight. The real Guinevere had wanted to become someone stronger so that she could. She had seen a vision in the water of who she would need to be to walk at Arthur's side, and even though she had not understood what she was agreeing to, she had wanted it to happen. It did not make the real Guinevere weak, or bad, or worthless. But she was not made for being queen of Camelot.

Guinevere had *literally* been made for it.

She put her hands to her mouth to muffle her sobs. She smelled the blood, the iron tang of humanity, from beneath her bandage.

Whoever she was, whatever she was, she was strong enough to rule at Arthur's side. To ensure that he did not make these choices alone. That the curse of the sword did not become so heavy and twisted that he became another Pendragon.

Excalibur could be her curse, too.

She had thought she was choosing Arthur, choosing Camelot, when she came here the first time, and then when she returned after leaving the blood-soaked meadow of the Dark Queen. But she had never really committed. Never really seen herself as the queen, as Arthur's partner.

She was not his protector. But she could be his *partner,* if she could accept the cost.

"I have to choose," she said. "I have to choose to let her go. She was innocent, Arthur, and I have to choose to be complicit in her ending."

Arthur drew her close and held her in the darkness. He did not say anything, and she was glad, because nothing could make this feel better. Nothing *should* make this feel better.

Guinevere was deciding to take her first life in the name of Camelot.

CHAPTER THIRTY-SEVEN

The day was gloriously warm, an autumn equivalent of false promises whispered between lovers. Tomorrow would probably be sharp and chill, but for now Guinevere luxuriated in the feel of the sun on her skin. At the very top of the mountain castle, in the garden Arthur had shown her, she could almost pretend she was out of the city.

Lily sat beside her, humming as she put the last touches on her wedding dress. Ever loyal, she had even included the split sleeves that Guinevere was quickly making fashionable.

The tournament was tomorrow. Lily's wedding would be the following day, assuming Lionel was knighted, which Guinevere had little doubt of. The days since her failed attempt with Excalibur had been filled with planning for the tournament and wedding, building her council of women, and arguing with Arthur over how to govern half an island.

Guinevere sighed and rubbed her injured palm. The healing process was at a dreadful itching stage. Lily took Guinevere's hand and traced her fingers down the angry red line left by Excalibur.

"I am not upset," Lily said, surprising Guinevere. After Guinevere had told Lily that her last hope of restoring the real princess had failed, they had not spoken of it again. Guinevere had thought they never would. As much as she wanted to talk about it, she would not place the burden of listening on Lily.

"I gave up on her, though." Guinevere had wrapped guilt around herself like chain mail. Some days she felt as though she were back in the lake, the weight of it dragging her to the bottom. Some days, though, it felt more like armor, reminding her of how hard she had to fight, how much she had to do, because she was here and the other Guinevere was not.

Lily squeezed Guinevere's hand, then tucked it in the crook of her elbow as she looked up at the view. "I have seen you working every hour of daylight and far too many hours of the night, too. You do not give up on anything. You—she—" Lily shook her head with a frustrated frown. "I am sorry, I cannot see you as two separate people. You always wanted to help everyone around you, and not having the power to do that broke your heart. Now you have the power, and you are using it. *That* is my sister. *You* are my sister."

Guinevere leaned her head on Lily's shoulder. "I wish you were staying in Camelot."

"I do, too, sometimes. But I want to help like you are. And I am determined to obliterate our father's legacy from Cameliard."

"You will." Guinevere had no doubts. "I could use you on my council, though. Oh! That reminds me. I want to add Ailith."

"Who is Ailith?"

"Right now, she is working in the kitchens. But she was raised outside of Camelot by women who were banished for using magic. I think her perspective will be useful."

Lily laughed. "You are going to seat a kitchen maid next to Lady Tegau Eurfron, Sir Caradoc's infinitely prideful wife? Now I really do wish I could stay, just to watch."

"And now I wish I could go with you, just to escape." Guinevere cast her eyes over the land beyond the lake. The fields were brown, already past the harvest and slowly preparing to sleep for the winter. A plume of dust drew her gaze to a rider streaking toward Camelot at a gallop.

Coming from the north.

Guinevere stood. "That looks like news," she said. They had had no word from Sir Tristan in the north, which meant she had had no word from Lancelot. Hoping desperately she was right, but not daring hope that the rider was Lancelot herself, Guinevere tracked the horse's progress all the way to the ferry as she helped Lily pack up her things. After delivering Lily and her supplies back to her room, Guinevere hurried down the exterior stairs.

Arthur was not in the castle. He was at the arena today. It was not quite proper for a queen to be seen running down the street, but Guinevere did not care. The castle guard attending her could barely keep up.

Guinevere was used to going to her observation box, but instead she went straight to the arena floor, reaching Arthur before the messenger. Arthur was there, surrounded by boys a few years younger than himself, laughing with such innocent happiness that it hurt Guinevere to hear. He was barely older than the boys and yet he had been carrying Camelot since he was a child.

Guinevere put a hand over her heart, imagining the real Guinevere nestled there somewhere. Every day, she would have to choose to keep this life. Every day, for the rest of her stolen life, she would have to choose herself over the girl whose body she had taken. She would have to choose Arthur and Camelot.

"My queen!" Arthur said, beaming. Other than their governing meetings, they had not spent much time together. Guinevere did not want to be in the same room as Excalibur, and she also did not want to find comfort in Arthur's strength. She needed to feel this pain. To live with her discomfort as a reminder to never take her existence and her duty for granted.

"A messenger is coming. From the north," she said. Arthur grew instantly serious, and he waved farewell to the youths before hurrying to her side. He apparently felt the same urgency she did, because as soon as the soldier—not Lancelot, not anyone Guinevere knew—delivered the sealed parchment, Arthur handed it to Guinevere and drew her to a shadowed alcove of the arena. She slid her fingers under the wax, breaking the seal, then held the letter out so they could read it at the same time. The letter was short, the ink splotched, clearly written in haste.

"'We are marching toward Camelot, two days behind the messenger, a day ahead of the Dark Queen's army,'" Guinevere read. "'Meet us on the border of the forest with Excalibur. Leave your men in the city, where they are safe. Trust no one, especially your own soldiers in the north. They are not yours anymore. Tell the queen the infection is spreading. Yours in alliance and fealty.'" Guinevere read the signatures, then looked up in surprise. "Nectudad, daughter of Nechtan and ruler of the people of the Branching River, and Sir Tristan."

"What more can you tell us?" Arthur said, looking up at the waiting soldier. The poor man was exhausted and covered in dirt and sweat.

"Nothing, my king. I was stationed at the border to the north. Another messenger, injured, gave me the letter, but no other information."

Arthur nodded and dismissed him. "Someone has taken my men, or they have defected. And Sir Tristan's handwriting looks odd." Arthur ran his fingers over the shaky letters. "Either he was forced to write the letter or he is injured. Or Nectudad wrote it. What does he mean, the infection is spreading?"

"It is a reference to when he was bitten by a wolf in the forest and I burned the fever out of him." Guinevere frowned, puzzled. "I wonder if he included it to prove that he is the one writing it, of his own volition?"

"But we do not know that for certain."

"No," Guinevere agreed, warnings buzzing through her like a swarm of bees. "Can you imagine any circumstance where your men would defect to Nectudad, or to the Dark Queen?"

"No." Arthur's expression was grim. "It looks like they are working together, but is Sir Tristan doing it willingly? All we know for certain is that Sir Tristan is telling me not to trust my own men, Nechtan's daughter will be within striking distance of Camelot in two days, and the Dark Queen has an army."

All the warmth of the day disappeared, and Guinevere could feel the phantom sensation of spider legs crawling on her skin. *I will be everywhere.*

CHAPTER THIRTY-EIGHT

Guinevere tugged distractedly on one of her braids. Midnight had long since passed and they were quickly burning toward morning. The arguments and discussions had gone in circles so many times she was amazed they had not worn a groove around the table.

"But we cannot trust a Pict," Sir Percival said.

"Fina has proved herself!" Sir Gawain protested.

"She has," Guinevere said, holding up a hand. "But she has not been in contact with Nectudad since her sister left for the coast, so she can offer no insight. Nectudad is honorable, but she is also fiercely protective of her people, so I cannot say whether this is a ploy for revenge or an attempt to get Fina back. Fina was not even mentioned in the letter. And I trust Sir Tristan. If he wrote this, I am inclined to believe it is not a trick."

"I am, as well," Arthur said. "But we all know there are points at which a man can be broken."

"We meet them, as requested," Sir Bors said. "But we take a full force and send some tomorrow to hide and lie in wait should we need to surround or ambush. We know the numbers Nectudad can command, and, assuming she has not turned the soldiers we left in the north against us, she cannot hope to prevail in battle."

"But we have no idea why Sir Tristan would tell our people to stay in the city, where they are safe, and we do not know where the Dark Queen found an army," Guinevere added.

"If she has one," Sir Bors countered.

Arthur nodded. "I think Sir Bors's suggestion is the best course of action. We will face whatever comes, and be prepared for anything. I have sent scouts out, too, to find the force from the north before they arrive and bring back numbers and information for us. I wish Sir Tristan had said more. It worries me that he did not." Arthur tilted his head from side to side, stretching his neck. "Now, since we still have time, we should finalize the plans for tomorrow's tournament. It appears we will need all the knights we can get in the very near future."

Guinevere stood. This, at least, she did not need to be present for. The knights all inclined their heads as she walked to the door. Arthur opened it for her. "Do not speak to Fina of this," he said. "We cannot be certain of her loyalties."

"I understand." It made Guinevere sad, but Arthur was right. Nectudad had been no ally of hers. If Nectudad was planning something, Guinevere would keep Fina out of it. It was the best way she had to protect her friend.

Instead of returning to her chambers, Guinevere took this opportunity for solitude. Since Guinevere's attempt with Excalibur, Brangien had gone back to sleeping in her room instead of the side room, and when Brangien was not with her, Lily was, or Fina, or Dindrane, or Arthur. Guinevere climbed the exterior stairs, her feet taking her unconsciously to Mordred's alcove.

Oh, to be back in the wilderness, with nothing to think about but losing themselves together. She would never go back to that, but tonight, if she closed her eyes and imagined herself elsewhere, she suspected she would end up in Mordred's arms.

Guinevere scowled at the lake as it spread, deceptively placid, beneath the night sky. She felt as wild and dangerous as a lightning storm, ready to strike at a moment's notice. Or to evaporate into a mere drizzle, fading without a trace. She sat with a sigh, resting against the wall and closing her eyes. She was so wretchedly tired. Tomorrow would be exhausting, and the next day would be even worse.

When she opened her eyes, everything was black. But not the blackness of night, which was something. This was the blackness of absence. The blackness of nothing.

"Here you are," Mordred said. "Late, as usual."

Guinevere rushed to him. His hair was beautiful, brushing his shoulders, and he wore a fine tunic of dark green. She studied his face, looking for some hint as to what had happened since they had been separated. "Where are you? Are you safe?"

He did not hold out his arms to her, as she had expected him to. Instead, he folded them and looked down at her with half-lidded eyes. "You mean unlike my mother."

Guinevere saw Excalibur piercing Morgana's heart again and again and again, the violent ending repeating forever in her mind. He knew, then. "I am so sorry. I—"

"She was right about you. She said it would never work, and here we are."

"What would never work?" Guinevere searched his face and then wished she had not. The malice and derision there were almost palpable. She took an instinctive step back, confused.

"I said **we** could manipulate you. Make you so confused and vulnerable that you would not know the sun was shining when standing beneath its noonday brilliance. And it worked." He laughed bitterly. "It was not even difficult. You believed I was there to protect you, believed that I would ever work against my mother and grandmother. You even thought I drank a *truth* potion. But that was not as pathetic as promising you I would not kiss you until you asked, knowing you would. And you did." His cruel smile dropped, eyes narrowing like knives. "But it worked too well, because you were so incredibly weak, so hopelessly incapable, that Arthur had to rescue you yet again. You might not have seen what was happening, but he had no doubts about us. My dear mother paid that price. I had the sense to leave early." He sighed, flicking his gaze up and down her with brutal dismissiveness. "I am finished with you. I have tried every way possible to make you useful, but other than your convenient blood helping my grandmother take form it has proved impossible. You really are useless."

Guinevere could not understand what she was hearing, what she was seeing. Here was the eel, the man everyone had warned her about. Had everything else been fake? A lie? Their history was rewriting itself with cold cruelty. Everything he had said and done, all the moments of truth and intimacy. Holding each other against the cold and the dark. All lies. Manipulations.

No. That was the Mordred the world had warned her about. But not the one she had experienced. And she trusted herself, if nothing else. She had *felt* him. Had understood him. "You crossed the line above Camelot. The magic trip wire I made that would kill anyone who intended me harm."

Mordred let out a dry laugh. "You are also not very good at magic, I am afraid."

"No." Guinevere shook her head, desperation rising. "No, you are— This is—"

"A lie? Everything is. Forget about me. I certainly intend to forget about you and how much of my time I wasted here." He reached up to his hair, to where hers was knotted in, connecting them.

"Wait—" Guinevere held up a hand, her heart racing. This *was* the eel. But the eel had been a pretense. A lie he told to survive, to try to save someone he loved.

Mordred was lying to her, and she did not know why. But she would not let him leave before she did. "Do you want to know what your mother's last words were?"

Mordred froze, and in that moment the facade cracked. He could not hide the raw pain on his face, his deep and agonized mourning.

"Why are you trying to make me hate you?" Guinevere whispered.

He struggled to replace the mask, but his face would not obey. His sorrow bled into fear and he stepped to her, grasping her painfully tight by the shoulders. "People *die*. People die all the time. It is not special, or unusual, and it is only a tragedy if they do not deserve it. I deserve it. Remember that."

"What are you talking about?"

"I brought it on myself, and you owe me nothing. You have given me so much more than I should have asked already."

Guinevere shook her head. "What are you saying? Why are you telling me this?"

"Forget about me. Stay. Stay with Arthur." Mordred's intensity was broken with a frown like he had tasted something foul. "Well, perhaps do not stay with Arthur. I hate that, and I always will. But stay with Lancelot, stay in Camelot."

"Mordred, what happened? Where are you?"

There was a sound like the soft fluttering of darkness. Mordred's eyes locked on hers, burning in the darkness. "Stay. Promise you will stay. And I lied—please, I do not want you to forget me. Think of me often. Think of me at the most inappropriate times. But think of me honestly, and remember that I am answering for my own mistakes."

Guinevere felt something land on her arm. She tried to look down, but Mordred pressed his forehead against hers, whispering urgently, "She wants to remake the whole world, to become humans since she cannot defeat them. Stay in Camelot. Stay with Excalibur. Let her beat herself against this rock until she fades to nothing. I was wrong to restore her." His voice broke, and her heart with it, as he said, "I am forever loving things that cannot love me back."

He brushed his lips against hers, and then, before she could decide if she wanted to kiss him, he was swallowed by the darkness.

But this was her dreamspace. Her mind. Darkness could not swallow him if she did not let it. She wanted sunlight, forest, their cottage. A chance for Mordred to explain. A real goodbye. They both deserved that. She closed her eyes and focused on light.

The rustling whisper of wings grew louder. She could feel them now, on her arms. She looked down to find herself covered with black moths. And there, in front of her—Mordred had not been swallowed by the darkness, he had been covered by it. He stood frozen just a few steps from her, his outline fluttering gently with the movement of wings.

Something new, a voice like the scales of a snake sliding over rocks said. *You changed everything.*

"Where is Mordred?" Guinevere asked, terrified.

He is whole now. Soon everyone will be. I will come for you, too. Do not fear.

"Arthur can stop you. Excalibur can stop you."

The sword cannot undo the knots you showed me how to tie. Come. We will kiss you, and you will join us, and everything will be soft and dark and gentle and whole.

The thing that was no longer Mordred held out its arms and walked toward her.

Guinevere ripped herself from the dream, the sensation of crawling things on her arms lingering. She looked down and found it was not a remnant of the dream. Screaming, she shook herself, swatting at her arms and her face, trying to banish the smudges of fluttering darkness, every beat of their wings promising death.

CHAPTER THIRTY-NINE

The remaining moths dropped to the floor, dead, as soon as Guinevere rushed inside the castle, killed by her iron knots that undid magic.

But not *all* magic. Not the magic that bound the Lady of the Lake into the real Guinevere's body, because it was shielded by her humanity. Fed by the iron in her blood to form a perfect hybrid of magic and mortal. That was why Excalibur made her sick but did not end her. That was what the Dark Queen had figured out.

"Arthur!" she shouted, bursting into his room. It was empty.

She ran down to the great hall and found him sitting at the large, round table, conferring with Sir Bors and a few other knights.

One look at her face and he swept his arm as though brushing away the rest of the conversation. "Very good. We have all earned some rest tonight." He stood and walked calmly to her side, escorting her out of the room as though nothing was wrong.

"What is it?" Arthur whispered as soon as they were in the hall.

"Not here." They made their way up the interior stairways, smiling and nodding at the night guards, then entered Arthur's room.

As soon as the door was shut behind them, Guinevere collapsed into a chair. "The Dark Queen did it. She learned Merlin's magic. She has used it to take human form."

"Who gave you this information?"

Guinevere sighed, reaching up to where her hair was neatly plaited thanks to Isolde and Brangien. This would not be easy. "Mordred. In a dream. Before the Dark Queen took him over."

Arthur's jaw clenched at the name. "He can talk to you in dreams now, too? How?"

"It is not important." The memory of him covered in those moths, the Dark Queen reaching for her through him, made her want to scream. "I saw him, and saw the Dark Queen take him over."

Arthur sat, his expression one of shock. "He used you to give the Dark Queen form. He kidnapped you. And you believe him when he comes to you with a story of imminent danger that only you can save him from?"

Guinevere shook her head. "He did not come to me for help. He—he told me that I should stay with Excalibur."

Arthur lurched back to his feet and paced, his jaw twitching with each step. "It sounds like a perfectly orchestrated trick to get you away from safety."

"By telling me to stay and let him die?"

"Yes!" Arthur threw his hands in the air. "He knows your goodness. How much you will risk to help others. And he is using it as a tool."

"But the Dark Queen does not lie. She does not need to. And he was not lying, either. Not about this. She has taken him, and he would rather I stay here, safe, and let it happen."

"If that is true, then good. He is at last doing the right thing."

"But we cannot let him die!"

"What do you think would have happened if he had been in the forest when I found you?" Arthur's tone was soft, with no accusation. His eyes were sad, but there was no reluctance in them. No apology.

Guinevere took a deep breath to calm herself, to turn her mind away from Mordred joining Morgana in the ever-repeating loop of death. "We have to find Mordred and stop whatever the Dark Queen has done to him. Free him from her."

"What is there to stop?" Arthur held up his hands at her incredulous expression. "Whether set by Mordred or the Dark Queen, this is a trap. For *you*. But she has nothing that can hurt us. And I realize now, that is what she is. Nothing. She had to use men to take you because she could not hurt me on her own. When I appeared, she ran. There was no attempt to face me, no fight. I rule the island that she would have destroyed. If Mordred is telling the truth, then he is right. The best way he can atone for bringing the Dark Queen back is by keeping you far away from her. You are safe, and she is nothing but the dregs of chaos draining from the land. If she has bound herself in Mordred, so be it. She will live and die as a human now."

"She would not do that. There has to be a bigger plan. She told me she would be everywhere. I felt her promise in those words, in her threat. And if we do not help, Mordred will be lost." Guinevere could not deny that was part of her panic. She did not want Mordred to die.

Arthur's face fell. He might have accepted Mordred's death, but it still affected him. "I am sorry for it, and glad I did not have to be the one to end him. But I will not risk anything for his life, least of all you."

Guinevere stood, twisting away from Arthur when he held out his hands to her, taking over his pacing, instead. "This is not the right decision. I can feel it. I said I would come back as queen to fight the Dark Queen. And you *promised* me that I could." There was something she was missing, something she had not figured out. The Dark Queen would not merely bind herself into a human body. What then? Try to lead armies? Try to rule as Mordred? If anything, she should have bound herself into Arthur's body. It did not make sense.

She said she would be everywhere. And in the dream, Mordred said something odd. He said . . .

"She wants to be *humans*. Plural. Sir Tristan said the infection is spreading. He was not referring to his own infection. He was referring to the infection of the Dark Queen!" Guinevere's mind spun with the terrible sense of it all. "She saw what Merlin and Nimue did, and she figured out how to do it without losing herself like Nimue. That is why you cannot trust any of your soldiers in the north. She is binding herself into every human she can, building an army where her magic is sealed away from Excalibur by skin and blood and bone."

"But—"

"I am right. I know I am right about this."

"You are assuming Mordred was telling the truth. And that Nectudad can be trusted."

"Yes! I am assuming both of those things because this foe is bigger than any of us. In the face of the Dark Queen sweeping like a plague to consume and possess every human on this island, we are all allies now! There is no telling how many people she has already infected. I cannot undo this magic!" Guinevere stopped pacing. She knew what had to be done. "We need Merlin."

Arthur sighed. He sat on a chair and pulled off his boots, then removed his sword belt and outer tunic. Finally, he pulled off his plain silver circlet, holding it in his hands and staring at it. "I think you still hope for some way to save that girl. But she is gone, and she is never coming back. Merlin can never—"

"This is not about me! We cannot win without Merlin. I wish there were another way, any other way. I know exactly how much harm he is willing to do. But we must free him."

Arthur placed the crown on his chair as he stood. "I know he was not good, Guinevere. And yet I also know everything I am, every life I can improve and save, is because of who he made me. So I will follow *all* his wishes, including that I never give him freedom again."

"What? When did he ask that?"

"You did not read the rest of his letter where he told me to keep you safe. He also asked me to ensure that he was never again allowed to walk this land. The Lady's power is gone. The Dark Queen is losing, whatever plot she may have right now. The island belongs to men, and Merlin knows better than anyone how to use men. He saw what it would take to give me power, and he also saw what would happen if he remained at my side. Or, worse, if he took the sword and crown for himself." Arthur held out his arms, inviting Guinevere into them, his eyes begging her to join him. "He put you at my side instead. Please. Help me. Help me be what our people need me to be."

Guinevere's feet moved of their own accord, and Arthur wrapped her in an embrace. Her head pressed against his chest, the steady beat of his heart more familiar than her own.

This was the promise in the water, the one that lured the real Guinevere to her doom, the one that both she and the Lady of the Lake wanted so much they became something new. The promise of this Arthur, and a Guinevere strong enough to stand beside him.

But that had been *their* choice. Not hers.

"We have to try," Guinevere said. "If I am right, it is the only way to stop her without fighting an entire army."

"I have fought armies before. I can do it again."

"Not like this! They will be your own men, your own soldiers, turned against you by the Dark Queen."

Exhaustion pooled beneath Arthur's eyes. He released her. "They *have* been my own men. My friends. My father. It is *always* like this. Every war is. Any man I fight could just as easily be my family, my knight, my friend, were we not on opposite sides."

"But fighting her army will be fighting symptoms. We have to destroy the infection itself. We need Merlin."

Arthur shook his head. "I will take my men and meet Nectudad and Sir Tristan. Once we have more information, we can plan how to defeat this threat. If it *is* what you think it is, and not simply a trick plotted by the Dark Queen and her grandson."

"If you are wrong, no one will be safe!"

"If I am wrong, Camelot will still be safe. When I leave, we will seal the city as you did before."

Guinevere narrowed her eyes. "You mean you will be on the outside, and I will stay behind the barrier."

"I can fight knowing my city and my queen are safe, and that, if anything happens, Camelot still has a true leader. I have no heir, Guinevere. I have *you*. Camelot has you. And you are what we all need. Now, will you come to bed?"

"Too much time spent around your sword," Guinevere said, offering Arthur a tight smile as she gestured to where Excalibur stood sentry against the wall. "It makes my head ache. I will see you in the morning." She bent over and pressed a gentle kiss against his cheek, then walked out before she could see his expression. Arthur and Brangien still would not let her sleep alone, but she would not, could not, take comfort sleeping next to Arthur tonight.

Her bedroom was dark, no light from beneath the door to the sitting room that had been converted to a bedroom for Isolde and Brangien. Brangien must have assumed Guinevere would spend the night in Arthur's room. Guinevere groped, trying to find her cloak without lighting a candle. Arthur was wrong. She knew it in her bones. And she did not have time to convince him.

She would have to do it without him.

CHAPTER FORTY

Only a monster could help them undo the magic of another monster. The idea of seeing the wizard now that she knew the truth, now that she remembered what the real Guinevere had endured at his hands, made Guinevere want to vomit. But it had to be done. She had no other options. If she could undo this magic, it would be undone already. She would be gone.

The real Guinevere would not have been able to face this threat. Guilt and relief warred in her yet again. She was still here, and because she was still here, the island stood a chance. But the real Guinevere continued to be the sacrifice.

No time for guilt, or fear. She needed to focus. She also needed her friends, but with Lancelot and Sir Tristan in the north, Brangien opposed to her, Dindrane fast asleep safe in her own home, Fina unable to join this fight, and Lily unsuited to it, she was out of options. "Where is it?" she hissed to herself, digging through a trunk, feeling for her thickest cloak.

"No ferries will allow you on."

Guinevere whirled, heart racing. Brangien stood in the doorway, barely visible in the dark of the bedroom.

"What?" Guinevere asked.

"No ferries will allow you on, and the secret passageway is guarded by men and blocked with heavier barriers than you can move on your own. Even if you get past the guards with magic, you will not be able to get through."

Guinevere shook her head. "You do not understand. I—"

"I do not *understand*?" Brangien's voice trembled. "I do not understand that you left before, exposing yourself to danger, and now you will leave again to unmake my best friend?"

"It is not that. The Dark Queen has Mordred, and—"

"*I do not care.* I will not lose you again. Not to some misguided attempt to save a girl we never knew, and certainly not to help Mordred, who has made his bed and now must sleep in it. How dare he ask you for aid!"

"He did not. He told me to stay away."

"Oh." Brangien deflated. "Well, maybe he really does have some sense then. He is right."

"Other people are being hurt, though. The Dark Queen has figured out a new, horrendous magic."

"Again, I do not care! I told you my love is vengeful and selfish, and I will do whatever it takes to protect you from yourself. Arthur and I are keeping you safe in Camelot, and you are welcome to hate me for it, because you will be alive to hate me, and that is enough. Now, get in bed or I will force you to sleep."

Guinevere perched on the edge of her bed, her heart so heavy she could not bear to stand. "I could never hate you. But the price of my safety is too high."

Brangien huffed a sigh, then came and sat next to Guinevere.

"Do you love him?" she asked. "Mordred, I mean. Though I suppose I also mean Arthur."

Guinevere stared down at her hands. The steady strength and assurance she felt when she touched Arthur. The spark and fire and need she felt from Mordred. Both things she took to try to fill herself. But she could never be filled by someone else. It was the same thing she had said to Arthur. She had been treating the symptoms of her own unhappiness, not its cause. Until she felt whole on her own, how could she be a partner to someone else?

"I thought I loved Arthur. But I cannot separate what is mine and what is the Lady's and what is Guinevere's. They both loved him before I ever met him."

"Set them aside. They are not here. You are. How do *you* feel?"

"Do I love Arthur, or did I crave the validation that his love would give me? I wanted to be seen. To matter. And what could matter more than having someone like Arthur love me?"

Brangien took Guinevere's hand. Most of her anger was gone, replaced with the usual edge of annoyance softened by sympathy. At least the incredible well of sadness Brangien used to carry was gone now that Isolde was here. "But Mordred always saw you."

"Yes. He offered me passion and urgency and a love that could swallow me whole. Something wild and free."

"Arthur is the order of Camelot, and Mordred is the lure of magic."

Guinevere felt the words strike deep and true. She had been torn between them because she herself was torn between two worlds, a changeling in either. "But I do not belong to order *or* magic."

"You belong to yourself," Brangien said, her voice firm. "Accept that you are worthy of your own love, and accept that you are worthy of the love of your friends, who will not see you harmed. At last this is something Mordred and I agree on." She patted Guinevere's knee. "He is clever. He will figure out a way to protect himself. He always does. And Arthur will face whatever the Dark Queen is doing and triumph, because he always does. And in the meantime, I will keep you here, protected, and we will love you so fiercely you will not be able to feel any guilt at all."

Guinevere leaned her head against Brangien's shoulder. "I am very lucky to have you."

She expected Brangien to agree with her, but, to her surprise, Brangien sniffled. "We are the lucky ones, and I hate that you cannot see that."

How could Guinevere keep trying to convince people who she loved, who loved her, that they needed to let her walk into danger? If Brangien were doing the same, would she not try to stop her friend? How could she blame Brangien—and Arthur, too—for trying to protect her? But why could they not see that she was strong enough for this—and, if she was not, that it was a fight she was willing to die waging?

"Can I go sit on the walkway at least? I need to clear my head."

Brangien nodded imperiously. "I will allow it."

"Thank you." She kissed the top of Brangien's head, then walked outside. She put her back against the stone wall of the castle and stared at the black lake beneath her.

If she were the Lady of the Lake, she could meet the Dark Queen head-on. If she were the real Guinevere, she would let Arthur fight this alone, however he saw fit. But she was neither of them. She had to arm herself with a wizard. And to do that, she needed to escape her city.

She stepped to the edge of the walkway, toes brushing open air. The beginnings of a plan were forming. There would be no time to waste, but first—

A hand came over her mouth, an arm around her waist to keep her from falling as she startled and thrashed.

"It is me," a voice she would know in any darkness said. The hand around her mouth dropped.

"Lancelot!" Guinevere spun and threw her arms around her knight. She had been ready to give up on ever seeing her again. Lancelot, here, flesh and blood against Guinevere's body, made her truly happy for the first time that she was still herself. That she got to have this moment, and that she understood how much it was worth.

"I am so sorry," Guinevere said. "For everything."

Lancelot let out a quivering breath. Guinevere braced herself for rejection, for Lancelot to still be angry, but instead, Lancelot embraced her as well, strong arms circling her. "I know," she said. "Promise me you will never leave me behind again, and all is forgiven."

"I promise. But how are you here?"

"I was sent with a message for the king. I did not know if it was safe, so I swam the lake and then climbed. The Dark Queen has taken over men's minds, Guinevere. They swarm the land like ants, following her whims. And they are coming here. Does Arthur know? Did any of the other messengers make it? Sir Tristan and Nectudad sent a dozen."

"Only one other made it." Guinevere felt a stab of terrible triumph that she had been right. It was a horrifying thing to be right about. But now Arthur would see, and—

It would change nothing. He would still meet this threat head-on in battle, because that was what he had decided. Because, even now, he was still following Merlin's commands.

Guinevere would not.

"I have a plan, but it means going against Arthur's wishes. Will you help me?" Guinevere asked, dreading the answer. Lancelot had already been punished for her loyalty to Guinevere rather than Arthur. And now, the moment she was back home, Guinevere was asking her to choose again.

Lancelot's voice was as clear as the ringing of an iron blade. "I am only yours."

Guinevere barely held back a sob of relief, but it was coupled with a surprising flutter of warmth. Lancelot was *hers*. "In that case, we have no time to lose."

"What are we doing?"

Guinevere kept hold of Lancelot's arm, needing every infusion of her knight's strength she could get. "We are going to steal Excalibur."

CHAPTER FORTY-ONE

Lancelot paced along the edge of the walkway as Guinevere finished explaining what she had seen in the dream. "I believe Mordred, and—"

Lancelot cut her off. "I do, too," she said, her voice gruff with reluctance. "That *idiot*," she added for good measure, then stopped, facing Guinevere. "But now you must tell me the truth. Are you freeing Merlin to undo only the Dark Queen's magic, or to try to undo the magic that binds you, as well?"

Guinevere's back was pressed against the wall of the castle. Inside, Isolde and Brangien and Arthur slept, unaware that she was plotting against them. She would have lied to them, but not to Lancelot. "The Dark Queen's. But, when this is over, if we win . . . I cannot promise I will not restore her if I can. She was an innocent, Lancelot."

Lancelot shook her head, clearly angry, but did not argue.

"How many men does the Dark Queen have?" Guinevere asked, hastily changing the subject.

"We do not know. Hundreds, at least. The north is sparsely

populated, but she got to many of King Arthur's men and some Saxon settlements, as well. We feared she might have infiltrated this far south."

The Dark Queen's form bubbling up from the earth in a torrent of black beetles skittered through Guinevere's mind. "Nothing I can do will unravel the knots she used. And Excalibur can only undo this magic by killing, so Arthur will have to wage war against innocent people."

Lancelot sat with a slowly exhaled, "Oh."

"We have to stop her, forever, before she can claim us all. The only person who can undo this magic is the man who designed it. And to free Merlin, I think I need Excalibur." The cave had been sealed by magic, which Excalibur could devour. It made sense that Merlin would leave his captivity in Arthur's hands, since he trusted Arthur would always obey his wishes.

"You cannot wield it," Lancelot said.

"I know. But you can."

Lancelot shook her head. "The Lady said it was not for me. She chose Arthur."

"Well, I *am* the Lady, and I choose you." Guinevere said it flippantly, but as soon as the words were out, she felt their truth. "I choose you," she said again, conviction strengthening her. It did not matter what Merlin or the Lady had wanted or chosen for this island. Lancelot was her champion. "It is up to us."

Lancelot's voice was as soft as the starlight. "Arthur will never forgive us."

"We will give him one last chance to help when you tell him what you know. But I do not think he will bend, and so yes, I will betray him. I can live with that, if it means the Dark Queen can never hurt anyone again." Guinevere paused. She doubted Arthur would forgive treason twice. "Can you live with it?"

"I will agree to free Merlin to stop the Dark Queen, but I will never help you undo what was done to make you. That is the one thing I could not live with."

Guinevere could not help the swelling of emotion at Lancelot's declaration. Maybe that was why Lancelot was the one person Guinevere could not bear to leave behind, why love had taken her to Lancelot. Only Lancelot made her feel whole, or at least like she would get there someday.

"How will we get out of the city?" Lancelot asked. "I can swim, but . . ." She trailed off meaningfully. If only she knew what Guinevere was thinking.

"I have a way. First, we need the sword. Arthur never leaves it in his room unattended. It is only in there if he is. And if he sees us taking it, he will know we are plotting." Guinevere tapped her fingers together.

"What are our resources?"

"My magic. Your skill. Against us is the fact that both Brangien and Arthur will be watching me very closely."

"Do we have any allies?"

Guinevere's first impulse was to say no, but she hesitated. "Lily will help in any way she can. And I know Fina would, too, though I hesitate to put her at risk."

A voice drifted down from overhead. "I like risk."

Lancelot drew her blade, staring upward.

"Fina?" Guinevere hissed. "Is that you?"

A figure jumped from the walkway above and landed in a crouch. Lancelot stepped between Guinevere and Fina, but Guinevere put a hand on her arm. "Lancelot, this is my friend, Fina."

"Oh, I have been looking forward to meeting you!" Fina, who wore only a nightshift, stood straight and stepped close, to examine Lancelot in the darkness. Which was perhaps a bit too close to

Lancelot, who stood rigid with discomfort. And then, to make matters worse, Fina grabbed Lancelot's upper arm. She let out a low exclamation in her own language, then laughed. "Magnificent indeed, as promised!"

"Magnificent?" Lancelot asked.

Guinevere cleared her throat. "We do not need to go into it."

"That was how Guinevere described you. We were drunk at the time."

"Oh," Lancelot said, her voice even.

"Drunk on a truth potion," Fina amended. "You were in the north. Is my sister alive?"

"She was when I left her."

Fina nodded. "All right, tell me what to do. I would prefer not to murder anyone, but I am ready for mischief."

"Actually," Guinevere said, looking from one warrior to another, her mind spinning with possibilities, "I think I have an idea."

"I will help, too," a soft voice said from the castle doorway. Lancelot spun with her blade pointed before Guinevere could process whose voice it was.

"Isolde?" Lancelot asked, incredulous. "I am a very poor knight. Is half the city out here?"

Isolde stepped out of the shadows. "Brangien sent me to spy on you, but I know what it is to be held in a castle. I will never participate in taking away the free will of another woman. If you need to face the Dark Queen, I will do whatever I can to help."

"Are you certain?" Guinevere asked. "Brangien will be furious."

"I am familiar with Brangien's temper. It has been my companion for many years." Even though Isolde's tone was sad, her smile could be heard. "You once rescued me. Allow me to return the favor."

"Camelot keeps surprising me," Fina said. "Though given their queen, I suppose it should not come as a shock that the entire king-dom is mad."

"Do we still need Lily?" Lancelot asked. "What if she sides with Brangien and the king?"

It was a possibility. But Guinevere had been a fool to think she could attempt this on her own. She was going on a quest, and she would need as many of her champions as she could rally. She understood why Arthur and Brangien felt the need to restrict her, but not everyone who loved her would express it the same way. Lily had trusted Guinevere to make her own choices; Guinevere would extend that trust back to her. "We will need everyone we can get. Lancelot, go wake the king and tell him what you know. Give him one last chance for him to change his mind. Isolde, if you would not mind staying out here so Brangien thinks I am being watched, I will go speak to Lily. Unless she is out here, too, and we did not notice? No? Good."

Guinevere was torn between happiness that she had Lancelot, Fina, and Isolde on her side and sadness that it meant there *was* a side in this conflict. That they were conspiring against the people they loved most.

Arthur had been right. Every battle was inevitably waged against friends and family. She hoped Camelot survived the one she was planning.

CHAPTER FORTY-TWO

Guinevere sat beside Lily in their booth overlooking the arena floor. It was not time yet. It would be soon, and Guinevere did not know what Lily would do. Last night—or very early this morning, really—when they had spoken, Lily had stared, silent. Guinevere had expected anger or excitement or arguments, but Lily had listened to Guinevere's plan, then asked if it would be dangerous. Guinevere could not deny that it would be. Lily had said she was tired, and they would speak later.

Lily held the power to ruin everything. It felt right somehow, that a girl who had never been given power, who had been forced to fight her way through the world to find a place she chose in it, would be the one who would determine everyone's fate this day.

Arthur stood in a corner of the booth, waiting for the aspirants to fight.

We should delay the tournament, Guinevere had insisted that morning.

I need knights now more than ever. We cannot hold the fate of the island hostage to whatever the Dark Queen is doing.

We know what she is doing. Lancelot confirms it.

Sir Tristan's letter said to trust no one, not even my own men.

Lancelot is herself! I would know otherwise.

Still. I do not trust Nectudad any more than I trust the Dark Queen. We will knight more men, and then I will ride to face the threat outside while you protect Camelot from inside.

Guinevere wanted to both strangle and embrace him. He was stubborn and bullheaded and still placing his faith in Merlin. Trusting that since Merlin told Arthur not to free him, any sacrifice made on that path was acceptable.

Guinevere watched as Lancelot entered the arena. If Arthur had not taken Lancelot's advice, at least he had not sent her away again. Instead, he had put her into the tournament. An aspirant had to beat at least three knights to be knighted, but this tournament was structured differently. They had many more hopeful knights than usual, and less time to get through them all. The aspirants fought each other in an elimination pattern before the top third could compete against the actual knights.

Brangien sat behind them in the booth, ostensibly sewing, but Guinevere could feel her friend's eyes heavy on the back of her neck. Guinevere hated that Brangien had become an obstacle.

Lily leaned close, her voice low enough that the noise of the arena kept her from being overheard by Arthur or Brangien. "If you have a chance to undo the magic that was done to your body, after you have defeated the Dark Queen," she said, "I want you to know: it is your choice. So long as some version of you comes back safely to me." Guinevere wanted to laugh at Lily's matter-of-fact statement that she would defeat the greatest magical force on the island, one who had slipped through Merlin's and Arthur's fingers time and again.

Guinevere did not have Lily's confidence in the outcome of this fight. But she squeezed Lily's arm reassuringly nonetheless, grateful that her friend—no, her sister, always—continued to offer her the grace of love, regardless of what she chose.

Lily nodded. "Right, then. When does the plan start?"

Arthur turned toward them, smiling, then walked over to sit by them. Guinevere had just enough time to whisper, "You will know it, trust me."

"Oh, Lionel is fighting!" Lily stood at the railing, waving her handkerchief.

"Did you sleep well? How is your head?" Arthur's hand drifted to his empty belt. He had left Excalibur in his room to keep Guinevere from having a headache.

Knowing what she was planning, and how badly it would hurt him should she succeed—or fail, and be discovered—Guinevere almost wished she *had* stayed with him last night. One last night curled against his steady, familiar strength.

"What news did Lancelot bring?" Guinevere asked, because, as far as Arthur knew, they had not spoken yet. She hoped—desperately—that he would tell her everything, and change his mind. That saying it aloud would make him face the enormity of the threat and admit that their best chance was her idea.

"Nothing I am not prepared for," he said instead.

Guinevere tried not to let her heartbreak show. Because today, *she* was what he was not prepared for.

She took his hand in hers, linked their fingers, and looked down at his darker skin against hers. Felt that strength she had loved and depended on so much during her time as queen. Whatever happened, whoever she was now or would be in the future, the one thing she had never lost was her belief in Arthur. Whether it came from the Lady and the real Guinevere, or whether it was entirely her own, did not matter. Camelot was not perfect, Arthur was not perfect, but she did not regret how hard she had fought for him.

She would not regret what she had to do to fight for him and for Camelot now.

"Guinevere?" he prodded.

She did not trust herself to speak, and so she tipped her face up and pulled his down to meet her lips. A kiss, stolen with these lips that were not hers. But she did not think the real Guinevere, who had chosen to follow Merlin and the Lady into the cave to chase the dream of Arthur, would mind.

Arthur's jolt of surprise pulsed through his skin and hers, but he kissed her back, tenderly and even eagerly. That eagerness was new, and it broke her heart that she could not enjoy it. They had never gotten their simple moment, their calm stretch of time to explore who they might have been together.

Guinevere might not feel the same overwhelming spark of passion for Arthur that she had for Mordred, but that did not mean she felt nothing. She had wanted this, and him, in so many ways for as long as she had been herself, and now she could not have any of it.

She pulled back, pressing her cheek to his. "I love you," she whispered, because it was true and she wanted him to know before it was too late.

"We are going to be fine," he said, his voice soft but ringing with the joy of a horse at full gallop, running for the love of motion. "You and I, together."

Then the crowd let out a simultaneous gasp of shock.

CHAPTER FORTY-THREE

"What is she doing?" Arthur asked, brow wrinkled in confusion.

Fina stood on the arena floor. Her gloriously tattooed arms were bare, and she wore her leggings and leather tunic. "My turn!" she declared, expertly twirling an ax.

All the men and all the knights turned as one to stare up at Arthur. Except Lancelot, who kept her head down as though hoping not to be noticed.

"I thought we gave her clothes to wear," Arthur said. "She still has to follow *some* rules. I should have had Lancelot speak to her about how to blend in."

"She will never be good at that, I am afraid." Guinevere stood and politely clapped.

Fina continued twirling the ax, feet set wide. "Do not make me fight these children first. I have bloodied my axes with the steaming viscera of warriors the likes of which they cannot imagine. I will fight the knights, or no one."

The arena fell silent. Not only was Fina unlike anyone they had ever seen, she was also making demands and flouting the structure of the tournament. How would the king react?

Sir Gawain hurried over to her. He raised his sword. "I will fight her first."

Fina grinned at him. "No. You like me too much. I want to fight the only other woman who has ascended to King Arthur's table. I want to fight Sir Lancelot."

Lancelot's expression was blank as she awaited instructions from her king.

"Fina of the Northern People," Arthur said, and Guinevere had a moment of pride that he remembered *Pict* was a term they despised, "because you are a special guest of Camelot, I will allow you to bypass the preliminary fights. But be warned: if you do not defeat three of my knights, you cannot be knighted. I will make no exceptions. And you are challenging one of Camelot's best."

Lancelot lowered her head, one hand over her heart. Guinevere's hand drifted to her own heart, wondering how it felt for her knight to hear that praise knowing what they had planned.

"I accept!" Fina shouted, charging straight at Lancelot. Lancelot barely had time to dodge a powerful blow. She held her hands up, saying something inaudible, but Fina answered by kneeing her in the ribs. Lancelot put one hand under her tunic, clearly in pain. She still had not drawn her sword. The crowd jeered, pointing in rage toward the rack of weapons the knights were supposed to choose from first.

"This is not how we—" Lancelot said at the same moment that Fina swung the blunt end of her ax. It caught the side of Lancelot's head, and the knight fell heavily to the earth.

"No!" Guinevere shouted. She pushed out of the booth, heedless of how it looked, then rushed down the steps and raced to Lancelot's side. She knelt and took Lancelot's motionless hand. Her knight's chest moving up and down was the only indication of life.

Fina stood awkwardly to the side. Her ax lay on the arena floor where she had dropped it. "I am sorry," she said, her voice soft. "I thought—"

"We follow the rules." Guinevere stared up at her friend, anger twisting her face and tightening her voice. "We follow them so that things like this do not happen."

Fina's shoulders drooped and she hung her head. Sir Gawain draped his cloak across her shoulders and murmured something indistinct.

Guinevere had been followed onto the arena floor. Brangien put a comforting hand on her back, and Arthur crouched at Lancelot's side, peering down at her to assess the damage. She was unconscious, but the blow had struck the side of her head and was obscured by her thick, curly hair.

"Fina," Arthur said, firmly but not harshly, "it is clear you do not have the discipline it takes to be a knight. I take the blame for allowing you to try when you were not fully prepared. I cannot allow you to continue in this tournament. Perhaps the next one, if you are ready."

Fina nodded once. "I understand," she said, staring down at Lancelot.

Guinevere stood. "I need to get Lancelot back to the castle. Brangien can help her. Right?" Guinevere looked desperately at Brangien, who nodded. Then Guinevere turned to Arthur. "Can you carry her?"

"What is the problem?" Lily demanded, striding toward them.

"We need to take Lancelot back to the castle," Arthur said.

"What? No." Lily frowned down at the unconscious knight. "I mean, I am very sorry she was hurt. But if you leave, the tournament will be halted. Lionel will not be knighted and I cannot marry him. Cameliard needs good rulers to help it transition to your laws. Every day we delay, I fear for what violence may be taking root there. Please, my king, stay here. Let the tournament continue. The needs of the kingdom must be greater than tending to one injured knight."

Everything Arthur was, every choice he made, always came down to the good of the kingdom. He could not argue with it. But he was clearly torn. "I—"

Guinevere waved a frantic hand at Lancelot's prone body. "We are wasting time! If the tournament must go on, then stay. Sir Gawain? Fina? Can you carry her?"

Sir Gawain looked relieved to have a task as he grabbed Lancelot under her arms and Fina took her legs. It would be awkward, but they would manage. Sir Gawain was careful to make certain that Lancelot's head was supported against his shoulder.

Guinevere tore her eyes away from her fallen knight and put a hand on Arthur's chest. "I will send word when she wakes up." She went onto her tiptoes and pressed a kiss to Arthur's cheek, wishing she could linger, but there was no time. As she hurried from the arena, Fina and Sir Gawain struggled to keep up with their unconscious burden.

Brangien stayed at Guinevere's side. "Lancelot is strong. I am certain she will be fine." But she sounded worried. Head wounds were frightening; the damage was often invisible until too late. And Lancelot had not yet stirred or shown any signs of waking.

Sir Gawain and Fina did not break stride even when they arrived at the castle and carried Lancelot up five flights of stairs. "You are very strong," Sir Gawain said, breathing heavily.

Fina grinned. "Just wait."

Sir Gawain's already ruddy face turned a violent shade of red.

Brangien ran ahead and opened the door to Guinevere's rooms. Guinevere pointed to her bed, and Sir Gawain and Fina put Lancelot down. Sir Gawain shuffled his feet, keeping his eyes on the floor, clearly uncomfortable.

"Thank you, Sir Gawain," Guinevere said. "You may go back to the arena. They need you for the tournament."

"What about me?" Fina asked. "I would like to stay until she wakes up. And I suspect I will not be very popular in the arena right now."

Guinevere nodded. "Stay if you wish."

Sir Gawain bowed, then hurried from the room. Brangien went to the table but found the basin empty. "Isolde!" she shouted.

Isolde entered from the other room and gasped. "Oh no."

"I am going to the kitchen for supplies. Stoke the fire. I will be right back!" Brangien rushed out.

As soon as the door closed, Guinevere reached into Lancelot's tunic and pulled out the sleep knots Lancelot had activated when she fell. Lancelot sat up with a groan as Guinevere took off her decorative cape and put on her travel cloak. She grabbed a pouch of supplies prepared by Isolde—including the iron thread that Guinevere had carefully knotted in the early hours of the morning—and fastened it to her belt. Lancelot, meanwhile, had peeled off her chain mail, leaving only her leather outer tunic, leather leggings, and a sword at her waist.

Fina grabbed her weapons from beneath Guinevere's bed and strapped them on with a grin. "That was fun."

Lancelot's scowl was fiercer than any blow she could have delivered. "I still do not understand why I had to be the one injured. It could have been Fina."

"Poor Lancelot! Did I hit your pride?"

Lancelot's jaw twitched, her eyes narrowed. "Someday we will have a rematch."

"I look forward to it." Fina's raised eyebrow and slightly parted lips made Guinevere feel a surge of something hot and angry that took her a moment to place. She was . . . jealous? Fina could meet Lancelot on her own level. Guinevere would never be that strong, that physically capable. That outrageous of a flirt.

She did not have time for this. Guinevere turned to Isolde, stomach twisted and chest tight, mostly because of what lay ahead of them. That was all she should be focusing on now. "Did you manage it?"

"I did. Good luck." Isolde embraced Guinevere. "Take care, and come back to us."

Isolde hurried out into the hallway. She would find Brangien and tell her the truth: Lancelot had awoken and Guinevere, Lancelot, and Fina had left.

Fina sighed, a longing expression on her face. "I really did want to be a knight, you know."

"I know," Guinevere said. "And I wanted it for you, too."

"I swear, Nectudad is never false. If she says there is a threat, there is a threat. She would not lay a trap for Arthur the way our father did. When Arthur goes to meet Nectudad and Sir Tristan, he will find allies, not enemies."

Guinevere hoped desperately that Fina was right. Either way, Fina would not be returning to Camelot after helping her trick Arthur. They might have just destroyed any chance at peace with the north.

"Are you certain?" Guinevere said. "Lancelot could hit you. Make it look as though you tried to stop us."

Fina looked Lancelot up and down, then shook her head. "I would rather face Arthur's wrath than Lancelot's fist. I am with you."

Lancelot went out first, then held open the door to the castle's exterior stairs. All the docks were watched and the ferries halted; the secret passage was sealed. Every avenue and path out of the city was blocked.

All except the one Arthur did not know about. The one no one would ever expect Guinevere to take. The one she would prefer to throw herself off the side of the castle and attempt to fly rather than face.

They walked up and up, their steps quick and furtive, until they reached the alcove where Hild's brother had tried to kill Lily and Guinevere and where, hidden behind a column carved like a tree, there was a tiny room with a hole in the center of its floor. A hole that dropped straight into the cold lake that lurked beneath Camelot.

Excalibur rested against one of the columns. Arthur had left it in his room so as not to aggravate Guinevere's headache. It made her feel even worse that she was taking advantage of his tender care, that his kindness had made it so easy for Isolde to steal the sword and leave it here for them.

Lancelot lifted the sword, her expression reverent, and fastened it to her back. She was careful to keep it sheathed. "The Lady gave it to Arthur," Lancelot said softly, almost to herself.

"Well, this Lady is taking it back. But only for a while." Guinevere walked to the edge of the landing, then swung herself around the column into the hidden room. She edged aside as Lancelot and Fina immediately followed her. There was barely enough space for the three of them.

Guinevere pressed against the stones behind her. The mountain that the Lady—Guinevere herself, in a way—had carved to create Camelot. She had created this drop, too. This one path to freedom, so long as Guinevere was willing to endure hell to get there.

"What if Nynaeve is waiting?" Lancelot asked.

"Oh, yes, the watery witch," Fina said. "Forgot about her. You have a lot of enemies for someone so small, Slip."

"If Nynaeve tries to stop us, we use the sword." Guinevere stared down into the abyss, remembering how it had felt in the dream as she had dropped into it. How certain she had been. How right it had seemed. She had none of that calm certainty now.

Fina did not count down, or even ask if they were ready. She jumped with a delighted whoop, the noise of her splash taking far too long to reach Guinevere and Lancelot.

"He will never forgive us," Lancelot said.

"I know." Guinevere held out her hand. Lancelot took it. Even amid the soul-crushing dread, Guinevere and Lancelot hand in hand was as true as anything she had ever felt.

They jumped.

CHAPTER FORTY-FOUR

Guinevere could not breathe. She knew—somewhere inside the tiny part of her brain that was still functioning—that Lancelot had her, that the arms around her waist were Lancelot's, that Lancelot would never let her drown. But the water was everywhere. She could not see anything, and though Lancelot hauled her upward, keeping her head above water, still the water splashed and slapped, trying to reclaim her. Trying to end her.

"Stop fighting," Fina said.

"I think I see light," Lancelot said, kicking. "I can get us—"

A surge ripped Guinevere away from Lancelot and sent her spinning and tumbling, trapped in blackness, alone. The water felt like hands around her arms, a viselike grip.

It *was* hands. Nynaeve had found her.

"Lancelot! Fina!" Guinevere screamed, but there was no answer. She could not even hear the sounds of swimming. Suddenly the fear of losing herself was replaced by something deeper and stronger: the fear of losing Lancelot. *"No,"* Guinevere said, pushing outward with everything she was. The water stilled, frozen, droplets hanging in the air around them. The luminescent, shocked face of Nynaeve appeared in front of her.

Guinevere pushed upward. The water responded, bubbling around her like a gentle fountain until as much of her body was out of the water as she could manage. She reached out her hand and *willed* Lancelot to come to her. A wave slammed Lancelot against her. Guinevere checked quickly to make sure she was conscious. Though her eyes were wide, Lancelot nodded with determination. Guinevere found Fina the same way, buoyed by the water and the strength of the woman at her side. Fina still moved like she was treading water, not trusting Guinevere's power. Which was probably wise of her.

"Nynaeve," Guinevere said. Now that she had seen Nimue, there was no comparison between the two. Nimue held human form with love and care. Nynaeve shimmered and wavered, unable to settle, her features running down and down like tears.

Please. Nynaeve's voice was a ripple echoing outward. *Please, we want her back. We need her back. We are not complete without her.*

Guinevere could feel her control slipping. Without the sheer animal panic of needing to save Lancelot, her fear and revulsion were returning. She did not know how much longer she could hold the water, or control Nynaeve. And if Lancelot drew the sword to banish Nynaeve, Guinevere would be unable to do anything.

"Whatever is left of Nimue is in me," Guinevere said, "and I need to get to the shore. If I die, so does she."

You are her? Nynaeve reached out one watery hand, and Guinevere tried not to recoil in horror. *We want to be whole again.*

Guinevere understood the longing to be restored. To reclaim something taken from you, something that split you both mind and soul. But could it ever be the same for Nynaeve? Even if Guinevere managed to extract Nimue, would the Ladies be reunited?

Merlin and the Dark Queen might have thought Nimue losing herself in Guinevere was a mistake, but seeing Nynaeve now, Guinevere wondered. Nimue had been so deliberate, so careful in her planning. Splitting part of herself off so the magic would remain in the water. Creating Camelot, and the sword. Finding the real Guinevere. It did not make sense that Nimue would have made a mistake at the very end.

Was it possible Nimue had known she would be erased, remade into something new—and that she had wanted it? The only way she could truly live as a human was to leave her eternal self behind and become something finite, with a beginning and an end.

An end Guinevere that did not want to be here, in Nimue's frigid lake. "Take me to the shore. We are going to Merlin."

He is dangerous, Nynaeve said. *You cannot unseal what we have sealed.*

"We have the sword."

A shudder rippled through Nynaeve. *You* should not *unseal what we have sealed,* she amended.

Guinevere knew that, perhaps better than anyone. But the Dark Queen was using magic created by the wizard. Without him, it could not be undone. Everyone she had infected would have to be killed, and that was unconscionable.

Guinevere was still terrified of what the cost of freeing the wizard would be, though. Magic always had a cost, and Merlin's magic always demanded others pay it.

Give the water back to us. We will take you to the shore.

Nynaeve was terrifying, but she did not seem capable of lying. Guinevere wrapped her arms around Lancelot, and Fina encircled her on the other side. She squeezed her eyes shut, and let go.

They dropped. And then they began to move. It was far smoother than riding a horse, and it was also far worse, being whooshed along on the inescapable current of the Lady. Nynaeve mostly remembered to keep their heads above water, and soon they were out of the caves and tunnels beneath the city. The daylight was a small comfort, which Guinevere, with her eyes squeezed shut as tightly as her arms squeezed Lancelot, was unable to take in.

Though they traveled swiftly, it felt like an eternity before they were dumped unceremoniously onto dry ground. Guinevere staggered away from the sound of the water and vomited until she had nothing left.

She wanted to indulge her misery, but there was no time. She did her best to wring out her cloak and skirts. Lancelot stood nearby, ready as always, none the worse for wear other than being thoroughly soaked. Excalibur was still sheathed on her back, her own sword on her belt. Fina was wringing out her hair. She looked thrilled, the wretched thing.

"Can she come with us?" Fina gestured to where Nynaeve shimmered nearby. "Could be handy in a fight. Or just fun."

Guinevere stood on the bank, looking at yet another creature broken and ruined in Merlin and Nimue's wake. "I am sorry Nimue did this to you," she said.

Nynaeve moved with a sound like weeping. *She will never come back to us. We see that now, and we cannot bear it. You have the sword. Unmake us. Return us to the water. Take away this desolate consciousness, this torment of knowing what we were when we were whole. What we can never be again.*

Lancelot looked at Guinevere, at a loss for what to do.

Guinevere hated herself for how calculating it was, but she had promised Arthur she would protect Camelot. She could not afford to be merciful. Not yet. "Keep the Dark Queen and all she has touched out of Camelot, and when I return, I will do as you wish."

Nynaeve held out a longing hand. Guinevere could not bring

herself to touch it. Then Nynaeve bowed her head in agreement and splashed back down to become the lake.

"So our plan now is to steal some horses?" Fina asked. Between them and the trees was nothing but an open field, stretching blank and offering no protection. They needed speed above all else. Once they reached the trees, it was a hard two-hour ride to Merlin's cave.

"Yes," Guinevere said, taking a deep, calming breath. "That way we can arrive well before dark."

"I do not suppose you ordered fifty horses brought to you and forgot to tell me?" Fina pointed at the dozens of mounted soldiers galloping toward them from the direction of Camelot's stables.

"How did they discover us so soon?" Lancelot drew her sword, assuming a fighting stance even though the soldiers would not arrive for several minutes. "And how did they know where on the lakeshore we would land when even we did not know?"

"They are not coming after us." Guinevere pointed in the opposite direction, toward the north, where dust rose from other horses. "We can trust no one coming from the north, and Nectudad and Sir Tristan are supposed to arrive tomorrow. We should run into the fields and hope no one notices us."

"There is nowhere to hide," Lancelot said, her tone grim. "We should run for the soldiers from Camelot. Overpower them, take their horses, and flee."

Fina twirled a knife idly. "While my skills are beyond compare, I do not even think the two of us combined can expect to successfully take on fifty men. I knew we should have kept the water witch with us."

Guinevere looked from one approaching force to the other. The one from Camelot would protect her, but the soldiers would also take her back to Camelot and Arthur, bringing her quest to an abrupt end. The other was probably led by the Dark Queen, but *possibly* led by Sir Tristan and Nectudad, who might be possessed.

Stuck between fields, the dreaded lake, soldiers loyal to Arthur, and ones whose loyalties no one could be sure of. "We take our chances with the northerners." Guinevere hitched up her skirts and ran.

CHAPTER FORTY-FIVE

Lancelot had her sword drawn, Fina held her ax, and Guinevere took two of her precious iron knots out of her pouch, ready to use if necessary. The first two riders became visible. Guinevere fought against her relief at the sight of Sir Tristan and Nectudad—there was still a chance it was not actually them. As soon as they got near, Nectudad threw herself from her horse and embraced Fina with such momentum they nearly fell over.

"Is she trying to strangle you?" Lancelot asked.

"No, this is just how she shows affection," Fina said, her face red from lack of air when Nectudad finished her hug.

"You were supposed to arrive tomorrow," Lancelot said as the rest of the force—a dozen or so soldiers—caught up.

Sir Tristan dismounted with difficulty, one arm bound to his side and one leg bandaged. "Things got worse. We had to split everyone up so the Dark Queen could not find us all together. It also allowed us to travel faster. Where is the king?"

Lancelot shook her head. "In the city. He is determined to meet the threat with force. We have a different idea."

"What?" Nectudad demanded.

"We are going to free—" Fina started, but Guinevere shouted, "No! Do not say anything. Step into the water. All of you." She pointed at the lake. It was impossible to tell whether the Dark Queen was infecting anyone, as much as Guinevere hoped she would recognize Sir Tristan, or that Fina would sense if something was wrong with Nectudad. But Nynaeve would know.

"Why?" Sir Tristan asked, even as he walked toward the lake.

The rest of the soldiers dismounted but remained by their horses. Four of them were from Camelot; the other ten were Nectudad's people.

"It's a test. You told us to trust no one," Guinevere said. "This is us not trusting you until we have proof."

Sir Tristan was already ankle-deep in the water. The fact that he obeyed her without question confirmed that he was not infected—he was definitely still Sir Tristan, loyal to the core. Nectudad nodded and stepped into the water, gesturing for the rest of the soldiers to do the same.

Nine of them followed her.

One, a northern woman with tattooed arms and brown hair shorn close to her scalp, did not move toward the lake. Perhaps she did not understand. Guinevere shared a look with Lancelot, whose sword was still drawn.

"Derile." Nectudad spoke in her language, gesturing toward the water.

Derile smiled, but her smile did not look quite right. It was as though strings were pulling the corners of her mouth up. "We already know where you are going," she said, and then she held out her right hand. There was a spider on her palm, swaying hypnotically back and forth, caressing her skin with its needlelike legs. "Why are you fighting us? It is easy here. So peaceful." Her smile twitched higher, a rictus grin. Then she flung her arm out and the spider sailed through the air, releasing silk strands so that it floated on the breeze and landed right on Nectudad's shoulder.

"Nectudad! In the lake!" Guinevere shouted. Nectudad plunged herself down.

Fina tackled Derile with a roar and threw her into the lake. The water bubbled to life around the northern warrior, seething and swiftly pulling her deeper. Everyone held their breath, waiting, watching where Nectudad had disappeared. Waiting to see if she would reappear as herself or as something else.

Nectudad resurfaced, gasping and swatting at her shoulders, but the spider was gone.

"Derile," Nectudad said, putting one hand over her heart. Her friend was surrounded by foaming water. Whatever Nynaeve was doing, she was not healing Derile or cleansing her of the Dark Queen's infection. Guinevere had asked her to keep the Dark Queen out of Camelot. It looked like that was all the Lady was capable of.

"It is too late." Derile laughed, choking and spitting out water. "The wizard cannot save you. He has never saved anyone. Only we can heal the island. You will understand. You will all understand."

The water swallowed her, and then the surface of the lake was smooth once more.

Nectudad and her people bowed their heads, then lifted their eyes to the sky. One moment of heartbreak showed on Nectudad's face before her features became fierce and determined. "What is your plan?" she asked.

Guinevere turned her back on the shimmer of light on the lake water as the uninfected slowly waded out. "Exactly what Derile said. We are going to free Merlin."

"Nectudad, you go with them. Take our horses," Sir Tristan said. He gestured for two of his soldiers to stay with him. Nectudad put a

hand on his shoulder and shook her head. Without needing more in-
struction, Sir Tristan pointed to one of the northern fighters instead.
Guinevere understood. He was staying with one man from Camelot
and one from the north. A united front.

Sir Tristan turned to where the force from Camelot was riding
ever closer. "We will update Arthur," he said.

"And delay them if they intend to stop us," Guinevere said.

Sir Tristan inclined his head, then turned to Nectudad. They
shared one last look before clasping hands and pressing their fore-
heads together. "On another battlefield," Nectudad said.

"In any fight," Sir Tristan said.

Guinevere met Fina's gaze, questions in both their eyes. What
had happened in their absence that bound those two so tightly, so
quickly? Sir Tristan and Nectudad released each other, and the
knight moved as fast as he could to intercept the incoming force,
accompanied on one side by a soldier of Camelot and on the other
by a warrior of the north.

Lancelot boosted Guinevere onto Sir Tristan's horse, then
mounted another. Fina leapt onto hers. "Hurry. We have an evil fairy
to beat to a wicked wizard," she said, kicking her horse's flanks and
flying into motion.

The rest followed. Guinevere hoped Sir Tristan was successful in
convincing Arthur of the threat that approached. She hoped Arthur
stayed in Camelot, where the lake would protect the city's inhabit-
ants. And most of all, she hoped she was strong enough for the task
ahead.

Derile's rigid smile haunted her. A puppet master's imitation of
humanity. She could think only of Mordred's green eyes being eaten
away by darkness. What if it had been Sir Tristan who was infected?
Or if the spider had gotten to Fina or Lancelot? Mordred had already
been taken, and soon the entire island might follow.

She could not fail. The whole world and everyone she cared
about depended on her.

As they galloped toward Merlin's cave, Nectudad filled them in,
shouting to be heard over the pounding of the horses' hooves.

"The Dark Queen has taken almost all of Arthur's forces. We had
to scatter. She controls a large group of Saxons, but they disappeared
before we could figure out how many or where they are headed. Why
are we freeing the wizard?"

Guinevere shouted back. "We cannot fight everyone she pos-
sesses, or kill more innocent people like Derile. We are going to free
Merlin. This is his magic, corrupted. Our hope is that he can undo
what she uses to bind herself to her victims and free everyone."

"Will Merlin help us?" Nectudad asked.

"He hates the Dark Queen, so I think he will. If he needs convincing, we have Excalibur." Part of Guinevere wished he would refuse so that she could have Lancelot threaten him with the sword.
But that was childish. Her own pain had to come second to the fate
of the island. The island Merlin had always been concerned with.
How had Merlin not foreseen what would happen, though? How
had he not known he would be needed?

Guinevere's hands cramped with how tightly she held her reins.
It was a painful few hours. They pushed the horses harder than they
should have, but they did not dare rest or slow their pace. Finally, the
trees ahead took on a nightmare quality of familiarity.

They were back.

Guinevere did not look at the rotting shack that Merlin had
tricked the real Guinevere into thinking was a cottage. She rode
straight past it, gesturing for Nectudad and the rest to follow her.

"Here!" she shouted, dismounting in front of the smooth rock face that had been the opening to the cave. The cave where Nimue and the real Guinevere had been transformed. The cave where Merlin had allowed himself to be sealed away forever, according to his demands.

He did not get to choose. Not this time.

"Are we certain we should free the demon?" Fina asked, nerves tightening her voice. Guinevere had seen her fearless in the face of death, but the wizard scared her.

She was right to be scared. Guinevere stepped up to the rock face and pressed her palm against it. She felt Nynaeve there, felt the traces of her mournful rage. "It is our only choice."

"How are you going to free him?" Nectudad surveyed the rock with a dubious expression.

Guinevere glanced back at Lancelot. "Magic first, and then its opposite."

Lancelot nodded. Her expression was determined, but there was reluctance and worry in the way she clenched and unclenched her fists. Lancelot still did not want to use Excalibur. Guinevere wished for both their sakes they did not have to do what came next.

Guinevere cut one of her fingers and drew the knot for age. The same one she had used to rust the lock on Isolde's door at King Mark's castle in what felt like a lifetime ago. This time, she let far more blood fall onto the stone. Days, weeks, months, perhaps even years of her own life, bled out to try to save this island.

With a gasp, she pulled her hand back and staggered away. "That is all I can do." Already, the rock was pocked and weathered. Where Guinevere's knot had been was a single crack.

Lancelot gestured for Guinevere to stand behind her, but it was not necessary. Guinevere was already scurrying as far from Lancelot and Excalibur as she could. She wanted to watch, but she could not afford to grow any weaker. She ducked behind a tree, letting it support her and keep her upright. She prayed to any god that might be listening that this would work.

She felt it the moment Lancelot drew the sword. Wrapping her arms around herself and breathing deeply, Guinevere jumped at the resounding crack that echoed through the air. She left the shelter of the tree as Lancelot sheathed the sword. In front of her was a jagged wound in the face of the rock.

Everyone held their breath, waiting to see whether a spindly old man would climb through. No one appeared. But still, it was an opening, wide enough for one person to enter at a time.

"You did it!" Guinevere said, hurrying to rejoin the group.

"We did it," Lancelot corrected.

"Thank you," Mordred said, stepping free of the trees. "We could not have managed that on our own."

CHAPTER FORTY-SIX

The movements were Mordred's as he prowled toward them, his steps more like dancing than walking. The way he twirled his sword through the air so that it sparked brightly in the afternoon sun was familiar, too.

But his *eyes*.

That was the worst part. Because, unlike in Guinevere's dream, they were not black. They were his own eyes, lovely and green, and absolutely lifeless. Gone was the winking familiarity, the sly glance, the hundreds of infinitesimal changes that were *him*. These eyes were as lifeless and unchanging as a snake's.

"Run," Mordred wheezed, his mouth not quite cooperating, his eyes staying cold. "Please, run."

"Mordred?" Guinevere took a step toward him. He was still in there!

"Stay," his voice sang with ease. "Join us. *No.* I am not strong enough," he said, tears tracing down his face. "I cannot fight her any longer. Please, run. As far and as fast as you can." His mouth spasmed into a smile as he sauntered toward them. Maybe he was able to resist the Dark Queen because he was a fairyson, or maybe because he was Mordred, and he always survived. But if the muscle memory of Guinevere's body was that of the real Guinevere, it was clear the Dark Queen had complete control of Mordred's skills, including those with a blade.

Lancelot drew her sword and took a fighting stance. "Mordred, stop."

"Go," he said, his voice agonized.

There was a snap of a twig, a footstep, and then a dozen, a hundred, an innumerable swarm of people walked free from the trees where they had lain in wait. Saxon, southerner, northerner, it did not matter. They walked in unison, as though controlled by a single puppet master. But they all had the same ghastly quality to their eyes: unanimated, lifeless windows with no soul behind them.

"Why are they all here?" Fina asked, panicked.

"How did they know?" Nectudad demanded.

"She was already trying to get in," Guinevere said, trying to dam her flooding despair. Guinevere had accomplished what the Dark Queen could not. She had opened the cave, and now the Dark Queen would kill the only being capable of beating her. Or, worse, infect him. This had been why Merlin warned Arthur to never open the cave. Guinevere had disregarded the warning because of her hatred for the wizard. And now she had ruined everything. "We cannot let them inside!"

"Form a circle around the cave!" Nectudad commanded. Fina grabbed Guinevere and tugged her back as Nectudad's group took a defensive stance. Lancelot strode toward Mordred, blocking his way.

"Please kill me, Lancelot!" Mordred begged. His fingers spasmed and then his voice became smooth again. "Give us Excalibur, Lancelot. Give it to us now, and we will spare her life." In a gesture at odds with his words, Mordred pointed his sword at Lancelot's neck and then at Guinevere's.

Because of their watery journey, Lancelot was not wearing armor. Neither was Mordred. It would be blade against blade, with nothing to protect their desperately human bodies.

"You cannot hope to beat us all," Mordred said. "And soon you will be with us."

One of Nectudad's soldiers cried out as the spiders surged toward them, carpeting the forest floor with seething black. Guinevere reached into her pouch. She had not expected the Dark Queen to beat them here, but nor had she come unprepared. Guinevere waited until the first spider got close enough to strike, then stabbed an iron killing knot into it, staking it to the ground.

As she had hoped, the magic was connected to the spider, and the spider was connected to all the rest of the encroaching arachnids. They twitched and withered away in a widening circle. Guinevere's heart swelled, then sank. A part of her had desperately hoped the magic would kill *all* the infection of the Dark Queen, but it had only stopped this particular method of delivery. The army surrounding them was still the Dark Queen's.

"Clever," Mordred said. "And vicious. We did not know you had it in you, soft, gentle girl. No wonder he loves you." Mordred's free hand tapped against his heart. "We can still feel him, how much it hurts. How scared he is that we will harm you through him. You have already hurt him so many times. Do not make us kill you. Give us the sword."

The Dark Queen's horde stepped closer. Fina and Nectudad raised their swords, shoulder to shoulder with the handful of soldiers that stood between the Dark Queen and the cave. They would be overwhelmed, and quickly, but none of them suggested retreating.

"At least we will die as ourselves," Fina said, her voice bright.

"That is the most anyone can hope for," Nectudad agreed. "Stay tight! Protect Guinevere and the sword!"

Lancelot turned her head and met Guinevere's gaze, her own grimly determined. She unstrapped Excalibur, still sheathed, from her back. Guinevere braced herself against the impending sickness. Maybe Excalibur could buy them time. But she knew from experience the sword could not undo this magic.

The horde surrounding them pressed closer. The Dark Queen was out of patience.

"Until we battle again," Nectudad said.

"In another field," Fina answered. She raised her sword and roared.

An answering roar echoed, amplified a thousandfold, from the east. They all turned, terrified of this new threat. But the pounding of hooves announced the arrival of Camelot's forces. The horde shifted toward the threat as Arthur himself crashed through, sword swinging, eyes blazing.

Arthur was here! Camelot was here!

But . . . he was too far away. Hundreds of infected bodies were between them, a sea of the Dark Queen separating them. They might as well have been on separate islands for all they could reach each other. Arthur looked across the heads of the charging army at Guinevere and then Lancelot. His eyes flashed with anger when he saw that Lancelot held Excalibur, still sheathed, aloft. But he nodded once, giving permission. Then he dove into the fray, sword swinging. The Dark Queen's forces fought with mindless frenzy, throwing themselves into blades, heedless of the damage they did to their bodies. Horses and men were pulled screaming to the forest floor.

The worst part, though, was that the Dark Queen's possessed died soundlessly, bleeding out into the dirt. They were not allowed to feel their own pain, to cry out at being violently torn from the world against their wills. She stole even their last moments from them.

"Come, Lancelot!" Mordred called over the battle's cacophonous din. "The tyrant cannot reach us in time. Give us the sword, or try to fight us. Either way, we will have it, and you."

Mordred was flanked by at least twenty of the Dark Queen's horde, held back from the larger battle by this smaller yet most desperate one. Guinevere could see how both conflicts would end, though. How could they fight an infection? How could they win when their attackers would pay any price to destroy them?

She was going to have to watch Arthur, Mordred, and Lancelot die.

"The sword, Lancelot!" Fina snapped. "It might save us!"

Instead of drawing Excalibur, Lancelot tossed the sheathed sword to Guinevere. "Do what you must to keep it safe from the Dark Queen. Get to the wizard. We will protect the cave entrance for as long as we can."

Mordred ran toward Guinevere. Lancelot blocked his path, sword raised. Fina and Nectudad screamed a battle cry and joined the fray, supported by the soldiers with them, who kept the cave entrance clear.

Guinevere slung the wretched sword over her shoulder. "Please do not die," she said to Lancelot. "And do not kill him, if you can help it."

"She cannot beat Mordred, and we are him," Mordred said, that pulled-string smile twitching once more.

"I have had a good teacher." Lancelot launched an attack with a flurry of steel, driving Mordred back. "Go!" she shouted to Guinevere.

Guinevere turned and crawled into the darkness.

CHAPTER FORTY-SEVEN

The sounds of ringing steel and agonizing deaths were immediately muffled as Guinevere crawled through the jagged opening of the cave and stood. Up ahead, there was light. Guinevere wanted to run, but her whole body seized with the memory of the last time it had entered this place. She had been another girl, full of hope. She had no such hope now.

She was back in the cave and once again about to throw herself on the mercy of a merciless creature. But this time it was not only her body on the altar but everyone's.

She took a step forward, and then another. Her mind screamed with the need for haste, but her lungs refused to draw breath, remembering a flood of warm water. She should have sent Lancelot. She should never have come. Not to this place, and its waiting darkness and silence.

But . . . it was not silent.

There was a humming and clicking above her. She looked up, but her eyes could not pierce the dim shadows. She lit a fire with her fingers, and then wished she had not. The cave's ceiling moved and shimmered with black beetles flying in drunken, clumsy patterns. A flutter of moths joined them.

Her army was outside, but the Dark Queen was *here*.

Guinevere began to run, desperate to reach the wizard first. A swirling tornado of life blocked her way. Guinevere wanted to laugh and cry and scream. She had worried so much about seeing Merlin again, and now it was likely she would not get even that far.

The light from Guinevere's sparks reflected a thousandfold, and it looked as though the Dark Queen was made of tiny points of fire, crawling and shimmering and making a mockery of the human form. Nimue had loved the Dark Queen, loved the fierce life of her. But that life had been corrupted, turned rotten and greedy out of desperation. Was it a coincidence that the Dark Queen, her natural state perverted by violence, now chose to form herself in imitation of people?

And not just a person but a queen. Stag beetles created a crown on the Dark Queen's head as two moths settled into place and blinked their eyed wings at Guinevere. Guinevere dropped her fire to the cave floor, where it continued to burn. She grasped the pommel of Excalibur.

Wait, the Dark Queen hummed. *I will pause the useless slaughter outside if you listen. You humans never listen.*

Guinevere swallowed, then nodded. Maybe it would buy her friends enough time to escape, or regroup.

You have already lost, the Dark Queen buzzed. She did not sound triumphant. She sounded almost tender. *Even now, everything you love is dying or killing something else you love. And it is all for nothing. If they would just accept me, everything would be better.*

"You are a monster," Guinevere said. "You cannot take lives like this."

If they were not doing it here, they would be doing it elsewhere.

Saxon, northerner, southerner. You know it is true. They were slaughter-ing each other long before I got involved, and they will continue to do so in an endless cycle of struggle and violence.

Guinevere tightened her grip on Excalibur. The Dark Queen hissed, twitching. *I can kill them all right now. Every body I possess. Stop their hearts with a wish.*

Guinevere released the pommel.

The Dark Queen's buzzing hit a higher note, a sweeter tone. *So many are being hurt, being lost, being left behind. I will be a benevolent god to this island. No others will arrive on the shore to kill and overtake. They will become one with us. All will become one with us. Life will flourish. No one will hurt or die before their time.*

"What about those dying outside right now?" Guinevere de-manded.

That is not my fault. Merlin had a vision for humanity and it was a vision that resulted in the systematic destruction of my magic, my power. Without nature to remind them of how small they are, without the constant struggle to eat, to stay warm, to hunt or to avoid being hunted, mankind turns its violence outward. They seal themselves away behind brick and stone, become cruel, conquering, covetous wretches. That is what Merlin has done with his progress. *Why should he get to decide what this island will be? After all, look what he did to you. Look what they made you, how they hurt you, so they could possess you.*

Guinevere let out a harsh laugh. "Do not pretend to care about me."

The Dark Queen raised one crawling, shimmering hand as though she would caress Guinevere's cheek. Guinevere jerked away from her touch. The droning continued as the hand and arm crawled back up themselves, disappearing and re-forming at her side. *I am Mordred now, as he is me, and I love you as he does. You broke his heart when you left him, but he understood. You could not turn your back on people in need. But now you can have that life! Life with him. Because when I am everywhere, I will take care of them all. I will take care of you. And even Arthur, that wretched boy. I will love him because I will be you and you love him, and I will love him because I will be him, and he will love me because his burden will be gone. He will be free. Everyone will be free.*

"At the cost of their freedom."

Nothing is without a price. Arthur takes their freedom, too, and still so many of them suffer and die. That will end. I can rule with a lighter touch. A whisper in the back of your mind, the flutter of a moth's wings against your skin. You will still be yourselves. You will be unified. One. Safe.

Guinevere shook her head. A moth alighted on her forehead and she could not brush it away before it whispered a vision into her mind.

Sunlight.

Trees.

Laughter and happiness. Mordred at her side, all traces of the eel gone, no more pain radiating from his skin. Now he had a family, the family he always wanted. Arthur on her other side, younger, freer, lighter than he had ever been. All burdens erased, all violence banished, the curse of Excalibur broken and only life left. Power given to those large enough to truly wield it, not crushing these poor children. Her heart swelled to see them like this, to hear their laughter, everything healed between them.

And Guinevere whole at last. Not lost, or struggling, or in pain. Complete and loved and—

Guinevere slapped her hand against the insect, snuffing it out. Tears welled in her eyes. Part of her wished she had stayed. Even for a few breaths longer, just to see who they could have been. "You are a liar."

You do not love my grandson enough to join him? You do not love Arthur enough to free him from his accursed calling? The insects hushed their humming and buzzing and then fell silent. The moths closed their wings, hiding the Dark Queen's false eyes. Then they lazily opened again.

I have Mordred's sword at your knight's throat, the Dark Queen hissed. *Drop Excalibur and I will let you both walk away. This is not your fight. It was never your fight. Let Arthur and Merlin and me finish what we started.*

The Dark Queen's gambit had the opposite effect intended. Instead of fear, Guinevere felt her resolve harden. Lancelot would fight until the end. So would she. "I will stop you." Guinevere reached for Excalibur again.

The Dark Queen shimmered with laughter, all of her shaking and skittering around to express her mirth. *You cannot wield it, and even if you could, I will merely scatter.* As if to demonstrate, the insects dropped to the floor in a cascade of darkness before swelling up to re-form the Dark Queen. *Surely you have learned that lesson through Arthur. I tire of this. Who are you to stand in my way? I am a god, and you are not Nimue. You are just a girl. Not even that. You are neither Nimue nor the princess. You are* nothing. *Let me make you something.*

The Dark Queen was right. She was neither Nimue nor the real Guinevere. But she did have that girl's determination. It was not weakness that had led her to this cave. It was hope. It was courage. And it was strength. The strength that the fairy queen never considered, never measured, never feared. Because Guinevere—the real Guinevere—had been human. And that meant she was small. Finite. Contained.

And able to do small, finite magic that could contain even those who considered themselves infinite.

While the Dark Queen was fixed on the hand resting on Excalibur,

Guinevere reached into her bag with her other hand and pulled out a tangle of iron thread. "You are just another tyrant, you absolute horse's ass," she said. Then she threw the thread she had poured herself into last night, bleeding power into the same knot of binding she had seen Merlin paint on her body. The knot landed with a gentle ping on the floor of the cave.

The Dark Queen looked down with a derisive laugh. She buzzed, then held out one hand. Nothing happened. She stared at her hand, moth wing eyes fluttering in confusion. The moths flapped frantically but did not leave her face. She remained in the form she had taken, all the thousands of creatures she made herself out of, the tiny bits of herself that would scatter and flee before being destroyed, bound in one piece and in one place: the floor of the cave.

"Very clever," Merlin said with a laugh.

CHAPTER FORTY-EIGHT

Merlin's laugh filled the surrounding emptiness. It hurt Guinevere to hear how warm his voice was, how paternal. How kind he sounded as he rounded a corner and joined them. "Oh, you wicked old hag. The girl has bound all your wretched pieces together so you cannot skitter away." His bushy silver eyebrows drew low as something occurred to him. "I did not teach you that knot."

"You did, though." Guinevere trembled with rage, looking at this man, this monster, this thing who had left a trail of women's bodies in his magic's wake. "You used it on her. The real Guinevere."

"Ah." Merlin tugged on his beard. "Well. I am surprised to be awake and find you still alive. I thought I would sleep for centuries. I did not see this. I did not see *any* of this." His face opened with surprise. "What a wonder! To have something new. Nimue was right. Her decision to become you has changed things. She stepped outside the current of time I control, and now nothing is certain." Merlin was staring at Excalibur, held at Guinevere's side, and Fina was right: his eyes glowed like coals.

Guinevere had thought Merlin's warning not to open the cave had been because of this exact threat. But if he had not seen any of this happening, what had the warning actually been about? Why had it been so imperative that they not release him?

"We need your help," Guinevere said.

Merlin laughed, shaking his head. "Another thing I never saw myself saying: I was wrong. *I* was *wrong*! I was wrong to allow myself to be locked away. I thought it was for the best, but clearly Arthur, dear boy, has not been handling things well. Here you are, and here she is—" He waved at the Dark Queen, who was emitting a high, keening buzz, all the beetle and moth wings fluttering so frantically that her edges blurred with their vibrations. "And where is my king?" Merlin sighed. "Arthur cannot do this alone."

"He is not alone," Guinevere said through gritted teeth.

Merlin did not acknowledge her. "I will take up the mantle once more."

"He has me."

Merlin finally looked at her, lifting a single eyebrow. "But you are not strong enough to help him shape the world. Here, give me the sword. I should have always had it, whatever Nimue said."

Guinevere had asked him for help and he did not even ask why she was here. He did not care. This dirty old man assumed that, whatever the problem, giving him more power was the solution. Guinevere shook her head. "Arthur does not need me because I am strong enough. He needs me because I am weak enough. I am weak enough to feel fear, to be hurt, to understand pain, to—to be human." She understood at last what Nimue saw when she looked at Camelot. What she longed for. Why she gave up what she was to become a limited, fragile creature. Nimue as the Lady could not be weak, and thus she could never be strong.

Merlin blew a puff of air between his pale, wet lips. "You are a silly child. There is not enough Nimue in you and too much of that girl."

Guinevere lifted her chin, her eyes narrowing with the rage of being dismissed. With the rage of the real Guinevere's life being dismissed. "I will show you that girl. And then maybe you will understand." She stepped forward and pressed her hand against Merlin's forehead, and she *pushed*.

She pushed every moment of suffering, all the terrible grief that the real Guinevere had not been able to escape. Merlin's eyes ceased to glow like coals.

She pushed all the ways she felt so deeply, so completely, until it paralyzed her. Merlin's eyes turned filmy blue and dull with age.

She pushed the hope that the girl had felt looking at the promise of a new life. Merlin's eyes filled with tears as his shoulders stooped.

And then, finally, she pushed the pain and terror of the ending Merlin had forced on that innocent creature. He gasped and staggered away as she finished giving Merlin the gift that Nimue had violently claimed, the thing Merlin could never have for himself.

Humanity.

"Now you know what it is to pay the price you always inflict on others," Guinevere said.

"Take it away," he pleaded, clawing at his forehead with gnarled fingers. He twitched his head as though he could shake away what she had shown him, like a dog flinging water from its fur. "No. No. It does not matter. I do what is right. The sacrifices must be made."

"Then make them yourself." Guinevere squeezed Excalibur's hilt, hating the way it made her head hurt, her hands freeze, but needing something to hold on to. "Show me how to undo the knots that made me. The ones that the Dark Queen corrupted to infect humanity with herself."

"Why would I make a way to undo my magic? My magic is pristine. Essential. My magic is *necessary*," Merlin said, his face turning red with anger. Then his eyes narrowed and he smiled. Already she could see him move past the humanity she had pushed into him. He was willfully, deliberately setting it aside. "But I can fix this. Give me the sword." He gestured, fingers crooking greedily.

The buzzing and humming grew louder. The Dark Queen's multitude of wings were working in unison, and her toes barely brushed the cave floor.

"If she can get away from the cave floor, she will break free of the binding!" Merlin said. "If I destroy her, her infection will end. I need Excalibur."

Something in Merlin's eagerness rose the hairs on the back of Guinevere's neck. She remembered Merlin's own warnings to Arthur that he needed to be removed from power. If Nimue had intended Merlin to have Excalibur, she would have given it to him. Instead, she had given it to Arthur. But she had also helped and protected Lancelot, made certain Lancelot had the chance to grow into who she would become. To eventually wield the sword.

And she had placed them both at Guinevere's side so that one or the other could give it to Guinevere. The sword was a curse, the weight of choice. The weight of violent endings to create new beginnings.

Nimue had made the sword for *her*.

This was a future the Lady of the Lake had wrested away from Merlin. A new future, created for the humans that Nimue loved more than anything. A future that could only be secured by a human. By a girl.

By Guinevere.

"Hurry!" Merlin demanded, his voice filled with urgency and authority so heavy it almost compelled her to obey. "Give me the sword and I can fix everything. I can reset the path I carved for this ungrateful island." Merlin bared his teeth in a skull-like approximation of a smile. No wonder he had disguised himself as an old woman. His real face was barely human, and he had no kindness in him. "I will free the girl, too. The real Guinevere. You live with her pain, you have showed me. Nimue tricked us both. I did not know what she was planning. I will remove Nimue and restore the princess."

"The sword is not for you," Guinevere said, but her hands had left the hilt and she could feel Merlin's words echoing in her head, drawing up all the pain of the real Guinevere. Was that not what she wanted? What she had tried to do herself? Merlin would restore her, and Arthur would be safe, and the Dark Queen would be defeated. She would have saved everyone.

"Give me the sword," Merlin demanded. "Do not sacrifice this innocent girl to your own arrogance."

"They need me," Guinevere said, looking over her shoulder in the direction where her friends, her family, her loves were fighting and dying. And even after today, even if they won, they would continue fighting and struggling and working. It would never end. Everything was pain and struggle and she was not helping anyone. Not really. Despair welled inside her.

"They do not need you. What can you do? These tricks with threads and knots, the dregs of Nimue's magic? You are not strong enough to be what Arthur needs. What Camelot needs. I am. I told you to fight like a queen, but you cannot. You are not a queen, you never were, and you never can be. You will ruin everything. You already nearly have. I *promise*," he said, his voice wrapping around her, "I will take care of her. She will never be hurt again. You will have saved her. Unless you think her life is not worth saving?"

Guinevere nodded. It was arrogance to assume the fate of the island rested on her shoulders, violent greed to demand to stay in the place of the real Guinevere. Her fingers brushed the sword's hilt and a cold jolt of pain stabbed through her. It was like her cleansing fire, burning away dirt and sweat. Cleaning out the magic of Merlin's voice, the poison of his words, the will he forced into her head.

She grasped the hilt again. "I am sorry," Guinevere whispered to the girl who was worth saving, because every girl was. She was sorry for the girl who had been stolen. The girl who would never come back. She would sacrifice her to protect every other girl out there from these two monsters, these two beings incapable of seeing the value of a human life.

The value of a single girl. And the incredible power there.

Guinevere unsheathed Excalibur. Her arms trembled, the expectant void already pulling at her, blurring and dimming her vision. Every bit of her strength was called for, and she felt it rushing forward, like when she had used it to stop Nynaeve in the water. She drew all Nimue's ancient power to the surface.

We are fools, the Dark Queen said. Her moths stopped fluttering, the buzzing and droning at last going still and silent. *She told me from the very beginning, in this exact cave, but I did not think it possible. She will unmake us all.* The wings drooped, and a single tear of Guinevere's blood rolled down the Dark Queen's face. Instead of the expected fight, one last burst of malevolence, the Dark Queen's moth eyes fluttered halfway shut, narrowing thoughtfully.

"No." Merlin stepped in front of the Dark Queen. "I need her! You do not get to destroy her."

"You left her on purpose," Guinevere said, realization dawning. The Dark Queen had not survived the battle with Arthur by accident. Merlin had let her live on in some form. Because as long as the Dark Queen was in the land, Merlin was needed, too. He let people be hurt, be controlled, be killed, so that he still mattered.

Both of us, or neither, the Dark Queen hissed. She grasped Merlin and pulled him into an embrace. He shouted incoherently, struggling to get free. The Dark Queen's moth eyes opened, triumphant, her fate sealed to Merlin's as ever.

"I accept that cost," Guinevere said. She drove Excalibur straight through Merlin and into the Dark Queen.

Her fingers were wrapped around the hilt, sealed there as the current of nothingness flowed, draining the life from Merlin and the Dark Queen. Merlin struggled, but his coal-fire eyes dimmed again. All the cold arrogance in his face disappeared as he sagged, his skin wrinkling and turning gray and lifeless.

The Dark Queen let out a slithering laugh. *He did not see this.* With a final whimper of moth wings, she collapsed into all her beautiful parts until they were empty husks. The Dark Queen had been bound by Guinevere's iron, and Excalibur had claimed every part of her.

There was too much magic, though, and Guinevere was too frayed to hold herself together. The same void that had unmade Merlin and the Dark Queen patiently invited Guinevere in. She felt the iron thread on the floor snap as the remaining knots in her pouch broke one by one. Her magic from Nimue had given her the power she needed to wield Excalibur, but now that same magic connected her to the sword, and the sword was draining her.

She had accepted the cost, and she had meant it. Not just the cost of taking away the final pillars of old magic from the world but also the price she would pay for doing so. With one last breath before Excalibur finished her, she exhaled love. The love that had built a girl out of nothing. The love that had given her the past she searched for, the future she longed for. The love that had shaped her from something stolen into something *real*.

She had never been the real Guinevere, but she had always been real, and that was extraordinary.

With a sigh, she released herself to the darkness.

And then someone's hands covered hers and pulled them from the sword.

CHAPTER FORTY-NINE

Guinevere had never felt anything like this sunlight on her skin. Even with her eyelids sealed shut, tears streamed due to the sun's brilliance. She was real, and she was alive, and she was different. So many things had ended in that cave, and she could feel some of those endings in herself.

At last she opened her eyes. Two faces, both beloved, hovered over her.

"Lancelot," she said. "Arthur."

She did not know whose hands had pulled her free. Whose hands had severed the connection to Excalibur before she could die. And she did not care. She lifted her arms and grabbed both of them by their necks, pulling them down and pressing their faces against hers. And, for once, she felt only their warmth. Nothing else.

It had not been only Merlin and the Dark Queen destroyed in the cave. An entire part of her—the part that had contained Nimue's magic—was *gone*. She was truly just a girl now. Whether this was what Nimue had always hoped for, or what the first Guinevere had wanted, she would never know. All she could do was live the fullest, truest life possible. She would mourn what was lost, but leave behind guilt. She had protected the whole island, and that, at least, both Nimue and the first Guinevere would have been proud of.

"Everything is different now," she said.

"You did what I could not." Arthur's eyes were red, his face hollowed out with grief. "I felt him die. And when he died, it was like—it was like shrugging off chain mail and realizing I had forgotten how heavy it was."

If Merlin had infected Guinevere's thoughts with just a few minutes of talking, how must he have invaded Arthur's over all those years? And the wizard had also been his family. Merlin had made certain that, for a long time, he was Arthur's *only* family. It had not been wisdom that led Merlin to take the baby, to give him to two horrid knights who could provide no real love or care. It had been selfishness. The same thing that drove Merlin to keep part of the Dark Queen alive. He needed to be *needed*.

"I am sorry," Guinevere said. She was sorry for Arthur, but not that she had ended the wizard. His violent manipulations across time were finished.

Arthur nodded numbly. He would grieve the wizard, and it would be harder because it was a complicated grief.

Lancelot helped Guinevere sit up. "The Dark Queen's army froze, unable to move. Some advocated slaughtering them, then and there, but Arthur commanded us to wait. To give you enough time."

Guinevere squeezed Arthur's hand. It would have been understandable to make the other call. But he had trusted her enough—and shown enough mercy—to risk defeat on the chance that she would succeed.

"Thank you."

Lancelot continued. "And then, minutes later, they all collapsed and woke up as themselves. You did it. I knew you would."

Guinevere laughed dryly, the exertion painful. "That makes one of us." She looked around the battlefield. There were bodies, too many of them but not as many as there would have been had she failed. Fina and Nectudad were working alongside Sir Tristan, Sir Bors, and Sir Gawain, assessing injuries. Everywhere Saxons, northerners, and southerners were helping, binding wounds or simply sitting beside each other in stunned silence.

And then Guinevere let out a small cry of dismay as she found who she was looking for. Mordred was propped against a tree, eyes closed, head at an awkward angle. She crawled toward him, reaching out and touching his cheek. But the extra sense was gone. She could not feel anything about him.

"I am not dead," he murmured. "Yet."

Guinevere lowered her head in relief, then smiled up at Lancelot with pride. "You fought him without killing him."

"Or being killed." Lancelot's smile was slightly off-center, as though she herself could not quite believe it.

Guinevere's stomach dropped with the realization that Arthur was here, and so was Mordred. And Mordred was in no shape to defend himself or run.

"Arthur," Guinevere said, but he walked past her and crouched at his nephew's side.

"Uncle King." Mordred peeled one eye open. Only he could be weaponless and half-dead, faced with the king he had betrayed, and still manage to look insouciant. "Am I to be executed?"

Arthur sat next to Mordred, one knee up, one leg outstretched. "You did try to warn us. And it seems to be a day for setting aside enmities in the face of a common foe." His voice was gentle with exhaustion, and he closed his eyes as he said, "I forgive you."

Mordred frowned in surprise. But then a twist of a smile tugged his lips up. "Ah, you forgive me. But you do not pardon me. So I do not have a home with you, or a welcome in Camelot."

"No. I am afraid that door is closed to you forever."

Guinevere remembered the sword driven through Morgana without hesitation. Whether it was because Arthur loved Mordred or because he finally saw that the rules and laws of Camelot had to make room for mercy and understanding, she had hope. And renewed determination. She did not think the Arthur of a few months ago would have made this choice. He needed her, yes, but more than that, Camelot needed her. Not to serve Arthur, but to rule with him. To shape the island not as conquerors, but as protectors and nurturers. Together.

"I will leave," Mordred said.

"Where?" Arthur asked. "I will not allow you in the south, and I do not trust you in the north."

Mordred lifted his eyes toward the heavens, exasperated. "That leaves very little island for me to inhabit."

"Go to another island, then," Guinevere said, squeezing his knee. "One you already found to give safe haven to others."

"Ah, Rhoslyn. I will go to Avalon, then." Rhoslyn and her village had gone there so they could live as they chose, free from persecution and violence. They had once healed Guinevere. She had no doubt they would help Mordred now. It would be the last harbor for magic in the land, a quiet fade instead of the violent end so many of the old powers had found.

"I am going to retrieve Merlin's body," Arthur said, standing. His hand moved as though he would place it on Mordred's head, in goodbye or blessing, but he withdrew it and disappeared into the cave.

As soon as Arthur was out of sight, Guinevere leaned close and wrapped her arms around Mordred. He spoke into her ear. "You can leave, too. Live free. Without worries or responsibilities. With me."

Guinevere had made this choice twice before. She had gone back to Camelot to protect it from the Dark Queen, and she had left the passion she found in Mordred's arms to try to save a lost girl. But the first Guinevere was sacrificed forever, and the Dark Queen and Merlin were vanquished. Guinevere had accomplished her own quest at devastating cost.

But she did not feel *finished*, because it was not actually a quest. It was not a story, neatly contained and tidily ended. The stories were all lies, leaving out the before, the after, and all the characters the tellers did not deem worthy.

Guinevere shook her head. "I cannot turn my back on the people who need me."

"On Arthur, you mean."

Guinevere drew away so she could look Mordred in the eyes. She brushed his hair back from his face. "No. On everyone. I will not leave the welfare of this island up to a table full of knights."

"I wish you were slightly less good." Mordred smiled ruefully. "But then you would be slightly less you, and I never wish to see you diminished." He held out his hand and Guinevere helped him stand. She missed the spark she had always felt from him, and knew she would miss it for the rest of her life.

She pressed a kiss to his cheek, but at the last moment Mordred turned his head to catch her lips with his.

He smiled through the kiss, then pulled away. "One last stolen kiss. I am not sorry. And I leave you with a promise: if you ever find Camelot too much to bear, I will rescue you. But I know you will have love until then." He nodded over her shoulder and she turned, expecting to see Arthur but finding Lancelot instead.

Lancelot nodded at Mordred, acknowledging her foe turned reluctant ally. Whether she had heard what he said, Guinevere did not know.

Before she could say anything else, Mordred stepped away and whistled. A horse responded immediately and Mordred gingerly climbed onto its back. "I will not stay for goodbyes and give Arthur time to change his mind about forgiveness, or me to change my mind about letting you go." He gave her one last smile, the smile that had intrigued and baffled and aggravated her, that had broken her heart and helped heal it, and then he rode away.

"Goodbye," Guinevere whispered.

CHAPTER FIFTY

The wounded were tended to, and the dead were buried. And then they all—people of the north, of Camelot, of the south, and Saxons—journeyed together to Camelot.

On the shore of the lake, Guinevere took Arthur's arm and whispered one last request. He drew Excalibur. She did not feel it. To her, now, it was just a sword, and the same threat as any other sword. Guinevere knelt on the shore of the lake and dipped her hand into the water. She felt the touch of water brushing her fingertips back.

"Goodbye, Nynaeve," Guinevere whispered.

Arthur submerged Excalibur in the lake. The water rippled in reverse, the waves circling and then disappearing into the center, where the sword ended the magic of Nynaeve, the only remaining Lady of the Lake.

One last terrible promise, fulfilled.

Arthur turned to Nectudad, who sat tall and proud and still quite bloody on her horse. "You can join us in the city," he said.

She dismounted and washed her hands in the lake. "No. It is time for me to return home. I wish to be allies, Arthur, king of the south. I do not want war with you. And I do not want my people, or any of the people of the north, to disappear. Though I wonder if that is our fate."

"You could unite them." Arthur handed her his own cloak to dry herself with.

She eyed him thoughtfully. "Would you consider it a threat if I did?"

"Would it be a threat?"

"If I unite the north, it will be to protect it from being erased. Not to threaten others with destruction. I will never be your enemy."

"Nor I yours."

The painful benefit to watching those around them be taken over by the Dark Queen was realizing they were all on the same side. There was no difference among them, only the desire to live and grow and thrive in whatever manner they best saw fit.

Arthur held out his hand. "The north is fortunate to have you as its protector. If you are ever threatened, you can call on me."

Nectudad clasped his hand in her own. "And the south is lucky to call you king. If you are ever threatened, I will . . . consider helping." At last her grim expression broke with a smile.

Arthur laughed. "Will you join us for now? We have a tournament to finish, and then a feast and a wedding."

Guinevere could not quite believe that Camelot was still the same city they had left. Of course there would still be knightings to accomplish, Lily and Lionel to wed, all the business of managing a kingdom to attend to. The world had not ended—thanks to her—but she was exhausted thinking of all the work ahead of them.

Nectudad inclined her head. "Thank you for the offer, but no. My sister and I must return to the north with all haste."

Fina dismounted, twisting her face up in a painful grimace. She flinched, as though expecting a blow. "Actually, I am staying."

"What?" Arthur, Nectudad, and Guinevere all said, in tones varying from surprise to anger to absolute delight.

"I really do want to be a knight." Fina shrugged, her expression sheepish. "And I can act as ambassador between our peoples."

"I am going north again," Sir Tristan said. Then his kind brown eyes widened with alarm at his own daring. He bowed his head. "If my king permits it. I thought I needed a quest to become the best knight I could be, but I need more than that. I need a purpose, and I found it at Nectudad's side. I want to help bring peace to the people of the north. To preserve what they have left."

Nectudad's glower softened at this. She nodded. "I would be honored to allow it."

"If that is what you wish," Arthur said, solemnly and with no small amount of regret in his face.

Guinevere did not know whether to cry from happiness that Fina was staying, or sadness that Sir Tristan had found something in the north that he wished to return to. She embraced him. "Will you come back and say goodbye to Brangien and Isolde? They have worried about you."

"Of course."

Surprising everyone, several dozen of the northern people who had been possessed or come of their own free will knelt and asked Arthur for permission to stay and become farmers.

"The land up north is shit for that," Fina said thoughtfully.

And, as though this sparked the realization that such a thing was possible, several Saxons asked the same thing. Then eighteen men from Arthur's forces asked permission to go north with Nectudad and Sir Tristan. With the land opening up, it gave everyone the opportunity to choose which path was best for them.

"And you?" Arthur asked, leaning close so that only Guinevere could hear. "Are you staying?"

They had not spoken about Guinevere breaking Arthur's trust by stealing the sword and going against his wishes, or about Arthur not trusting Guinevere enough to believe that she knew what needed to be done. The fact that she had been right was some help, but trust had been broken. By Guinevere, and by Lancelot, again. She did not know how long it would take to repair.

She linked her arm through his. She would stay at his side, help make certain he never lost sight of how complicated and fragile and wretched and wonderful people truly were. Whatever led to their marriage, whatever it became, she loved him. They were a family, king and queen, and they needed each other if they were going to succeed. For now, that meant partners. Maybe someday it would blossom into something else, something that had been cut short between them. But Guinevere found that did not matter so much to her anymore. Camelot would come first, for both of them.

"I am sorry I did not have enough faith in you, and that you had to depend on Lancelot, instead," Arthur said.

"And I am sorry that we stole your sword."

Arthur nodded. "I am glad you were both worthy of it. And I hope that I never have reason to distrust Lancelot again." He looked troubled as he glanced toward where Lancelot was helping injured people onto the ferry. "She is a champion of Camelot, and she is your friend. I would like her to be both to me, as well."

"She would like that too, I am sure. And as to your question, of course I am staying. You do still need a queen, right?"

"Yes," he said, the word coming out a relieved rush of air. "I do not want to do this alone anymore."

Guinevere rested her head against his shoulder. "You do not have to."

CHAPTER FIFTY-ONE

Guinevere watched the tournament from her box, which was more crowded than usual thanks to her newly appointed women's council. She would have them with her at every public event, to make certain their faces and their authority were as familiar to the city as the knights'. Lily sat beside Guinevere, periodically taking her hand, as if to reassure both of them Guinevere was still there.

The tournament ran smoothly this time, and Guinevere was not in the least surprised when Fina bested the first four knights she faced, losing only to Lancelot but still securing her spot as a knight. Nor when Lionel, sweet and gangly but showing great promise, *miraculously* defeated his father in combat to secure knighthood.

She cheered for them all, her council joining her, except Brangien, who sat with Isolde in the corner. Brangien sewed with deadly force while Isolde patiently endured the waves of her silent wrath.

"She will forgive us," Isolde had comforted a distraught Guinevere when Brangien refused to greet her upon their return. "Let her finish feeling the anger she needs to."

"And stop talking about her as though she cannot hear through this door!" Brangien had shouted, causing Guinevere and Isolde to bury their faces in Guinevere's mattress to try to muffle their laughter. It was good to be home, and even better that it felt like home.

When the tournament was finished and the knighting ceremonies complete, Guinevere strolled with Dindrane and Lily back toward the castle. Arthur and Lancelot were close behind, escorting the new knights to the chapel, where they would spend the night in prayer. Guinevere wondered with amusement how Fina would handle that much boredom.

"A wedding tomorrow!" Dindrane said, breathless with happiness. "And so much to prepare! It is nicer to plan someone else's wedding than one's own. All the fun and none of the fear."

Lily blushed, but she glowed with happiness and, more importantly, purpose. She had spent more time planning for Cameliard than she had for her wedding.

Guinevere embraced her sister outside the castle gate. "It is such an honor to know you."

"I am so glad you came back," Lily whispered, squeezing her. Then she joined Brangien and Isolde to go up to her rooms and prepare for her wedding. It would be a day of celebration and sorrow, a beginning of her time as a wife and leader and an ending of her time in Camelot.

There was one last task to accomplish, and only three people to see to it. The three people who knew the truth. Stories were already spreading, stories of how Merlin had defeated the Dark Queen, of how Arthur had defeated the Dark Queen with Merlin's help, even several stories that Merlin was not dead but sleeping in case the island ever needed him again. None of the stories were correct. None of them included Guinevere, or the pain, or the before and after of it all.

Perhaps it was human nature to cling to simple stories. Stories of right triumphing over wrong, of wizards who were powerful and good, of kings who always saved their people. Stories that made sense, with a beginning, a middle, and an end. Guinevere could not say whether the stories helped—inspiring and comforting the listeners—or hurt, leaving out the messy truths in favor of shining falsehoods. But they would continue to be told, she had no doubt.

Guinevere waited at the gate for Lancelot and Arthur to arrive. The three of them solemnly climbed the exterior stairs to the top of the castle, where it became mountain once more.

The pyre was waiting for them. Guinevere absentmindedly tried to call fire to her hands, but it was not hers anymore. She wondered when she would stop feeling loss every time she reached for magic that was no longer there. She suspected that day would never come.

Arthur lit a torch and touched it to the wood. They stood in front of the pyre, watching it burn bright against the night sky, consuming the body of Merlin. The wizard. The man who walked through time. The engineer of Arthur's existence, the destroyer of Igraine and the first Guinevere, the creator of this Guinevere. More than a man and thus so much less.

It was the end of an era. The Ladies of the Lake, Morgana, the Dark Queen, and the wizard were gone. Magic and all the chaos, violence, beauty, and wonder it brought sunk into the earth or burned before their eyes. The path forward was unknown and unknowable.

Arthur took Guinevere's hand. Guinevere reached out her other hand and took Lancelot's. She startled, staring down at their intertwined fingers. Even though she was no longer magic, Lancelot's hand in hers still felt *right* in a way that could not be denied. Guinevere looked up and met Lancelot's eyes. Lancelot's smile was surprisingly tentative, and as sparks rose and crackled around them, Guinevere felt a kindling of them in herself, as well.

Duty, passion, and love. She had known the first two with Arthur and Mordred. She could wait patiently to see what the third became.

She turned back to the flames, feeling the greedy heat of destruction and life on her face. A long path lay ahead of them, and they would journey it together, the three of them. She had been sent to Camelot as a lie, fought for it as a witch, abandoned it as a queen. Now she would make the choice to serve it for as long as she could, however she could, as the most powerful thing she could be.

A girl.

ACKNOWLEDGMENTS

First and foremost, I guess I should thank all the many, many Arthurian stories that participated in the long history of treating their women characters like garbage. My rage fueled this trilogy. All your women belong to me now, and you can't have them back.

To the ones who do right by the women of Camelot, come sit by me. We're friends.

Speaking of friends, I am so fortunate to be supported in my career by tables both round and rectangular, filled with tremendously talented and infinitely intelligent people. My agent, Michelle Wolfson; my editor, Wendy Loggia; my publisher, Beverly Horowitz; the entire team at Delacorte, Get Underlined, and Penguin Random House; my publicist, Kristopher Kam; assistant editor Alison Romig; editor Hannah Hill; cover designer genius Regina Flath; cover artist extraordinaire Alex Dos Diaz; copy editors Colleen Fellingham and Heather Lockwood Hughes (I'm so sorry, I will never get hyphens right); and everyone I have the absolute delight of working with at Random House Children's as a whole. Book people are my favorite people, and you're the most bookish and my most favorite.

Stephanie Perkins literally took care of me during the first draft of the first book, and though we had to be apart during this one, she was there to answer all my desperate, triumphant, and everything-in-between texts. I love you, Steph.

Also always on the other end of my phone and behind the scenes in every book I write is my forever-friend Natalie Whipple. There's no one I'd rather whine to. Move next door to me and bake for me and my life will be complete.

To my family—which, if you read the acknowledgments in *The Camelot Betrayal*, you'll know is legion—thank you for all the support and pride and help. I feel so fortunate to be surrounded (sometimes literally) by such love.

My children are constantly, almost unnervingly delightful, and though this book was birthed during a historically difficult time, they never complained about sharing my attentions with a bunch of fictional characters getting into way worse situations than any of my own teenagers would dream of. (My seven-year-old would probably volunteer for some sword fights, though, so I'm glad Camelot is inaccessible to him.) People often ask how I balance motherhood and writing, and the truth is my kids are all better, more organized, more interesting people than I could ever hope to be. I take no credit. (Okay, maybe a little credit.) (Okay, a lot of credit, but only when bragging about them on my private social media accounts.)

I write about teens in extreme situations, and I write a lot about those same teens pondering love, falling in it, falling out of it, and otherwise making huge decisions that will impact the rest of their lives. But after spending half of my life with my favorite person, I know sometimes teens get it right. I sure did. Thanks, my love, for the brainstorming sessions, the suggestions that are rarely helpful but always make me laugh, the unwavering support, and the absurdly shapely bottom.

(I hope his mom reads that part, or at the very least several of his coworkers.)

I loved going on this journey through Camelot. I will miss these characters fiercely, but that missing is softened by knowing I get to share them with *you*. Thank you, as always, for lending me your imagination for a few hundred pages. There is truly no greater honor than telling you stories.

Now go pick up a sword, a needle, a pen, or whatever tool you'll use to create your own magic as you claim your future.

ABOUT THE AUTHOR

KIERSTEN WHITE is the *New York Times* bestselling author of *The Camelot Betrayal, The Guinevere Deception, The Dark Descent of Elizabeth Frankenstein,* the Slayer series, the And I Darken trilogy, and many more novels. She lives with her family near the ocean in San Diego, which, in spite of its perfection, spurs her to dream of faraway places and even further-away times.

KIERSTENWHITE.COM

The complete
Camelot Rising trilogy
is available now!